A More Obedient Wife:

A Novel of the Early Supreme Court

Natalie Wexler

✳ *Kalorama Press* ✳

D1021487

This book incorporates a number of historical documents, but it is essentially a work of fiction. Although most of the characters are based on real people, and many of the events described actually transpired, much of the plot and virtually all the dialogue are invented. Spelling and punctuation in the documents have been modernized.

Acknowledgments for permission to quote from various historical documents can be found in the acknowledgments section at the end of the book.

For my own James

*... Could you wish a more obedient Wife, my dear Mr. Iredell?
I wrote you last night, and am now attempting another letter ...*

—Hannah Iredell, September 15, 1790

A Note to the Reader

The genesis of this book lies in a treasure trove of letters I came across years ago, when I was an associate editor of a multi-volume documentary history of the United States Supreme Court in its first decade, the 1790s. I was particularly intrigued by the intersecting stories of two of the early Justices, James Iredell and James Wilson; but what intrigued me even more were the stories of their respective wives, both named Hannah. Although at first I contemplated a biography of some kind, I quickly realized that these women—like almost all 18th-century women—had left behind far too little documentation to support a work of nonfiction. If I wanted to get at their stories, I would have to use my imagination.

Although I did a little archival research—fingering with awe and reverence the same paper that some of my characters had actually held in their hands—the vast majority of the letters and other documents that I have relied on in constructing this story were painstakingly collected and photocopied, over a period of ten years, by the staff of the documentary history project before I joined it. Many of them have also been transcribed and published in the project's volumes. But quite a few others were put aside as being concerned solely with personal or domestic matters, and thus irrelevant to the Court's work. From my perspective, of course, these were often the most interesting letters of all. I spent many hours at a spare desk in the project's office, sifting through boxes and filing cabinets to find documents that would help me reconstruct the details of my characters' lives, my eyes aching from the effort of deciphering 18th-century handwriting (which often looks like chicken-scratches to the uninitiated) and contending with smudges, ink blots, and stubbornly illegible words.

At some point it occurred to me that I should use these documents not only as background research for the novel, but as part of the actual text. There is an immediacy to the letters that I find thrilling—candid glimpses written not for the historian or the public record but for a wife or husband or close friend—and I hope others will respond to them similarly. In addition, I hope that by including the letters side by side with my fictional imaginings, I have enabled the interested reader to separate the two—to distinguish the factual, historical skeleton from my novelistic addition of meat to those bones. Accordingly, I have put anything that is drawn from an actual historical document in italics. These passages are unaltered from the original, except for the omission of irrelevant material and the modernization of spelling and punctuation—and the occasional educated guess at an illegible word. And while I have omitted any number of real details in my fictional narrative, I have not consciously contravened any established historical fact.

Although the historical record has served as a basic road map to my characters' lives, I have taken quite a few fictional detours along the way. And of course the thoughts and words I have placed in my characters' minds and mouths are, with very few exceptions, entirely my own invention. It is quite possible that, were they magically to be revived and shown this book, the people whose lives I have appropriated here would be horrified at the way I have imagined them. But though I have invented freely, I have tried to be faithful to the glimmers and hints of character I have been able to glean from the few documents that have come down to us. Even if my characters did not do or say all the things I have attributed to them in my narrative (as is surely the case), I like to think that they *could* have.

London, England

March 1808

At the age of thirty-four, Hannah Gray Wilson Bartlett lay on her deathbed.

Shapes and shadows flitted across the walls and the coverlet, propelled by the dimming light from the window and the flicker of the fireplace—shapes that sometimes formed themselves into faces, the faces of people she had once known. She could hear voices—her husband's, the maid's—wafting up to her room from downstairs, but sometimes she was certain that she heard other voices, voices from long ago.

She reached for the book by her bed; perhaps reading would steady her. It was a volume of poetry that she had long treasured, but now she found the familiar words dancing away from her, their meaning just out of reach. As she closed the book, a letter fell from the inside cover, slightly yellowed with age. It was folded, and the outside was addressed, "Mrs. Wilson." Smiling at the familiar handwriting, Hannah opened it.

My dear Madam:

Having accidentally met with a very neat edition of Thomson's "Seasons," I take the liberty of requesting your acceptance of it, in the hope ... that it may sometimes be the means of recalling to your recollection the person who presented it. You will, I flatter myself, forgive this selfish motive ... in consideration of the earnest wish I naturally feel to live with some esteem in your memory as long as I possibly can.

> *With the greatest respect,*
> *Your obedient servant,*
> *James Iredell*

She gently tucked the letter back into its resting place, returned the book to the table, and picked up the hand mirror that lay beside it; her face was pale, but her complexion was still smooth, her neck still graceful, her auburn curls still lustrous, and her eyes—if anything—even brighter than they had been ten years before. But that was the fever, of course. She sighed and put the mirror aside. Suddenly exhausted, she soon fell into a deep but restless sleep.

Half an hour later, the maid entered the room with a cold compress, which she began to apply to her mistress's burning forehead. Mrs. Bartlett's head turned back and forth on the pillow, and her lips began to move. Opening her eyes, she caught the maid's arm and said urgently, "Mrs. Iredell, there is something you must know."

The maid dropped the compress and drew back in surprise. "But it's only me, Ma'am—it's Sally!"

Mrs. Bartlett seemed not to understand; she began speaking of things that made no sense: someone crossing a river and falling through the ice and being in mortal danger, and then something more that Sally could not quite make out—something about an "indiscretion."

"Please ma'am," Sally interrupted, "you must rest now, you must be quiet!"

"But you must let me finish!" Mrs. Bartlett insisted. "It is what Mr. Iredell said and did next that I must tell you."

And so Sally, not knowing what else to do, allowed her mistress to finish, although it all came in such a rush of words and so low a voice that she could make neither head nor tail of it. At last the story appeared to come to an end, for her mistress clutched her once again.

"Forgive me, Mrs. Iredell, only please forgive me," she pleaded, her eyes wild and bright. "There is no one in the world whose good opinion I crave more than yours." Her voice dropped to a whisper. "I haven't led an exemplary life, I know—there are others I have wronged as well as you. But if I could only have your forgiveness, it would all be put to right, somehow. Please, I beg you, don't make me go to my grave without a kind word."

Sally raised a hand and placed it on her mistress's shoulder; a tear began to roll down her cheek. Poor Mrs. Bartlett: so young, and still so beautiful. Whatever it was she was on about, there was surely no harm in sending her to her rest with a kind word.

"Of course, ma'am, of course I … forgive you."

Mrs. Bartlett's eyes closed now, and her grip on Sally's sleeve loosened. She sank back onto the pillow, her lips forming a smile.

1790

From Hannah Iredell to James Iredell:

Edenton, North Carolina, May 6, 1790

I have had the satisfaction of receiving your kind letter from Greensville. I hope you were as well as you said. Our dear Children continue quite well. Annie was much distressed at parting with you—she told James in a very doleful tone that Papa was gone. He clapped his hands and repeated very gaily, "Pa's gone." He is in a sweet sleep now, and our dear Girl sends her love to you and says please to come home soon...

When you think of your children, my dear Mr. Iredell, let it remind you to take care of your health, for to you they must look for everything under Providence... I should think nothing of this voyage if you were with us (or I was to meet you at the end of it), but it seems hard to be traveling to the very opposite points of the compass. However, I trust to the same good Providence which has never yet forsaken us, that you will return to us safe & well ...

You will hear no more from me till I get to New York ..., for we shall certainly sail I believe before next Tuesday. You may be assured that I will take every possible means to guard your dear Children from danger... They are both as lively & lovely as you could wish them. Annie has given me some kisses for you, her first conversation this morning was about you... There is no danger of her ever forgetting you. No Child can have a more affectionate disposition than she has...

Pray my dear Mr. Iredell, I must again repeat it: take care of yourself. You never had so much occasion for discretion as on this journey. Think of us often & come to us as soon as possible. I shall not know what to do with myself until you come. . .

From James Iredell to Hannah Iredell:

Camden, South Carolina, May 10, 1790

... I feel inexpressible anxiety about you & my poor Children. How hard it is to be so much out of the way of hearing from you! My imagination is continually at work, but can be never satisfied. I trust in the infinite goodness of God that you will have a safe & pleasant passage to New York, and that we may be all so happy as to meet there quite well ... Kiss my ever dear Annie and my lovely James with the greatest warmth & kindness, & tell them no Father ever more doted on his Children than I do on mine. May God preserve them & make them useful Members of Society! Tell Annie I will come & see her as soon as I can ...

From the *State Gazette* of Edenton, North Carolina, May 15, 1790:

On Tuesday last, the sloop Virginia Packet, Captain Andrews, sailed from the port for New-York, in which went as passengers the families of the Honorable Samuel Johnston, Esq., Senator in the Congress of the United States for this state, and of the Honorable Judge James Iredell, lately appointed to the Supreme Court of the United States. We unite our wishes with those of their numerous friends, that pleasant and propitious gales may waft them in safety to their destined port.

Diary of Hannah Iredell

New York, New York

Friday, May 21, 1790

All is confusion here. Never in my life have my ears been so assaulted by the clatter of wheels over stones, the squeals of pigs rooting in gutters, the shouts of vendors in the Markets. And the odors that afflict my poor nostrils! Edenton's stagnant waters gave rise to their own repugnant Perfume, but the sheer agglomeration of people here yields something far worse. Surely Nature never meant for so many persons to congregate in one place. Oh, to be back on the vast empty expanse of Ocean that cradled us just days ago, the only sounds the lapping of waves and the keening of seagulls—mingled, of course, with the shouts and laughter of my Children and Nieces and Nephews, as they played about the deck.

It was never the Journey I feared, but the arrival, and all that would follow. When the ship was safely tied to the Dock, what I felt was not relief at our safe landing, but a creeping dread. Cramped and foul as the ship's quarters were, I was loath to leave them for the ramshackle shanties and rough-looking Characters that lined the shore, so unlike the neat buildings and dignified merchants that greet the seafaring visitor to Edenton. But Mrs. Johnston and her family eagerly began to disembark, once they spied my Brother waving from the dock, and Annie hurried to follow her Aunt and Cousins; I hung back on the ship's deck with Sarah and the other Negroes, who took their time gathering up our bundles—their faces betraying the wariness that was in my own heart, for neither they nor I have ever set foot outside of Carolina. If it had been my own Husband down below, gaily lifting his hat in welcome, I shouldn't

5

have hesitated for a moment. But my own Husband is hundreds of miles from here—in Charleston, if his plans have held, en route to hold Court in Savannah.

But little James cried in my arms to follow his Sister, so there was nothing for it but to go, my knees trembling and my legs feeling strangely not my own. They say this is the normal course after a sea Voyage, and that one must patiently await the return of one's "land legs," but in my case I fear it was something more, that my real legs, even my real Body, has been lost somewhere—perhaps at Edenton, perhaps at sea. Certainly my knees have not yet stopped trembling, and it has been two days now.

At least my Brother's house here is well-appointed and large—befitting a Senator, I suppose, and convenient to the Federal Hall where Congress meets. It is made of red brick like its neighbors, and has a small Garden at the back that may serve me as something of a refuge, despite the clatter from the street. It is on Broadway, a thoroughfare that well deserves its name, many yards in width from one side to the other, equipped with raised walkways on either side and lined with fine buildings—Sam tells us the President himself lives on this Street, at Number 39. It seems several worlds away from the nearby clatter and menace of the Docks. But they say New York is like that—like some jagged mountain range, dizzy heights of extravagant wealth soaring right next to murky depths of depraved poverty, each seeming all the more extreme by the sudden contrast to its Opposite. Sam has already warned me against venturing into certain areas only a few streets away: a place called Canvas Town, where many unfortunates, routed from their homes by the Fire of '76, make do even to this day with flimsy cloth shelters; and an unsavory neighborhood surrounding The Collect, a reservoir whose water is said to be equally unsavory. But Sam needn't worry about my venturing abroad in this place on my own—although, if Mr. Iredell (from whom I have had as yet no Letter, as I had earnestly hoped I might) does not make his way here soon, I daresay I shall have no choice.

Sam assures me that the courts in the Southern States will have little or no business (the idea of a Federal court being such a novelty, he says, that few will yet know what they may ask it to do), and that my Husband will be here in the Capital before the end of June. If only he were by my side, I flatter myself I could do nearly anything, even in this alarming City. But without him—with no News of him, with anxiety as an ever-present and unwelcome companion—I can do no more than peer out the window near the table where I sit and contemplate with horror the

6

passing Show: an endless stream of proud-looking Gentlemen, and Ladies wearing brocaded gowns and feathered bonnets such as I have seen only in the plates of London magazines. Indeed, the Tableau strikes me as one of those London novels come to life, with fashionable Society having nothing to do but promenade and greet their acquaintance. It is a World into which I cannot imagine inserting myself; and yet it is the World I must somehow contrive to call my own.

My true World, my very universe, is left behind in Edenton—a poor thing, as the Bard once wrote, but mine own. I yearn for the simple wooden houses, the narrow unpaved Streets, the familiar faces of home: for my few but faithful Friends, for Mr. Iredell's brother Tom and all his merry foolishness, and—most of all—for Nelly, my own sweet Nelly, her eyes a-sparkle with gaiety and mischief.

I feared this Separation nearly as much for Nelly as for myself. Though she has an excellent Husband and no doubt will soon have Children to occupy her, it is less than a year since her Mother died—and now she must lose me as well! Though I remind myself I am by rights no more than her Aunt, I have since her birth felt such an attachment as though I were a second Mother to her. And yet, being but fifteen years her senior, I have also acted the fond elder Sister, sometimes gently correcting her youthful high spirits, and at other times allowing them to carry me aloft with her. There is no Word, in short, adequate to describe what Nelly and I are to one another, our lives being so closely braided that each Conversation seems but a continuation of the last. We have rarely been apart for more than a few days, till now; and now I cannot tell if we shall ever see one another again.

Just before I boarded the ship at Edenton, Nelly and I stood at the dock, saying our farewells, and trying mightily not to weep—an Endeavor at which both of us, I confess, failed miserably.

"Whatever shall I do without you?" I whispered to her as we embraced.

"Now then, Aunt," she said in what was meant to be a playful scolding tone, but contained a tremble, "you know I shall be eager to visit, and see the Capital for myself." She drew back and put her hand into the pocket she wore at her waist. "And in the meantime, you shall have this."

She then withdrew a small Book, bound in red leather. "Not a book to read, though I know what store you set in those," she said, as I opened it and saw the pages were blank, "but a book in which to write, to record your Thoughts and all that transpires. Think of it as a companion, a trusted Friend, ever eager to know how it is with you, and capable of keeping any confidence you may repose in it."

"I shall think of it, then, as a Simulacrum of yourself," I said, and kissed her.

She wrinkled her nose in that way she does whenever I employ a Word she deems too elevated, and told me saucily, "Think of it as you will—only write a few lines in it now and then, and let it remind you of me."

And so I have, for what I have set down here today is very much what I should have told Nelly, if she were by me; and though the Book does not call me a "poor Lamb," and squeeze me about the shoulders, as *she* would, I yet feel the better for having written in it.

From James Iredell to Hannah Iredell:

Charleston, South Carolina, May 23, 1790

... I arrived here last night in company with Mr. Rutledge, from whom I have received the greatest and kindest civilities, and at whose house I now have the pleasure of staying. He is one of the most agreeable men I was ever acquainted with; and his wife seems a truly respectable and amiable woman, who has received me in the most obliging manner ... On Friday we are to set off for Savannah ...

Thursday, May 27, 1790

Yesterday Doctor Romaine was here (I had not seen him since he was in Edenton to visit his relations, some years since) to put us all under inoculation against the Smallpox—all but Sam, that is, as he has already been inoculated. I had thought I should be brave, for I have heard and understood all the arguments in favor of the Procedure: that it nearly always produces an extremely mild case of the Disease (far milder than when it is contracted in the natural way, they say), and then confers a lifelong immunity. Certainly I don't class myself amongst those who still rail against the idea of inoculation as a blasphemous interference with the ways of God. And yet—to voluntarily infect my precious Children, and myself, with a Disorder that yet *may* be fatal, or at least disfigure us permanently—it was a prospect that filled me with Trepidation. The Speckled Monster, I have heard some call it.

But the preparations had all been made: the Children given Rhubarb as a purgative, myself and Mrs. Johnston purged and bled two days before. Dr. Romaine had sent word that he had obtained fresh "Matter," as he termed it, from the pustules of an infected Patient, and it would not retain its efficacy more than a day or two. Mrs. Johnston shared my Doubts, I know—I could see it in her eyes—but she dared not defy Sam's wishes. Nor could I have faced my own Husband, were he to arrive and learn that, fearing a small risk of harm to our Children, I had left them exposed to one far greater.

But I confess I was quite paralyzed with fear, when the Doctor arrived at last, brandishing his Lancet; and the Children clung to me and whimpered pitifully. In the end it was Sarah who stepped forward, rolling up her sleeve to expose a smooth, dark arm. (Dr. Romaine glanced at me first, to make sure I meant to pay to have my Negro inoculated. I nodded to him, for of course Sarah must be protected as well as the rest of us.) After that, she held the Children on her lap for their turns, and they exhibited a commendable bravery, for a Girl four years of age and a Boy only two. I went last, with my fear well concealed—or so, at least, I flatter myself.

Odd, now, that we feel nothing; I have the sense that we are suspended above a deep Ravine, held by a rope which will shortly break. We are to expect chills and fever at the seventh day following inoculation, with the eruptions appearing several days after that. We are, of course, confined to the House and its grounds for the next few days, and may entertain no Visitors—restrictions which, I confess, are so congenial to my Mood that I view them as nearly adequate compensation for the Ordeal we may be about to endure.

From James Iredell to Hannah Iredell:

Savannah, Georgia, May 31, 1790

... I have been much better pleased with Savannah than I expected; it is really a pretty place, though on a bed of sand; but I cannot say I am sorry that the Court adjourned today, and that Mr. Rutledge &

myself are to leave it tomorrow. I thank God, I preserve my health remarkably well… Tomorrow I shall begin to advance towards you…

Friday, June 4, 1790

We have all been suffering from Fever and headache and the like, some of us more than others; it is a good thing Sam thought to hire two Servants, already inoculated, to wait upon us until we are recovered, for the Negroes are as sick as anyone else.

James has weathered it better than Annie—they say younger Children feel it less, and that it's best to inoculate while babes are still suckling, or at least before all the teeth have come in. And James is fleshy and robust, like his Father, while poor Annie (like her Mother, alas) is scarcely more than a stick of a thing. She gave me quite a scare, the Night before last, shaking and chattering so much with her Fever that I nearly sent for the Doctor. Surely we have kept these bedside Vigils over a sick Child many a night in the past four years, Mr. Iredell and I, praying fervently and wiping away our anxious tears. But it matters not how many times I sit and watch and pray, nor how many times my prayers are answered and the Fever breaks: each time I am seized with a cold Fear that what befell our first-born will strike us again—that a Child will once more be cruelly snatched from us.

Perhaps all Mothers who have lost a Child endure these torments—which is to say, of course, nearly *all* Mothers. But I cannot help thinking it is even worse for Mr. Iredell and myself than for most: after eleven long years of barrenness—during which I had prayed as earnestly as my namesake, the Hannah of the Bible, that a Child might be given to us—to have our little Thomas sicken and expire, after a mere two days' taste of Life. Can it be six years since then? The Pain is nearly as sharp as though newly inflicted. I thought myself dead as well then; though Friends assured us we should go on to have more Children, I could not contrive to believe them. I considered that I was already thirty-six years of age; it seemed that if I were meant to have Children, the Lord would have provided them already. I never then imagined He would extend such mercy as to give us not one more Babe, but two.

And yet to be in such constant fear of losing them! Were it not for that Fear, indeed, we might be in Edenton still. For I was quite deaf to all Mr. Iredell's entreaties, after the Letter arrived from President

Washington. What cared I that the Federal government was like to fall apart, if men of Character and loyalty refused to accept posts in it? What cared I that the appointment of a North Carolinian to the Supreme Court might secure the allegiance of the State to this new endeavor? Surely there were others to answer the call. But when Mr. Iredell begged me to think of the Children, and their health—when he reminded me of how close we'd come to losing them to the intermittent fever last Summer, and laid out the evidence of a healthier climate in the North—when he urged that his acceptance of this post, and our removal from Edenton, might well save their very lives—how, then, could I refuse him?

But now, as I sit by my dear little ones' sickbed and cool their burning brows, or pile blankets on them to ward off their chills, I cannot help but entertain my doubts. We never had Smallpox to worry us in a town as small and remote as Edenton! And there's another Disease here that I have never encountered before, which they call the Influenza—such a pretty name, more suited I think to a musical instrument; as one might say, "Why yes, I play the Influenza." But it nearly carried off the President himself last month, just about the time we arrived here, causing everyone the utmost Consternation. And they say that it has struck Mr. Jefferson and Mr. Madison, and that Mr. Adams' entire household suffers from it, with the exception of the Vice-President himself.

And of course, when I agreed to remove to the Capital, I had thought my Husband would be here with me—I did not yet understand that Congress, in its wisdom, had decreed that Supreme Court Judges must not only hold the Supreme Court in the Capital twice a year, but must also roam the length and breadth of the Nation in Spring and Fall, holding Circuit courts! Sam assures us that the flaws in the Plan are clear to all, and that Congress will soon alter it. God grant that they alter it before the Fall, or Mr. Iredell will be required to set off once more over rutted roads and swollen Rivers, assaulted by inclement Weather, and no doubt forced to put up in verminous Taverns. Perhaps if I had remained in Edenton, I could have managed to bear this anxious Separation; but here in this strange place, with myself and my Children ill, I fear it is too much for me.

Ah, but Annie is waking now, and calling for me. We have still had no word from Mr. Iredell. I pray the Lord no mishap has befallen him!

From James Iredell to Hannah Iredell:

Charleston, South Carolina, June 7, 1790

... Mr. Rutledge and I returned here from Savannah on Friday last... Nothing can exceed the universal kindness I have experienced... I have had the honor of several visits, particularly in a high style from the British Consul in his chariot... I have met with such extreme attention and politeness in this country, that I cannot avoid feeling some degree of pain in parting from it, notwithstanding the delightful prospect I have in view...

Saturday, June 12, 1790

At last, a Letter from Mr. Iredell—written a full month ago, in Camden! At that time, at least, he was safe and well, and I can only trust to Providence that he remains so. So relieved was I, even at this stale news, that I could not help but shed a few tears—hiding them from the Children, of course, as I wouldn't want them to realize what secret Fears I have been harboring. But they paid me no mind; I let Annie take the Letter, once I had perused it, and pretend to read it to her Brother. It was enough to divert all our minds—at least for a while—from these horrid spots our Bodies are covered in, oozing their foul matter.

I am greatly relieved that the Children have not only recovered completely from their Fevers, but also have had no eruptions on their faces. I myself have not been so lucky. Though I doubt anyone acquainted with me should consider me Vain, I cannot help but cringe and shudder when I accidentally catch sight of myself in the Glass. A Speckled Monster, indeed! They say the spots caused by inoculation generally leave no permanent trace, but of course it is too soon to be sure of that, and difficult not to fear the worst. Mrs. Johnston has far fewer spots on her face than I—and Fanny has fewer still—yet to hear her go on about her lost looks and Fanny's ruined Marriage prospects, one would think their visages had been entirely ravaged.

"Look now, my dear Sister," I said at last, when I could bear no more of her moaning and hand-wringing, "is not my Face more roundly attacked than yours?"

"Well, yes, but"—she started to say, then stopped suddenly and looked away.

I could tell what she had meant to say, before she thought better of it: that I had no looks to lose in the first place. It's true, of course; I have nothing to rival her round blue eyes and plump, rosy cheeks, which Fanny has luckily inherited. But even a plain Woman can dread being made plainer. And though I am under no illusion that Mr. Iredell married me for my beauty, I wonder if he will not shrink from me in Disgust if he arrives to find my face not merely thin, sallow, and hatched with lines—such as he has come to expect—but disfigured as well by Pock marks.

Alas, even without the marks, I fear Mr. Iredell would have found me sadly wanting in comparison to the fashionable and alluring New York Ladies I have been spying at from my window. And who knows what youthful Beauties are paraded before him in the various Towns he stops at along his circuit, at dinners and balls and tea parties? Old fears and Questions, long buried (or nearly so) have begun to plague me once again: Why would a Gentleman like Mr. Iredell—a man who charms all he meets, and whose admiration for feminine beauty has been only too evident to me over the years—choose as his Bride someone like myself: four years his senior, timid and bookish and (as Mr. Iredell himself once described me, in a letter to his Father) *"not what is generally called handsome"*? Was it perhaps not for myself, but for the advantages that such a marriage might bring to a young man of keen Ambition? My Brother Sam (as Mr. Iredell, being his pupil in the law, well knew) was already one of the first Men in the Province, and my Family in general was not without importance, my Uncle having been a Royal Governor. No doubt Mr. Iredell believed, as well—seeing the Manner in which Sam lived, and which I then shared—that I would bring him a substantial dowry; alas for both of us that he was so sadly mistaken!

There is one Memory in particular—one image, or a series of them, that has lately persisted in taking up residence in my mind, try as I will to banish it forever. It is now a good ten years since that Calamity occurred, and yet the recollection, when it comes, makes me shudder and wince and catch my breath, and my Stomach begins almost to heave: A ball at the Courthouse in Edenton—Mr. Iredell gone out to take some air and not returned—myself stumbling through the blackness of a moonless night, seeking to ask him some Question I have now forgot. And then discerning a familiar Form, a laugh I know as well as my own. I move towards him, my mouth open to speak. But the darkness reveals another figure—a Lady of our acquaintance, one whose handsome face and figure and lively Conversation Mr. Iredell has often praised to me—their arms about one another, his lips pressed against her neck! And then a Scream, a Scream that must have come from me, a Scream that alerted *them* to my presence and all of Edenton to my Shame. And all my Suspicions, which he had ever dismissed as baseless Jealousy, confirmed in an instant!

But no more, no more; I tremble so as I write this that it becomes difficult to hold the Pen. I must rid myself of these ancient Miseries, these doubts that feed so unhealthily upon themselves. My Husband has, since that exceedingly painful Encounter, given me no further cause for grief, or at least none that I have been able to discern. And his protestations of Remorse after it occurred, his avowals that he loved me and me alone, are truly heart-rending to recall (although I nevertheless remained unyielding to them for some six Months, six long Months spent in blackness and despair). It is on those memories I must dwell, and not on the Circumstance that gave rise to them.

It would be far more prudent for me to muse on our first Meeting, and the very first words my dear Mr. Iredell addressed to me, when he and Sam surprised me in the parlor at Hayes Plantation with my nose in a Book (a novel, I confess—though I had intended to continue my study of the history of the Church of England).

"Ah, my Sister!" Sam said by way of introduction. "Quite the reader, she is. I daresay she prefers books to People."

I felt tears rise to my eyes at what I knew was meant as a gibe; but before they could spill, Mr. Iredell rose to my defense. "And quite right, too, Mith Johnthton." He had a pronounced lisp, yet he seemed untroubled by it, smiling at me with approval and Sympathy. (Such kind brown eyes, I noticed; such charmingly unruly hair; what an attractive countenance entirely! And his Manner was altogether so smooth and confident that I little suspected he was then but seventeen.) "A Book is far more reliable than a person. One needn't worry about amusing or pleasing or making a good impression on a *Book*. A Book's job, its mission in Life, is to entertain and instruct its reader. And if it fails, one can simply banish it back to its place on the shelf, with no anxiety about having wounded its feelings or offended its Pride. How many human companions would be so accommodating?"

I believe it was at that moment that Mr. Iredell won my Heart; for never had I heard someone put into such clever and precise words the very thoughts that had so often entered my own head (and the power of those words was such that, after a moment, I no longer heard the lisp). I knew that I had found a Gentleman who—though outwardly so different from myself, so affable and confident—possessed a Soul that was the very twin of my own. My Nerves were such that I found it impossible to utter a word (and indeed, for many weeks afterwards I remained nearly mute in his increasingly frequent Presence); but my eyes met his, and I thought I saw in them an exact reflection of my own Sentiments.

And yet, I cannot help but wonder, from time to time, if I was right.

From James Iredell to Hannah Iredell:

Wilmington, North Carolina, June 18, 1790

... I arrived here on the evening of the 15th, and received immediately the delightful intelligence of your safe arrival at New York, for which I am devoutly thankful to that good Providence to which we owe so many blessings... Had the weather not been so hot, my Circuit would have been quite a jaunt of pleasure, for I have been everywhere received, by everybody, with the utmost distinction & politeness, and by many of the first Families in South Carolina with a degree of unaffected kindness which was gratifying indeed...

Monday, June 21, 1790

A terrible Day!

This morning after Breakfast Mrs. Johnston observed that it was high time we ventured abroad: our spots are nearly gone (or hers are, in any case), and the weather was fine. She proposed a promenade down Broadway to the Bowling Green, where she was certain we should encounter many of the most fashionable Characters of the City. As I had no appetite for such an outing, I demurred. She said she would go herself, then, but insisted that I must go *somewhere*, for my health; and then, with a sparkle in her eye, declared that I should go to the Market with Mrs. Simmons.

"You must learn your way about the City, you know," she said with mock sternness, "for you'll soon have a House of your own to manage.

And I know you: *you*'ll want to oversee the purchases yourself, so as to procure the best Victuals for the lowest price."

A shudder of fear went through me at the thought of leaving this place, where I am safely tucked under my Brother's wing. But of course Mrs. Johnston was right. The Plan was for us to stay here only while under inoculation, and to find a House to rent before Mr. Iredell arrives.

Mrs. Simmons is one of the Servants Sam hired to see us through the inoculation, but she has proven so valuable, with her knowledge of the City, that no one has yet made a move to dismiss her. I decided to bring Sarah along, as it was equally necessary for her to be acquainted with the Market, and Mrs. Simmons bustled us out the door with business-like efficiency, anxious to begin the day's Purchases. We would go to the Fly Market, she announced, at the foot of Maiden Lane.

As soon as we left the house, my senses were assaulted, as they had been on my arrival weeks before: the glare of the Sun, the clatter of the hooves on cobblestones, the shouts of vendors in the street. It was if anything worse now, after so many weeks of confinement to the quiet dark of Sam's house. I immediately felt Faint, but forced myself to follow Mrs. Simmons' determined lead. She picked her way among the cobblestones and wove through the streams of people so quickly that it took all my Concentration to keep up with her. Sarah hung back a bit with me, but it seemed that she was as fascinated by the Tumult as I was repelled, her mouth slightly agape with amazement, her eyes open wide so as not to miss a thing.

We followed Mrs. Simmons from Broadway onto a street of more ordinary width, called Crown Street. The noise grew louder, and the Crowd, now packed into a narrower space, seemed to be crushing me from all sides. The people here were clothed with far less elegance than those on Broadway—a thing to which I would have had no occasion to object, which indeed I would have applauded, had not their Manners also been considerably less elegant as well. I was not moving quickly enough to suit some of them, and a number—both Men and Women—pushed me aside in their haste to get to the Market. Within seconds I had lost sight of both Sarah and Mrs. Simmons, and had lost as well all sense of which Direction I was to proceed in.

I began to feel a kind of Suffocation, as though the air too had abandoned me, and my head began to spin. I came to a dead stop, uncertain of where to go, and indeed of whether I could go on at all. My heart pounded in my breast, and my hands and knees were shaking violently; perspiration soaked my armpits and trickled down the front of my Chemise. A Man's voice, coming from behind me, barked at me to move, and a rough hand pushed me aside so that I stumbled and began to fall. Terrified now, I staggered to the side of the Street and held on to the wall of a House until I could catch my breath.

I could not imagine begging directions of any of the Strangers hurrying by, their faces set, their mouths grim, their manner more suited to fleeing some natural Disaster than to shopping for the day's provisions. I tried to call out to Sarah, in hopes that she would be close enough to hear me over the din, but I could make no sound emerge from my throat. I was close to tears of Despair when I saw them at last, Sarah and Mrs. Simmons both, scanning the crowd for me, Mrs. Simmons looking irritated and Sarah frightened. I mounted the front steps of a nearby House and waved my hand in hopes of attracting their attention.

They spotted me after a few seconds and pushed their way through the Crowd until they reached me, upon which I fell into Sarah's arms and, much to my embarrassment, began sobbing onto her shoulder. I could feel people turning and staring, pausing at last in their hurry to wonder at the cause of this Scene, but I could not stop myself.

"It's all right, now, Mrs. Iredell," Sarah whispered in my ear. "I'm here, you ain't lost no more."

When I raised my head at last, I saw Mrs. Simmons standing beside me, hands clasped before her and her head cocked to one side. Her irritation had subsided, but she now looked alarmed and puzzled. When she spoke to me, she did so slowly and gently, as though to a Child afraid of Goblins.

"Shall we go home, then, Mrs. Iredell? I can come back to the Market later, on my own. Perhaps another day ... "

But why should it be better any other Day than it was today? How shall I ever bring myself to venture out there again? And yet I must, I must. I promised Mr. Iredell I would endeavor to overcome my cursed Timidity, that I would comport myself as befits the Wife of a Supreme Court Judge: calling on the Wives of the other Judges and Government officials, attending the levees and teas and Dinners that we will as a matter of course be invited to, even acting as a Hostess myself—all those things that Mrs. Johnston is so eager to embark upon, and which I view as Ordeals that must somehow be got through. Mr. Iredell is so fond of Company, and eager to make a good impression here; why should he be constrained by a Wife who wants nothing more than to hide under the bed?

Before we parted he told me that he knows that I can overcome my Fears; for had not he overcome the anxieties caused by the Lisp that afflicts his speech? Had he allowed it to interfere with his ambitions in Law and Politics? Indeed, no; like Demosthenes, he had applied himself to correct it. But more important, he had shaken off his foolish concern with what *others* might think, trusting that if he treated the Impediment as no more than a minor matter, others would follow suit, and attend more to the substance of what he said than the way he said it. That is the Course I must follow, he advised; cease to dwell on what others might think, and be my own self. He was certain that once I relaxed my guard and spoke freely in Company, that others should admire me—for my Wit, as he said, and my benignity—as much as he did. "I only want the Gem I cherish in secret," he said, "to sparkle as brightly in the presence of others."

His words of praise fell upon me, as ever, like the Sun's warmth upon a struggling bud. Smiling, pressing his hands in mine, I pledged to him that I should change my ways. In Edenton, in our own cozy Parlor, it seemed a Task I could surely master. But how am I to attend a dinner at the President's House, or invite the Chief Justice's Wife for tea, if I cannot even manage a walk to the Market?

From Nelly Tredwell to Hannah Iredell:

Edenton, North Carolina, June 22, 1790

... My last letter was such a complaining one that I reckon, my Dear Aunt, you will be afraid to read this; for you have so many troubles of your own it is a pity to seize you with idle complaints. I have always set down determined to write you word when I was satisfied and happy, but my spirits are always so affected I fall into a complaining way without intention—& indeed, your absence is all I have to distress me. Mr. Tredwell is as affectionate as you, my Dearest Aunt, who I know are more anxious about my happiness than anyone else in the world, could wish him to be—but I am continually wishing for you. It seems impossible for me to speak freely to anyone, & as I cannot bear to go abroad, nor do I feel the least inclination for company at home.

Before this time the small pox is, I flatter myself, happily over with you & my dear Annie & James. How did they bear the inoculation? Poor little Annie was frightened almost to death, I reckon. Oh, my Dearest Aunt, is it possible I shall ever again have the happiness of seeing you and them? ...

Thursday, June 24, 1790

Not yet feeling sufficiently fortified to venture abroad again, I have endeavored to make myself useful about the House by means of a few modest Offices in cooking and cleaning (I find that Mrs. Johnston's Servants, both White and Black, are unacquainted with certain rudimentary methods of protecting Silver against tarnish, and the like), and in beginning Annie's instruction in her Letters and numbers. She is an eager pupil, for she hopes to show off her newly acquired Erudition to her Papa, when he arrives—which I am in hopes he will do within a fortnight.

I was fortunate enough to receive another letter from Mr. Iredell this morning, this one from Savannah some three weeks ago; I was relieved to discover that he is faring much better than I had feared, and seems to be thoroughly enjoying the hospitality so generously offered him along his route. It appears, indeed, that he is having a better time of it than I am here, and feeling rather less distress than I on account of our Separation. I confess (for why not confess my true feelings to this little Book, which can be trusted to keep my secrets?) that mingled with my relief was some Anxiety that he was perhaps enjoying himself a little more than he should.

Saturday, June 26, 1790

Sam has fallen ill—now that the rest of us are well at last. He insists it is nothing more than a severe Chill, but the Fever he has had for some days has worsened, and Mrs. Johnston has sent for the doctor. Sam appears concerned only that he be able to attend at the Senate, for he says the Residence question is soon to come to a head, and every vote will be needed. I have asked him repeatedly (or as often as I dare) when the Senate will take up the question of the Courts, and abolish this Cruel system of having Supreme Court judges risk life and limb in riding Circuits across the country. But he always dismisses my inquiries, and tells me that the Residence question must be settled first—that until the permanent location of the Capital is fixed, the Senate cannot turn its attention to less pressing matters.

The location of the Capital! Yet another thing that no one thought to mention to me. It seems that New York is only to be the temporary seat of Government, that in some period of time (some say ten years, some fifteen), the Government is to move to a location, somewhere on the Potomac River, that is now little more than a desolate Fen. But even before that time, any number of towns are clamoring for the Honor of becoming the temporary Capital: Baltimore, Annapolis, Philadelphia of course—and places that are far more obscure. It seems every miserable village has discerned in itself the attributes that uniquely qualify it to become the Capital of a proud new Nation; really, the spectacle is as unedifying as that of a pack of Brothers squabbling over the estate of a deceased Parent.

Sam says that he and the other Members from the Southward care only that the Capital ultimately be seated on the Potomac, closer to the Southern States; and that the prime consideration in choosing a temporary Residence is that it be a place unlikely to insist on becoming the permanent one. It is for this reason that he believes the Government must be moved from New York; no one seems to trust the New Yorkers, and indeed they have already begun building a grand, and very permanent-looking, mansion for the President down by the Battery, though the question is obviously far from settled. There have been a great many meetings, at this House and elsewhere, on the subject, and much plotting and whispering and covert accusation. Mr. Iredell's friend Major Butler—now *Senator* Butler of South Carolina—has been here frequently, as he has taken a leading Role in the debate; indeed, he called on Sam this morning, and was much distressed to find his condition worsened.

It matters little to me whether the Capital remains here or is removed to some other equally strange place; unless it be put in Edenton (which is perhaps the only town in America, alas, that has not been advanced as a candidate), I care not. I simply want the question decided, so that Congress will be at liberty to turn its attention to the only matter that truly concerns me: whether my Husband will once again be forced to take to the Roads, come this Fall, leaving his Wife and Children bereft of his company and anxious for his Welfare.

But that is Dr. Romaine's voice I hear now, in the Hall, come to see Sam; I must go and speak with him, for Mrs. Johnston cannot be entirely trusted to recount his symptoms correctly.

Friday, July 2, 1790

A most unpleasant Scene has just transpired. Mrs. Johnston went out this morning to pay some calls, leaving me in charge of Sam, who is still alarmingly ill (the Doctor, to our horror, has declared it to be the Influenza). Almost as soon as she'd shut the door, Sam rose from his bed and began ordering the Negroes to help him dress. I asked him what on Earth he was doing, and he replied that the Residence question was coming on for a vote in the Senate today, that it was expected to be exceedingly close, and that it was his bounden Duty to be there if he could. I pleaded with him to think of his Health, to think of what Mrs. Johnston would say when she found out, but he would hear none of it. Within a few minutes Caesar had brought Sam's horse from the stable and hitched it to the chair, and soon Sam—pale and coughing but determined—was on his way.

When Mrs. Johnston returned home to find him gone, her Wrath was indeed something terrible to behold, and the brunt of it, of course, fell on me. Knowing my Sister, she will repent of this (surely, in a calmer moment, she will realize how impossible it is prevent my Brother from doing a thing he has firmly set his mind to); and yet some of what she said reflects, I am sure, her resentment that I am still here in this house, trespassing on her Hospitality (though I have offered to pay my expenses and those of the Children, Sam has only waved me away), when by rights I should long ago have found a Situation of my own. And Mr. Iredell—whom I trust to Providence will be here soon, perhaps within days—will surely be most disappointed if he arrives to find that I have done nothing to procure us some independent Lodging.

And so I have resolved to find a House to rent, though I know not exactly how to go about it—and although, thanks to the vote on the Residence question, we will soon be forced to move again. Sam is quite satisfied with the Result: it appears that before this Winter the Government is to be moved to Philadelphia for a period of ten years, after which time it will take up permanent Residence on the Potomac. As for me, New York is not much to my liking, but I scarcely relish the thought of removing to another strange City—and one that is yet larger!

From Senator Pierce Butler of South Carolina to James Iredell:

New York, New York, July 5, 1790

... The House of Representatives are now debating the questions of Permanent and Temporary Residence ... Mr. Johnston was really dangerously indisposed with [the influenza]; in this situation, contrary to my pressing recommendation, he suffered himself to be brought in a chair to the House to vote on the question of Temporary Residence. He is now recovered ...

Friday, July 15, 1790

We have now removed to a House of our own, obtained through the assistance of Mrs. Johnston, who had heard of a likely place not far from hers. It is an odd little structure, built of brick in what Mrs. Johnston tells me is the old Dutch style: only one and a half storeys high, with a peculiar jagged roof that climbs like a set of stairs up to a central chimney. Inside, the house is low and dark and close, almost cave-like—not a thing like the houses in Edenton, built so as to take advantage of whatever breezes may come off the Sound. And yet, I was unaccountably charmed when I saw it; it seemed a den where I could burrow like a mole with my Family, a Refuge where I might contrive to forget, for a time at least, the world outside and all that was expected of me. The rooms were adequate to our needs, though small. Indeed, the size of it was such that even Mr. Iredell would have to agree that entertaining Company was out of the question, at least until we removed to Philadelphia. And the garden at the back was spacious enough to allow the Children, and myself, to take some exercise without the necessity of venturing abroad. At the back stood a handsome apple Tree that would provide us with an abundance of fruit come Fall; would we still be here then, I wondered?

Mrs. Johnston, I could see, found the place distasteful—too small and dark, the very qualities that rendered the place so appealing to me. Nevertheless, she began making inquiries as to the rent and the terms. I had said little, allowing Mrs. Johnston to take the lead, but when the Owner—a Mr. Vanderbeek—named a price of forty dollars a week, I could not stifle a little gasp. Mrs. Johnston (anxious, no doubt, that we should find a House, whatever the cost) was about to give her assent, when I heard my own Voice, firm and forthright.

"Come now, Sir," I said. "You know as well as I that within a short time the Government will be gone from here, and you'll be begging someone to occupy this House. Why, even now, I cannot imagine you'll find many takers, for nearly all of those attached to the Government secured their lodging long ago. I should think you would consider yourself lucky to receive no more than half of what you've asked."

There was some further haggling, but in the end we agreed on thirty dollars, which seemed to me fair enough. On our way back, Mrs. Johnston fretted over the size of the House, apologized for taking me to the place, and nearly refused to believe that I sincerely wished to live in it.

"Well," she said at last, "I suppose it will do as your ... *Temporary Residence.*" She laughed gaily at her little pleasantry. "And I must say, Sister, you were so *remarkably* forceful in bringing down the Man's price. You were right, of course, he was expecting far too much for such a hovel. But I should never have been able to bargain with him as you did!"

I shrugged off her compliment, but in Truth it pleased me to hear it. It is odd indeed that what for Mrs. Johnston appears to come as easily as breathing—making idle chit-chat with Strangers, and plucking topics for genteel Conversation out of the thin air—is for me a daunting and near impossible task; while negotiating a fair price in some business dealing—a thing I have never hesitated to do—strikes her as commensurate with one of the Labors of Hercules! I pray that Mr. Iredell (who himself pays less attention than he should to matters of Economy) will be equally impressed at my accomplishment in procuring us such inexpensive lodging. And I pray daily—nay, hourly!—for his safe arrival.

From Arthur Iredell to James Iredell:

Gravesend, England, July 27, 1790

My Dear Brother,
    Thank God my Mother is at length within a few hours of embarking on board the New York ... *May the voyage be no less propitious than the circumstances under which it will commence. The only one I have to regret is the necessity I am under of drawing upon you for one half of the passage money...*
    The seeing a mother, whom you have not seen for so many years, possessing as you both do great sensibility, will be an affecting, interesting scene, and it will engross all your thoughts. Instead of apologising therefore for the shortness of, I shall entreat you to forgive the <u>length</u> of this letter...

Friday, July 30, 1790

I thank the Lord that he has come at last—my own dear Husband—safe and well, only rather fatigued from the Journey.
    Yesterday afternoon Sam sent Hannibal to tell us that a Ship from Edenton was then docking in the Harbor, and—forgetting all my alarm and anxiety about this City's streets, and particularly those fetid, crowded alleys in the neighborhood of the Harbor—I grabbed up the Children and raced out the door with Sarah, stopping only to put on a clean apron and glance quickly at myself in the glass (alas, the pox has left my Face with some few marks, but fortunately not deep). Sarah seemed as eager as I—for of course, Mr. Iredell would be accompanied by Peter; no doubt she has suffered anxiety on Peter's Account, just as I have suffered it on Mr. Iredell's, though she has spoken of him little.
    The Ship was just tying up when we found the Dock, and Sam was already there (Mrs. Johnston had pleaded indisposition, but I suspect she preferred not to pick her way through the pigs' leavings and offal that litter the Harbor streets). And then, there was his dear face, beaming at us from the Deck—oh, the Joy, the relief I felt, is beyond expression! Gone were the distress, the despair, of the past two months and more—gone the nights when I have sobbed myself to Sleep, yearning for the comfort of my Husband's presence—gone as well the base

Suspicions of his unfaithfulness to me; in their place was nothing but the purest Happiness. It is almost worth enduring prolonged pain and anxiety, in order to experience such giddy wonderment when—in the stroke of an instant—they are gone.

We made a merry procession through the Streets, me pointing out the sights to Mr. Iredell as though I were a native New Yorker—there the Fly Market, there the Federal Hall, there the Exchange, where Mr. Iredell will take his seat on the Supreme Court in just a few days time. One might have thought I'd been promenading daily in the Streets, instead of burrowing into my dark little Dutch-built hole and dispatching Sarah to attend to any errands that needed doing. It so happened that we met our old Friends Mr. and Mrs. Pollok on our way, and they exclaimed over Mr. Iredell and inquired after their acquaintance in Edenton; we are now engaged to dine with them tomorrow afternoon, and I find myself almost eager to attend. Though there are likely to be Strangers at the table, I feel confident that I can do nearly anything, now that Mr. Iredell is by my side.

I had then a few Moments of anxiety; for when we arrived at the door of our little House, which I proudly presented to Mr. Iredell, I could see a cloud of dismay pass over his features.

"I know it's nothing grand, of course," I said quickly as I showed him our few rooms, "but it's only till Fall. And the location, you know, is quite central. Did I tell you how cheap it came? The Gentleman asked for much more, of course, but I"—

"Hannah, my dear." He drew me close to him, and I breathed deep of his scent—sweat and stale tobacco, but dear to me as the rarest perfume. "It's a lovely little House, a charming House." He kissed me tenderly, then held me at arms' length and smiled, the edges of his eyes crinkling just as I remembered them. "It's only that ... there will be more of us living in it than you expected."

He then sat me down and began to tell me some momentous News: there had been a Letter waiting for him in Edenton, from his brother, Arthur, in England. Now it was *his* Voice that was a-tremble; he gripped the edge of a tea table, and I could see tears forming in his eyes. Mr. Iredell has never been one to hide strong Emotion.

"In short, Hannah, he is sending to us one who is very dear to me—as dear as Life itself—and whom I trust and pray will soon become equally dear to you—someone I have longed for you to meet since first

I came to know and love you." His face now spread into a broad grin, as he announced, with outstretched hands, "My Mother!"

I was struck dumb for a moment. Though Mr. Iredell had long talked of bringing his Mother from England to live with us—a Mother he has not seen since he left his native land some twenty-two years since—there had always been some obstacle to the Plan: at some times her understandable reluctance to part with all that was familiar to her, at so advanced an age; at others, her Health, which I had understood was not such as to permit her to undertake an arduous sea Voyage. I had come to believe that the yearned-for Reunion between Mother and Son would never come to pass.

As Mr. Iredell chattered on about when we might expect his Mother to arrive, and where in the House she could be lodged, I found myself gripped by apprehension. I had long yearned for a Mother—a Mother to replace my own, ripped cruelly from me by Death when I was but a Child of three. But old Mrs. Iredell, I knew, had not been pleased that her eldest Son had chosen an American as his bride; she had hoped he would return home and marry an English girl. Might she not still hold me to blame for his settling permanently in this Country, and causing so long a separation? And even aside from that stroke against me, would she not perhaps find me unworthy, in my person and my Character, to be the Wife of her darling Son—who was, from what I have discerned, always her favorite?

"Do you think," I began with some hesitation, interrupting Mr. Iredell's consideration of the various Bedchambers, "do you think she will find me to her liking?"

"My sweet Hannah!" said Mr. Iredell, shaking his head at me, "But how could she not? Only be free and easy—don't fret and measure every word, as though it were the last precious coin in your purse. For my Mother has a lively disposition, and she does relish a good Conversation."

These words served to cheer and fortify me somewhat, and now that I have had some time to consider the matter, I am becoming rather eager to welcome Mrs. Iredell—Mother—into our home. For I sorely miss the presence of a Friend, someone in whom I can confide and trust entirely—someone who might become what Nelly has been to me (I mean no offense to this little Book in which I write—but it cannot take the place of a living, breathing Soul). I have nearly despaired, now, of seeing Nelly herself again, for Mr. Iredell has brought with him news that

26

she is expecting a Child; and though I am heartily glad on her Account, I confess that, selfishly, I felt a shiver of dismay when I heard it: with a Babe in tow, it will be far more difficult for her to keep her promise and pay me a visit.

From the *Gazette of the United States*, New York, New York:

August 4, 1790

On Monday last the Supreme Court of the United States met at the Exchange, in this city. Present, his honor Chief Justice Jay; associate Judges, their honors James Wilson, William Cushing, John Blair and James Iredell, Esquires; Hon. E. Randolph, Esq., Attorney General. Adjourned till yesterday, when the Court again met, and adjourned till February next...

Wednesday, August 4, 1790

The Court made a fine spectacle on its opening day, all the Judges looking solemn and distinguished in their wigs and robes—my own Husband, to my mind, appearing the finest of them all. I was seated next to Mrs. Jay, whose appearance was so grand and haughty that I could think of scarcely a word to say to her; but fortunately there was little call for Conversation, as we had only a few minutes before the Court was brought to order, and I excused myself to go and greet my Husband nearly as soon as the proceedings were adjourned. But what proceedings! Aside from the reading of Mr. Iredell's letters patent, and a few other administrative matters, they consisted of nothing more than the admission of a few Gentlemen to the Bar. And from what Mr. Iredell has told me of his Southern Circuit, the Courts he held there did little more.

It pains me to think that we have endured all this travail and uprooting for so paltry a business; but Mr. Iredell assures me that things will be altered soon—that Federal statutes will be enacted, Federal cases brought, great Federal questions decided. We shall see. A part of me, I confess, is in hopes that Mr. Iredell's prediction is mistaken, for if the Court continues to lack for business, perhaps I shall be able to prevail on him to resign his Post and allow us all to return to Edenton.

Indeed, I made such an Argument to him only last night, but to no avail. I could not help speaking my mind, for we have had a terrible disappointment. Mr. Iredell returned home late from a meeting with the other Judges with the news that in fact, there is to be no Rotation of Circuits—that he and Mr. Rutledge are expected to endure the adversities of the Southern Circuit in perpetuity, when the other Circuits are far shorter and are known to have better roads! The matter appears to have been determined at the very first Meeting of the Court, last February, when neither Mr. Iredell nor Mr. Rutledge was present—indeed, before Mr. Iredell had even received his Commission.

We both sat for a moment, after he had imparted this intelligence, in a state of mournful Shock. He assured me that he would make his case to his Colleagues when next they met—he had been taken so much by surprise yesterday evening that he been scarcely able to speak—and surely the arrangement would then be altered. Poor Mr. Iredell; to have his new Colleagues—Gentlemen whom, I know, he holds in the highest regard—treat him so shabbily; it must have been a stunning blow indeed.

I should, I see now, have tried to offer him comfort, but instead I forced him to comfort me. For a panic at the thought of my own Situation seized me: to have him gone again for Months, so soon, and exposed to God knows what perils! And my Brother and his family gone as well—for Sam has been concerned that his fields are being neglected, and he intends to return to Hayes until Congress meets again in the Winter. I fell to my knees before Mr. Iredell, and, like a Supplicant, took both his hands in mine. "No please—please, dear Lord!—do not leave me again for weeks on end, alone and friendless, fearing every minute that some disaster has befallen you on the Road. Please, my dear Mr. Iredell, resign this post and let us go home to Edenton and resume the peaceful, quiet life that suited us so well!"

Tears were coursing down my cheeks—I could not stop them. Mr. Iredell took me into his arms and held me close. It pained him beyond measure to see me so distressed, he said softly into my ear, but there was no question of his resigning; did I not recall what we had discussed, when he had decided to accept the Position? How essential it was for Men such as himself to assist in the great project of knitting this vast and fractured terrain into one unified Nation? Why, even now there were signs—near every day—that the whole Endeavor might come to naught, States flying off in all directions like sparks from a Roman candle. No, returning to Edenton was unthinkable. And as for the more selfish considerations of the Climate, and the Children's health—well, surely he need scarcely remind me of those. Nor should I be alone and friendless while he was gone, for had we not many acquaintances from Carolina now residing in this City? Not to mention his Mother—whose ship, with luck and a fair wind, will have docked in New York before the time comes for him to leave.

Although the thought of our Carolina acquaintance failed to cheer me (for these were people I knew only slightly, and on whom I should no doubt be expected to pay tiresome calls), I managed to take some comfort in the thought of having old Mrs. Iredell to keep me company. And I shall have my Children as well, of course—my greatest comfort, indeed, for when I look into their clear, unclouded eyes, I can for a time become as unconcerned as they are with the cares that otherwise weigh me down. It is to their Welfare, and their nurture—and their small, soothable Distresses—that I shall happily devote myself.

Wednesday, August 18, 1790

I have been caught up in a veritable Hurricane of social gatherings, these last few weeks, with Mr. Iredell by my side—levees, and Dinners, and teas, and theater parties. The leading Ladies of the City all have their evenings: Mrs. Knox, the wife of the Secretary of War, on Wednesday; Mrs. Jay on Thursday; Mrs. Washington on Friday. All of these involve a great deal of curtsying and bowing, and the ceremonial ingesting of tea or coffee; but one is required to stay no more than half an hour, during which a few mild pleasantries concerning the Summer heat or the Government's impending move are exchanged. Mrs. Washington's evening was so crowded that one could scarcely enter the Room, and the din was such that (to my secret relief) even the most cursory attempt at Conversation would clearly have been futile. Even so, I stuck close by Mr. Iredell's side, my heart pounding at the thought that the Throng might inadvertently separate us; while he forged ahead, gaily greeting those of his acquaintance on this side and that, so that together we must have resembled a grand frigate at full sail with a reluctant skiff in tow.

It was at Mrs. Washington's that I was introduced to Mr. Iredell's colleague Mr. James Wilson, of whom Mr. Iredell has often spoken with great awe. Indeed, Mr. Wilson's name has long been known to me—as to many others—as one of those few Gentlemen who had the honor of signing both our Declaration of Independence and our Constitution, and as one of the most brilliant legal Characters in the Nation. They say he is quite wealthy, as well. Mr. Iredell presented me to him with great fanfare, but I fear neither of us made a particularly favorable Impression on the other; for I scarcely managed a smile before he was off, perhaps to greet someone of greater importance. All I recall is a tall Gentleman with a round face and a small nose that he held high in the air, a pair of Spectacles perched precariously upon it.

And that was one of my more successful encounters! I have endeavored my utmost to ape the ways of those fashionable Ladies who abound here, the Wives of Gentlemen attached to the Government as well as those who are members of New York Society: their Manner so easy as to be almost languid; their smiles somehow at once both cool and inviting; their wit ever at the ready; their Dress cut to the latest style, so as to show off their bosoms to great (indeed, some might say scandalous) advantage. But alas, my efforts have led me only into embarrassing blunders—or one such, at least. At Mrs. Knox's last week (my first "evening," which gave me a severe case of Nerves), I was sure the Gentleman Mr. Iredell and I were conversing with was the Secretary of the Treasury, Mr. Hamilton, and so I called him by that name. There was a moment of awkward Silence, at the end of which the Gentleman said, "Madam, you do me too great an honor; it is not the Secretary of the Treasury to whom you address yourself, but merely the Secretary of State."

I was immediately mortified—not to have recognized the famous Mr. Jefferson! And to have confused him with one who is, from what Mr. Iredell tells me, rather repugnant to him! I fear I turned a deep shade of crimson; great torrents of tears threatened to pour from me, and I felt I could not remain in the Room another second. Mr. Iredell later assured me that Mr. Jefferson had taken not the slightest offense, and I imagine now that he was right (why, after all, should an eminence such as Mr. Jefferson care that an obscure personage like myself had confused him with Mr. Hamilton?); but in that moment it seemed to me the World had never before witnessed such a *faux-pas*. I whispered to Mr. Iredell that we must leave at once; and he complied, though I know he was greatly disappointed. Once in the Street, I could hold back the tears no longer, and I was still shaking when we at last entered our house.

To my exquisite shame, this trivial incident has haunted me ever since, a ghost that springs out upon me from the recesses of my Mind in unguarded moments. I relive it in excruciating vividness while slicing potatoes in the Kitchen with Sarah—wince with mortification over it while letting down a hem for Annie—groan audibly while lying awake in my bed. I have even, when no one is looking, slapped my own face as punishment, so hard as to leave a red hand print on my cheek. I know not what distresses me more—that I committed the error, or that I have not the wit to simply laugh it off, as a Mrs. Jay or a Mrs. Adams surely would have done. What Mr. Iredell has told me is true: the mistake would have amounted to nothing had I but treated it as such.

Ah, if only I had the composure of one of those characters in a novel of Society, able to toss off a clever quip or smooth reply in the most awkward of circumstances. My brain has teemed, in the days since our Encounter, with responses to Mr. Jefferson that, if not sparkling, would at least have been such as to spare me further embarrassment. "Why, Sir, the honor is all mine," I might have said, with a careless smile. "I know not how the Cabinet is ranked, but I can think of no greater pleasure than to make the acquaintance of a Gentleman whose reputation has so illustriously preceded him." But characters in Novels needn't think on their feet, of course; the authors who place words in their mouths may take days or even weeks to compose and polish the conversation of their creations—a luxury in which those of us made of flesh and blood are not permitted to indulge.

Today, indeed, I am in such a state of anxiety that I confess I have actually resorted to the pages of Fiction for guidance; for we have been invited to the President's House for dinner tomorrow, and I fear it will prove my severest Trial yet. I thumbed through Mrs. Burney's *Evelina,* and the third volume of *The History of Emily Montague* (the only one I could lay to hand), in hopes of discovering some elegant dinner party scene in which the various characters outdid themselves in clever repartee. But alas, all I could find in my frantic search were various depictions of attempted seduction, or other situations in which the Heroine delivered herself of outraged variations on the theme, "Fie on you, Sir!" It seems unlikely that such monologues will prove useful at the President's table. I now see what people mean when they say that Novels impart no useful information!

I thought I should faint yesterday as we approached the grand Mansion near the Trinity Church, surrounded by carefully tended gardens, with the President's gleaming white coach-and-six standing idle next to the stable. It seemed I could scarcely catch my breath, and the nearby trees and buildings suddenly took on an alarming aspect of fluidity. Mr. Iredell had no black velvet coat and breeches to wear, nor could we afford to procure him any, and my own gown was several seasons out of date; would his new silver shoe buckles and the blue ribbons I had purchased for my hair render us sufficiently presentable? Would I unknowingly commit some breach of the rigid etiquette all visitors to the President's House are expected to observe? Would there be a repeat—dear Lord forbid it!—of the sort of appalling incident I had experienced with Mr. Jefferson?

In the end, it was not nearly so bad as I had feared; indeed, I was saved by that very etiquette whose breach I had so much dreaded. For all the guests appeared to be waiting to take their instruction from the President, who remained mute as a stone. There was a hush of expectancy, as at a Theater just before the entertainment is to begin—indeed, the Table was set as elaborately as a stage, decorated in the middle with fruits and artificial flowers and small replicas of the National flag. But the curtain, as it were, refused to rise. As the sumptuous Meal was served, course after course (soup to start, followed by fish roasted and boiled, Gammon and fowls, apple pies and pudding and fruit—practically none of which I could bring myself to eat, for my Stomach was in a knot), the minutes ticked by in excruciating silence, the only sounds the pinging of silver against China, here and there a muted cough, and the tapping of the President's fork, which he occasionally struck idly against the edge of the table. The room could have been no quieter, I reflected, had I myself been the Host.

At length, after the Cloth had been removed, the President filled a glass of wine and began to drink with great formality the health of every individual by name around the table. This was followed by a general buzz of "Health, Madam," or "Health, Sir." A semblance of conversation then ensued, sparked by the President telling a story of a New England clergyman who had lost a hat and wig in passing a River; he smiled at the end of it, and everyone else laughed. Others then, encouraged, sallied forth; there was some discussion of the Theater season, and the success of Mr. Dunlap's play, which the President said he had heartily enjoyed.

Now that the Silence had been relieved by a conversation that did not appear to require my participation, I felt my nerves begin to relax a little. The Gentleman to my Right—who had been presented to me as Mr. Maclay, a Senator from Pennsylvania, and who it cheered me to see was, like Mr. Iredell, not clad in the requisite black Velvet—now began to whisper occasional remarks in my ear. I suppose I should have taken offense at this effrontery, but I found his observations so amusing that I could not help but smile. When a heavy-featured Gentleman at the other end of the table went on for several minutes, in a slow and deliberate manner, about recent intelligence concerning the political situation in France, this Mr. Maclay identified him to me as Mr. Ellsworth, a Senator from Connecticut. "Endless Ellsworth, we call him in the Senate," he said drily. And when Mr. Adams took up the same subject, crossing his hands importantly over his round Belly, Mr. Maclay again leaned towards me and shielded his mouth with his hand. "The Gentleman is so fond of titles," he whispered, "that we have conferred on him that of `His Rotundity.' " A laugh nearly escaped me at that, but I managed to disguise it as a cough.

I had quite lost the thread of the conversation, thanks to Mr. Maclay's distractions, but a moment later I heard a Gentleman refer to what he termed *Homer*'s description of Aeneas carrying his father out of flaming Troy. "*Virgil*," I could not help but mutter under my breath; for Sam's library at Hayes contains a translation of the Aeneid, and I had taken great pleasure in reading the passage in my youth. Mr. Maclay must have overheard me, though I did not intend it, for he leaned towards me once again and remarked softly, "Quite right, my dear Lady—and if he had ever read it himself, he would know."

Eventually the Ladies withdrew from the Table, and the most difficult part of the evening commenced; for I have found that when Ladies are left to themselves, with no men to crowd the stage, the Contest to outshine one another in wit and eloquence often becomes more heated. But Mrs. Washington, thankfully, was kind and solicitous of me; when I confessed to suffering from homesickness, she smiled warmly—revealing a set of lovely white teeth—and assured me that she heartily wished herself back in Virginia. It gave me some comfort to hear that I was not alone in my distaste for life in the Capital—that indeed, the President's Lady herself not only understood but shared my sentiments.

"We must bear up, you and I," she said, placing her hand gently on my arm. "For the sake of our Husbands, and our Country. It is a great endeavor these Gentlemen are engaged in, and though I daresay no History will record the role we play in these matters, we must play it nonetheless."

I nodded gravely, vowing to take her words to heart; and a moment later there came a knock at the door, signaling that the Gentlemen had finished their Port and Brandy and were ready to collect us. It so happened that we left the House at the same moment as Mr. Maclay, who bid us farewell with a slight bow.

"It was a pleasure, Madam," he said, "to take Dinner in the company of a Lady who doesn't feel obliged to prattle on about nothing in particular—and who knows her Homer from her Virgil!"

I felt a blush come over my face, and Mr. Iredell smiled broadly. But later, as we turned from Broadway onto Wall Street, he remarked that he was glad I had made such a favorable impression, but that I should be careful who I charmed. "Your Brother says that Senator Maclay is not fully to be trusted. Apparently he's taken it into his head that he's the only true democrat in a den of Monarchists, and takes every conceivable opportunity to ridicule and rail against his colleagues."

I reflected that Mr. Maclay's jests *had* been rather disrespectful; and I was seized with regret that the one Gentleman I had contrived somehow to impress proved to be one whom it was better to avoid. Ah well, at least these social engagements are likely to subside soon, as those attached to the Government take their leave of this place. The President departs in a week's time, and Sam and his Family have already embarked for Carolina—Sam eager to plant some tomato seeds he obtained from Mr. Jefferson (he scoffs at the notion, held by many, that the fruits are poisonous). Mrs. Johnston's Sister, Mrs. Mackenzie, is with child, and she and her Husband will be lodged at Hayes during her confinement. But Sam has assured me that he will return here before the end of October, in order to assist me in moving to Philadelphia; for it is uncertain whether Mr. Iredell will be finished with his Circuit before the Weather turns cold and travel becomes difficult. Most likely Mr. Iredell won't return here at all, but will simply come to us in Philadelphia.

Ah, how I dread Mr. Iredell's departure! And yet, I keep reminding myself, I shall have his Mother here by my side in his stead. Indeed, last night, after Dinner at the President's house, I had a dream that Mrs. Iredell had arrived, and she was all that I ever wished for in a Mother:

kind and lively and wise. I felt all my cares, all my silly fears, all my Melancholy melt away, replaced by a steady warmth as palpable as that which radiates from a fire. The oddness of the dream lay in this: that old Mrs. Iredell's face was exactly that of Mrs. Washington.

Monday, September 13, 1790

Mr. Iredell must be off tomorrow, and still no sign of his Mother! Needless to say it pains him greatly to leave without so much as a glimpse of her—and it pains me too, to think that I must greet her without him. But there is nothing for it, he must meet Mr. Rutledge at Augusta to hold the Georgia Court on the fifteenth of next month. Imagine how disappointed Mr. Rutledge would be to travel all the way from Charleston and discover that, because of Mr. Iredell's absence, the Court was to fail for want of a quorum!

Ah, surely Mr. Iredell suffers from this cursed court System as well as I. But Mr. Jay has written a Letter to the President, urging that the practice of Circuit riding is both inexpedient and contrary to the Constitution—the draft was delivered to Mr. Iredell just this morning. Something to the effect that as the Circuit Courts are subordinate to the Supreme Court, the same Men cannot serve as Judges of both. Certainly the President will not be able to ignore a missive subscribed by all six Justices of the Supreme Court!

The Children have both been ill this week, Annie complaining of an earache and James coughing in the alarming fashion I know to be a sign of the Croup. Mr. Iredell was all for summoning the Doctor, but I thought we might spare ourselves the expense. We have found a decent Apothecary's shop not far from here, and I was able to wet some cotton wool with sweet oil and Paregoric for Annie's ear, and to prepare a mixture of camphor, spirits of wine, and Hartshorn for Jamie. They have begun to show signs of improvement, but I know it adds to Mr. Iredell's anxiety, and to my own, for him to leave when they are not in the best of Health.

And yet, for all that I know he is genuinely reluctant to take his leave of us, I also detect in him a certain—well, I should not say eagerness exactly, but a sort of Anticipation: though his body is still with us, I sense that his mind is already roving over the Roads he will soon travel, thinking on whom he may meet and what legal questions may come before him. Complain as he will, I am convinced—from what he has told me of his previous Circuit—that a part of him enjoys it all: arriving in some outpost as the representative of the National Government, being feted by the leading Families, delivering a charge to the Grand Jury that the local newspaper requests for publication.

And, if I am to be truly honest, I must confess that some part of myself regards Mr. Iredell's departure with a degree of relief. Oh, I would give anything to have him remain, of course; but the thought has occurred to me that once he has gone I needn't go out so much. If I choose to stay home with my Children and my books on occasion rather than to prance about paying visits, or attending at levees and evening parties, who will be here to chide me for it? These last few weeks, following about in Mr. Iredell's wake, I have been nearly free of the Melancholy that often plagues me in his absence; but the effort of it has left me exhausted. Sometimes it strikes me that he is like a shimmering, quick-running current of Water, and I am the rock over which he continually courses—giving me life and vigor, yet wearing me down in the process.

From James Iredell to Hannah Iredell:

Philadelphia, Pennsylvania, September 15, 1790

... We arrived here today after a very agreeable Journey about two o'clock... I like what I have seen of this City very much.
... Give my tenderest love and a kiss to each of our dear children, and remember me as you know I would wish to be to my other friends. God grant I may receive a favorable letter tomorrow! ...

From Hannah Iredell to James Iredell:

To be left till called for at the Post Office in Baltimore

New York, New York, September 15, 1790

... Could you wish a more obedient Wife, my dear Mr. Iredell? I wrote you last night, and am now attempting another letter. Indeed,

36

writing to you and attending to my Children will be the most pleasing amusement I shall have in your absence.

Our dear Children both continue better, they seem to have got quite rid of their disorders. James has been fretful this afternoon, but it appeared to me to have been occasioned altogether by his teeth... Annie never had finer spirits in her life than she has now. She seems very anxious that I should give a good account of her to you.

I had a Letter this evening from Mr. Tredwell of the 31st August... Nelly was not very well, but wished very much to come and stay with me while you were from home. I know of nothing that would give me greater satisfaction, if she could come without too great risk to herself. Sea sickness and the small pox would prove too much for her in her present situation ...

... Mrs. Romaine and Mrs. Williamson drank tea with me; and Mrs. Jay did me the honor to call for half an hour. I wish you had been here. Where shall I get the spirits to pay all the social debts I owe, now that I have not you to go with me?

You are so good that I know I need not ask you to write often to me, though I shall expect to hear from you by every opportunity... Yesterday I had a fever the greatest part of the day but am quite well now. See what long letters I write! Do not you think I shall expect to be paid at least line for line, not written in so great a hurry?

How much pleasure it would give me if Nelly would come, but it is too much to expect. My God, when shall I have the happiness of seeing you again? Heaven bless you, my dearest Mr. Iredell. Take care of yourself—that, I shall always repeat, is a thing of the greatest consequence to your ever affectionate

H. Iredell

Sarah sends her love to Peter, she is well.

Wednesday, September 22, 1790

Old Mrs. Iredell—Mother, as I must accustom myself to calling her—arrived at last two days since, on the 20th. She is not quite as I expected, but a very charming and friendly Lady indeed. Her good cheer is such that she seemed scarcely disappointed at the absence of her son—"Ah well," she said, "if I have waited this long to see Jemmy, I suppose a few more weeks makes little difference." Her vitality was hardly affected by the sea Voyage, and she appeared to have made friends with a good many other passengers—even some of the crew, who bade her a raucous and hearty farewell as she left the Ship. One of the sailors even asked where he might find her, while the ship was still docked here, but as Mother did not yet know our Address, and as I did not think it proper to give it to him, he was left unsatisfied.

As we were leaving, the Captain approached me and demanded, in a rather ill-mannered tone, the remainder of Mrs. Iredell's—Mother's—passage money, some forty pounds. I was taken aback, because Mr. Iredell had given me to understand that his Brother Arthur would be paying the whole of the passage, but Mrs. Iredell told me that Arthur had only been able to afford half, and indeed I later discovered that there was a letter from him to this effect among her belongings.

I have not much left from what Mr. Lenox advanced to me on Mr. Iredell's account; I hope it will be possible to draw on him for more. Our Finances are indeed in a sorry state. I must try to exercise more economy, although I am hard pressed to see how. Better to remind Mr. Iredell to collect on the monies that are owed him in Carolina, although I know such dunning tasks are not to his liking. The situation is beginning to make me feel most anxious.

But Mrs. Iredell has good spirits enough for both of us. Her complexion is ruddy and her constitution sound, her only apparent infirmity being an attack of Rheumatism in her right leg—and were it not for that, I think she would join right in with the Children's games of running and jumping. The Children are quite taken with her, for she has already enthralled them with fairy stories she learned in Ireland in her youth, and which she relates with great vivacity. They are the only Grandchildren she has at present, and she is full of praise for their looks and their sweet tempers and quick wit—all of which, need it be said, endears her to me no end. We are bound, at least, if not by Blood itself, then by affection for those who share our Blood.

I had thought that she would be fatigued after her Journey, and—seeing that Mr. Iredell was no longer here, and that she might require peace and Privacy—arranged things so that she would have my bed Chamber, whilst I would make do with a bed in the parlor. The arrangement suits her quite well, but I fear it will take its toll on me, for she is content to remain awake long after my usual time of retiring, sitting in Mr. Iredell's chair by the fireplace and chatting away with great animation, so that there is no way for me to go to sleep.

Last night near 11 o'clock, when I was quite fatigued and imagined that she, at her age, would be ready to retire for the night, she instead turned to me and said, "My dear, I feel a powerful thirst coming on. Have you any more of that Ale we drank at supper? And perhaps some bread and cheese to accompany it?"

After I brought what she requested, and she had slaked her Hunger and thirst to some degree, I thought she might at last move towards her bed chamber. For the candle was burning low, and my eyes were now blurred with weariness. But Mother showed no inclination to end the conversation.

"Ah, this leg of mine," she sighed, rubbing her right thigh. "It gives me no end of trouble, and the Doctors can do nothing for it—for I have tried them, a number of them, though Arthur always objected to the expense. But I reminded him that he has but one Mother, indeed but one Parent living, and that he would suffer torments of remorse after I'd gone to my grave if he did not do what he could to restore me to a condition in which I could at least take a few steps without pain. And so he agreed, but grudgingly. It did no good in the end, though—those Doctors will put on a grave countenance, pretend to a great deal of skill and knowledge, and then merely guess at what might make a body feel better."

"Yes," I began, thinking to suggest some remedies for the Rheumatism that I had reason to believe were efficacious, "I quite agree—"

"Although there was one doctor who prescribed a Cordial I became very fond of, very fond indeed—it had no effect on my ability to walk, mind you, but it helped a great deal with the pain, so that although I knew I was in pain, I didn't really mind, do you see?"

"I suppose—"

"But then Arthur said I was using too much of it, I shouldn't have it any more, and that was that. Arthur seems to have the impression that he is the Parent and I the Child, really he treated me with barely any respect whatsoever—I won't repeat the things he's said to me, my dear, it would shock you. It's a terrible thing to say about one's own Son, but I confess I wasn't sorry to part with him, not at all—and he was delighted to see the last of me, I warrant you!"

This only confirmed for me the impression of Arthur I had already formed, but still it seemed a harsh statement, coming from a Mother; before I could express surprise, however, Mother continued.

"Ah, but I am fortunate to have two other Sons who still respect their Mother as they should, and who will make my remaining years a pleasure rather than a trial, I am sure. And a Daughter as well, such a sweet, kind Daughter—and your two lovely Babes!" Then she stopped, shook her head fondly at me, and softly repeated the word Daughter. "Ah, to say `Daughter' after all these years—nothing but Sons for me—it brings my heart such joy! A Son is a wonderful thing, to be sure, but how I have yearned for a Daughter." She patted my arm and smiled, tears brimming in her rheumy eyes.

Tears now came to my own eyes, adding to the blur of weariness. "And I have waited nearly my whole life to say `Mother,' " I replied, so moved by the Harmony of our sentiments that I forgot, for the moment, not only my surprise at her harshness towards Arthur but also my fatigue.

And yet, grateful as I am to have a Mother at last, I have become so accustomed to keeping my own Company, and having long periods of quiet and solitude, that it is not easy for me to adjust to her constant conversation. She does not seem to be one for reading, and walking or moving about is sometimes painful to her. And so, conversing with me is her only Pastime. (Indeed, I write this in the Kitchen because to do it in the parlor, with Mother so close at hand, would be impossible; she is under the impression that I am making preparations for Dinner.) I suppose we should pay some calls, as I had intended, for at least she would then have someone else to talk to; and yet I hesitate, for I am not sure that her Manner, so simple and direct, would be well received in these parts.

The Children are both sleeping—poor dears, they are still unwell—and I have sent Sarah out to buy some dry Mustard for Mother's Rheumatism. Her son (not Mr. Iredell, fortunately, but his Brother Tom) suffers from the same complaint, with the wet climate in Edenton causing him a good deal of misery, and I have sometimes been able to provide him relief by means of a plaster made of Mustard and water—though, if I remember correctly, Horseradish leaves may be substituted for the Mustard, dried first before the fire, then dipped in hot vinegar, and applied warm. (Ah, would that old Sappho were still alive to advise me in these healing arts! Sarah does not seem to remember nearly as many of her recipes as I do—though Sappho was *her* Mother, and only my

40

Nurse.) If the plaster doesn't prove efficacious, I suppose we can send for Dr. Romaine; but we already owe him a good deal of money.

I have had but two letters from Mr. Iredell, the last written a week ago, from Philadelphia. Where is he now, I wonder? Perhaps already in Edenton, where he intended to stop for a few days on his way to Augusta, to see Sam and Nelly and the rest. Ah, to be there again, even for a short while—to have an *actual* conversation with Nelly, instead of the imaginary ones I continually conduct with her in my Mind. I suppose it was too much to expect that I should find in Mother an immediate substitute for Nelly; yet perhaps, in time …

Well, Sam and his family, at least, will return here soon, as promised, to assist me in moving my Household to Philadelphia. I expect Mrs. Johnston's Sister has been delivered of a child by now, and if all has gone well, I suppose I may look for them here within a few weeks. The Children miss their Cousins and ask daily, it seems, when they will see them again. And how I too yearn for their Arrival! For Sam will know all that must be done in preparation for the Journey to Philadelphia; without him, I would surely be lost.

From Hannah Iredell to Samuel Tredwell:

New York, September 27, 1790

… I know not when I shall have it in my power to visit your Mother, though I wish very much to do it. I shall be prevented for some time at least by the arrival of Mr. Iredell's Mother, who got here the 20th after having had an eight week's passage and not one hour's sickness the whole time. I lament very much that Mr. Iredell could not have had the satisfaction of seeing her before he set off. She is very cheerful and looks quite hearty. I like her very much, she only talks a little too much for me.

My dear little Children have not recovered their health yet. They are some days better and then worse again for a few days, so that I hardly ever get out of the house. I need not tell you, I am sure, how happy it would have made me to have had Nelly with me during Mr. Iredell's absence—nothing could have given me greater satisfaction—but it would be too dangerous to her for me to desire it in her present Situation. But I indulge myself in the hopes of seeing her some other time, I hope not very distant.

Nursing, playing with, and sometimes instructing my children form my principal amusement in this large City, where every afternoon the whole people seem in motion, either riding or walking.

Mrs. Iredell desires her compliments to you and Nelly and all my friends…

From Samuel Johnston to Hannah Iredell:

Hayes Plantation, near Edenton, North Carolina, September 27, 1790

I had the pleasure of hearing of you yesterday by Mr. Iredell, who notwithstanding his long and fatiguing Journey, appears in perfect good health and no doubt will write to you by this opportunity.

I wrote to you last week that Mrs. McKenzie was lying in here. She was so unfortunate as to lose her son on the fifth day after it was born. She is very weak and low but as she has no unfavorable symptoms about her, I hope she will do well and be more fortunate next time.

As I cannot ask Mrs. Johnston to leave her sister till she recovers, this circumstance will inevitably delay my return, so as to make it uncomfortable for you, for the old Lady if she arrives, and for the children, to travel. I would therefore advise you not to wait for me, though I will endeavor to be with you as soon as possible. But as soon as Mrs. Iredell is rested, and you think it unsafe to wait longer, you had better proceed to Philadelphia, where Messrs. Hewes and Anthony have provided houses for us. Mr. Lenox has been so obliging as to offer to assist you in your removal and to accompany you to Philadelphia if necessary…

… If I do not come to you in New York, I shall certainly meet you at Philadelphia on your arrival or very soon after…

From James Iredell to Hannah Iredell:

Edenton, North Carolina, September 28, 1790

… Your brother now almost repents his having left New York. It is his intention to go for you as soon as he can, but as … the condition of Mrs. McKenzie may make the time uncertain, he wishes, and I earnestly

do, that if you meet with a good opportunity you should go to Philadelphia without waiting for him, as soon after the middle of October as you can. At the same time he thinks, as well as myself, that it would not do to go in a common stage, as the early hours of their traveling might endanger the health of all of you. He therefore mentioned you hiring a coach, or, if you could command your own hours so as not to be too early in the morning ... and could meet with agreeable company, your engaging the whole of a stage, which our company did when we left New York. By all means put not the expense, whatever it is, in competition with you and our dear children's health.

I think it very probable you may be able to go with Mr. and Mrs. Pollok, which would be extremely agreeable... So many will be going that I shall think it very unfortunate if you don't meet with some agreeable company.

... I am greatly distressed that you should be left in this manner to yourself—and so is your brother—but I trust in God we shall all meet and spend a happy winter in Philadelphia. I flatter myself I shall hear from you today...

Remember me most dutifully and affectionately to my mother, if arrived.

Tuesday, October 5, 1790

Mother's leg is improved, though whether the improvement is due to the Mustard plaster or the change in the weather I cannot tell; she did a few days since suffer a fit of lax, which she attributes to an intermittent disorder of the Bowels she contracted aboard Ship.

But it is not her health that most concerns me at the moment. Yesterday evening I witnessed such a scene as I can scarcely credit, and which I pray will prove to be a singular aberration in her behavior. In the afternoon—the weather being fine, and Mother for the first time since she arrived being neither lame nor ill—she expressed a desire to look about the City. I had scarcely left the house myself since her arrival, what with tending to her and nursing the Children, and I thought a short walk would do us both some good. I therefore instructed Sarah to watch the Children carefully (for they are still not entirely in robust health), put on a clean apron, and set out with Mother.

She seemed less impressed than I had expected—but, I suppose, having come from London, she finds nothing particularly astonishing about New York. I led her, at a slow pace, through the crowded streets, past the Federal Hall and on to Broadway, then down past Trinity Church and what used to be the President's mansion, to the Bowling Green. I believe we passed two or three People I should by rights have greeted; but I busied myself with attending to Mother, pointing out this sight and that, and prayed that these Gentlemen and Ladies would not notice me, not recognize me, or consider me not worth troubling to speak with. In this I was apparently successful. But it seemed that Mother barely heeded my commentary, looking around instead at buildings that were not the ones I was pointing out to her.

When we reached the Bowling Green—which is quite a lovely place, with bricked paths running under leafy poplars—Mother said she needed to rest on one of the benches. I sat beside her for a while, noticing that she was unusually quiet and ascribing it to fatigue.

"Ah, daughter, it may be some time before I regain my strength," she said at last, "and I know how anxious you are to return to the Children. You needn't stay with me. Go on home now, I beg you, and I shall return presently at my own speed."

I protested that I must stay with her, that she might have difficulty finding her way back or that some other ill might befall her, but she insisted that she was perfectly capable of managing on her own. It was true that I was anxious about the Children, and it was no more than four blocks back to our house; and so I relented and left her, though I felt uneasy.

A full forty-five minutes passed at home without any sign of her, and I saw rain clouds beginning to threaten; soon, I knew, darkness would come on. Anxiety seized me: even allowing Mother time to rest, and considering her slow pace, she should be home by now. Throwing on a cloak, I returned to the Bowling Green, retracing the route we had taken, but could not find her either on the way there or back. The clouds unloosed their contents, and I returned home soaked and distraught.

Sarah laid out Supper, but I was unable to touch any of it, imagining all manner of horrors that might have come Mother's way. Perhaps, in the confusion of the Storm, she had wandered into one of the more unsavory sections of the City, where robbers—and worse—were known to prowl. A lame old Woman would be defenseless against one of these brutes, and I shuddered to think of her rain-drenched body lying lifeless in some rubbish-strewn alleyway. To lose a Mother once more, to have death again snap asunder bonds of affection that were just beginning to form and strengthen! And poor, wretched Mr. Iredell—would he ever recover from the shock of discovering that the longed-for reunion, which he had come so close to effecting, was not to be? Would he, could he, ever forgive me for allowing such a thing to happen while his Mother was in my care?

I put the Children to bed and paced the Parlor, unable to read or take up my needlework, pausing only to peer out the small front window or stare into the fire, which melted and danced through my tears. At last, when the hour was going on ten o'clock and the wind and rain had quieted some, I heard loud voices outside, one of which sounded distinctly like Mother's. I flung open the door and indeed, there she was at last, and accompanied by two others, a Man and a Woman considerably younger than herself, and dressed in shabby clothing. Mother herself was disheveled in her appearance—her bonnet gone, her hair wet and coming loose, a drop of rain poised to drip from the end of her nose—and at first I surmised that some harm had come to her at the hands of these two, that perhaps they were bringing her back to me to make a demand of ransom.

But then I saw that they were all three laughing merrily, and that Mother had an arm around the shoulder of each of her companions. Evidently she had lost her walking stick somewhere and needed their assistance. The three of them were swaying slightly with their laughter, so that I feared any further hilarity might cause them all to tumble like a line of bowling pins.

Still uncertain as to the circumstances, I exclaimed over Mother and thanked the couple for escorting her home, but told them it would not be necessary for them to enter the House. I offered Mother my shoulder to help her inside, but as soon as I drew close to her I was struck by a strong smell of Spirits, such as I have never encountered on a Lady before, and on hardly any Gentlemen of my acquaintance. In the light from the fire, I could see that her face was ruddier than usual.

"Mother," I said, when I had her settled in a chair, straining to keep my voice calm, "what have you been doing? Where have you *been*? Have you any idea how anxious I have been about you these last several hours?"

She smiled and shrugged, appearing not the least bit ashamed about her Condition. "I was overcome with a powerful thirst of a sudden," she said simply, "and so I decided to break my journey home in one of the Taverns along the way."

"You went into a Tavern? Alone?"

Again she shrugged, this time accompanying the gesture with a yawn. "Such has been my custom in London, and indeed, I have made a good many friends at some of the better public houses there. This one, mind you, was not equal to those I generally frequent at home, but I did become acquainted with some merry folk, and we passed the time pleasantly enough."

I knew not what to say, and so sat there for a few moments, my mouth hanging open. Small wonder that Arthur was so eager to send his Mother across the Ocean, then!

Mother's head was now nodding forward, her eyes fluttering closed, and it was all I could do to get her to her bed (or my bed, as it used to be) and out of her wet clothes. I left her there, snoring heavily, and sobbed myself to sleep in the Parlor. Alas for poor Mr. Iredell, to find a Mother so changed from his memories and expectations! Surely his disappointment will be inexpressible. For my own, though undoubtedly a mere shadow of what a true Daughter's would be, is almost too painful to bear.

And yet, perhaps it was nothing more than an unfortunate accident—perhaps Mother, being of a naturally friendly disposition, happened to strike up a connection with People she did not realize were of the meanest sort, and who led her astray. True, she said she was accustomed to frequenting public houses in London, but for all I know there are some in that City that are respectable enough; perhaps customs differ there. She is still asleep now, but when she wakes I am in hopes she will express regret and mortification over what occurred, and will assure me that such a Scene will never again be repeated.

Wednesday, October 6, 1790

Alas, what transpired yesterday afternoon was yet more distressing—if that be possible—than what I had witnessed the night before. While Mother was still snoring in her bed, there came a knock at the door. As Sarah was hanging Laundry in the garden (and as I was still too distracted to think clearly), I went to answer it—only to discover, to my horror, Mrs. Jay! Last week I had finally mustered the courage to call on her, and was greatly relieved to find her not at home; but I was obliged to leave my card, of course, and now she was repaying the call.

Never have I met so elegant a lady as Mrs. Jay: she was a Livingston before her marriage, her Family one of the most distinguished in these parts, and her illustrious Father a Governor of New Jersey. (My own Family is one of the most distinguished in Carolina, to be sure; but I take it from Mrs. Jay's manner that having an Uncle who was Governor of North Carolina is no match for having a Father who was Governor of New Jersey—no more than being the Wife of an obscure Associate Justice of the Supreme Court compares with being the wife of the Chief Justice.) She was wearing a rose-colored gown of the latest fashion (to wit, immodestly cut) and a bonnet the size of Gibraltar, complete with meadows of artificial flowers. Thinking of the possibility of Mother staggering out from the bedroom in the Lord knew what state of dishevelment, I felt my heart sink clear down to my ankles.

I presented the Children to Mrs. Jay (despite their lingering illnesses, they comported themselves creditably) and sent them out to the garden with Sarah (for the sky had at last cleared, and they needed the air), then hurried to the kitchen to prepare Tea. When I returned a few minutes later, I saw to my dismay that Mother had entered the Parlor in my absence and was comfortably settled in my chair, chattering gaily to Mrs. Jay, who wore a polite but inscrutable smile.

"Ah, Tea!" Mother exclaimed when she saw me. "Such a considerate Daughter, to bring me my Tea when I've just awakened—and with such a monster of a headache, the likes of which I wouldn't wish on my worst enemy."

At least she had cleaned herself up a bit this Morning: her hair was in place, and her cap pinned on. But she was giving off a sour odor, and I could only pray that Mrs. Jay was sitting upwind of her.

I poured Tea for the two of them—my nerves so agitated that I fear my hand was shaking noticeably as I did so—then quickly fetched another cup and a chair from the kitchen for myself. I could barely speak, for added to my usual nervousness in the presence of someone such as Mrs. Jay was the heart-stopping knowledge that at any moment Mother might do or say something unspeakably embarrassing, something that could endanger Mr. Iredell's Reputation and even his position on the Court. But in truth, the visit was proceeding remarkably well: Mother was regaling Mrs. Jay with the story of her Atlantic crossing, which she had by now, in repeated tellings, polished to a fine tale, no matter that each version varied a bit from the last. It was difficult to see beneath Mrs. Jay's thick veneer of politeness, but from what I could tell she was genuinely charmed. I began to breathe more normally: not only was Mother behaving presentably, but she was also thoroughly relieving me of the burden of entertaining Mrs. Jay. I even began to allow myself to imagine that perhaps the previous evening had been but a fevered Nightmare.

"How unfortunate," Mrs. Jay now said to Mother, "that Mr. Iredell did not stay a few days longer before leaving on his Journey, so as to be here when you arrived." She shook her head sympathetically, the field of flowers waving as though caressed by a breeze, and turned to me. "Ah, Mrs. Iredell, our lot is a hard one, is it not? I have done little but fret about Mr. Jay these last two days, him on the road to Hartford in all this wind and rain!"

I felt a wave of dismay and Fury—for the Road to Hartford was surely but a garden path compared to what my own poor Husband was traversing. Why, at this very moment Mr. Iredell might be mired in some foul Swamp, shaking with Fever in a squalid tavern, swept off a bridge into a swollen River. For a second I had a vision of tossing the contents of my teacup into Mrs. Jay's pale and beautiful face: her dark eyes wide in surprise, brown liquid dripping from her chin.

I expect I would have thought better of this impulse, but in any event I was prevented from committing such a profound breach of Etiquette by a sharp knock which then came at the door. As Sarah was still in the Garden I again answered it myself, which proved to be a fortunate thing, for there before me was the rough-looking Man who had escorted Mother home the night before, now dressed somewhat better but wearing a far less friendly demeanor.

"Where's the old Lady?" he demanded, attempting to peer past me into the Parlor. Although the distance was not great, fortunately the Parlor was at such an angle to the front door that I was fairly sure the man was not visible to Mother or, more important, Mrs. Jay. But he had spoken loudly, and I feared that his voice would carry.

"And what may your business be with her, Mr.... ?" I said in a low tone, stepping outside and closing the door behind me. The thought of conversing with this rough Stranger made my head spin; yet the thought of him barging in on Mother and Mrs. Jay was far worse.

"Carver, Madam, Mr. Carver. My *business*," he said, sneering, "my *business* is that she owes me money, and I'm here to collect it."

"Owes you, Sir? You mean, for her ... for her refreshment yesterday evening?" I glanced nervously behind me at the door, desperate to return to the Parlor, for I had still my lingering doubts about Mother's sense of propriety. I reached into my pocket, where I kept a few Shillings. "I should be glad to repay you for that, as well as to offer you a Shilling for your trouble in escorting her home, for which I assure you we are most grateful."

"Hah!" Mr. Carver shook his head at the coins in my hand and laughed. "That won't near cover what *she* owes, Missus."

Dear God, I thought, how much could she have drunk?

"Didn't she tell you," he continued, "that she had a run of bad luck, playing at Whist? No, she didn't tell you about that, then?"

Again I glanced at the door behind me, feeling my stomach flutter unpleasantly. "How much ... how much did she lose?"

He adopted a swaggering stance, his thumbs in the lapels of his coat, as though to signal the seriousness of his intentions. "Fifteen Pound, that's how much."

"Fifteen Pounds!" I had not more than ten Pounds in the house. I leaned back against the door for support.

"If you don't believe me, here's the paper to prove it." And he extended a crumpled, stained document, with what looked very much like Mother's name, Margaret Iredell, at the bottom. "She told us she's got a son who's a Judge, on the Supreme Court no less." He looked dubiously behind me at the house, so ancient and modest. "Now, *if* that's true, I'm sure the Family won't want any trouble—wouldn't want this matter bandied about, as it were. Wouldn't want to read about it in, say, *The Daily Advertiser*, would they now?"

I swallowed hard. Steady now, I told myself. The main thing was to get rid of this scoundrel, return to the Parlor, make sure Mother never left the house unattended again. "Come back at 10 o'clock tomorrow morning," I said in as firm a voice as I could muster, "and I shall have your fifteen Pounds for you."

"Eight o'clock this evening would suit me better."

It was already three in the afternoon. I would need to wait until Mrs. Jay was ready to leave, go to Mr. Lenox's House, prevail upon him to advance me a further fifteen Pounds ... And what if he was not at home? I would have to return the following morning, perhaps. No, I could not guarantee that I would have the money this evening, and I did not want more than one further visit from Mr. Carver.

"No, sir," I said. "I cannot have it for you before ten tomorrow."

He looked displeased, but to my great relief he turned to go. "Ten o'clock, then," he said over his shoulder as he began to walk down the Street. "But I advise you, for your own welfare and that of your Family, to see that I am not disappointed."

I had an urge to burst into tears as soon as he was out of sight, but the thought of Mother and Mrs. Jay, alone together in the Parlor all this time, had a steadying effect on me. I took a deep breath and reentered the House, excusing my absence: it had been an exceedingly persistent merchant, I explained, harassing me about a floor cloth I had expressed an interest in but had since decided against. Mrs. Jay nodded sympathetically—some of these shopkeepers truly overstepped the bounds, she agreed—and soon, to my great relief, took her leave, regretting that she couldn't stay longer but lamenting that she had a great many other calls to pay, as she was sure I did as well, and expressing her hope that we might all meet again in Philadelphia—et cetera, et cetera.

As soon as I had shut the door behind her I turned to Mother, so furious that I scarce knew where to begin. But then, I reminded myself: she is your Mother, and whatever her weaknesses, whatever her failings, she is due that respect and consideration which is owed to any Parent, as the Bible commands. And so I took a great breath, and clenched and unclenched my hands a few times, until at last I was able to find a voice that was, I hope, such a one as a Daughter should use to address a Mother.

"That was not a merchant at the door before, Mother," I said. "It was Mr. Carver."

She looked at me without comprehension. "Mr. What, you say?"

"The Gentleman—the Man—who brought you home last night."

"Ah … last night. I never got his name, I think, or I've forgotten it."

"Well, he got yours." I took another breath. "He says you owe him fifteen Pounds. That you lost it at cards."

Mother shook her head. "Ah now, could it have been that much?"

"You signed a paper. He showed it to me."

"Well, if he showed it to you, I suppose I did." She chuckled a bit and spread out her hands, palms upward. "But I haven't got fifteen Pounds, you know."

"No, nor I. But I must get it, by tomorrow morning, or he threatens to tell the whole City about the matter."

"Does he? But he seemed such a nice man." She sighed and shook her head sadly. "You can never tell about people, these days."

"No," I remarked, unable to suppress completely some of the bile I felt rising within me, "you certainly can *not*."

But Mother seemed not to catch my meaning, which perhaps was just as well. I had not the time then to speak further with her, as I needed to hurry off to Mr. Lenox's house to procure the money. I was fortunate enough to discover him at home, and though he gave me a peculiar look (perhaps occasioned by an agitation of manner that I could not sufficiently disguise) he did not hesitate to advance me what I requested. When Mr. Carver appeared at the appointed hour this morning, I was able to quickly give him what he came for and bid him Goodbye and good riddance. Scandal has been averted, at least for the time being.

But for how much longer? Will the World not eventually learn that the Mother of the esteemed Judge Iredell is a common drunkard, and a gambler to boot? For it seems to me, from the way she has conducted herself, that this episode was no mere aberration, but the result of vile Habits of long standing. If such intelligence should become public—oh, the disgrace, the mortification, would be unthinkable. Ah, if only Mr. Iredell were here to speak convincingly to his Mother, and impress upon her the grievous error of her ways. And yet, might he not be too overcome by strong emotion to engage her calmly? But Sam will be here soon, any day now I expect; perhaps he will take the situation in hand.

Wednesday, October 20, 1790

A Letter has come from Mr. Iredell, written from Edenton three weeks ago, along with one from Sam—I cut them open with such eagerness, only to find in them Intelligence that has quite distracted me. I have done little but fret and weep since I read them this morning. To journey to Philadelphia on my own—how can they ask such a thing of me, when they know my Situation and the paralytic anxiety that attends me in any such undertaking! And Mr. Iredell should know as well that he left me with insufficient funds for such a Journey. How am I to procure us places in a Stage, or hire a Coach—run after all my acquaintance and beg them to escort us—arrive in a strange City all on my own?

All this would appear impossible enough, even without Mother; but *with* her—I cannot imagine how I shall manage. What if we were to travel with the Polloks, or Mr. Lenox, as Mr. Iredell suggests, and she were to commit some unthinkable indiscretion? I have kept a close eye on her, but still she has gotten into the Wine and ale in the Pantry on more than one occasion, drinking herself into a stupor. And once I returned home from the Market to discover her missing, poor Sarah distraught and apologetic: Sarah explained that she had slipped out to the Garden to tend to a tub of laundry, Mother being apparently safely asleep in her chair in the Parlor, and had returned a few minutes later to find the chair empty, the walking stick gone—and gone as well, a few shillings I keep in a box near the door. I ran back out of the House at once and set off for the Bowling Green, peering into every tavern I passed along the way, until in the third one I found her, a cup of Gin in her hand, and evidently not her first. I was able to settle her bill and remove her from the place before much damage was done. But I fear it is only a matter of time before we have another incident such as the one with Mr. Carver, or worse. I cannot be her jailer!

I have tried to engage Mother in conversation about her behavior, pleaded with her to remember her Son—his Reputation, his career—and her poor Grandchildren. But she only smiles vaguely and nods agreement, as though I were talking about matters that have nothing to do with herself, and changes the subject. Once or twice I have been unable to stop myself from shedding tears, thinking on how Mr. Iredell will view the situation when he discovers it, and on looking up I have caught an expression on Mother's face that more nearly mirrors comprehension, and with it such a profound Sadness that I begin to suspect she does understand the gravity of the situation, but feels herself powerless to do anything about it. So confused are my feelings towards her, so overpowering is the mixture of grief, anger, disgust and Affection—yes, Affection still—that at times I can barely bring myself to speak to her. And to think that I looked forward to her arrival with such eager anticipation!

But now I must steady myself to reply to Mr. Iredell's Letter, to explain to him the difficulty of what he asks of me. I have written to him of his Mother's arrival, of course, but I have not yet been able to bring myself to tell him of her distressing behavior. Twice I have tried, but on each occasion I have crossed out the words, imagining him reading them alone in some flea-infested Tavern, the noise of revelers drifting up from the public rooms below, no one about in whom he might confide, no other Soul to comfort him in his distress. It has even occurred to me that perhaps he would not believe it, would dismiss my description as exaggeration, and think ill of me for it, a thing I could not abide. But most important, I yet have hopes of altering the situation, of prevailing on Mother to mend her ways before Mr. Iredell returns from the South. Perhaps, if I can find some way to penetrate the fog of vagueness with which she has surrounded herself, if I can more fully prick her conscience, her son need never know of what has transpired.

From Hannah Iredell to James Iredell:

New York, New York, October 21, 1790

I have had the pleasure, my dear Mr. Iredell, of receiving all your letters from Edenton. Your request that I go to Philadelphia without waiting for my Brother has really distressed me very much, though I intend to comply with it in part. I believe I shall stay here till about the time I expect my Brother will be there. I can surely go one hundred miles in such weather as he will have to travel four hundred in.

It is not so light a task as you perhaps think it to go a Journey with two Children, your mother who has been lame for several years, and myself, who am almost as helpless as a Child amongst Strangers, and no others. Shall we have to deal with a strange coachman all the way, & at the end of our Journey with Strangers? And no great stock of money, considering our expenses on the Road, and when there, for furniture and all the fees of housekeeping. I shall be in a disagreeable situation, I fear. For already Mr. Lenox has advanced eighty pounds, near fifty of which was paid for your Mother. The remainder I had, but have very little of it now remaining ... The Doctor's bill is to pay, too. What then shall I have, my dear Sir, to answer all the expenses above mentioned? You must perceive there will be great necessity for my considering my expenses and for you doing the same, and I wish both together may be sufficient to keep your affairs from embarrassment. My dearest Mr. Iredell, do not think me impertinent in mentioning such things, but join with me in reflecting on them.

However vexatious other things may be to me, thank God our dear Children are well. Nobody would believe they had been sick that had not seen them so. Annie has not recovered her flesh, but her complexion and spirits are good. As for James he is lively, florid, fat, and saucy. There cannot be a finer boy than he is, nor a lovelier girl than my Annie.

Your mother complains sometimes of her thigh, something of the Rheumatism I believe, but she has a very good appetite and spirits. I am very well.

I have paid very few visits notwithstanding your injunctions. Had you been here, I could have gone anywhere with you with pleasure; but how could I find spirits to go alone? At a distance from all my Friends, what satisfaction could I find in visiting Strangers? I never was intended to move out of the circle of my own Family; it is only there that I can either give or receive pleasure...

From Samuel Johnston to Hannah Iredell:

Hayes Plantation, North Carolina, October 27, 1790

Mrs. Johnston is ... very ill, she had nearly gone off two nights ago with a violent pain in the side which almost took away her breath for some hours... I still cannot fix a day to leave ...

From James Iredell to Hannah Iredell:

Charleston, South Carolina, October 30, 1790

I have passed my time here in the usual agreeable manner. I stay at a boarding-house, but have never once dined at home... I had last night the pleasure of dancing with Mrs. Kinloch at a ball, and was not in bed till 2 o'clock; nevertheless I got up at sunrise, and am perfectly well...

Monday, November 1, 1790

This morning Sarah asked me when we would be leaving for Philadelphia. "Winter coming on now," she declared, darting her head towards the window. "Those roads, they be covered with snow in a few weeks."

Indeed, the change in the Weather is hard to deny: yesterday and today have been chill and gray and rainy, the sky a sheet of streaked pewter. The fruit on that apple Tree in the garden has all long since ripened. We ate what we could, made pies and apple sauce, and the rest is rotting on the ground, wormy and shriveled. And yet I could not bring myself to agree with Sarah, for I have as yet had no word from Sam; if we leave now, how can I be sure that when we arrive in Philadelphia he will be there to greet us?

"We have plenty of time," I assured her. "It's only October."

She narrowed her eyes and stuck out her lower lip. "Today November the first, Ma'am," she said in that wary, careful way she uses with me now—like a cabin boy on a Ship whose Captain appears to have lost his sense of direction. The look on her face was the same one I see when I send her to the Market instead of going myself, or when I instruct her to give it out to a Visitor that I am not at home—as though I had entirely lost my senses. I cannot bear that look; she has no right to look at me in that way.

"Well, we cannot arrange anything without first making some inquiries," I said with angry briskness. "Indeed, it was my intention to go down to Fraunces Tavern this very day and see about getting us places on the Stage."

This of course was a lie—I had conceived no such intention until that very moment—but I could not bear that look of hers. So I continued, propelled by anger—throwing on my cloak, kissing the Children, bidding farewell to Mother (who only grunted in response)—until I reached the Street, where I almost immediately felt my heart begin to pound, my breath to catch. The noise, the crowds; I had not been out of the house in at least a week, perhaps two, I suddenly realized (or can it have been three?). I had a wild impulse to return to the House, but that would never do: what would I say to the Children, to Sarah? And so I only walked about Town for twenty minutes, keeping to the smaller, quieter streets; and on my return merely told Sarah that the Gentleman who kept the stagecoach schedules had not been at the Tavern, and I should return another day. Judging from the glance she gave me, I doubt that she believed me.

Oh, would that we were leaving for Edenton instead of Philadelphia! I fear that I shall never contrive to change myself to suit Mr. Iredell's wishes; if I am a "Gem," as he once told me, perhaps I am one that can sparkle only in the comfort and Security of its own home. Can he not love me as I am?

From Hannah Iredell to James Iredell:

New York, November 7, 1790

... You see my dear Mr. Iredell, I am still where you left me, & I know not when I shall get resolution to leave it, though I am determined to set about preparing this week. It is a task that must be performed, however disagreeable, I suppose, for I see no probability of my Brother's getting Mrs. Johnston from Carolina till the middle of winter.

I intend to go tomorrow and speak to Mr. Lenox to settle Dr. Romaine's account, and then I shall know how much remains for our other expenses. Both myself and the Children must have something warm to ride in... I am very apprehensive that with the greatest economy I shall hardly have sufficient to bear our expenses until you come. The Doctor, you know, has been attending our family near six months, his bill I daresay will be no trifle. Our Children have had and have still a cold, but are very lively & look very hearty. I should be happy indeed, my dear Mr. Iredell, to know that you were as hearty as they & I are. Your Mother has a complaint in her bowels which she brought with her; it is sometimes troublesome and at others pretty well.

Major Butler called on me today. He was so polite as to say he would go with me himself if Mrs. Butler was not so ill. He desired I would give his affectionate compliments to you when I wrote.

I have made no visits. I could not prevail on myself to run about the town alone after people whom I had never seen & whom I did not care if I never saw again. It is impossible for you to make a fashionable woman of me, & therefore the best thing you can do with me I think will be to set me down in Edenton again, where I should have nothing to do but to attend to my Children & make perhaps three or four visits in the year. What a dreadful situation that would be for a fine lady, but to me there could be nothing more delightful, with the company of a few friends whenever [they] would be pleased to call on me...

Monday, November 8, 1790

I vowed I should go today and see Mr. Lenox, and indeed wrote a letter to Mr. Iredell stating that as my intention—and yet my feet refuse to take me there, or anywhere else. Sarah long ago obtained the

56

particulars concerning the Stage, but they only served to convince me further that this is a Journey I can never undertake. To transport all of us—Mother and the Children—and all our belongings, to Fraunces Tavern in the dead of night! For the Stage departs at three in the morning.

Yesterday when Major Butler called, I could see the look of concern on his face when I confessed to him that I had not yet set a date for our Departure. The only reason he has not yet left the City himself, he told me, is that his Wife's ill health has become quite dire. I felt a good deal of Sympathy for the Gentleman, and reflected that great Wealth such as his is no protection against ordinary grief. But so self-centered am I that I soon found myself wondering how it should be with *me* if I were to face the imminent prospect of losing my Spouse—surely far worse than it is for Major Butler, who is possessed of many strengths and Resources that I am not. It is a thought that has occurred to me more times than I care to number in recent days, as it has been some weeks since I have had any news of Mr. Iredell. Dear God, grant that he is well! Surely, if he is, I shall receive a Letter within the next few days.

Thursday, November 11, 1790

I have just woken from the most alarming Nightmare, of a type I have had before, but never so vivid. I saw before me Mr. Iredell's face, the dearest face I know, but in this dream terrible to behold: pale and devoid of that lively spirit which in reality animates it. His head lay against a pillow—I suppose my Imagination had placed him in some dreary roadside inn—and his reddened eyes, surrounded by gray skin, gazed blankly into the distance. Sweat beaded on his brow, and his breath came with a gulping, rasping sound—a sound that I know generally means but one thing, and that too horrible to contemplate.

"Mr. Iredell! Mr. Iredell!" I cried in my dream, but his eyes seemed to look past or through me, as though I were not there.

I threw myself upon his body, sobbing, pierced to the heart by the thought that he was dying here, alone and untended, and that his last moments would not even be comforted by the knowledge of my presence. A Desolation swept through me that seemed to suck the life from me.

"James, James!" I cried at last, using his Christian name. Why, I now berated myself, had I denied him this simple wish?

At this sound, his eyes fixed upon me. His breathing calmed; he lifted his head, even propped himself on an elbow, and smiled at me benevolently.

"Hannah," he said, "you've come at last."

And then I awakened.

I am not one to maintain, as some do, that dreams betoken Reality; I know that my having dreamt of Mr. Iredell on his deathbed does not make it any more likely that he is in fact there. And yet, my mind will not rest until I have some evidence that he is well. A letter, please dear God, a letter!

And if my Husband is restored to me, safe and well, shall I comply with the sentiments of my Dream and address him as James? Would it not signify to him that I am capable of altering myself, of suiting myself to modern fashions as he would wish? Alas, though, I know that I cannot; the name would stick in my throat. To me he always has been Mr. Iredell, and always shall be; and I can only pray that he understands that my adherence to an Appellation of respect does not signify that I love him any the less than do those modern Wives who gleefully concoct pet names for their Husbands.

From Hannah Iredell to James Iredell:

New York, Thursday, November 11, 1790

... My anxiety about you is very great. I have not had a line from you since you left Eden House in early October. If I do not hear from you in a few days I shall really be very miserable. I never can think of your Journey, the distance and risk you run, without shuddering almost. If I could but hear you were well I should endeavor to make myself easy on other subjects. But my dear Mr. Iredell, you know not how painful a situation mine altogether is.

Your dear Children are perfectly well & playing around me now in so noisy a manner that I hardly am able to do anything. Your little Annie will be able to read to you very prettily when you come, & James will entertain you with a great deal of very sensible conversation in good language very well pronounced. Come, my dear Mr. Iredell, and enjoy these pleasures as soon as possible, and make us all happy by once more having you with us...

Saturday, November 13, 1790

Of all the impertinence! Sarah has just returned to the house and told me she has reserved seats for us all on the Wednesday morning Stage to Philadelphia. I had sent her to the market, but instead of buying chicken and potatoes with the few Shillings I gave her, she hied herself to Fraunces Tavern and used it as earnest money for passage on the stage.

I could have told her to march back to that Tavern and get our chicken money back; I should at least have scolded her and warned her never to do such a thing without my permission again. I suppose there are many Mistresses who would have sold a Negro for such disobedience; and indeed, some of my Friends in Edenton (including Nelly) have urged me to rid myself of Sarah, with her sullen silences and her impudent manners. But I could never part with her—and alas, she knows it; for we were raised together, after my Parents died. What would I have done without her and Sappho—the only familiar and affectionate Faces I saw, after I was sent off to live with Strangers (Cousins of mine, yes, but Strangers still)? I have grown used to her ways, even fond of them. True, she never before did anything quite as bold as this; but some part of me, I confess, was relieved she had done it.

She has even arranged for a Man to take us all, and our belongings, to the Tavern in the middle of the night—a free Black man she met at the market. This too, is a great relief, although it concerns me to hear that Sarah has been consorting with free Negroes. I suppose I should have expected it, in this City. I shouldn't wonder if keeping such company has been giving her notions, if perhaps this Man or some other put it into her mind to go down and use the chicken money to book those tickets. And from what I have heard of Philadelphia—teeming with Quakers who consider Slavery an abomination, and containing in its population a goodly number of free Blacks—it will be even worse.

Dear Lord, if she should take a notion to run away, what would become of me? But no, surely she is bound to me by ties of affection as well as those of Property; I have only to think on that terrible day, months ago, the day we tried to go to market with Mrs. Simmons—the way she let me cry on her shoulder, and gave me such comfort. Surely she needs me quite as much as I need her.

59

Philadelphia, Pennsylvania

Tuesday, November 23, 1790

Tis done at last: I write this in my own house in Philadelphia—the lease for which was obtained some weeks before our arrival, at Sam's and Mr. Iredell's request, by the firm of Hewes and Anthony. It is a brick house of three storeys, far grander than what we require—how we shall afford the rent on it I cannot begin to tell. Certainly, if the decision had been mine, I should have chosen a more modest and less expensive residence. But it would be ungrateful in me to complain, considering that I was spared the distasteful—nay, impossible!—task of seeking out lodging here on my own. In any event, what is important is that I somehow contrived to get us all here, and settled—and not so tardy, really, for the President himself arrived in this City only yesterday.

Sam and his Family, alas, are not yet here—Mr. Iredell likewise, though I was greatly relieved to find that he had left a letter for me in care of Mr. Anthony. The last Court on his Circuit was to meet at New Bern on November 8; even if he passes a few days in Edenton before he returns, he should be with us, God willing, within a week or two.

The Stage deposited us at the George Inn here late on Thursday evening; I was so weak and exhausted from the difficulties of the Journey (of which more later) that I could not think what to do, but only stood silently in the public room of the Inn, surrounded by our trunks and boxes, James heavily asleep on my hip and Annie clinging to my skirts. Mother was peering longingly at the kegs behind the bar, which held ale and all manner, I suppose, of other spirits. It was Sarah who spoke at last, to suggest that we take rooms at the Inn for the night and seek out Messrs. Hewes and Anthony in the morning. Fortunately there remained to me sufficient funds to cover the cost of the rooms, though little more.

The next morning Sarah offered to inquire as to the whereabouts of the offices of Hewes and Anthony, and indeed to act as a Scout; she actually ventured out into the streets on her own and found the address!

She appears to have acquired a great deal of resourcefulness and courage during our Months in New York. Within twenty minutes she returned to the Inn and began to lead us down what is called Second Street, past a bustling covered market, and confidently turned left on a Street called Lombard. Quite a strange and ragtag band, I'm sure we appeared: a lame and disheveled old Lady, two small whining Children, and a haggard Woman with terror in her eyes—all obediently following the confident stride of a Negro wench. And now that we are settled here with all our belongings, I have no intention of leaving again until my Brother or Mr. Iredell arrives; for this City is even noisier and more crowded than New York. In any event, I believe it will take me several more days to recover from the travails of the Journey.

Indeed, I am amazed that we all survived that Journey with no ill effects other than fatigue and sore throats. If I never travel in a Stage again I shall certainly not have cause for complaint: hard benches with no backs; stones and roots in the Road jostling us as though we were all so many pennies in a beggar's cup; freezing rain that made its way through the roof of the carriage, dripping on our heads and running down our necks. And the Tavern where we passed the night was distinctly unsavory, the mattresses lumpy and no doubt ridden with vermin; I shared a bed with the Children, and I don't believe any of us slept more than an hour or two. I have more sympathy than ever for Mr. Iredell, thinking on what he must suffer traveling Roads far worse than those between New York and Philadelphia. Twice we were stuck fast in the mire, which required all of us to alight, and the Gentlemen to doff their coats and assist in the lifting of the wheels. The Children behaved as well as could be expected in these conditions, poor things, but with little sleep and nothing to do, there was a good deal of whimpering, which did not endear us to our fellow Travelers.

The worst occurred at one Tavern somewhere in Jersey, where we stopped for fresh horses and food: Mother slipped away from us and could not be found when the driver was ready to go. I pleaded with him to allow me a few minutes to search for her, which he did grudgingly, and at last I found her in a back room that smelled of sweat and spilled Liquor, swigging gin and in the thick of a card game with an assortment of Characters to whom I did not care to be introduced. I pulled her up and hurried her as best I could back to the stage, hampered not only by her limp but also by what was now an impaired sense of balance on her part. When at last we got there, the Driver was scowling and James and Annie wailing loudly, convinced that the coach was going to leave me and their Grandmother behind, despite Sarah's best efforts to reassure them.

I did not recognize anyone in the carriage—fortunately so, for Mother's inebriation was, I fear, rather apparent. But to my great dismay, shortly after that disastrous stop in Jersey, Mother took it into her head to engage the Man seated across from her in a conversation. It took her only a few minutes before she began boasting, in a loud voice, that her Son was one of the Judges on the Supreme Court; I could feel all eyes in the carriage upon us. But she then, mercifully, drifted off to sleep before anyone could inquire his name.

From Arthur Iredell to James Iredell:

Guildford, England, November 30, 1790

... I had ten Days ago the inexpressible Happiness of receiving a letter from my Mother, in which she gives me the best accounts of her arrival at New York, and kind reception in your family. It was particularly unfortunate that you had but the day before left that place ...

I can conceive nothing more truly gratifying than the meeting between my Mother and you! After a Separation of so many Years, with so entire an Affection on her Part, and a Duty unimpaired on Yours, it must be all that Feeling can make It! May it be succeeded by Many Years of mutual Gratification! To our Parent, it is a great change indeed! And the joy of giving her a <u>new existence</u> has been reserved for <u>you</u>! ...

Wednesday, December 15, 1790

The Johnstons and Mr. Iredell arrived at last, ten days since, fatigued but otherwise in fine health, thank the Lord; Mrs. Johnston, only, has some lingering complaints. But it seems scarcely worthwhile for Mr. Iredell to have traveled so far; for two of the three courts—those at Augusta and New Bern—failed for want of a quorum. So all that wandering was only to hold a two-day Court at Charleston, where little business was conducted! Mr. Iredell has promised me that he will write a letter to the other Judges, setting forth his objections to being permanently assigned to the Southern Circuit (for who can tell when

Congress will turn its attention to a complete alteration of the system). But he betrays not nearly as much irritation at this situation as I would have expected—indeed, not nearly as much as I myself feel—recounting instead tales of the various Dinners and balls to which he was invited, and what distinguished Gentleman and charming Ladies he met.

Of course he has been quite overcome with joy to be reunited with his Mother at last. I am now greatly relieved that I considered it best not to mention anything of Mother's problems in my letters to Mr. Iredell, for it seems that—as I had so fervently hoped—the seeing her dear eldest Son once more has worked a marvelous transformation on the old Lady. When Mr. Iredell first arrived, the spectacle of their Reunion was even more affecting than I had anticipated: the two of them weeping freely, exclaiming over each other, embracing again and again—for Mother and Son share an inclination to surrender themselves to the strength of their Emotions. Since then Mother has maintained a near perfect Sobriety, has even engaged in some needlework, and has resumed spinning her fairy stories for the Children. Annie and James seem delighted to have once more the Grandmother they knew when she first arrived, and fortunately are too young to tell their Papa of the changes they witnessed in her shortly thereafter.

"You see, Hannah?" Mr. Iredell has said more than once. "I knew that you and Mother would come to treasure one another."

And indeed, when we all sit of an evening with our few chairs pulled up before the fire, I have so acute a sense of peace and contentment that to my amazement I sometimes feel tears spring to my eyes, and must resort to some subterfuge to conceal my emotion. I suppose it comes of having had so few such Scenes in my own childhood: never knowing my Grandparents, never even having any hopes of traveling all the way to Scotland to meet them; and of course losing even my Parents when I was quite young. And I always suspected those Cousins of mine took me in after Father died largely in order to gain the Income I brought with me; in any event, they bestowed little affection upon me. I never again felt part of a Family until Sam sent for me to come and live with him at Hayes, by which time I was nearly grown. But now I have it again, that downy nest of affection and easy familiarity that makes a true Home: the casual brush of hand on shoulder, forehead gently bumping against forehead—these little things are the World to me.

For myself, I should be content to never venture beyond this cozy haven; but Mr. Iredell is urging me to accompany him this afternoon to attend Mr. Wilson's first Law lecture at the College of Philadelphia. He says that a great audience is expected, including the President and Mrs. Washington and many other members of the Government and of Congress, and of Philadelphia society; it is only fitting that the other Judges of the Supreme Court—and their Wives, if in the City—should attend. Indeed, Mr. Iredell seems so delighted at the prospect of one of his colleagues being honored in this way that one would think he himself were delivering the lecture! He says the lectures are confirmation, if any were needed, that Mr. Wilson is the foremost legal scholar in the Nation, and most likely the next Chief Justice, should Mr. Jay take it into his head to resign.

Saturday, January 22, 1791

A letter today from Mr. Tredwell brings the joyous news that Nelly has been safely delivered of a Daughter—to be named Elizabeth, after Mr. Tredwell's Mother, and called Betsey. And Mr. Iredell and I are asked to be the Godparents! How I should like to hold and admire the infant. Does she have Nelly's dark hair and eyes, I wonder, or does she more resemble Mr. Tredwell, with his copper-colored hair and ruddy complexion? What I would give for just a glimpse of her. But no more on that now, lest I grow Melancholic.

We have made the acquaintance of an amiable family living just next door to us—or, I should say, Mr. Iredell made their acquaintance and brought me along, as I had neither seen nor spoken to them before his arrival here. Their name is Bond, and they have two daughters of about eighteen or twenty, Fanny and Becky, who seem quite taken with Annie and James—and vice-versa. Mrs. Bond appears a clever and lively Woman, and yet not one to put on airs or flaunt her wit, like so many of the Ladies here and in New York. She dresses well, but with sobriety and modesty, and has such an open, engaging manner that I dare to hope that, someday, I may come to know her as a friend.

I believe that if I had just one friend—one true friend—in this City, it would make a world of difference to me: it would so strengthen me to have someone of my own Sex with whom I might talk freely, and laugh, and perhaps even gossip occasionally. I had hoped, of course, that

Mother might prove to be that friend; but—for all that her behavior of late has been irreproachable—I cannot, after all that has transpired, bring myself entirely to trust her.

Of course Mr. Iredell would say that in this City I am quite surrounded by Ladies who might be my friends, if I would only allow them to know me. He has begun to chide me again, as he used to, for my timidity, as I feared he might—and as, indeed, I chide myself. Last Wednesday we went again to one of Mr. Wilson's lectures on the Law (for though he is no eloquent speaker, yet his erudition is great, and I consider that I am gaining some understanding of the principles of our Constitution—a document on which Mr. Wilson himself is said to have had great influence). I happened to spy, across the room, Mrs. King, whose acquaintance I had made at some Evening or other in New York—the wife of a Senator from New York, rather grand—and whom I had not seen since. Alas, I made the mistake of remarking on her presence to Mr. Iredell.

"Why, you must go and greet her!" he cried heartily, much to my dismay; left to my own devices, I would surely have pretended not to notice her, and prayed that she would not have noticed me.

I pointed out, with feigned regret, that there was no time, the lecture was about to begin; but Mr. Iredell made me promise that I would seek out Mrs. King at its conclusion. I gazed at Mr. Wilson, noted how his thick dark eyebrows wiggled up and down whenever he wished to emphasize a particular point, and the way his spectacles were continually slipping down his short nose; but I found myself scarcely able to attend to what he was saying—something concerning Natural Law, and the Natural rights of individuals, I believe—so agitated was I at the prospect of speaking to Mrs. King: What would I say to her, and she to me? Would she recall my face, or should I give my name? If I gave my name and she indeed remembered me, would she be offended that I had presumed otherwise? If I were fortunate enough to engage her in some semblance of conversation, how would I extricate myself from it without appearing too abrupt? These and a host of other Questions entirely occupied my mind; but I consoled myself that at least I should have Mr. Iredell at my side to assist me.

But as soon as the lecture was done and the applause had died down, Mr. Iredell not only reminded me of Mrs. King but also announced that he would stay at his place whilst I greeted the Lady on my own. Trembling, I tried to protest; but he told me—kindly but quite firmly—that if he always accompanied me on occasions of this sort I should never learn to fend for myself in his absence.

"Go!" he whispered urgently. "Hurry, before it is too late."

I cannot say I entirely obeyed that injunction, but Mrs. King was apparently in no great hurry herself, and was just rising from her seat when I approached. She was engaged in conversation with another Lady, who I did not know, and I stood near her in awkward silence for what seemed like some minutes. At last she turned in my direction; I curved my lips into a smile and opened my mouth, but to my horror, I could make no sound. I was conscious only of the blood pounding in my head, my heart fluttering in my breast like a bird in its death throes.

After a moment's puzzled silence, a gleam of recognition seemed to light her eyes. "Mrs. ... Iredell, is it?"

"Yes," I managed to whisper.

She rattled on for a minute or two about how nice it was to see me again, introduced me to the other Lady (whose name, if I even heard it, I immediately forgot), and sallied a few casual Inquiries—how was my Journey from New York, was my family well, et cetera—to which I responded with one-word answers, and even those barely audible. At last she said something about how I must call on her some afternoon, and gave me her address in the City; I had enough wit about me to understand I had been politely dismissed, and made my way back to Mr. Iredell. Fortunately, he was now surrounded by various Gentlemen and Ladies, engaged in an animated discussion of the lecture, and I had a few moments to collect myself, and calm my shaking body.

"There, now," he said, when he had bade farewell to the assembled company and we were on the Street, heading at last for home, "that wasn't so terrible, was it, my dear?"

"Why, no, not at all." I smiled at him brightly. "She invited me to call on her."

"Excellent!" he cried, squeezing my hand, which rested in the crook of his arm. "And so you shall, of course. Why, I warrant that within a few months you'll be nearly as much at home here as you were in Edenton."

He was so pleased that I nearly forgave myself for deceiving him; and yet the lie has continued to plague me, for it is clear to me that the Woman he was so pleased with is nothing like the Woman that I am.

From Samuel Johnston to Nelly Tredwell:

Philadelphia, Pennsylvania, January 23, 1791

... I sincerely congratulate you on the Birth of your Daughter and am very happy to hear from Tredwell that you and the child are like to do well. Take care that you are not too fond of it ... Your Aunt desires her love to you and wishes you a great deal of happiness in your Daughter ...

Sunday, January 30, 1791

Alas, what I most dreaded has come to pass. Yesterday afternoon Mother slipped away and had not returned by nightfall. I feared the worst—although in a way Mr. Iredell feared even worse, engaging in the same round of anxious Speculation to which I had succumbed when Mother first disappeared that day in New York. It was a bitter cold night, as indeed the whole Winter here has been bitter, and Mr. Iredell's imagination painted for him vivid pictures of his Mother having somehow lost her way, wandering miserable and frozen, or waylaid by thieves. I yearned to speak, to reassure him; and yet what reassurance would it be to tell him she was undoubtedly safe and warm, but drinking herself into a stupor and gambling us into Bankruptcy?

At last, shortly after the clock struck ten, Mother appeared at the door, and in a sorry state: her cap gone, her hair half unpinned, and her Person generally stinking of drink. When I saw Mr. Iredell's face as he greeted her—that initial joyous Relief yielding first to confusion, then to the horror of comprehension—it was clear to me that he genuinely had no prior inkling of her weakness. She staggered to a chair, where she collapsed, her knees spread wide, and let out a loud belch.

"Mother!" Mr. Iredell exclaimed. "What is the meaning of this?"

Mother replied with a shrug and that vague smile I have unfortunately come to know well, as though her Condition was nothing to do with her. Mr. Iredell looked at me then, helplessly, and with such a degree of Pain in his gentle brown eyes that I felt tears rush to my own; distressed as I had been at my discovery of Mother's weaknesses, it was as nothing to what I felt watching Mr. Iredell's anguish.

I put my arms around him, and he seemed to Collapse against me. "Only help me get her up the stairs and into her bed," I whispered to him, "and then I will tell you all."

After we had done what was necessary—tears running down Mr. Iredell's cheeks all the while, and a Sob escaping him now and then—I sat him down in the Parlor and related the entire sad history. Painful as it was for me to describe and for him to hear, I considered it necessary that he understand the situation in full.

"Ah, Hannah, what a Trial I have subjected you to," he said when at last I had finished. "But why did you not tell me this before?"

"I had thought that the sight of you might at last work a Reformation on her that my pleading could not," I replied. "But I see now that I was mistaken. It is a Habit that must be deeply ingrained in her."

Mr. Iredell turned his back to me and stared into the dwindling fire. His hands gripped the mantelpiece so tightly that the skin over his knuckles was pulled taut. "Damn her!" I heard him mutter. "She's no Mother of mine."

"Mr. Iredell!" I rushed to his side and placed my hand on his back. Certainly this was no time to reprimand him for swearing, as I have so often in the past. "She has her faults, to be sure, but she is still your Mother, and always will be. Think on what she has given you: life itself, her Mother's milk, the many pains she must have taken with you in your childhood. For you could not be, I feel sure, the Man you are today had not a Mother loved you and taught you well."

My words must have had some effect, for I felt a loosening of the muscles in Mr. Iredell's back, and then his whole body began to shake with sobs.

"Be not angry with her, but rather consider how together we may perhaps yet inspire her to reform herself, and become once again the Mother you so cherished," I said softly, my head now against Mr. Iredell's shoulder. "I couldn't manage to prevail on her myself, though I tried—but I see how much she dotes on you. And I am convinced that, somewhere within her, she truly desires to rid herself of this demon, and only requires the urging of someone she loves and admires." Mr. Iredell's sobs had quieted, and I now embraced him. "No, if you must be angry, better to think on someone else—someone who should have prevented her from taking this Road before it was too late."

Mr. Iredell was still for a moment, then straightened his posture with such violence that I was forced to stumble backwards.

"Arthur!" he pronounced with venom.

Despite the pain of this Scene, and the circumstances that had led to it, I confess I felt a small warm current of Satisfaction run through me, now that Mr. Iredell's Wrath had found an Object who is, I daresay, nothing less than deserving of it.

Saturday, February 5, 1791

Last night Mr. Iredell addressed his Mother for the first time since the night she came home in that disgraceful state, but I fear the exchange did not proceed quite as I had hoped. Alas, his anger got the better of him; indeed, his tone was almost as stern as the one he took in the letter he wrote to Arthur, some days since. He expressed disbelief, consternation, outrage; and all the while Mother merely gazed at a spot on the ceiling.

"I do not understand this, Mother," he finished. "Surely you, who taught myself and my Brothers the meaning of propriety, the meaning of Dignity—surely you of all people must realize how improper such behavior is for one of your sex, your age—your position in Society!"

At this Mother made a sort of snorting noise, and at last looked directly at Mr. Iredell. "*My* position in Society!" she said, her voice quite as shrill as her Son's. "I think you mean *yours*, Jemmy, do you not? Just like Arthur, you are—always worrying that I would embarrass him in front of his fancy friends." She shifted forward in her chair, rubbing her bad leg, before continuing with her Speech, which she pronounced with such rancor that she fairly spat the words out. "But I'll tell you something, Jemmy my boy. I've had a hard life, I have. Your father suffering that paralytic Stroke, leaving me to support the four of you—not that he was much good at bringing in Money before that, mind you. You sailing off to America when you were barely seventeen. Then Charles going off to India, and dying there, poor Soul—Tom disappearing to America as well—leaving me with that prig Arthur, who never did treat me as he should. I've had a hard life, I say, and I deserve to have a little harmless Pleasure in my old age."

Although there was great bitterness in these words, they inspired in me some Sympathy for the old lady; her sorrows had evidently borne heavily upon her. But the effect on Mr. Iredell was rather different; as I have seen happen before in conversation between Parents and

69

Children—or indeed, between close relatives of any kind—one party seizing on a portion of what has been said by the other: the part that concerns himself.

"My sailing off to America when I was seventeen—that is what you hold responsible for the sorry State I find you in now?" Mr. Iredell railed. "Had I a choice? Did I not have to find a way to provide for you and my Brothers, when I was barely more than a Child myself? Did I not faithfully remit to you all that I earned, save for what I needed to eke out a modest Existence of my own?"

"I'm not saying you didn't." Mother tightened her shawl about her. "All I'm saying is that I've had a hard life, and now that I'm in my declining Years, and I've got my Children established in life, I'm entitled to amuse myself a bit, and no harm done."

Mr. Iredell's face was now very red. "No harm done! On the contrary, Mother, there's a great deal of harm done. For one thing, if news of your drinking and your gambling should become Public, just imagine the consequences for my Reputation, my career!"

"There! You see?" said Mother, beginning to struggle up to a standing position, and reaching for her walking stick. "Just like Arthur, always thinking of himself." She paused, and turned back to Mr. Iredell, the harsh lines on her face softening for a moment. "But you, Jemmy, I thought you were different. I thought you would have some feeling for your poor Mother in her old age." She turned and began again her slow limping. "I see now that I was mistaken."

She made her way up the stairs, while Mr. Iredell slumped into his chair and held his head in his hands. When at last we heard the click of her Bed chamber door, I went to kneel by Mr. Iredell's chair and embrace him.

"You see?" he said, not looking up. "It's hopeless, hopeless. She is, alas, entirely depraved. She has lost the gentlewoman in her." He reached for my hand and pressed it to his lips. "And I cannot bear the thought that you and the Children should be left alone with this … this *Monster* … when it is *my* Mother, *my* cross to bear. When I think of what you must have been through …" He suddenly dropped my hand and rose to his feet. "I shall begin writing that letter immediately."

I knew what letter he meant—the one he had promised to write to the other Judges, setting out his objections to the Southern Circuit. I had asked several times if he had yet begun it, and each time the answer was No; it is a task, I know, that he approaches with distaste, for he is always loath to appear to be asking any Favor for himself. But he was at his desk late into the night, and even now, at Eleven in the morning, I can hear his pen scratching at the paper. (For there is no time to be lost; the Court begins its session on Monday.) Mr. Iredell is a most persuasive writer; if his pen could convince the wild Rebels of Western Carolina to ratify the Constitution, as it once did, surely it can convince five Judges to do what is only just.

Monday, February 14, 1791

The Court is adjourned, the Circuits assigned—and Mr. Iredell's letter, so carefully composed and cogently argued, has fallen on deaf—nay, cruel!—ears. His colleagues have refused to relieve him of the Southern Circuit, each of them proffering some reason or other why it would be impossible—all but Mr. Blair, who was prevented attending this sitting by illness. And it appears that Mr. Iredell may be constrained to ride the Circuit alone this Spring, as the rumor is that Mr. Rutledge is soon to resign his seat on the Court in order to become Chief Justice of South Carolina. The inequity of it leaves me entirely speechless: Mr. Iredell, who only returned home in December from a three months' arduous journey, is now required to embark on the same Journey in but a month's time! And I am to be abandoned again in this still strange City, nearly friendless (alas, I have not yet had the courage to try and make a friend of Mrs. Bond), and with a Mother who is capable of bringing all sorts of difficulties upon us. Ah, would that Mr. Iredell might follow Mr. Rutledge's example and resign his seat; surely North Carolina could be induced to give him some honorable position similar to what Mr. Rutledge is said to receive. But I dare not mention such thoughts to Mr. Iredell; though he appears dejected over the way his colleagues have used him, I fear that he would yet bristle at any suggestion that he resign.

Indeed, he is almost as distressed—and at the same time, I think, rather delighted—over the first Case of any importance that has made its way to the Court: two Dutch merchants have sued the State of Maryland on a debt; and though it appears that Maryland has no objection to being sued in a Federal Court, Mr. Iredell fears that other States will take it as a grave insult to their sovereignty, and insist that it is only in their own State courts that they may be sued—and even then, only when the State gives its consent. It is a point, he says, on which the language of the

Constitution is not entirely clear; but he is certain that many States—including our own—would never have ratified the document had they believed such a result might ensue. The merits of the Question have not yet come on, but when they do, Mr. Iredell says, it will be one of great significance; the eyes of the Nation will be fixed on the Supreme Court. And indeed, there was such a gleam in his own eyes as he spoke these words that I fear I shall never be able to tear him away from this cursed Court!

From Hannah Iredell to Nelly Tredwell:

Philadelphia, Pennsylvania, February 27, 1791

I should not, my dear Nelly, have been so long silent, but I have really not had spirits to write, nor indeed has my Health been much better. But whatever Situation they may be in, it will always be a particular Satisfaction to hear from you, my dear child.

I am glad to see so much of the Mother in your letter. I am not much less pleased than yourself with the Praises of your little girl. I wish you would bring her to me that I may judge if the dear little Creature deserves them, though I have no doubt but she does. However, I should be much better pleased to see her loveliness than to hear of it ...

Mrs. Johnston often complains, and my Brother still has a cough, but they both look very well. And thank God our children are all well... My little Annie and James talk of nothing half so often as their cousin Nelly and Carolina, and there is no place in the world, I am sure, that their Mother would prefer to it, not out of love to the Country, but the tender friends she left there...

Thursday, March 10, 1791

At last, some good News has come our way: Mr. Blair, who has recovered his health, has agreed to take the Southern Circuit in Mr. Iredell's stead! Mr. Iredell will take the circuit assigned to Mr. Blair—the Middle, which includes Pennsylvania. For one of these Courts, then, Mr. Iredell need only stroll the four blocks up Chestnut Street to the City Hall! Short of a declaration from Congress that Circuit riding is to be abolished, or Mr. Iredell resigning his post, I cannot imagine any turn of events that might have delighted me more than this.

Mr. Iredell is particularly pleased that he will be riding the Circuit in the company of Judge Wilson, whom he so greatly admires. To be sure, the Gentleman is eminent and learned; and yet he appears to me to be one of those people who is so fond of himself as to make it unnecessary, if not impossible, for anyone else to experience such feelings towards him. Last week we were invited to take Dinner at his house, the table being presided over by his eldest Daughter—a sober and modest young lady of about twenty. Mr. Wilson spoke at such length, and with so few pauses, as to make it impossible for anyone else to insert a word. He began with a Disquisition on the institution of Juries—going back to the times of the ancient Romans—and then moved on, by slow degrees, to the jurisdiction of the Federal courts, and then to a catalogue of all the crimes and offenses known to the Constitution and laws of the United States. It was all very impressive, but I confess that my mind began to wander after he described, in gruesome detail, the exact method of drawing and quartering by which Treason is punishable in England—a subject I found, in any event, ill-suited to the Dinner table.

But there is Sarah now, back from the market. Mr. Iredell has decreed we must have a celebratory Dinner, and invite our neighbors, the Bonds. Surely our Dinner will be a jollier affair than Mr. Wilson's; I feel quite sure that no one will see fit to bring up the subject of drawing and quartering. I do hope the Bonds have no expectation of elegance or strict formality; but then, how could they, when we were forced to ask them to bring their own chairs?

Chief Justice John Jay to James Iredell:

New York, New York, March 16, 1791

... I was this Moment favored with yours of the 10th Instant. It gives me Pleasure to find that by Mr. Blair's consenting to go the Southern Circuit, every Objection to your attending the middle one with Mr. Wilson is removed. The Circuits press hard on us all; and your Share of the Task has hitherto been more than in due proportion ...

From Arthur Iredell to Tom Iredell:

Guildford, England, April 5, 1791

... I have had the pleasure of a letter from James a week or two ago. He gives me a melancholy account of my Mother's indulgence in a failing which I had reason to think she would have got the better of in his family. Did she used to make too free with Liquors when you were in England? It is a most disgraceful habit, and has given James the utmost unhappiness. I pray God he may induce her to surmount that only Bar to her happiness...

Friday, April 8, 1791

The Circuit court is to begin here next week, but alas, it appears I am to be deprived of my Husband's company yet longer—for he writes that he must stay in Trenton to preside over the business there, which was greater than expected, while Mr. Wilson returns to open the Court here. At first I was rather vexed at Mr. Wilson for taking upon himself the privilege of returning home; but then I reflected that the poor Man (for all that I find his manner rather unpleasant) is a Widower with six Children—the youngest, I believe, no more than five or six and the eldest girl acting as Mother to the rest. Surely it must be even harder for the Wilson Family to part with their Father than it is for us. And it must be difficult for him as well, raising all those Children with no Spouse to assist him.

But such reflection on the misfortunes of others, I fear, cannot entirely rid me of my own selfish disappointment. The longer Mr. Iredell stays away, the more likely it is, I fear, that Mother will commit some serious indiscretion; he has only been gone a week now, but already she has slipped away twice and returned home some hours later much the worse for wear; I can only hope she told no one her name, or her Family connections. I have taken to hiding my Money, as well, for several shillings have disappeared from my purse, and I can ill afford to lose any more.

We must go now to Mrs. Bond's, for she has been so kind as to invite me to take Tea with her—and she has asked Mother to come as well. It is a risk, of course, but I prefer to be accompanied by *someone*—even someone as risky as Mother—when I go visiting; Mrs. Bond was exceedingly amiable when she came to Dinner (as indeed, was the entire Family), but I am still not entirely at my ease in her company.

From James Iredell to Hannah Iredell:

Trenton, New Jersey, April 9, 1791

... I am much mortified in seeing Judge Wilson going to Philadelphia before me, but there is no help for it. My duty requires me to stay here, and therefore I stay contentedly ... In the meantime, my dear Hannah, pray write to me as often as you can, for this place I assure you is a very dull one, and I want something to support my spirits. I was disappointed in not getting a letter from you yesterday. Pray write to me if Mr. Cox has enclosed the Warrant for my Salary. I am most afraid you are already in want of money ...

Monday, April 11, 1791

All my charitable feelings regarding Mr. Wilson have been quite dispelled by certain intelligence communicated to me yesterday by Mrs. Bond.

Our Tea at her house last week having gone well (Mother keeping herself rather quieter than usual), Mrs. Bond invited us to accompany her Family to Church yesterday, and on the way home I found myself confessing to her some of the torments that have afflicted me this past year, with Mr. Iredell being away so much of the time. Her murmured expressions of sympathy filled my heart with such emotion that I feared tears would soon be falling from my eyes.

When we reached my doorstep, I mustered my courage to ask her if she might spare a few minutes to take some Tea with me; she readily agreed. My heart fairly leapt in my breast; anxious though I was at the prospect of entertaining her, I felt as elated as a young Girl who has been smiled upon by some ardently admired playfellow.

Before long our discourse turned to my disappointment at Mr. Iredell's being detained in Trenton. "But of course," I added with a sigh,

"I suppose that Mr. Wilson—with six Children and no Wife—has a greater claim to return to the bosom of his Family."

Mrs. Bond paused and took a sip of tea before she spoke. "I believe, my dear Mrs. Iredell, it is not family concerns that bring him back so urgently. Polly Wilson can manage quite nicely without her Father around—she's had quite a bit of practice in doing so, I fear. She's a Friend of my Daughters, and quite a capable Girl."

We then both sipped from our cups, leaving a pregnant but uncertain silence. I am not one for Gossip, nor do I believe that Mrs. Bond is generally so inclined. But under circumstances so closely affecting myself and my family, I felt further Inquiry was not only justifiable, but appropriate.

"You believe, then," I said, "that Mr. Wilson was anxious to return to Philadelphia for some other reason?"

Mrs. Bond set down her cup, dabbed at her mouth with her handkerchief, and leaned towards me slightly. "It is generally known, my dear Mrs. Iredell, that Mr. Wilson is one of those who has speculated quite extensively in Western lands. Some say rather too extensively. They say he has gotten himself into a good deal of Debt, counting on the prospect of reaping enormous profits. That is why he prefers to take these Circuits that keep him closer to home, or so I understand—so that if a crisis should arise in his Finances, as it frequently does, he can rush back to put out the fire before it spreads. No doubt some such conflagration has recently erupted."

I thanked Mrs. Bond for imparting this interesting intelligence, though I did not reveal to her the Fury seething within my bosom. That Mr. Wilson should be able to run home to see to his grand financial schemes, while Mr. Iredell—who has suffered more than any of the other Judges, and certainly far more than Mr. Wilson, in this Circuit riding business—should remain separated from his Family for the Lord knows how much longer! And we, far from having vast Tracts of Western land to attend to, are very nearly running out of the wherewithal to purchase our next meal. Last night we made do with a Supper of beans and bread, with Mother reminding us throughout the meal that such fare would take a toll on her Digestion.

As to Mother, I believe Mrs. Bond may be of great assistance there as well. Mrs. Bond has been so kind, and seems so trustworthy, that I thought it would do no harm to mention our domestic Difficulty; and it has been so long since I was able to have a frank conversation with a true

Friend. I have confided in no one to this point, not even my own Brother or Mrs. Johnston, as I know all too well her disposition to wag her tongue.

I did not tell Mrs. Bond all, only that Mother has a tendency to overindulge, and that I wished she had some worthy Endeavor with which to occupy her hours. Mrs. Bond put a finger to her lips for a moment; she then told me of her widowed Aunt, who is a member of a Circle of older ladies that meets at Christ Church under the patronage of the Assistant Rector, to engage in Prayer and discussion and perform good works such as knitting socks and gloves for the poor. I clapped my hands for joy, for I believe it is the one thing that might save Mother from herself: a group of women of her own age who would provide a salutary Influence, and virtuous and useful Tasks to distract her from yearnings for the vicious Amusements of her past. Mrs. Bond has offered to give Mother and myself an introduction to the Assistant Rector as soon as she can, perhaps later this week. What a welcome surprise that would be for Mr. Iredell, to see his Mother busy at Charitable endeavors, and with a new set of respectable and pious friends! And to see as well, that I have made a Friend; for such, I believe, I can begin to consider Mrs. Bond.

Friday, April 15, 1791

Mr. Iredell, and Peter, returned home yesterday evening, none the worse for their Sojourn in Trenton, and will remain here close to two entire weeks before setting out again.

Despite the brevity of his Absence, and the short distance that separated us, Mr. Iredell appeared extremely moved at seeing his Family once again, as we were to see him. Indeed, last night in the Privacy of our bed he embraced me with an Ardor that he has scarcely exhibited since the first months of our Marriage, so long ago. I can only attribute this enthusiasm in him to the dearth of Amusement, and of beautiful Ladies, in Trenton, a place that Mr. Iredell describes as dull and entirely lacking in Charm—for surely I am no different, and certainly no more a Beauty, than I was before he left. Would that all Circuit Courts were held in such Wastelands of diversion!

Mr. Iredell also appeared somewhat cheered by the news of Mrs. Bond's suggestion for Mother. I pray that Mother will be amenable to this Scheme; while she seems to have little fondness for the Church (for Arthur has taken Holy Orders, and she says that if the Church will admit to its ranks such a man as he, what good can there be in it?), I am in hopes that her native sociability will incline her at least to visit the Circle as an Experiment.

My only apprehension is that if Mother's behavior and disposition do improve, Mr. Iredell will insist that we begin to receive Visitors—a thing we have been wary of doing, not knowing what indiscretions Mother might commit. Nor have we accepted many invitations ourselves, fearing to leave Mother alone for long, or even with Peter and Sarah. I am ashamed to admit that I have sometimes felt grateful for Mother's condition for this reason; but of course there is no question of my wanting it to continue.

From Arthur Iredell to James Iredell:

Guildford, England, May 3, 1791

... I am happy to hear that my Mother's Health is so well established... You, who possess so large a share of Feeling, may form some Idea of the Shock my Pride and my Affection experienced at hearing that One, who could so easily call them both into Action, had degraded herself by the meanest of all Indulgences!

I write, my dear James, with no Reserve, even upon this painful Subject, as well because you are entitled to my utmost Confidence, as because it is most proper that you should be upon your Guard. We owe all imaginable Duty and Respect to her who gave us Birth; and it is, for that reason, incumbent upon us, whenever she loses sight of her own consequence, and endangers her own life, to exert an Authority over her, which is necessary, and can be exerted by no other Person. I have often ventured to do this, when She was in this Kingdom, from the purest Motives. It was a severe Exercise of Duty, which I cannot think of without Horror, but which I never shrunk from. She gave me no Credit for the Sacrifice I made, and I fear, should she read this, she will judge harshly of this new Proof I give of my Concern for her Welfare...

I have not had occasion to write in this little Book lately—which is, I suppose, a sign of good spirits, for it is true that I am more inclined to unburden myself of Melancholy than happiness. And indeed, life has proceeded smoothly enough these past two Months: Mr. Iredell scarcely away from us at all; Mother overindulging in Spirits only in the evenings, and only at home—which seems to be the best we can hope for, alas—and in somewhat better humor now that she has begun attending the Ladies' Circle at Church; and none of us suffering more than trifling Illnesses. Mrs. Bond and I have grown quite fond of one another, and sometimes go visiting together; though I still derive no enjoyment from performing these social obligations, it pleases Mr. Iredell, and I find them far less obnoxious when I am in the company of a Friend.

But I now take up my pen to report a Suspicion that brings me both great joy and some apprehension: If I am not much mistaken, I am once again with Child, and this at the age of forty-three! If my calculations are correct, the Conception occurred upon Mr. Iredell's return from Trenton in April. Should I carry the child to Term, and should it be healthy, it will perhaps owe its existence to the extreme Dullness of that place.

I have not yet breathed anything of this to Mr. Iredell, for I may not be pregnant at all; and it is still so early that there is a great risk of Miscarrying, as has happened to me once before; our Disappointment on that occasion was so profound that I would prefer not to inflict it once again on Mr. Iredell, although Heaven knows it would be a painful Secret for me to bear.

It is difficult enough now to keep all my teeming thoughts and emotions caged beneath a placid exterior. I am at times elated beyond words, thinking of another precious Child in my arms—I, who for so long considered that Providence had for some reason deemed me unworthy of bearing Children. The Child will be not much younger than Nelly's Betsey, who is now about six months, and in my idle fancies I see them happily at play together. But the next minute I am gripped by fears of losing the Babe, either before Birth or—like my poor tiny, wrinkled Thomas, frail as a nestling—shortly thereafter. And then of course there is the possibility of my own Life being taken, especially as I am at such an advanced age for childbearing—not that I should shrink from meeting my Maker, should it please Him to take me; but how can I leave two, or perhaps three, young Children bereft of their Mother, and Mr. Iredell with no one to aid him in their care and education?

But I must not allow my mind to lead me into such melancholy corners, dark Crannies that I strive to keep tightly shut—especially as gloomy or agitated thoughts during a Pregnancy are apt to have an unfavorable effect on the Character and Health of the infant. For the Child's sake, then, I must strive to remain calm and cheerful. I must, for example, face with equanimity, if not delight, the dinner that Mr. Iredell intends to give in celebration of the day of our Independence—for Mother has been on fairly good behavior for some weeks, and Mr. Iredell believes it is now safe to risk having company. Dear Heavens, the Fourth of July is but a week from today.

Were I to tell Mr. Iredell of my condition, or what I suspect it to be, he would almost certainly yield to my pleas and postpone, or even cancel, the Celebration. But that I will not do, not yet. No: I shall write out the invitations, this very afternoon, and have Sarah deliver them. Indeed, when I look at the list we have agreed on, it is not so fearful a group: my Brother and his wife; Mr. and Mrs. Bond; Major Butler—who has been rather broken in spirit since his Wife's death—and his eldest Daughter; and, at Mr. Iredell's urging, Mr. Wilson and *his* eldest Daughter. We still, alas, have not sufficient chairs for so large a number, but I imagine Mrs. Bond will again oblige us by lending us a few. I hope that Mr. Wilson and Major Butler are not so grand that they refuse to sit on mismatched chairs!

Tuesday, July 5, 1791

Thank the Lord *that* is over. The only good thing to be said about our Dinner party is that it was so disastrous that Mr. Iredell will likely not want to repeat the Experiment for quite some time.

The roast of veal, I suppose, was acceptable—I wouldn't know myself, having been so nauseated throughout the meal that I could not bring myself to swallow a mouthful. It did not help that the Weather has grown quite uncomfortably warm, and the room, despite our having opened all the windows, was stifling.

Mother persisted in asking for more wine, and as it would not do to refuse her in front of Company, we were forced to oblige—with the result that her speech became increasingly loud and slurred, and in the end she excused herself from the table before the pudding was served and fell asleep in her chair in the Parlor. Her snores reverberated all the way to the dining room, and it was decidedly awkward when we Ladies adjourned to the Parlor for coffee and found her still there.

Even worse than Mother, though, was what occurred between Major Butler and Mr. Wilson during dinner. Things began peaceably enough, with the two of them fondly recalling their experiences in the Convention that drafted the Constitution—although as I look back on it, it seems that they were already subtly vying at this point in the conversation, each one taking pains to prove that his role was the more important. But then Mr. Wilson got onto the subject of his Western lands: the glorious Opportunities they present for men of vision and courage, the possibility of reaping great personal Rewards while at the same time contributing to the strength and wealth of the Country. Major Butler, I noticed, began to frown and rub his long and rather prominent chin in a way that betrayed some skepticism.

At length he said, in that aristocratic drawl of his that ever seems to contain a polite sneer, "But my dear Wilson, have you actually *seen* these lands for yourself? One hears stories, you know, about unscrupulous Speculators who entice these poor wretches over from Europe, promising them milk and honey and all that sort of thing—and then of course it turns out to be swampland, or barren hillsides, or some such."

Mr. Wilson clearly took offense at this, for his round cheeks grew rather red, and his bushy eyebrows began bobbing up and down. "I have seen quite a few of my holdings myself, Sir, but the extent and remote location of the lands, and the demands of my Judicial duties, of course make it quite impossible for me to examine them all personally. However, even those I have not seen have been described to me in great detail by my Agents and surveyors, and I haven't the least hesitation in describing them as exceedingly fertile, and abundantly endowed with coal, and running water, and other valuable features."

"I *see*." Major Butler arched his eyebrows. "Well—call me fastidious if you will—but I could never bring myself to *buy* a parcel of land that I had not personally inspected, let alone endeavor to sell one."

At this Mr. Wilson rose from his place and leaned over the table towards where Major Butler sat, planting his hands on the cloth. "Are you implying, Sir, that I make claims for my lands that I cannot justify?"

"My dear Mr. Wilson!" Mr. Iredell called out quickly, with a nervous laugh. "I'm quite sure Major Butler meant nothing of the sort. I myself have heard that many of these Western lands are beginning to show great promise. Mr. Bond, you recently journeyed to Pittsburgh, did you not, on business? Tell us, please, how did you find the place?"

At this cue Mr. Bond happily embarked on a rather detailed narrative of his Journey, and Mr. Wilson within a moment or so resumed his seat. I was exceedingly relieved, and grateful for Mr. Iredell's quick wit; for though I had seen disaster looming just seconds ahead, I could not think of anything to say or do that might avert it.

When all the guests had taken their leave, Mr. Iredell and I sat for some minutes in a somber silence that was broken only by Mother's rasping intakes of breath (for, now that the guests were gone and it made no difference, her snores had at last quieted).

"Well," Mr. Iredell said at last, "it was unfortunate, but great Men will sometimes clash. By Jesus, though, what a damned row!"

"At least Mrs. Johnston will have something to talk about," I replied, "other than Mother's drinking herself into a stupor. And, Sir, how many times must I ask you not to swear?"

Mr. Iredell took my hand and kissed it, by way of apology I suppose—although I have spent so many years and so much breath begging him to break his Habit of swearing that I feel certain he no longer pays me any mind on the Subject. There then came a last loud snore from Mother—so deep and grating that it seemed to emanate from her very gut—which caused us both to flinch and Mr. Iredell to drop my hand, and we turned what remained of our energies to the unpleasant business of getting Mother into bed.

From Nelly Tredwell to Hannah Iredell:

Edenton, North Carolina, July 17, 1791

It seems like an Age since I wrote to you, my Dearest Aunt, but unavoidable circumstances have prevented me. My Child & myself have both been very ill... Betsey had the Thrush, & it was broke out on my Breast—never did anyone Suckle a Child in more agony than I did for four weeks... . Whenever she would go to suck I was as much Convulsed with the violence of the Pain as if I had been going into a fit ... I was taken with an intermitting fever, & not knowing the consequences, I continued to Suckle my little Cross Pet; & in two Days ... She was taken with a fever that for Eleven Days was never off ... I know not how I got better, for after she was taken sick She would not let anyone touch her but me, & all the Sleep I got was in the Day with her dozing at the Breast. For after the Family went to Bed I never Slept for fear of her having fits, & so much did I dread Them that if she started the Least in the World I was in a violent tremble & as sick as Death in a Minute ...

[Betsey] now mends very fast indeed & Sleeps well at Night & is quiet all Day—I am out with her at five o'clock every Morning the Weather will permit ...

From Arthur Iredell to James Iredell:

Guildford, England, August 1, 1791

... I have ... received [a Letter] from you ... containing little more than one Subject most painful to us both! Believe me, my dear Brother, I sympathize most sensibly... You do me, however, great injustice in hinting at a charge from which I am wholly free—the utmost I knew amounted only to Suspicion, & that she now and then exposed herself in that way—I had not the smallest Idea that it had Grown to a confirmed Habit, and might not easily be done away in your Family...

The money she drained from me far exceeded what she ought to have spent in her Style of Life... If your Pride be wounded at the Disgrace She now subjects you to, what must mine suffer, whom in this & many other ways she has subjected to the most serious Mortifications! ... She was from the Time she first came to London till she quitted it, in that Quarter of the Town where she could do me the most mischief—She was acquainted with many strange People (strange for her) who were, in different Ways, connected with great Families—her idle Vanity led her, naturally fond of talking, to vapor away about her Children, & as I had many Friends in high Life, chiefly about Me...

I should have received her into a Family of my own, if I had had one, rather than have permitted her to remain in the State in which I had the Mortification to see her. You invited her strongly to America—could I hesitate? Allow me, however, before I close this very unpleasant Subject, to observe that, were I in your Situation, I should think it my

Duty to exert an Authority over her, which surely would put it out of her
Power to indulge a Vice that perhaps is out of the reach of Argument ...

Friday, September 2, 1791

Mr. Iredell departed yesterday, amid great expressions of tender anxiety and veritable freshets of tears, for the Southern Circuit once again—to go it alone this time. Mr. Rutledge, his erstwhile traveling Companion, was only recently replaced by a Mr. Johnson of Maryland—who, apparently having been well warned, made it a condition of his acceptance that he *not* be required to ride the Southern Circuit! I believe Mr. Iredell has at last despaired of appealing to his Colleagues' sense of Equity; for he has been engaged in serious discussions with Sam about what sort of Bill might be introduced in the Senate to require a Rotation of the Circuits. And yet he still will not allow a negative word to be spoken against his fellow Judges—and especially not against the esteemed Mr. Wilson, whom Mr. Iredell now considers as his particular Friend.

Thank the Lord Mr. Wilson understands that we haven't the wherewithal to invest in his Land schemes; for though I have no particular reason to doubt their soundness, I confess that Major Butler's remarks at Dinner did give me pause. And yet I suppose they did not have that effect on everyone who heard them, for Mrs. Bond tells me that Mr. Bond has decided to become a partner of Mr. Wilson and some other Gentleman in a land company by the name, I believe, of Indiana. For the Bonds' sake, I hope Mr. Wilson continues to prosper.

At least I have Mrs. Bond to keep me company in Mr. Iredell's absence; and while he is gone, I needn't make such a show of paying these tiresome Visits to other Ladies. Indeed, I have no intention of accepting any invitations that may arrive while Mr. Iredell is gone, for being some five months pregnant, I can easily plead indisposition. And yet, it is that very pregnancy that causes me such anxiety: what if something were to go awry during the three Months Mr. Iredell must be away? What if the Child comes early, or is lost? Difficult as such a thing would be to bear with Mr. Iredell by my side, the Idea of undergoing it in his absence is nearly impossible for me to contemplate. But most likely, he will return well before I am truly in need of him—and, he hinted, he may bring Nelly and her little Betsey along with him! Such inexpressible happiness it would be to me to see them both.

From James Iredell to Hannah Iredell:

Alexandria, Virginia, September 7, 1791

... My health was not very good the day I left you, owing I believe to the great agitation of my mind at the thoughts of parting, and it was very indifferent the first day after my arrival in Baltimore—but I thank God it is now recovered, and my spirits, which were greatly dejected indeed, begin to revive... I had a view this morning as I passed to George Town of several of the new Federal Streets, which will quite eclipse Philadelphia ...

Thursday, September 15, 1791

I have had no word from Mr. Iredell since he left Baltimore a week or more since. I tell myself it means nothing—that I have gone far longer than this without hearing from him, and no reason for alarm—but I cannot entirely calm my mind. I imagine it is because I am with Child that I fret so. And yet it is because I am with Child that I must *not* fret, lest the poor innocent suffer by it!

Little things disturb me beyond all reason: James crying when there is no more Pudding, Sarah misplacing the Spirits of Turpentine, Mother belching after meals, Annie pleading with me to help her at rolling hoops in the yard when I am fatigued. And larger things, too. I noticed this morning that a silver snuff box, much treasured by Mr. Iredell, was not in the spot where it usually resides, on the side table in the Parlor. Sarah and I searched high and low for it, as I grew increasingly anxious—for it was a present from Major Butler, in gratitude for our hospitality when he was in Edenton during the War, and I suspect it is worth a great deal. Mr. Iredell will be much put out if he finds it missing on his return, not only for its value but because of his high regard for the Donor.

I did not want to accuse Sarah, but she swore without being prompted that she had no knowledge of its whereabouts, and I am inclined to believe her. She can be sullen and moody—especially now, with Peter gone—but I have never known her to be Dishonest. No, it is not Sarah I suspect, but Mother. I must confront her, ask her what she knows of it, but it will be hard. It goes against everything in my Nature to accuse an elderly Lady, and one to whom I owe a particular duty of respect, of such a disgraceful act, even were I to do it obliquely. And I suspect that, no matter what the Truth is, she will only profess bewilderment and Ignorance.

I am at a Loss as to what to do with her—aghast that I must entertain such thoughts concerning her. She continues to go to the Ladies' Circle, quite faithfully, but I cannot discern that it has yet worked much improvement in her Character. And yet I know—I refuse to forget—that within that depraved exterior, there is trapped a woman of Virtue and Character, a woman I could hold to my Bosom and be proud to call Mother. If only I can devise a way of releasing her!

From James Iredell to Hannah Iredell:

Salisbury, North Carolina, October 2, 1791

... It has been this time very much crowded indeed—I suffered very much the first night, having to sleep in a room with five People and a bed fellow of the wrong sort, which I did not expect ...

Monday, October 2, 1791

Mrs. Bond has just been and gone, leaving me in a state of great agitation. For she told me that her Aunt—the Aunt who is a member of the Ladies' Circle at Christ Church—had inquired most particularly after Mother's health. Why ever would her Aunt imagine that there is anything amiss, I replied? For Mother has only her usual complaints—her leg pain, and the slight disorder of her bowels—and those in less than the usual measure. Indeed, her spirits have been quite cheerful of late, I added.

Mrs. Bond gave me a peculiar look. "But my Aunt tells me that Mrs. Iredell has been unable to attend at the Ladies' Circle—indeed has not been seen there these past six weeks—and they have all assumed it was because of some Ailment."

I must have blanched, for Mother has been claiming to attend Meetings of the Circle now three times each week, and I have been much impressed by her Dedication. Stupid woman that I am! That minty smell I have noticed on her breath when she returns—I see now it was a ruse, mint leaves she chewed to mask the smell of spirits. Where has she then been going—to what Hell hole, what Den of iniquity? And no wonder objects have been disappearing: first the snuff box, then this week a silver Candlestick from the dining room. Mother of course has claimed ignorance of their whereabouts; she is adept at Dissembling, I will give her *that* much.

Mrs. Bond soon made some excuse to take her leave, no doubt recognizing my Distraction. For I was turning in my mind what should be my proper course of action. To confront Mother, and meet with some vague but impenetrable denial? No—I must have incontrovertible Evidence before I accuse her. But how long can I bide my time, watching our valuables disappear one by one, and daily fearing that Mother's indiscretions will become the stuff of common gossip?

Oh, if only Mr. Iredell were at my side to assist me in this distasteful Endeavor! Would that I could at the very least write to him and ask for counsel, but it would be a Month or more before I would receive a reply; and of course such news would only distress him to the point of distraction, when he should be devoting all his Faculties to his judicial duties. Nor can I appeal to Sam, for he left for Carolina weeks ago, keen to experiment with a system of Fertilization suggested by Mr. Jefferson; he is not expected here until near the end of the Month, when Congress begins its next session. Perhaps if I put all the remaining silver under lock and key, I might contrive to hold the situation at bay until then. But how am I to prevent Mother from going off to the next Ladies' Circle meeting—or rather, wherever it is she *truly* goes?

I sincerely hope, for *his* sake, that Mr. Arthur Iredell never sets foot on this side of the Atlantic, as he has sometimes threatened to do; for at the moment I feel quite sure that I would do my utmost to cause him some grievous bodily Harm. But I now feel the Babe kicking at my insides; no doubt the violence of my emotions has disturbed the poor thing's rest. I must try to calm myself.

Wednesday, October 5, 1791

What I have most dreaded has come to pass: a Letter arrived this morning, from a Stranger—a Mr. Sharpe. It was addressed to Mr. Iredell, but something impelled me to open it rather than lay it aside. I am still suffering such Agitation from the reading of it that my heart is pounding, and I cannot seem to breathe properly.

This Mr. Sharpe is apparently well acquainted with Mother and her recent activities—far better acquainted than I was before reading his letter, for I have not yet had the courage to confront her concerning them. It seems she has spent many hours at a private house, where a party of no doubt unsavory Characters gather daily to engage in gaming and, I suppose, drinking; this Mr. Sharpe is one of their number. The import of the Letter is that Mother has lost a great deal at cards, so that she is now indebted to Mr. Sharpe and others, for whom he acts as agent, to the tune of four hundred and seventy five Dollars! I cannot imagine where I am to find such a sum, when I have less than half that at my disposal, and that to last until Mr. Iredell returns in November.

At first it seemed to me the Man might be alerting us out of concern, for he wrote that it pained him to intrude upon Mr. Iredell's privacy on a subject of such Delicacy, but that he had no other recourse: "My repeated attempts to impress upon your Mother the gravity of the Situation have been met only with vague assurances that 'all will come right in the end.'" Certainly I could sympathize with the Gentleman's frustration. But the final paragraph I read with alarm, for it seemed to contain a calculated threat: "Mrs. Iredell has often spoken with great pride of the high Position you have attained in the legal Profession, for which I congratulate you. And yet I fear that your Mother's own indiscretions may soon come to tarnish that very Reputation which is so evidently the Comfort of her declining years. For the sum she owes is large and cannot be overlooked; if we do not receive satisfaction of the Debt within these two weeks, I cannot guarantee that this unfortunate Matter will not reach the Public ear."

Two weeks! Not even time enough to wait on Sam's return. I have no one by me I can turn to, no one I may confide in; for I am loath to entrust even my dear Mrs. Bond with such scandalous Intelligence, knowing how often she has gleefully relayed to me gossip concerning the disgraces and misfortunes of others. To think that our Family should be one of those whispered about in Parlors, and mentioned in disreputable

Newspapers. I know the sort of Article, for I have seen them often enough: under a heading such as "Interesting Intelligence," there will be a paragraph informing readers that the Mother of a certain prominent Judge, *Mr. J___ I____*, has been observed consorting with those in low Life—drinking—gambling—et cetera, et cetera. If Mr. Iredell were to return to such a situation, I fear it would be a Shock from which he might never recover. But alas, what can I do? The very thought of seeking out this Mr. Sharpe on my own—not only a Stranger, but an unsavory one no doubt, perhaps as bad as that Mr. Carver in New York—fills me with such Panic that I am like to faint. And what should I say to him? How on earth would I convince him to have Mercy on us?

Tuesday, October 11, 1791

I have just had an exceedingly distressing Conversation with Mother; indeed, I can scarcely credit the words that issued from her wrinkled lips. And yet I heard them, clear as the cries from that Man out in the street now, hawking kindling. My God, to think I am sharing a roof with such a Creature!

I would have spoken to Mother sooner about that Letter, but Annie took ill the very day I received it. Doctor Mease's diagnosis was a Dropsy in the head, possibly occasioned by unnatural forcing of the Intellect. I confess I had my doubts about this assessment, for though I have undertaken Annie's education, there has been no force involved—the Child is a natural student. But I kept my thoughts to myself, and only asked the Doctor what course of treatment he would recommend. To my surprise he prescribed a remedy of the sort I would have expected old Sappho to counsel: shave the child's head, he said, and then cover it with a Poultice of onions slightly stewed in Vinegar, and also bathe the feet in warm water mixed with Mustard. He had heard of a case, worse than Annie's, that had been effectively cured by such a Regimen. I followed the doctor's advice, and indeed Annie's condition has improved—though she still smells faintly like that cabbage the German Women sell in the market here.

But as for Mother, and that Letter from Mr. Sharpe—I showed it to her just a little while ago, and asked her for an explanation. She began mildly enough, saying she might have lost a few Pounds at cards here and there, but nothing like the Sum quoted in the letter. I fear I then began to lose patience with her vagueness, addressing her in tones unsoftened by Daughterly respect.

"Have you no Shame, no Conscience—no Motherly feeling for your son?" I cried. "What has Mr. Iredell done to deserve such treatment from you? All his concern has ever been for your Welfare, for your Happiness—and this is how you repay him? Would that you had never set foot in this Country, to blight our lives in this way!"

To my surprise, she answered calmly that she had no desire to remain longer in this Country, especially when it was so clear she was not wanted. She had decided to return to Ireland, she said, and live with her Sister. "We were girls together, before I married—the McCulloh girls, as we were known." She folded her gnarled hands beneath her chin, where they brushed against a few wispy hairs; her voice became softer, and a gentle smile appeared at her lips as she entered her Reverie. "Inseparable, we were, and much in demand during the Season. We would ride out together in our Father's carriage to the Great Houses of the Neighborhood, dressed in our best silks, and come home days later—with holes in our dancing Slippers." Her rheumy eyes closed, and she breathed deeply, as though inhaling the memory.

I felt, even then, a pang of Sympathy for her, imagining the sprightly young Girl she must once have been, her Life nothing but endless and alluring possibilities. There was no question now of her undertaking another Journey across the Atlantic, let alone resuming the pleasures of her Youth. If she could harbor such fantasies, I thought, perhaps her poor aged Mind had grown so clouded that she truly could not comprehend the consequences of her Behavior; perhaps she was more deserving of my Pity than my Fury. But in the next instant she opened her eyes and glared at me with a look of cold Hatred such as I have never seen before, and hope never to see again.

"I've had done with my Children, and their meddlesome Notions concerning how I should conduct myself." The change in her was as startling as though a babbling rill had of a sudden turned to ice. She rose now, with some difficulty, her mouth set in a grim line, and began to move towards the stairs. "My Sister Mary would never treat me the way I've been treated by my Sons—like a Dog kept on a chain! Like a common Criminal."

She turned and pointed a swollen-knuckled Finger directly at my Belly. "Mark my words: someday that Child you now carry will cause you as much Grief and pain as my Children have caused me. And then you will understand the Wrong you do me!"

A terrible shiver ran through my body. I clutched at my Belly, as though to protect the babe, and fled from the outstretched Finger as though from a cocked Pistol. Perhaps she meant the words as no more than a prediction, but to my ears they had the ring of a Curse. A Curse, on her own Grandchild!

Wednesday, October 12, 1791

My God, what I have done today! Such things as I had not thought I was capable of. I am weak and trembling with exhaustion; and yet there is a Satisfaction mingled with it, to think what I may have accomplished.

I lay awake all last night, greatly troubled both by those unnatural words Mother uttered, and as well by the thought of that Letter, lying in the desk drawer like a venomous, sleeping snake. Two weeks, that Mr. Sharpe said—two weeks in which to pay the Debt, or he would be unable to guarantee "that this unfortunate Matter will not reach the Public ear." And now a week has passed since the receipt of it, I thought, staring into the Darkness and trying not to weep, and I have done nothing. How to procure four hundred and twenty five dollars in the space of a week? Impossible, I sobbed quietly to myself, impossible; we are lost, ruined. But you must plead with the man, I instructed myself sternly; for the sake of your Husband and your poor innocent Children, you must.

And so I rose and dressed and told Sarah, after Breakfast, that I had some shopping to attend to. Once out in the Street, I withdrew the now-tattered Letter from my pocket, where I had secreted it, to examine the address once more; between the shaking of my hand as I held it, and the watering of my eyes, I could scarcely read it. I saw, when I found it after a walk of about ten minutes, a modest house in the neighborhood of the Southwark Theatre, where Mr. Iredell and I had passed a pleasant evening the previous Spring, though the play itself was but a trifling Comedy; the memory of that evening, and the desire to experience similar ones in the future—unburdened by disgrace and unsullied by Scandal—helped to fortify my resolve, which I felt beginning to flag once again as I stood before Mr. Sharpe's door.

There I stood for several minutes, staring at the door's dull red paint, peeling in spots to reveal a duller brown. At last I raised a

91

trembling hand and knocked; and soon saw the door opened by a little buck-toothed Maidservant. She said nothing when she opened the Door; and I found that, when I tried to speak, I could make no sound.

"Madam?" she said at last. "Do you wish to see the Master, then?"

I nodded then, and to my great dismay, felt my knees begin to buckle. I clutched desperately at the door frame for support. No! I scolded myself: now is not the time to give in to your cursed timidity.

"Mr. Sharpe!" I heard the Girl call. "Come quick!"

A plump little man emerged from somewhere behind her within a few seconds, but I had already collapsed onto the front step, my head spinning. The two of them helped me up and led me inside to a small Office off the front hall, where they guided me to a chair.

"Bring her a Cordial, Sally," I heard Mr. Sharpe say, "and be quick about it. Something to do with her—with her Condition, I imagine."

I patted my swollen Belly, encouraging him in this belief. After I had taken a few sips of the Cordial, I began to feel calmer—this Mr. Sharpe was no monster, at least—and managed to murmur my apologies and thanks.

"Please, Madam, don't fret yourself, it was nothing," he said with a wave of his hand, taking a seat behind the desk. He smiled; he had a pock-marked complexion and squinty eyes, and one of his front teeth was missing. "But—may I ask—to whom do I have the pleasure of addressing myself?"

I then produced the Letter from my pocket and laid it on the desk. "She—Mrs. Iredell—she is my Husband's Mother."

"Ah, I see." He picked up the Letter for a second, then let it fall. "And your Husband is …?"

"From home. Away on business." Words still came to me with difficulty, and my voice was so low I was surprised that Mr. Sharpe could make them out.

"Ah, that *is* a pity." Mr. Sharpe sighed and shook his head. "And when, may I ask, do you look for him to return?"

"I cannot tell for sure," I said, encouraged now, "but I should think by the end of next Month, at the latest. Another six Weeks or less. And so, if you could only wait that little time—or accept a part of the payment now, perhaps fifty dollars, with the rest to come later—I'm sure that when my Husband returns he will see to this Matter, and do whatever is necessary to"—

"My dear Lady," Mr. Sharpe interrupted, sticking his Thumbs into a waistcoat stretched tight across a Belly nearly as round as my own, "I assure you, I am very sorry for your difficulties, very sorry indeed. If it were entirely up to me, I would agree to your proposal without hesitation. But, you see, I have … Associates, whom I cannot entirely control. There are some among them who are growing quite impatient—we all have our own Bills to pay, you know, and we have been waiting some time now to collect the monies owed us."

These "Associates," he went on to say, were capable of doing something rather rash and regrettable; some had talked of instituting a lawsuit to recover the sum, others of going to the Newspapers. It was indeed a shame, he said as he shook his head sadly, to think of a Gentleman of such an excellent Reputation as my Husband being tarnished in this way; but alas (here, a deep sigh), these hotheads refused to listen to reason.

I was now recovered enough of my Senses to be able to discern in this speech a mere Pantomime of sympathy. I was skeptical, even, that these conveniently hot-headed "Associates" existed, that it was not Mr. Sharpe himself who was so insistent. The kind smile, the expressions of regret, were nothing more than pretense, a wrapping of feathers concealing a core of unyielding metal; for he had hardly paused a Moment to consider my request. I now felt a great surge of Anger rising up within me; and I was grateful for it, for it carried with it a Strength I never suspected I could muster. At the same time, a Plan came to my mind—an Plan I might never had the temerity to conceive without the impetus of Anger.

"Very well, then, if that is how it stands." I began to rise from the Chair; Mr. Sharpe moved to assist me, but I waved him away. "I shall return within the Week."

I took my leave and headed, as quickly as my girth would allow, back along Fourth Street, past Mr. Bingham's grand mansion and the Friends' Meeting House, until I found myself before the grand four-storey brick structure belonging to Major Pierce Butler. For this was my Plan: to reveal all to Major Butler and throw myself on his mercy, begging for the loan of the necessary Sum. Major Butler, I had considered, has ever held Mr. Iredell in the highest regard; and of course, he is wealthy—wealthier than anyone else we know, with the possible exception of Mr. Wilson (whom I scarcely know well enough to approach in such a Matter). It goes against everything in my Nature to borrow such an amount, even from a Friend; and yet I could think of no alternative.

Major Butler's door was a far shinier affair than Mr. Sharpe's: freshly painted an elegant cream, the brass knocker gleaming in the sun. I closed my eyes, took a Breath, and let the knocker fall; a liveried Negro soon admitted me. As I waited in the well-appointed library—with its fireplace of rich green marble, its crimson velvet drapery, and walls of leather-covered books—I yet again felt my Courage flag. What if Major Butler should take offense at my Boldness, indignantly refuse me, turn me out of the house? I had an impulse to run; but I summoned the Memory of Mr. Sharpe's face—oily, and thinly coated as well with that expression of feigned commiseration—and once more was strengthened by the Anger it provoked.

Major Butler soon entered, bowed, smiled, kissed my hand, asked after the health of my Children and whether I had any news of Mr. Iredell. But as I began to reveal the reason for my Visit, I watched in alarm as his genial manner faded, obscured by what seemed to be ominous storm clouds gathering at his expansive brow. All I had said (and this while trembling with shame and apprehension) was that a Relation (I did not say who) had fallen in with some ill-suited companions and had managed to contract a sizeable Debt. I was beginning to explain that I had just now come from the Gentleman who held the Debt, and had found him most insistent, even threatening public exposure, when I suddenly fell silent, alarmed at Major Butler's aspect, and fearing that I had incurred his displeasure by my Impertinence.

"Scoundrels!" Major Butler burst out. "Damned lot of rascals!"

I allowed myself to take a breath, now understanding that Major Butler's wrath was directed not at me, but at my Adversaries. He turned to me, his eyes narrow and furious. "I shouldn't be surprised if there's some Politics mixed up in this. You would be surprised, Madam, at the degree to which Faction has already reared its ugly head in this Republic."

That there might be some political Object behind this threat had not occurred to me. Certainly (though Major Butler seemed to believe I pay little attention to the Newspapers) I am well aware of the unfortunate divisions arising between public Characters over the recent troubling events in France—particularly between Mr. Adams and Mr. Jefferson, though both ostensibly serve the same Government. But Mr. Iredell is a Judge, not a politician; surely he has done nothing to offend any Faction!

I was not inclined, however, to take issue with Major Butler's assessment of the matter, especially as it seemed he was on the verge of coming to my aid.

Indeed, in the next moment, he asked what was the amount demanded; and upon being told, instructed me to apply to him on Friday after 4 o'clock, and he should have it ready for me. A wave of such relief came over me that I could barely catch my breath; my body had been held taut by anxiety, and now—the Crisis over—felt on the verge of collapse. I felt a tear begin to trickle down my cheek and began to try to express my thanks, while bemoaning the fact that I could not give him a date of repayment with any certainty.

"My dear Mrs. Iredell," he interrupted me, "what I do is surely no more than what Mr. Iredell would do for me, were the circumstances reversed; for I well know what a generous and unfailingly loyal Fellow he is. It gives me great Pleasure, I assure you, to do whatever is in my power to relieve the Distress that is being so unjustly inflicted on him and his Family."

I thanked him once more, rather tearfully, and took my leave. Relief and joy swept over me; but as well, the odd sensation that all that had just transpired was only a kind of dream—for it was so unlike my real self to do what I had just done. And yet, as I trod slowly home, one clear thought penetrated the daze that enveloped me: Mother must be removed from our midst, from our house, and soon—before the time of my Confinement. I understand there are Families, in the country, who will take in old people for a fee. There, at least, she would be out of the way of Temptation. And perhaps it was no Curse she uttered, on my unborn Child; but my mind will rest easier when she is in a Place where she can do no further harm to herself, or to us.

Saturday, October 15, 1791

Never shall I forget the surprise on Mr. Sharpe's face when I appeared at his door yesterday evening with the four hundred and seventy five dollars in hand—and that several days early!

"Well, well," he said, recovering his oleaginous manner. "You are apparently fortunate, Madam, in having ample resources on which to draw."

Lest he believe that we were blessed with far more Wealth than was at our disposal, and therefore resolve to prey on us again, I told him only that I had been able to borrow the money from a Friend.

"Ah, dear lady, would that we all had such Friends." He put a pudgy finger to his multiple chins and knit his brow in the apparent effort of recalling an apt phrase. "'A faithful Friend' …No, that isn't it." He chewed a knuckle . "Ah! 'When Fortune is fickle, the faithful friend is found.' Pliny, I believe."

"Cicero," I corrected him, having no patience politely to tolerate his Misattribution. "And Fortune is, in my view, not the only one to blame for the Predicament in which I find myself, Sir. As Pliny *did* observe, 'Most of Man's misfortunes are occasioned by his fellow Man.' "

Mr. Sharpe's smile faded quickly, and he turned his attention to emptying the purse I had brought with me. The money having been counted to his satisfaction, he escorted me to the door and extended a hand, which I regarded for a Moment as though he were offering me a putrid slab of meat. I then turned, leaving the hand untouched, and walked purposefully in the direction of Fourth Street.

I imagine Mr. Iredell, when I reveal these events to him, will perhaps consider that his timid mouse of a Wife is capable of more than he expected. It now remains to find a Place somewhere for Mother; I perused the advertisements in the Newspapers today, in hopes of finding something suitable, but saw nothing. She has scarcely spoken to me since we had our words about Mr. Sharpe's Letter (except to inquire whether any Letters have come for her from Ireland—there have been none); but neither has she slipped away and returned stinking of drink, or even of mint. Perhaps she has been chastened, at least for the time being.

But I will not be lulled into believing any permanent change has come over her. The Babe is kicking quite regularly now, as though to remind me that Mother must be gone before its arrival. And I sometimes allow myself to hope, against my better judgment, that Nelly will be here to take her place.

Hannah Iredell to Nelly Tredwell:

Philadelphia, Pennsylvania, November 15, 1791

… I expected to have had a letter from you today, my dear Nelly, by the Post, but am disappointed. I wish I could prevail on you to write more frequently, for I am extremely anxious to hear from you…

I wish I knew whether to expect you with Mr. Iredell or not. I know nothing that would give me greater pleasure than to see you with him, but I dread your undertaking such a Journey at so late a Season lest you or your dear little girl should suffer. The cold and fatigue would be greater than either of you could bear. It is a great piece of self-denial in me to press you not to come, but I know your Uncle will be so pressing on the other side that you will be hardly able to refuse him, though it should be ever so contrary to your own Judgment and Inclination.

I am writing about your Uncle's returning as if I was sure of it, though I have not heard a word of him or from him since he left Augusta. I trust in God he is well; I cannot bear to think otherwise.

I shall send you a gown pattern ..., a few pounds of starch and of Salt Peter. I have begged of Mr. Iredell to get the favor of Mr. Tredwell to get us some pork and have some bacon made for us... They may say what they will of their Northern Bacon, it is by no means equal to ours...

The Assemblies and concerts are just beginning... I have been out very seldom since Mr. Iredell left me, to Mrs. Washington's room but once, and that was last Friday, when it was so full I could hardly squeeze through to make her a curtsey... We have got a very handsome House, but very little furniture in it. Our rooms are so much larger than [formerly] that our carpets do not cover half the floors...

...The only message I can get Annie to send is her love to you and that you must come. She has got pretty well again, thank God, and James is one of the heartiest fellows in the City. He is a fine boy, I assure you, and will make Betsey a smart husband by and by. Annie has finished a sampler and has done it with great ease and very well...

... If you should not come with your Uncle I shall write often to you and I beg you will do the same ... You must give my love to Mr. Tredwell ... Give a kiss for me to my dear little Betsey. God bless you, my dear Nelly ...

Arthur Iredell to James Iredell:

London, England, December 6, 1791

... I must inform you of the deep affliction into which I have been plunged by a most extraordinary Letter from my Mother. I see but too clearly the shameful Influence that horrid Vice she is addicted to has

over her—and I sincerely wish you could devise some Means by which its Effect upon your family may be removed. Is there no Place in America where you could procure her comfortable accommodation? So much she certainly has an unalienable Claim upon you for, but surely You are not bound to Sacrifice every Domestic Comfort, and to submit to such dishonourable Practices.

The Letter I have received was evidently written when She was by no Means in a proper State of Mind, at the House, as she calls it, of a <u>friend</u>. It states her Dissatisfaction where she is, & resolve of leaving America in the Spring, & of going to her Sister in Ireland. Poor woman! <u>She</u> has a very bare Subsistence, for herself, & to live with her would be impossible... It would be the height of Folly, as well as of Injustice to my Aunt. Indeed the Crossing of the Atlantic again, under any Terms, would be [Folly] at [my Mother's] Age...

Thursday, December 8, 1791

Mr. Iredell returned home from his Circuit five days ago, greatly fatigued but—thanks be to Providence—otherwise well. His return was the occasion, as always, of a Scene of great rejoicing, the Children running over and over again to their Father to be hugged and kissed, and Annie proudly showing him her sampler and her first efforts at copying a few Psalms. I did my best not to reveal my disappointment that Nelly had not come; surely it was for the best that she did not, at this risky Season, and with Mother still here.

I waited until yesterday evening to relate to Mr. Iredell the story of Mother and Mr. Sharpe, not wanting to dampen the merriment surrounding his arrival home. And indeed, his agitation was extreme as I recounted the entire sordid tale; he exclaimed over his Mother's perfidy, Major Butler's generosity, my own Courage. By the end of it, he was on his knees before me, the tears streaming from his eyes, his expressions of sympathy and Admiration for me quite fervent. I was exceedingly affected myself, seeing him so distraught, and recalling all that I had endured. When I at last broached the subject of sending Mother off to live with a Family in the countryside, Mr. Iredell hesitated but a moment before expressing his agreement.

"All right, then. I shall find a place for her, somewhere, before the next Circuit."

"No!" I cried. "I cannot wait that long. You must do it now—before my Confinement."

But why so soon, he asked me several times. I would not tell him—for how could I reveal to him that I feared for the Babe to be in the same house with the Woman who had given him life, and nurtured him through Childhood? It seems unreasonable even to myself; and yet I cannot deny the cold Dread that fills me when I contemplate the prospect. At length he saw I would remain unshakeable on the point, and gave me his promise: she will be gone within the Month. It seemed that I could demand no more, and I agreed; I pray the Child will hold off its arrival for so long.

From James Iredell to Arthur Iredell:

Philadelphia, Pennsylvania, January 10, 1792

... In two or three days I will remove my Mother into the Country. The duty of coercion you urge upon me is alien & contrary to my nature. I can't without distraction even speak to her on the subject, much less act as her Jailer and her spy.

I confess I was extremely shocked at one of your letters. Any Stranger who was to read it would think I had done you a grievous injury. In what did that injury consist? In nothing more, I believe, than lamenting that before you sent my Mother to America you had not informed me of what you knew, or suspected at least, of foibles which in that very Letter you acknowledge prevented your living even in the same kingdom or province with her. Whether these foibles would probably be corrected, during her passage to America, or after her residence for some time in my house, I think I ought to have been permitted to judge of as much as you when it was proposed she should come ...

Saturday, January 14, 1792

Mother left at last, this Morning, with Mr. Iredell. Watching the chaise wobble off along the cobblestones, I felt myself grow lighter with every foot it traveled. It is as though a great Boulder has been weighing on me for many Months and has been rolled aside at last, only a few moments before it was too late. For I can feel that my time is drawing near.

Mr. Iredell learned last week of a couple with a Farm a few miles beyond Germantown—just the right distance from us, remote but not inaccessible. Decent, simple folk, Mr. Iredell reported after visiting them, of the German farmer type common to these parts—though their poor command of English caused him some hesitation. But the amount they proposed to charge was reasonable, and time was growing short; besides, Mother is certainly able to keep up a lively Conversation without any assistance. Mr. Iredell agreed that it was likely the best we could do, and fortunately Mother put up no resistance. Though she continued to ask if any letters had arrived for her from Ireland, I believe she some time ago gave up any fantasy of joining her Sister. And she is probably as anxious to be rid of us as we are of her.

I can now turn my thoughts with some clarity to my Confinement, which brings of course its own anxieties. Mrs. Bond has been most insistent that I call in a Doctor—she says all the Ladies here avail themselves of Doctors if they can afford it, and it doesn't signify anything untoward concerning the condition of the Child, as it would in Edenton. She said I might still have my Women with me, when the Forcing pains began—which here, of course, means only Mrs. Bond herself and Mrs. Johnston, the latter being no doubt as useless as always in these situations, crying out and fainting at the least provocation. But I shall also have Sarah, of course; Sappho was with me at my previous Confinements and was well experienced in the delivery of Infants—I pray that she passed on some of her knowledge to her Daughter.

The thought of a Doctor attending at such an event still strikes me as indecent; but Mrs. Bond assures me they are trained to perform their examinations without visual inspection of a Woman's Parts. And Mr. Iredell has no objection—indeed, he is quite anxious that all possible precautions be taken, especially as I am so advanced in age. I shall be forty-four within a Month's time, should I be blessed to reach that day.

May it please the Lord to preserve my life, and that of the Child. But if it should please Him to take me to a better Place, I am ready to go there. I have given my Instructions to Mr. Iredell: in the event of my Death, Annie is to have my gold ring and the little Pincushion sewn by my beloved Sister, her namesake, embroidered by her with her initials; James is to have the Clock I inherited from my Father. I would like to leave something for the unborn Child, should it survive and I perish, but as it is still a Stranger to me I cannot think what to give; perhaps I shall write it a Letter, so that in years to come it will have some sense of who its Mother was.

From Tom Iredell to James Iredell:

Edenton, North Carolina, February 10, 1792

... I most cordially congratulate you all on the interesting and happy event of Mrs. Iredell's safe delivery...

I dread ever making any enquiries about my poor deluded Mother. I have not received a Letter from her for some time... My God, what misery does this one Event involve us all in. Good God, how could Arthur act so? ...

Kiss my lovely Annie & James for me, and tell them how much I love them ...

Sunday, February 12, 1792

I have not written in this Book in some weeks, being too fatigued from the Birth and as well the care of my sweet little Girl, born on January the 19th—Helen, we have called her, after my Mother; and so Sam and I now each have our own Helen. She was a scrawny thing, but my milk has been abundant, thank the Lord, and she has begun to gain some flesh. I look upon her tiny flailing fists, feel her bury her heavy bare head in the crook of my neck, and laugh to think I ever trembled at Mother's words about the Child bringing me Grief and pain.

The Birth itself was not an easy one—indeed, more difficult than any of my other confinements, even the first. My pains began promisingly enough, on the morning of the 18th, but then progressed but slowly. In the evening, Mr. Iredell sent for Dr. Shippen, highly recommended by Mrs. Bond and other Ladies for his expert skill in Midwifery; he, alas, was busy with another patient, and sent a young associate. This Doctor, who looked scarcely out of boyhood, immediately began to order my Women from the room, saying that he wanted no crowding, or unnecessary noise. I gave him to understand that my Women were to remain with me and that, if it should come to it, I would prefer their Presence to his. This he seemed to accept, for he said nothing further on the matter.

After examining me (his hands under the bedclothes and eyes averted to the ceiling), he announced that the Child was in a footling position and attempted to turn it, but with no success. Sometime after midnight, the Doctor said the only thing to do was to bleed me and administer a dose of Laudanum, then use his forceps to deliver the Child. This sent me into a panic, as I have heard tales of Babes being torn apart by forceps in the Womb, and delivered piece by piece.

"No!" I heard myself scream. And then again, over and over: "No, no, no!" The screams seemed to come of themselves; I felt powerless to stop them.

Dr. Hale seemed to hesitate, uncertain how to overcome the resistance of so recalcitrant a Patient. Then, through my screams, I heard Sarah's voice, low and strong: "You give me a chance, Sir, I reckon I can get that Child turned."

I saw the Doctor begin to shake his head; perhaps he was offended by what he saw as the impertinence of the Wench. But my "No"s immediately turned to cries of "Yes, Sarah, yes!" To my relief, the Doctor shrugged and stepped aside.

I felt Sarah's hands upon my Belly, rubbing and pushing; and heard her voice, now gentle, cooing, "Come on now, little one, come on." Then the odd, and exceedingly welcome, sensation of a small body moving within my own, the sight of waves of limbs rippling against my Belly; Sarah calling, "Push, now!;" the exertion of what seemed every muscle in my weakened Body; and at long last, the Babe's head slipping out.

"Make way, make way," the Doctor now called out, pushing Sarah aside so that he might catch the Child. She began to move towards the corner of the room, perhaps to rinse her hands in the Basin, but before she could I flung my arm out and caught her and clutched her to me, unable to speak.

"It's gonna be all right now, Ma'am, don't you worry," she whispered to me before moving off.

I thank the Lord I had her by me, for I shudder to think what might have transpired had she been absent. Mr. Iredell, who had been extremely agitated at the sound of my screams and therefore greatly relieved at the successful Delivery, insisted that we send a bottle of Claret to the Doctor along with his fee; but I am certain it was Sarah saved the life of our Child—and perhaps my own as well. I intend to make her a present of a new muslin Chemise, and, as soon as I can spare her, perhaps a day's Liberty as well.

Alas, Mr. Iredell now has little time to enjoy his new Daughter, for the Supreme Court has at last begun its Session (the first four days, it failed for want of a quorum), and he has been quite distracted by his duties. Another suit for debt has been brought against a State—New York—and Mr. Iredell is apprehensive; for he says that while Maryland was willing to appear in Court voluntarily, New York has failed to enter an appearance, and the Plaintiff yesterday moved to compel it to do so. Mr. Iredell is at the desk in the Parlor now, hunched over a draft of an Opinion that already contains many crossed-out passages. So exercised is he concerning this question that he has even criticized Mr. Wilson, who is otherwise the object of his extreme veneration; it seems that Mr. Wilson once remarked, in private conversation with Mr. Iredell, that in his opinion the Constitution permitted such suits against States—and that, having been so instrumental in the drafting of the Constitution, *he* should certainly know what it meant.

"But it wasn't the *drafting* that made it Law," Mr. Iredell said to me with some vexation, "but the ratifying. And I'm reasonably certain that most of those who voted to ratify had no intention of enacting Mr. Wilson's meaning. Certainly not in Carolina!"

Monday, April 2, 1792

Mr. Iredell sets sail for Charleston tomorrow, in the company of Major Butler and his Daughters, for there is a good Road from there to Savannah, where he must open Court on the 25th of the Month. After he is done with the Circuit, in June, he intends to linger a few days in Edenton, and has hinted again that he may persuade Nelly to accompany him back here; certainly this would be a healthier climate than Edenton in which to pass the Summer months. And yet I imagine some obstacle to the Plan will arise.

We all traveled yesterday, at Mr. Iredell's insistence, to visit Mother in the Country; he felt it necessary to bid her farewell before his Journey, and said it was time that she met her new Grandchild, who is now nearly three Months old. I had, until now, been able to use the excuse of recovering my Health to avoid accompanying Mr. Iredell on his visits to her, which he has undertaken weekly; but as I am now entirely well, and Helen is growing robust, I had no choice but to assent.

The farmhouse, where we arrived after a bumpy ride in a hired Coach, was small but neatly kept. The dour-looking Farmer and his flaxen-haired wife, by the name of Muller, spoke little English, but welcomed us inside with smiles and gestures. The Wife had the sort of placid demeanor one associates either with great Wisdom or bovine stupidity, and in her case I thought the latter the more likely cause. Poor Mother, I found myself thinking—to be shunted off here, where she knew no one, and to be cared for by People with whom she could scarcely communicate! I had wanted her out of my House, to be sure, but never intended to condemn her to a life of such miserable Isolation.

But there, by the hearth in the Kitchen—seated before a rough-hewn table bearing a steaming pot of coffee and a plate of little cakes—sat Mother, plump as a Piglet and grinning merrily from ear to ear. Her eyes sparkled, her hair was neatly tucked beneath her cap, and her apron was spotless.

She greeted Annie and James warmly—though they at first hung back, perhaps recalling her former sourness—and soon asked to hold Helen. I hesitated, remembering my fears; but there was no way to deny what was certainly a reasonable enough request. Mother exclaimed over the Babe in delight, so that if one hadn't known better, one might have thought her to be any doting Grandmother. Once again, I nearly softened towards the old Woman; perhaps, I thought, she may yet return to us, after a period of virtuous living that would purge from her those vicious Habits to which she has fallen victim. Perhaps we might yet again all sit by the hearth, and I might be once more a Daughter as well as a Mother.

But then she called the Farmer's Wife, Mrs. Muller, to sit beside her on the bench. Taking the blushing Woman's hand in hers, Mother cried, "Ah, my dears, you don't know what a Godsend Maria has been to me! She bakes me lovely cakes, and brushes my hair so gently, and tends to my every Need, she does."

I wondered how they contrived to understand one another; but before I could inquire, Mother clasped Mrs. Muller's plump hand to her bosom and said, in tones of wonderment, "Why, Children, I'll tell you what Maria is to me—she's the Daughter I never had, but have yearned for these many years!"

Mother looked straight at me as she said this—indeed, it was the first Remark she seemed to address directly to me—as though she knew what a blow her words would deal to my Heart. Was it possible that she preferred the Simplicity of a connection that demanded so little of her, and provided her endless opportunities to prattle on at will? Or was the fault in myself; had I but been kinder, or more patient—or perhaps more firm—might Mother have thrived in our own house, and formed so tender a fondness for me?

I spent the remainder of the Visit in a state of utter melancholy, scarcely able to speak; and indeed, I have since then been unable entirely to recover my spirits.

From James Iredell to Hannah Iredell:

Charleston, South Carolina, April 8, 1792

I saw young Mrs. Rutledge last night, who is a very pretty young Lady... My passage was on the whole very agreeable, though we had very rough weather. I had scarcely any sickness, or Major Butler. The young Ladies had a great deal. They improve extremely upon an acquaintance...

Friday, April 13, 1792

Fie on superstitions! For Friday the 13th is surely our lucky day. Sam has just been here, direct from the Senate, to inform me that the Bill which he introduced requiring a rotation of the Circuits—the one Mr. Iredell drafted himself—has indeed passed. I shall write at once to Mr. Iredell, for this news will surely cheer him as he suffers the discomforts of the Southern Circuit—to know that he will not be required to undergo them again, by Law, for at least another year! And I and the Children will no longer have to endure so frequently the anxiety and loneliness of these lengthy Separations. I had thought—with Mrs. Bond here to amuse me, Mother gone, and the City now being less unfamiliar to me—that I shouldn't mind his being gone as much as I used to. But I long for him nearly as much as I ever did.

I find, indeed, that I much prefer hearing about the goings-on in the City from Mrs. Bond than going out and experiencing them for myself—though she has been very kind in offering to accompany me on visits. Yesterday afternoon she and Mrs. Johnston both came to take tea with me, which raised my Spirits some. But, after Mrs. Johnston had finished delivering her usual catalogue of complaints (this time including headache, backache, a disturbance in her bowels, and a constant fluttering of her heart), Mrs. Bond communicated some alarming news from New York. It appears that after several months of frenzied speculation in Stocks and such like, the Bubble has at last burst (as burst it always will), and the great William Duer—the grandest Speculator of them all—has been thrown into Debtors' prison. A fierce Mob has gathered outside the Jail, Mrs. Bond said, including not just his wealthy Creditors, but also those unfortunates of modest means who entrusted to Colonel Duer their meager life savings: shopkeepers, widows, orphans.

Mrs. Johnston snapped her fan shut at this Intelligence and pressed it to her chin, her round blue eyes seeming to have grown larger than ever. "Do you hear tell that any of our local Gentleman are involved?" She flicked open her fan once more and whispered loudly from behind it, "Judge Wilson, perhaps?"

I felt a shudder of alarm. To have a Judge of the Supreme Court implicated in some fraudulent speculation, perhaps even thrown into Jail like Colonel Duer—the thought was horrifying. (And of course the Bonds now have a good deal of money invested in Mr. Wilson's schemes.) But to my great relief, Mrs. Bond shook her head. "No, I've heard nothing like that. It's true that Mr. Wilson has been associated with Colonel Duer in some of his endeavors, but the Bubble that burst was all to do with bank stock and government securities and the like—mere Paper, worth nothing in itself. Whereas Mr. Wilson's speculations are, I believe, almost entirely in Land—far more trustworthy, and respectable."

I said nothing to this, not wanting to cause Mrs. Bond any anxiety; but surely Land, in the hands of the wrong sort of investor, can be as risky a speculation as Paper.

From James Iredell to Hannah Iredell:

Charleston, South Carolina, April 19, 1792

... I receive such great civilities that I have been engaged to dinner every day since I came, and shall till I go ... I dined on Friday with young Mr. Rutledge, where there was a very large and genteel company, and

very elegant dinner. His wife is not only very handsome, but appears to me very accomplished and agreeable...

From James Iredell to Hannah Iredell:

Savannah, Georgia, April 26, 1792

... We have a great deal of very important business to do here. My horses turn out very well, but owing to my carelessness in driving, I had like to have suffered a good deal. Having understood that the horse in the chair was very gentle, and the road being a remarkably fine one, I was going on at my ease, when part of the rein getting under his tail, he ran away, the chair struck against a tree, and overset, throwing me out, and one of the wheels went over my leg. I was able to proceed however (as the chair was not broken) about ten miles, but then was in so much pain, I was under the necessity of staying very inconveniently at a house on the road. Fortunately, however, the hurt was only a swelling in my ankle that subsided next day...

From Hannah Iredell to Nelly Tredwell:

Philadelphia, June 18, 1792

... I received your short letter, my dear Nelly, the other day by Post... How came you to forget little Betsey? You do not even mention her name—your Uncle would hardly believe such a thing possible. I am sure the dear little creature was well, or you would have thought of her.

You say you have received the things, but you do not tell me how you like them. I have sent you ... a little neat Hat—the bow you can wear either to one side or higher up, as you like. The Ladies generally wear them here without any other head dress, or sometimes with a cap. They are not worn on one side now, but on top of the head. There is also a little Bonnet for my dear Betsey, which you must give her with a kiss from me. It is rather large for her, I fancy, but it will keep the sun off the better, and when your hat and it are soiled, if you will pour some boiling water on the skins of scarlet radishes and set them with a bit of alum, you may dye them a very pretty pink and they will look as well as ever. I hope to send you a looking glass too. I was out last evening to look for one, but could not please myself. I shall try again in the morning.

... What has become of Mr. T. Iredell? Remember me to him if he is still there. I sent his letter out to his mother; she is pretty well. My dear Children are quite well. James had a little fever, but a little tartar carried it off. Helen is very quiet and grows fast. I have got a very decent young woman to nurse her. I enclose a line of Annie's writing—she has been but a short time in letters, but she would try to write to you. I hope she will write pretty well by the end of the Summer. She is just as wild as ever, and though she seems never to be still, she is very quick in learning everything I attempt to teach her. James has grown very fond of his book since he went to school...

Your Uncle I hope is with you at this time, though I have not heard from him since he left Columbia... I wish my dear Nelly you could contrive to write to me oftener, for although I am always anxious to hear from you I am still more so in Summer. God bless you, my dear Nelly ... I am very glad to hear our Bacon is coming...

Wednesday, July 11, 1792

It has come to pass at last, that which I dared not even allow myself to hope for, for fear of being too grievously disappointed—Nelly has come, with her Betsey in tow! They arrived with Mr. Iredell on the clipper from Edenton three days ago, and so surprised and overcome with Joy was I when I spied them on the deck that my head began to whirl and I nearly dropped Helen, who happened to be in my arms.

Ah, it has been lovely, lovely beyond words. Betsey is even a more charming Child than I had imagined, with her Mother's dark eyes and dimples and ready laugh. And already a chatterbox, though Nelly is the only one able to understand what the girl is trying to say. What a delight to see Nelly so taken with the Child! There's no one I love better, of course, but Nelly's Character has always been slightly marred by a streak of stubborn selfishness and impetuosity—a streak that now appears entirely erased by the experience of Motherhood. Indeed, I fear she dotes too much, and may spoil the Girl in time. When I hinted as much, Nelly took some offense: Betsey had been ill before they left, she protested, and her concern was only to prevent any recurrence. It seemed, in any case,

108

best not to press the matter, for surely I don't want to ruin this longed-for visit with a trivial disagreement.

Every moment with them here is so precious to me, I yearn to make it last for Hours; for I am ever aware that it is but a temporary Paradise that I enjoy. Nelly intends to go from here to Long Island, where Mr. Tredwell's parents reside; surely they are entitled to meet their Granddaughter, and yet, if I could, I would imprison the two of them, Nelly and Betsey, right here in Philadelphia, for my own selfish sake. And for the Children's as well, for James and Annie are as taken with Betsey as I am. Even little Helen adores her, waving her hands and whimpering in frustration whenever Betsey tires of her and toddles away. Nelly says she will remain here till the end of the Month at least; perhaps I can prevail on her to stay longer.

Sam, too, has begun to talk of leaving—resigning his seat in the Senate and returning to Carolina and his beloved fields and agricultural experiments: like Cincinnatus (he says rather grandly), the time will soon come for him to once again take up his plough. He complains he has grown weary of Public life, dismayed by the factions and Cabals that are ever increasing, and he says that his Fortune is being depleted—both by the lower crop yields that he attributes to his absence from his farms, and by the expense of living in this City (though as to the latter, I believe Mrs. Johnston's penchant for luxury and show are partly to blame). I earnestly hope it is nothing but talk, for it has been such a comfort to have Sam here, and his Family; I should be quite bereft without them. And James and Annie would be desolate without their Johnston Cousins to play with—indeed, Annie has become nearly inseparable from her Cousin Fanny, who comes to us nearly every day. She has a quick Mind, much like Annie's, and I have undertaken to give the two of them some instruction in their Letters and Numbers. (The poor things are quite jealous of their Brothers, who are privileged to go off to school!)

But I shall try not to think on what the future may bring, and revel instead in the domestic Joys that now surround me—all of us dining together every day, either here or at Sam's, in easy familiarity, finishing one another's sentences and reminding each other of fond memories with the aid of nothing more than a word or two. Ah, how strong and soft a Web a Family can spin—and I am happily caught within it, a contented Fly, with no desire to explore the Ether any further.

I write this as I sit by Betsey's bed, in the room we have made up for her and Nelly. The poor little dear fell ill a week ago and gave us all a terrible scare, with high Fevers and near constant vomiting; Nelly was nearly beside herself with anxiety. But yesterday the Fever began to subside, and I believe her color is returning; with luck, she will be good as new by the end of the week.

Poor Nelly has scarcely left the Child's side for days, and yesterday, when I saw Betsey was improving, I insisted that Nelly go out this evening. We have all been invited to a Ball at the Binghams'—Mr. Iredell and myself and Nelly, the Bonds, the Johnstons—and it was clear that Nelly, having heard of the grandeur and elegance of the Mansion House and the Binghams' entertainments there, was eager to attend. As for myself, I was quite pleased with the prospect of a quiet evening at home, watching over Betsey.

One of the Bond girls was obliging enough to lend Nelly quite a stylish Gown for the occasion, and she looked a veritable Vision; I smiled as I watched her admiring herself in the Glass.

"Ah, if only Mr. Tredwell could see me!" she cried gaily.

Then Betsey whimpered slightly in her sleep—nothing more than a bad dream, I warrant. But Nelly rushed to the bed, her face suddenly drawn tight, and stroked Betsey's brow until the Child quieted.

"She's hot to the touch," she declared, rising now and beginning—to my dismay—to undo the hooks on the lovely Gown. "The Fever must be coming back. I cannot leave her."

"Don't be silly!" I cried. I could hear the disappointment in her voice. I touched Betsey's forehead myself, lightly: warm, perhaps, but nothing to worry about. Inexperienced Mothers are apt to startle at the least sign of illness. "There's no Fever there. You *will* go out, I insist—for when will you ever have another opportunity to attend such a grand Ball? Betsey will be fine with me, I promise you. When she wakes, I'll give her a dose of the Bark, as the Doctor recommended, and that will put her to rights."

"Well ..." Her hand hesitated above the next hook. "If you really think it's all right ..."

"Trust me." I began to do up the hooks for her. "Go, my dear, and enjoy yourself."

110

Nelly smiled gratefully and kissed me, then finished hooking the Gown back up and set off on the arm of Mr. Iredell. I expect they will stay out late, as both are so fond of dancing. But there is Betsey now, stirring and beginning to whimper; I must go and prepare the Bark.

From James Iredell to Dr. Tredwell:

Philadelphia, Pennsylvania, July 31, 1792

At the request of my dear Mrs. Tredwell, I write to you much sooner than I could have otherwise brought myself to do [concerning] a most melancholy event which has happened to her and to us.

We had flattered ourselves on Saturday that her lovely little Girl had got much better, and anxiously expected she was in a fair way of recovery. But to our inexpressible distress, she had a relapse on Sunday evening, and this morning, about 3 o'clock, expired. The sufferings of her poor Mother are past all description, but she has obtained some relief by abundance of Tears, and ... by expressing the terrible sensations she feels. We shall do everything in our power to mitigate a grief so naturally and justly felt, and with the utmost anxiety shall watch over her health.

She has desired me, with the strongest expressions of respect and affection for you and Mrs. Tredwell, and all your Family, to tell you that she now must decline a satisfaction from which she promised herself very great pleasure, in visiting you on Long Island, as it is her determination to return as soon as possible to her Husband, whose situation will require all the melancholy [comfort] her presence & society can afford him. Poor Fellow! I know not how to break it to him. I must do it by the intervention of a third Person & therefore beg the favor of you not to intimate a word of it to him very soon. His whole Soul almost was wrapped up in this charming Daughter, whose loss I feel exquisitely myself. Everything possible was done for her. But she could not retain Bark, which I believe was absolutely necessary for her recovery—nor indeed scarcely anything else.

Mrs. Iredell shares in a most affecting manner in this severe misfortune. She joins me in very respectful Compliments to you and Mrs. Tredwell, and all the Family, and in the sincerest sympathy for this truly unhappy event...

My God, my God—what have I done? Sweet Betsey gone, and Nelly beside herself with grief—and all of it, I fear, my fault.

I tried the Bark on Sunday evening, as soon as Betsey awoke, but she could not keep it down, poor thing. Alas, I had no snake-root with which to make an infusion, but I had Sarah make some strong Coffee and gave Betsey a teaspoonful, without sugar or milk, every fifteen minutes, as it is said to have great power to tranquilize the stomach; alas, that came up as well. Betsey grew more and more feverish, and by the time Nelly returned home from the Ball, at nearly two in the morning—all flushed and gay, and entirely unaware what horrors lay in wait for her—the Child was burning to the touch, and the convulsions had begun to come upon her. Nelly cried out in alarm, and then she looked at me—a look filled with such accusation and Blame, I believe I shall never recover from it.

"I knew it," she whispered, tears spilling from her eyes. "I should never have left her."

Nelly insisted that we send for the Doctor, despite the lateness of the hour, and persisted in asking me why I had not already done so. Yet—as Mr. Iredell has told me repeatedly, in hopes of comforting me—the Doctor's efforts were as powerless as mine: the Fever refused to relent, and the Convulsions continued unabated. And yet, perhaps if I *had* sent for him sooner, he might have been able to do something; I cannot be certain.

I am sick at Heart, mourning that sweet Child, who shed Happiness wherever she went, as the sun sheds light; and fearing, as well, that my dearest Nelly will never look on me again with anything but loathing and disgust; for she has kept her distance since it happened, scarcely uttering a Word to me, though all my desire is to offer her some comfort. Mr. Iredell says I mustn't worry, that she will come around in time, that the wound is still too fresh. I pray the Lord that he is right. But perhaps, indeed, I don't deserve her love; perhaps—no matter what Mr. Iredell says—I don't deserve to be forgiven.

Wednesday, September 19, 1792

They have all gone off and left me: Mr. Iredell on the Stage today to New York, on his way to Connecticut to begin the Eastern Circuit in the company of Mr. Wilson and his elder Daughter. And Nelly boarded a Ship for Edenton last week, with Sam and his Family—all except for Fanny, who will stay with us in hopes that she, along with Annie, will soon be able to attend a school for girls that a Gentleman here, by the name of Wigdon, has proposed. So it was not just idle talk: Sam was in earnest about leaving this place. Though he himself will return when Congress reconvenes in the Fall, the Family are gone for good, and Sam intends to resign his seat in the Senate at the end of the Session.

Nelly kissed me goodbye and assured me all was well, but there was yet a distance in her manner, a restraint that was never there before. For the six weeks before she left she scarcely spoke and barely ate—though I tried to tempt her with her favorites, caraway cake and custard. Just when I would think it was impossible for my Heart to ache any worse, I would look on her—pale and red-eyed, staring blankly, all her spark and Spirit gone—and suffer yet a further blow. It seemed she could not bear the sight of me with Helen—the knowledge that I still had a Babe and she did not, the suspicion that the reason for it was my own carelessness. If I could only be near her, day after day, a cushion of other Memories, soft and pleasant, would pile up on top of that most terrible one, so that soon it would be nearly buried. But as it is, from now on, when Nelly thinks of me, she will be overcome with grief and Anger, thinking of Betsey's death.

Alas, I feel myself abandoned and alone, so melancholy that I turned Mrs. Bond away this afternoon on the excuse of indisposition. Even the Children, my great Joy, are too much for me, with their romping and their loud voices; their cries afflict me like tiny arrows shot directly to my brain. I have taken to my bedroom and left them to Sarah and the Nurse. I am the victim of some cruel Tempest, that has swept away only those I hold closest to my heart, while leaving behind an entire City of people whose existence is to me a matter of complete Indifference.

What I would give to be back in Edenton, safe and surrounded by those I love. When I close my eyes I see the Bay, the tall spire of the Courthouse, our little wooden house just beyond it; I smell the fresh breeze, hear the clamor of the docks, feel the paddle in my hand and the cool splattered drops of water on my skin as I take the canoe across the Creek to Hayes. I hear Nelly's throaty laugh; the shouts of the Johnston Children at play; Sam's deep voice describing, in loving detail, his latest method of fertilization. I shall will myself to dream of Edenton tonight, for at present it is the only way I can think of to get there.

From James Iredell to Hannah Iredell:

New York, September 20, 1792

... I find I unluckily brought away the key of my desk. I will send it to you if there be an opportunity.

God almighty knows what I suffered in parting from you yesterday morning. The thoughts of your being left in a manner quite alone affect me inexpressibly ...

Thursday, September 23, 1792

I yesterday went to the desk in the Parlor, where we keep our Money, so that Sarah might go to the Market (for I have not had Spirits to go myself, of late). The desk was locked, which in itself was not so unusual (we began locking up such things when Mother lived with us, and the habit has not left us); but the key to the desk was not in its usual hiding place. Sarah and I searched the house, high and low, but could find no sign of the key. We were in great need of provisions, and so, much distraught, I went to the Bonds' and was able to borrow a few Dollars of them, some of which I gave to Sarah.

Now today comes a Letter from Mr. Iredell telling me he brought the key away with him by mistake! What does he expect me to do for Money? Shall we become beggars in the Street? I have written him a letter, rather disordered I fear, asking him to send the key to me at once, if he can find someone who will carry it here. If he cannot, I swear I don't know what will become of us.

From James Iredell to Hannah Iredell:

Hartford, Connecticut, September 30, 1792

... Wilson has resolved to return on very urgent business to Philadelphia, though with an intention still to meet me at Boston, as it is absolutely necessary both of us should be at New Hampshire, the District Judge there being incapable to act ...

From James Iredell to Hannah Iredell:

Hartford, Connecticut, October 2, 1792

... Judge Wilson carries this. He proposes to meet me at Boston. Be so good as to write me by him ... I shall be inexpressibly anxious. I write this in Court in the midst of great business...

Thursday, October 11, 1792

Judge Wilson has come and delivered a letter from Mr. Iredell—but alas! no key. The Gentleman was in so great a hurry as almost to be rude, not even taking the time to step inside the door and remove his hat. I was indeed relieved to find that I would not be required to entertain the fellow, whom I find stiff and awkward at best; but I would have greatly appreciated some particulars of Mr. Iredell's Health and such like. But Mr. Wilson was quite adamant that he had pressing Business to attend to, which was indeed the reason he had hurried back from Hartford, and he had but a few days left to him before he rejoined Mr. Iredell in Boston—as, he said, he *very much hoped* he would be able to do.

Very much hoped he would be able to! Does the man see his position on the country's highest Court as merely an interruption of his business Endeavors, to be put off or ignored if inconvenient? Mr. Iredell would no more think of missing a Circuit Court than of slitting his own throat, unless he were prevented from attending by serious illness or some other unavoidable obstacle.

Ah well, I suppose I must do without the key until Mr. Iredell returns, sometime towards the end of next Month. Mrs. Bond has been exceedingly kind in lending me Money, and jests that she certainly knows where to find us should dunning become necessary. It is a trivial sum to be sure—certainly nothing that compares with what speculators such as Mr. Wilson must owe, or what we ourselves owe to Major Butler—but it causes me anxiety to be in Debt to anyone, for any amount. I know that Mr. Iredell is distracted by the press of Business, and yet I cannot help feeling rather vexed with him for forgetting to send that key.

I am vexed a great deal these days; my Spirits simply refuse to rise. Mrs. Bond has been most kind and patient with me, but I fear she is tiring of my gloomy face. I cannot muster even any pretense of interest in the various bits of gossip or other intelligence she relates to me—whether the President will agree to a second Term, what rumored horrors the Jacobins are now committing in France.

All that I have the inclination to do is to tend to my precious Children, among whom I now number Fanny—almost more a Daughter to me than a Niece. James has proven himself quite a Student, even though he is not quite four; Helen grows well, though she will never have the flesh her Brother sports, and has become more spirited; and Annie and her Cousin are engaged in sewing Samplers that would make any parent proud. Once a week I set them the task of writing Letters to their relatives in Carolina, for they are not too young to begin to learn so vital a skill. And while they hunch over their Papers, their ink splattering and quills scratching and their little pink tongues caught between their teeth with the effort, I sit by them and write to Nelly, every week. As yet I have received no answer.

From James Iredell to Hannah Iredell:

Boston, Massachusetts, October 13, 1792

... I am very sorry I forgot to send the key by Judge Wilson. It was very careless in me...

I went to the Ball on Thursday evening. Very few Ladies (only about 29) attended, which was partly owing to many Families having sickness or being in distress, & partly to a kind of etiquette many Ladies have here of not going the first night... I danced down two Dances, & that was all. All the Ladies were handsomely dressed, and there were at least 6 Beauties out of the small number present—and several more that were nearly such...

From the *Columbian Centinel*:

Boston, Massachusetts, October 17, 1792

On Friday last, the Circuit Court *of the* United States *opened in this town. After the Rev. DR. LATHROP had addressed the throne of Grace, in prayer, the Hon. Judge IREDELL gave an elegant charge to the jury, and the business of the session commenced. The Hon. Judge WILSON is on the circuit—but has not yet arrived.*

From James Iredell to Hannah Iredell:

Exeter, New Hampshire, October 25, 1792

... We left Boston on a Monday morning, and ... came on here yesterday, where our stay will not be long as there is very little business to do...

I don't think I should have left this Country quite so soon, as I was desirous of seeing more of it, but Judge Wilson wishes to press on immediately to Newport, as he has some important business which makes him anxious to be as near Philadelphia as he can. I think I shall spend most of my time in Boston till near the time of going to Providence. I am in a manner domesticated there in several agreeable Families...

From James Iredell to Hannah Iredell:

Boston, Massachusetts, October 28, 1792

... I do indeed find every part of this country highly agreeable, and it would be perfectly so were you and my children with me. As it is, I assure you, Philadelphia would be much more so.

Judge Wilson talks of going to Rhode Island on Tuesday. But I don't think I can leave Boston so soon... I refused a seat in a coach with a very fine young lady, to come home and write this letter. However, I must go and drink tea with her ...

From James Iredell to Hannah Iredell:

Boston, Massachusetts, November 1, 1792

... I spent yesterday evening at a Gentleman's house, where there were a number of Ladies & Gentlemen—among others Mrs. Hancock, the Governor's Wife, whom I had not seen before. She is rather handsome,

and uncommonly pleasing; her manners altogether untinctured with any pride or affectation...

Wednesday, November 7, 1792

Every letter I receive from Mr. Iredell contains some compliment paid to a Lady—it appears that near every woman in Boston is elegant or beautiful or fine. No wonder he is so well pleased with the Place! The letter that has just come tells me he must break off writing to go drink tea with some young Vixen—whilst I needed to break off the reading of it because James scraped his knee badly rolling hoops in the yard with the Girls and required tending to, though he was trying to be brave. Fortunately I had put up some Balm-of-Gilead buds in a bottle of New England rum last Spring, and was able to soothe the wound.

How can it be that Mr. Iredell professes great affection and respect for me, as he so often does, and yet proceeds so lavishly to praise other Ladies for their beauty and charm—the very Qualities I lack? It is hard to resist the conclusion that he wishes me to be other than I am; and yet I cannot change—for I have tried, and failed miserably. Indeed, I fear he will be much disappointed in me when he returns, for I have become again nearly as I was in New York: loath to venture outside, even to the Market; hardly speaking to anyone other than the Children and Sarah—and, on occasion, Mrs. Bond. I cannot seem to rid my mind of terrible thoughts: of poor Betsey, and how she grew sicker and sicker as I watched; of how Nelly must be thinking dark, malevolent thoughts of me, and how I deserve them; of Mother, who scorned all my efforts to win her affections; and of Mr. Iredell, dancing till dawn with a bevy of charming Beauties, and thinking of me scarcely at all. I fall to weeping twenty times a day, though I try to hide it from the Children. But Sarah has begun giving me those looks again.

Mrs. Bond has proved herself a loyal Friend, and continues to come calling, even though I fear I give her little encouragement. I am in some way glad to see her when she appears at my door, but the gladness feels so remote, so buried deep within me, that I cannot even manage a welcoming smile. And yet she seems not to take offense, but manifests only concern for me, and for my Welfare. Yesterday she pressed me to leave the confines of the House, at least to go walking with her along the High Street.

"This really won't do, you know," she gently scolded me. "You cannot go an entire Season without mingling in society. People will talk, and perhaps take offense. And you know there's a good deal of highly interesting intelligence to be gleaned at these events, respecting the Government and politics and the like. Mr. Iredell, when he returns, will want to know what has transpired in his absence—and what will you be able to tell him?"

Though I knew she was right, I simply could not go, not even for a short walk. Indeed, the very thought of it made my throat tighten and my heart beat faster.

Sam is due to arrive from Edenton soon, for the opening of the Congress; I earnestly pray that once he is here, and residing under our roof, my Spirits will return to me.

From David Leonard Barnes, Massachusetts attorney, to Benjamin Bourne, Congressman from Rhode Island:

Providence, Rhode Island, November 8, 1792

... The Circuit Court was opened here yesterday. His Honor Judge Wilson gave us a learned dissertation on the first springs of Government, & the trial by jury in general—not a word, as I recollect, respecting the peculiar situation of this Country, or the nature of the crimes the Jury were to inquire about ...

His Honor Judge Iredell puts on his hat, upon the Bench, when his head is cold, and looks as if he was at home. He has won the affection of the Bar at Boston, by his urbanity and politeness, and everyone here seems charmed with his civility & frankness...

Thursday, November 15, 1792

Sam has been here nearly a week, much occupied with Senate business of course, but still a most welcome presence in the household. The Children like to crowd around him of an evening—Fanny especially, of course—clambering up to his bony lap and hanging on his limbs like Squirrels on a bare autumn tree. Sam pretends to suffer this attention grudgingly, with half-closed eyes and a weary face; but the Children and

I know he is in fact delighted to be the object of it. When I look upon the Scene, my eyes begin to fill with tears—in part out of happiness for his being here, and in part out of anticipated grief at his inevitable Departure.

I had thought he might express dismay at the Hermit existence I have been leading, but he appears to take little notice of it. Mrs. Bond came by the other Day, to try and convince me to go to Mrs. Washington's room with her, but of course I made some excuse—as she must have known I would. She then sighed and shook her head and said to Sam, "You must try and talk some sense to your Sister, Sir—she quite refuses to go out."

To my delight, Sam only gave a sort of grunt and said, "Quite right, too. Why waste time taking tea and gossiping at levees and Dinners and such—assembling with a great number of well-dressed people for the unmeaning purpose of seeing and being seen?"

He then admonished Mrs. Bond to tell the President, if she met him, that it was past time for him to make up his mind about a second Term.

"Tell him there's no other Man can keep this damned Country together," he barked at her. "Mr. Adams will never be able to keep the States united, and that scoundrel Jefferson will surely do his utmost to drive them apart!"

Sam was only teasing, of course (for who would have the temerity to make such remarks to the President?), but his manner is at all times so severe that those who don't know him well are apt to misinterpret his occasional pleasantries. Poor Mrs. Bond gave a trembling sort of smile and hurriedly took her leave. As soon as she had shut the door, the two of us fell into Laughter; it was perhaps disloyal of me, but I couldn't help myself.

Ah, how easy it is to share a life with someone of the same stripe as oneself—someone with the same preferences and assumptions! And yet we each of us, Sam and I, have chosen to bind ourselves to Spouses who are quite unlike ourselves, and whom we love, perhaps, for that very unlikeness—we the solid, craggy rock, they the quicksilver water coursing over us, ever just beyond our reach. Poor Sam: he tells me Mrs. Johnston pines for Philadelphia, with its shops and balls and general liveliness, and complains endlessly about the dullness of the Farms he loves with all his heart. He quite understands my yearning for Edenton—"Nothing wrong with you that being at home in Edenton wouldn't cure," he's remarked—and has urged me to speak to Mr. Iredell, on his return, about whether he would agree to a removal there.

His words are such a tonic to me; for, being surrounded by those—not only Mrs. Bond, but Mr. Iredell as well—who view my behavior as inexplicable, I have sometimes begun to think I am losing my Wits. Perhaps it is only that I have been separated from my natural element, and my Distress is no more unnatural than that of a trout flung into a dry basket. And yet, I wonder if I can find the courage to speak to Mr. Iredell about leaving this place, for I know if I were to launch such a Plea it would cause him the most severe disappointment.

And I should be disappointed in myself, as well: much as I long to return to Edenton, it strikes me that doing so would be an admission of defeat—an acknowledgment that I shall never be anything more than timid, fearful Hannah Johnston, the burdensome Cross which the gay and charming Mr. Iredell must bear through life. Is it truly impossible for me to graft onto myself those qualities that Mr. Iredell so admires—the way Sam might graft some brilliant and alluring flower onto a plain, leafless stalk? Would that Humanity were as malleable as vegetation!

Of course I anxiously await Mr. Iredell's safe arrival; and yet a part of me half-wishes that Sam and I might continue on our own a bit longer. I am reminded, these days, of when we lived at Hayes so long ago, Sam and myself and my dear Sister Annie, now gone to her rest. It was a time of such simplicity and, I think now, innocence: no Husbands or Wives or Children to fret ourselves over, little to occupy us but Books and conversation and, for Sam, farming and his law practice. Before the War came, even the Politics was simpler—or at any rate, more theoretical, which is perhaps much the same thing. Everything was as yet in the future; we were on the brink of life, free to imagine that governing a Nation—or, for that matter, conducting a Marriage—would prove to be a thing of sweet harmony and ease.

Thursday, January 10, 1793

I have just come from Mrs. Bond's, who this morning invited me to take Tea with her (hers is nearly the only House I still visit—though I can scarcely give myself much credit, as it is next door). While I was there she let fall a remark that has quite distracted me, though it is possible she meant nothing by it.

Yesterday was the day of Monsieur Blanchard's balloon ascent from the Walnut Street Prison Yard—it has been quite the object of general fascination, though it seems to me a great waste of time and energy. Why ascend to the Heavens, with no means of guiding one's craft, at the mercy of wind and Weather—and, needless to say, at great risk to life and limb? Any sane person who desired to travel to New Jersey would surely prefer to take the Ferry. But a great Crowd apparently gathered to watch the ascent and wish the Gentleman well—including Messrs. Adams and Jefferson, the French Minister, and President Washington himself (who has at last agreed, to general relief and rejoicing, to serve another Term).

Mr. Iredell, of course, was all for attending this event—for which the organizers had the temerity to charge five Dollars admission. Five Dollars, when anyone with one good eye would be able to see the thing floating overhead within a few minutes after the ceremony. I told him it interested me not one bit, and that I had the Girls' lessons to attend to in any event (for Mr. Wigdon has not yet made good on his proposal to open a Girls' school); and so he went alone. He has become quite accustomed to venturing out without me; I haven't been out, except to go to the Market or to James's school, in over two weeks—a refusal that I now have reason to fear will cost me dearly.

The Bonds were at the Prison Yard too, it seems, but on the other side of the Crowd from Mr. Iredell. They spied him, Mrs. Bond said, but could not catch his eye, and so he was unaware of their presence until later, when the Crowd dispersed.

"He appeared to be enjoying himself immensely," Mrs. Bond remarked, as she poured me a second cup of Tea. "He had an attractive young Lady on either side of him, and they were all laughing gaily. I believe one of them was Mrs. Andrews—that young widow I saw him with at a Ball last week? You weren't there, I think—in any event, he danced every dance with her. I'd keep an eye on that Gentleman if I were you, my dear—he's quite the charmer!"

I quickly excused myself, leaving my second cup untouched; for Mrs. Bond's words produced in me such agitation that I couldn't trust myself to remain there a moment longer. She seemed surprised by my hasty departure; perhaps in her mind the remark was merely an innocent jest. She has no knowledge, of course, of what once transpired between Mr. Iredell and myself, how he long ago violated those sacred Bonds that unite us. Dear God, give me the strength not to fall once again into that Swamp of suspicion in which I was once so mired; allow me to retain that trust in my Husband without which there can be no domestic harmony; banish from my Mind the horrors that now swim before it.

He is here now, in the next room, poring over some law Books; I need only go to him, and ask him if there be any Truth to my fears. Perhaps he would smile and reassure me, telling me that his heart is mine alone. But perhaps he would fly into a Rage, and rail against my suspicious nature; or perhaps he would reassure me falsely, as he did once before. How shall I ever discern the truth?

But no! I will not allow myself to fret in this way. It is certainly nothing; for if there were anything to be concerned about, would Mrs. Bond have mentioned it so casually? I will leave Mr. Iredell to his labors, for he is much occupied with them of late. He is convinced that, when the Supreme Court convenes next Month, they will at last be forced to squarely meet the question that has so long caused him anxiety—that of whether a State may be sued in the Federal Courts. That New York case, it seems, will be delayed; but another case, brought by a Mr. Chisholm against the State of Georgia, is to come on. Mr. Iredell says that Georgia surely will not willingly submit to the jurisdiction of a Federal Court, and he is determined to be prepared: for numerous reasons, including some respecting the Constitution, he intends to argue that such a Suit cannot stand. We have discussed the Question at length—Mr. Iredell and Sam and even myself, of an evening—and I am convinced that he is right, though he is apprehensive that his Colleagues may disagree.

So, no—I cannot worry Mr. Iredell with my silly fears when he is engaged in Business that is so vital to the future of the Country.

From the *Gazette of the United States*:

Philadelphia, Pennsylvania, February 6, 1793

The Supreme Court of the United States opened on Monday last... Yesterday the Court appointed to hear the Attorney-General of the United States, on the interesting question—Whether the Supreme Court can take cognizance of actions against a State, at the suit of one or more individuals of another State?

Monday, February 18, 1793

The Court delivered its Opinions in the Georgia case today. I suppose the rest of the Country is engaged in absorbing the shock of the result, but I confess that my own alarm at the Decision has been dwarfed by a shock of a far more personal nature.

I had not gone to hear the Argument, some two weeks ago, but Mrs. Bond urged that it was only my wifely Duty to hear my Husband deliver his Opinion in so momentous a case (even though, having copied the Opinion over for him, I am quite familiar with its every word). I wavered until the last minute—indeed, until after Mr. Iredell had already departed for the City Hall, so that he did not anticipate I would be in the audience. I imagine he was quite sure I would keep myself at home, as has been my recent Habit.

The room, on the second floor of the City Hall, was so crowded that Mrs. Bond and I were forced to take seats towards the back. Ladies and Gentlemen were smiling, chattering, greeting their acquaintances; an air of interest and expectancy filled the room. In a few minutes, the Marshal banged the gavel, a hush fell, and in marched the Judges to take their seats. So distinguished they all looked, in their crimson-trimmed robes, seated on a raised platform before three grand arched windows. I swelled with Pride to see my Husband there, looking perfectly at ease, the eyes of the Crowd fixed upon him; and I was glad that I had come. Perhaps, I thought, he will spy me back here, and I will be rewarded with a smile of surprise and delight.

And then—he *did* smile, only slightly, and nod his head; but not at me! My eye followed the direction in which he looked, and I saw, near the front and apparently returning his smile, the profile of a Lady. Though I was not close, I could see that she was young—no more than thirty, I should think—and exceedingly pretty.

Mrs. Bond, who must have been following both his gaze and mine, then leaned towards me and whispered, "Mrs. Andrews!"

I cannot say I took in much of the learned speeches that then followed; so absorbed was I in watching Mr. Iredell and the Lady—Mrs. Andrews—and trying to discern if they exchanged any further smiles or glances, that I confess I had no idea what conclusions Mr. Iredell's colleagues had reached. But after Judge Cushing ended his brief remarks, I noticed a sort of buzzing go through the room, and turned in puzzlement to Mrs. Bond.

"It is decided," she whispered urgently. "Three are in favor of allowing Georgia to be sued. So even if the Chief Justice agrees with Mr. Iredell, the State has lost."

Mr. Jay, as it happened, did not agree with Mr. Iredell; *all* the other Judges were of the opinion that states might be sued. Of this knowledge, however, and the apprehension for the future of the Country that it produced, I was only dimly aware. All my senses, all my energies, were yet engaged in the vigil I kept over Mr. Iredell and Mrs. Andrews. But now it seemed that Mr. Iredell was in no Spirits to exchange glances, much less smiles, with anyone; his brow was deeply furrowed and his chin rested in his hand.

The moment the Marshal declared the Court adjourned, the Courtroom began to clear; only a few, mostly Ladies, lingered to pay their respects to the Judges. Mrs. Bond began to move towards the front, but I hung back, still watching. I saw Mrs. Andrews sweep gracefully towards Mr. Iredell, as he rose from his seat; her Gown was cut so that her bosom fairly overspilled its bounds. Again I saw him smile at her warmly, then bow and kiss her hand. I was frozen as a statue, gazing on the scene, until Mrs. Bond asked me somewhat impatiently whatever was the matter.

And so we made our way towards the dais, my face no doubt flushed and my heart beating wildly with trepidation. But when Mr. Iredell saw me at last (for his eyes were so closely trained on Mrs. Andrews that we were nearly upon him before he noticed us), he exclaimed in surprise that he had not realized I would come. He then said something about the Business that had transpired—a sad day for the Nation, or some such phrase—while I waited for him to introduce Mrs. Andrews.

"Ah, Mrs. Iredell—at last!" said Mrs. Andrews, in a confident and mellifluous voice, once the introduction had been made. "Your Husband has spoken of you in such admiring terms that I have been most eager to meet you."

A ruse, I thought, a bald-faced lie, to cover a flirtation—or worse. For I cannot imagine that, what with my recent timidity and Melancholy, Mr. Iredell could do anything other than complain about me—if he thinks to mention me at all.

"I was remarking to Mr. Iredell," she continued, turning once more to him, "how utterly persuasive his Opinion was—far more so, to my mind, than those of his Colleagues. Though I am but a woman, and possessed of only a limited understanding of Politics, I should think his words will give much encouragement to those in Congress who are no doubt already hatching plans to overturn this ill-conceived Decision."

"You are too kind, Madam, too kind," Mr. Iredell replied. "Let us pray that this great Question may be resolved through peaceful means, and not by any rash actions that would destroy our precious domestic Harmony."

They gazed solemnly into one another's eyes for a long moment, until I could stand no more. "Come, Mr. Iredell," I managed to say. "Our Dinner awaits us."

I have not yet had the opportunity, nor the strength, to demand from Mr. Iredell a true accounting of his relations with this Woman. But I cannot live with this torment much longer; I must speak to him before I burst, no matter what the Consequences.

Domestic Harmony, indeed! Mr. Iredell professes to be so exceedingly concerned about the effect the Georgia decision will have on the Country; and yet what Disharmony may he be causing in his household by his own rash actions?

Thursday, February 21, 1793

I managed to hold my tongue until last night. I had not wanted to speak until the Court's session ended, which it did yesterday. And at Dinner Sam brought home the news that a Resolution had been introduced in the Senate, proposing a constitutional Amendment to be sent to the States designed to overturn the Court's decision in the Georgia Case (a similar Resolution having been introduced in the House the day before). Mr. Iredell was clearly pleased by this; indeed, his mood was lighter than it has been since the Judges announced their opinions.

I waited until we were in the privacy of our bedroom, preparing to retire. At first I mentioned, with seeming innocence, the name of Mrs. Andrews, and inquired who she was and how Mr. Iredell had happened to make her acquaintance. I thought I detected a certain hesitation, a pause as he undid the stock at his neck. A Widow who had recently moved to town, he replied, her husband having been a merchant and trader of some means; she was frequently in attendance at Balls and parties, and I would surely have met her myself had I chosen to accompany him to such events. (Though he kept his voice mild, I nevertheless detected a certain tone of Accusation.)

"It seems you are well acquainted with one another," I continued, though I could hear my voice beginning to shake.

"As I said, we have encountered each other frequently at one gathering or another." He now began to undo the buttons of his shirt. "Are you not going to bed, Hannah?"

"It seemed to me that you ... admired her."

His hands went to his hips, leaving his shirt buttons half undone. "She is generally considered a Beauty, and quite charming. I suppose I concur in the general opinion."

I was silent a moment, attempting to read his face; but all I saw was a wariness that told me far less than I needed to know. I took a deep breath and leaned against the chest that stood behind me. "Mr. Iredell, do not think me impertinent, but there is a Question I must ask of you; and before you answer, I charge you to recall the sacred Oath of fidelity that binds us, and which has once already been violated. Has there been any ... intercourse between you and Mrs. Andrews of a private nature—or anything improper?"

"By Jesus, Hannah!" He sighed wearily and shook his head. "I cannot tell what put such a damned foolish idea into your head. I can only think that you have, by your own choice, removed yourself so far from the normal course of relations in Society that you mistake mere cordiality for love-making!"

He then drew me to him, and made so many protestations of his love for me, and which sounded so sincere, that after a time I could not help but apologize for my Suspicions. (I refrained from remarking on his Swearing, as in other respects he was being so solicitous of me.) He then renewed a theme he has sounded much of late—namely, that I must no longer keep exclusively to the company of my Children and my Books, but accept of an invitation now and then. My spirits bolstered by his expressions of Affection, I promised I would do so. And surely, I told myself, it is better for Mr. Iredell to have his Wife by his side at these gatherings, distasteful as they may be for me, than for him to seek amusement or comfort from such as Mrs. Andrews.

Tuesday, March 5, 1793

I am in a state, a terrible state. This evening we went to Mrs. Knox's—Mr. Iredell *and* myself, for I have been trying my best to obey Mr. Iredell's wishes. We have been out together several times since our Conversation concerning Mrs. Andrews, and though certainly no one would say I have illuminated the Room at these occasions, I yet flatter myself that I have caused no great embarrassment. People have been kind, I suppose, inquiring after my health as though my absence from Society were doubtless due to illness; it has given me something to say, at least. I tell them I am well, or sometimes allow that I am much better now. Let them assume that I have been ill, then; it seems a far more acceptable Excuse that what has truly afflicted me—whatever that has been.

Mrs. Knox was making just this sort of inquiry, this evening, when I happened to spy Mrs. Andrews at the far side of the room. I fear I blanched, and stumbled over my replies to Mrs. Knox—but I imagine she attributed my confusion to my supposed recent Illness. Mrs. Andrews soon made her way to us, no doubt seeking Mr. Iredell; we at that moment formed part of a small group that included, in addition to ourselves, Mrs. Knox, our old friend Major Butler, and Mr. and Mrs. Powel.

The Conversation—being conducted, as it was, by skilled practitioners of the art—proceeded fluidly, like a River; whilst I stood aside and watched from the water's edge, as it were, aware of its sparkling surface but too distracted to plumb its depths (assuming, of course, that it possessed any). At length, however, I gathered that the talk had turned to Books, and reading—a subject on which I supposed I might, with some effort, bring forth a modest contribution. The topic of Novels, and their worth, was broached, with Mr. Powel rehearsing the familiar view that the vast majority were nothing more than a waste of time or worse, distracting readers with idle Fancies when they might be otherwise occupied in gleaning useful Information concerning history, or the Classics; and that such studies were particularly vital at the delicate juncture where our Nation now found itself, when the wisdom of the Ancients might serve as a model for the conduct of our affairs.

Mrs. Andrews then flicked her fan and raised her dainty chin in the air (her cheeks and lips were obviously rouged, I noticed), and said that Mr. Powel was certainly correct that history and the Ancients merited study, but was there not time enough in life for amusement as well? And did not many Novels manage to slip in valuable moral lessons along with the sometimes sensational adventures they depicted?

"But indeed," she continued airily, "I take great pleasure, myself, in reading nearly anything, as long as it's well written. I confess that I've turned down many an Invitation to stay at home with a good Book."

I was thinking that I could scarcely credit this Remark, considering how often she was seen abroad, when Mr. Iredell began to speak. "Indeed, my dear Mrs. Andrews, you show excellent judgment, as always. For is not a Book the most reliable of Companions—and generally among the most stimulating as well? No need to worry about amusing or pleasing or making a good impression on a *Book*, when its only purpose is to entertain and, perhaps, instruct. And if it should fail in that purpose, one can merely return it to its shelf, without so much as a by-your-leave—and no occasion for anxiety about its wounded Pride, either."

As the others in our party emitted small approving laughs at Mr. Iredell's Soliloquy (and Mrs. Andrews bowed her head in acknowledgment of the compliment paid to her judgment) I was seized by a terrible, near paralytic shock. For were not these the very Words, almost to the letter, that Mr. Iredell had uttered to me long ago, at our first meeting—the Words that had echoed the secret thoughts of my own mind, and convinced me that, despite the marked differences in our outward demeanors, we were in fact cut from the same cloth, and destined to be joined to one other? How could he so blithely repeat them to this simpering, painted hussy? Was this speech, to him, merely a set piece, to be trotted out at Dinners and parties, or whenever he sought to exert his charm on a Lady? How often, indeed, might he have said those Words, without my knowledge? Perhaps, to him, they had no meaning particular to myself—to *us*; perhaps he had even forgotten he once spoke them to me. Hearing them now, in this Company, it struck me that they did not emanate from his heart—that they were no more sincere than Mrs. Andrews' declaration that she had refused Invitations to remain at home with a Book. Surely he did not believe what he said about her choice revealing good Judgment; for if he did, how could he berate *me*, as he so often has these past weeks, for making that very choice myself?

I could not stay longer: I pleaded a sudden headache and Fatigue, and nearly dragged Mr. Iredell from the room. When I revealed to him, at his insistence, the true cause of my distress, he shook his head and furrowed his brow and seemed unable to comprehend: supposing he had said such a thing to me, some twenty-five years before; what was the harm, exactly, in his saying it to someone else? I could not speak, could not explain. How to explain to him that that Moment twenty-five years ago—that Moment which, it seemed, meant so little to him that he now scarcely remembered it—was the Instant I became convinced that our minds harbored the same thoughts, our hearts beat the same rhythm, our eyes perceived the same world? How to explain that I must now question all my Faith, all my trust in him?

Friday, March 8, 1793

My head is swarming with the blackest, most distressing thoughts; I want only to quiet them, but short of somehow separating my head from my Body, I cannot tell how.

My relations with Mr. Iredell have been most unhappy since the night we were at Mrs. Knox's. He continues to profess complete puzzlement at my agitation, and appears quite irritated with me; while I am still profoundly shaken by what I heard him say, and have become convinced that something has transpired between him and Mrs. Andrews—I cannot tell what exactly, but the looks I have seen pass between them betray some Intimacy that is certainly improper. And then, I think, why should this surprise me so? For is my Husband not one of the most handsome and charming Men in Philadelphia, and is she not among the most beautiful and elegant of Ladies? And what am I? Plain and dowdy and tongue-tied, too timid to venture from my own house. Would not any sane person match him with *her* rather than with me? And yet it wounds me so, to think I may have lost him to another; for I still love him dearly, whether we are well matched or not.

And then, yesterday afternoon, Mrs. Bond came to call. I believe she could see at once that something was amiss, but was too polite to inquire. At length it all came out, in whispers—about Mrs. Andrews, and Mr. Iredell's little speech about Books, and my suspicions. She was quiet for a moment, then took my hand and gave it a little squeeze. Perhaps I was assuming too much, she whispered back; from what she had seen, it was no more than a Friendship. But it was *you* who first put it into my head that something was between them, I said softly but urgently, with your remark about seeing them at Monsieur Blanchard's ascent! Oh that, she said with a nervous laugh; I meant nothing by *that*.

I could not tell, indeed, whether she *now* meant what she said; if People will say things that mean nothing, how are we to know when to believe them? In any event, I said to her, thinking of Mr. Iredell's past transgressions, there are things I know that you do not; let us leave it at that.

Well, she said, a little too brightly, clearing her throat, I have come to give you a piece of news: Mr. Bond has accepted a post that requires us to move to Baltimore, and we are to leave in two months' time. I shall miss you and your Family very much, of course, but you must come and visit us.

I was exceedingly distressed to hear this—especially as it was delivered with no apparent distress or regret on Mrs. Bond's part. No doubt she is happy to get away from me, as I have become poor Company indeed, more a burden than a Friend. But what shall I do without her? She is the only person of my own Sex in this town with whom I can converse easily; when she is gone, I shall have no one. I shall be entirely alone.

Ah, I have made a mess of everything—of my connection to Mrs. Bond, who was once so kind to me; to Mother; to Nelly; and, worst of all, to my Husband, without whom I am lost entirely. My only hope is to shake off this Melancholy and remake myself into what I know I should be; and yet this Melancholy is the very thing that prevents me.

I once saw an old Raft abandoned in the shallows of the Bay at Edenton—no more than a few sticks it was, held together with rope. I would pass by it every few days, and each time I did, would see that another piece of it had drifted away, out to Sea, gone for all time; for the rope that held it together was slowly dissolving in the brine. Each time I saw what remained of the Raft, it appeared more pathetic and forlorn, the few sticks buffeted by the tide, the frayed cord no match for the forces of Nature. One day, when I passed by, I saw that there was nothing left of it, no trace. I have an odd sensation now that something of the like is happening to me: pieces of me floating off, drifting away, never to be retrieved. And yet I am convinced that if only I could return to Edenton, I could contrive to collect the scattered, weather-beaten fragments, and begin to create myself anew.

Sunday, March 10, 1793

A most extraordinary thing has occurred; I feel myself entirely changed.

This morning I had not Spirits enough even to attend at Church, though I sincerely wished to go, and Sam and Mr. Iredell went off without me. Not long after their return, Mr. Iredell came into the bedroom—from which, I confess, I had not yet emerged. He settled himself on the bed, where I had been dozing, and took my hand.

"Hannah," he said softly, "I have been engaged in a good deal of contemplation about our Situation—yours and mine."

I felt agitation rising within me; I wondered wildly whether he was going to speak of his connection with Mrs. Andrews.

"I had hoped," he continued, "as I know you did as well—that in time you would grow to like this City, and to feel yourself at home here. To venture out into—indeed, to enjoy—what is perhaps the most accomplished and amusing Society in this Nation, to partake of all that the Capital has to offer." He stopped himself sharply and shook his head. "But I see that it is not to be." His tone was gentle, but his hands were clenching and unclenching, as though they had a Will of their own.

I felt my tears begin to flow, and feared I was coming in for another scolding. "I have *tried* ..." I began.

But Mr. Iredell interrupted me. "I know, I know! I am not here to take you to task."

I waited, now utterly confused, for further explanation.

"I have decided, my dear Hannah, that we must move back to Edenton, if that is what you wish." Tears were now brimming in his eyes as well, and he stroked my cheek with his hand. "I cannot bear to see you so unhappy."

"Back to Edenton?" I could scarce believe my ears: the very thing I had yearned for, prayed for. My body began to tremble with emotion, and more tears—tears of Joy now—cascaded down my cheeks. "Oh, my dearest Mr. Iredell, I wish it with my whole soul. You have no idea how much I wish it!"

I threw my arms about his neck, and we wept into one another's shoulders for some time; and I believe I loved him more at that moment than at any other time in our mutual History. Mr. Iredell's one condition—that we remain here until the Fall, so as to avoid the sickly season in Edenton—seemed but a trifle, compared to the rapturous Vista now stretched before me.

Since that moment, just hours ago, doubts have begun to intrude roughly on my Delight: Perhaps, I have considered, Mr. Iredell has his own purposes in this: might he not prefer to keep me in Edenton, so that he may be more at liberty when he returns here—on his own—to attend Court? Is it possible that his tears and emotion were no more than crafty Pretense? But I have tried to fling these Suspicions from me—or at least to assure myself that what I do not witness will not trouble me so. For there is no help for it: I cannot remain in Philadelphia. For the sake of my Children, for the sake of my own Sanity, to Edenton we must return. The very thought of it—the Spires and the harbor, Nelly and Sam waiting at the dock, my own little house—sends such a peace and Calm through me that I know I have no other choice.

From James Iredell to Hannah Iredell:

Trenton, New Jersey, April 2, 1793

... We arrived here very well a little after eight, or rather I should say I did, for poor Peter happened to be out of the way when we left Bristol and I never missed him till some time after. The Carriage stopped as long as I could decently permit it, but no sign of him appeared. I was in hopes he would have waited for the Mail Stage, but much to my surprise he came about an hour after us, having walked the whole distance from Bristol. It fatigued him very much, as you may well imagine, but he is otherwise well. It mortified me extremely, but there was no help for it. The business here is in a state of uncertainty, but I have reason to hope I shall be in Town on Friday...

Sunday, April 10, 1793

Mr. Iredell returned from Jersey late yesterday evening, having managed to avoid travel on the Sabbath, but greatly fatigued. He told me, before he fell asleep, that there was something we must discuss with Peter and Sarah today. This in itself was so unusual that my mind immediately began grasping at explanations; but never in my imaginings did I foresee what was to transpire.

After Dinner, when the Children had gone upstairs, Peter and Sarah appeared at the threshold of the Parlor. They came in awkwardly, unaccustomed to being there for any reason other than to serve—Peter rubbing his roughened hands together as though he were washing them under a stream of water, Sarah clutching the hem of her apron and darting her eyes around the room. I noticed how worn Peter's shoes were and

133

made a note to myself to send him round to the bootmaker, if we had the money to spare.

"Well then, Peter," Mr. Iredell prompted after a brief silence, during which it became clear that they would not speak unless spoken to first, "you have something you wish to say?"

"Yes, Mr. Iredell, Sir, I do." Peter ducked his head, perched atop a long neck with a prominent Adam's Apple, towards where Mr. Iredell sat, and shifted his weight from one worn shoe to the other. Then he glanced sidelong at Sarah, took a breath, and seemed to stand up straighter. "Sarah and I, we been talking, and we decided that we want—when you all go on back to Carolina in the Fall, like you all planning, what we want to do is, well—we going to stay here in Philadelphia."

"Stay!" I rose to my feet, looking at Sarah, who kept her gaze trained on the floor. "What do you mean, stay?"

"Hannah," Mr. Iredell was standing now, too, his arm at my elbow. "It's the Law here—they are free to stay, if that is what they want."

Amazed, I could only say, "The Law?"

Mr. Iredell looked from me to Peter and Sarah and back again; something must have passed amongst them of which I was ignorant. "You see, my dear," Mr. Iredell began cautiously, "the State—the State of Pennsylvania—has decreed that Slaves who are brought here—whose Masters have come here to live—are no longer Slaves, but are entitled to their freedom."

A dozen questions sprang to my mind—foremost among them, why I had not been told of this before—but they could wait till later. I looked again at Sarah, whose eyes would still not meet mine. She had as yet said nothing.

"Sarah." I was surprised to hear a tremble in my voice, and to recognize the weight of gathering tears behind my eyes. "Is this what you want, then? Never to see Carolina again? Never to see"—here I almost said "me," but something made me think better of it—"the Children?"

She covered her eyes with her hand for a moment, and I wondered if she too was struggling against tears. But when she brought away her hand, her face looked hard. "I'll miss them Children, that's for sure. And you and Mr. Iredell been good to us, Ma'am—I don't have no complaints." She cast a quick glance at Peter. "Neither of us got complaints. But we free now, that's what the Man said."

What Man is that, I wondered? I resolved to add that to my list of questions for Mr. Iredell.

"And if we go back to Carolina," Sarah continued, "we ain't free no more." She pressed her lips together, as if to seal in any further words that might escape from her.

"But …" Something impelled me to move a step closer, to take her hands in mine. I thought of how we had been Babes together, nursing together at Sappho's breast; how as Children we had rolled hoops and drawn stick pictures in the mud behind my Father's house; how she had been with me—she and Sappho—at my Cousins', after my Father died, the only reminders of my Home and childhood and all that I had lost. And when Sam at last brought me to Hayes, of course she and Sappho came as well—always by my side, my dark shadows. I then remembered Sarah at my confinement, stepping forward and struggling to turn the Infant, saving her life—Helen's life—and possibly mine as well. Sarah is to me often a mystery, her silences cloaking I know not what. But she has been *my* mystery, always with me, the only living being who knows all of me: my infancy and Childhood, maidenhood and marriage. All of this was in my Heart, but none of it would come to my lips. I searched desperately for something I could say, some words that would convince her to stay by me.

"But what of *your* Children?" I said at last. "What of Mamie and Sukey, down at Hayes? Don't you want to be with them again?"

"Yes, Ma'am, we do." Sarah gave Peter another glance, then looked down to where my hands still held hers; something made me release my hold. "We want to be with them, but not in Carolina. We going to work until we get the money to buy their freedom, then we going to bring them here."

"Oh, Sarah! That will take a lot of money—it could be years before you have enough."

"Yes, Ma'am. But that's what we going to do." Again Sarah pressed her lips together; I knew, somehow, that further importuning would be useless, not to mention unseemly.

"Very well, then." Now it was anger that propelled the tears towards my eyes, but I swallowed them back down. "If that is what you want."

"Peter has promised me that I can hire his services whenever I'm in Philadelphia," Mr. Iredell put in cheerily, "if he's at liberty. We shall miss you both greatly, of course." Mr. Iredell paused, his face reddening with emotion. When he spoke again, there was a slight choke to his voice. "You have both served us well, exceedingly well. We wish you Godspeed, and the best of luck in all you undertake."

"Indeed, for I warrant you will need it," I burst out, the anger rising in me. "Do you think that Masters who pay wages will look after you when you are sick, and send for the Doctor when you need him? Do you think they will keep you on and feed and clothe you when you are old and infirm and unable to work?" At this, Peter looked down at his feet, seemingly abashed, and I added, "And I was just about to send you round to the bootmaker, to be measured for new shoes. Do you think your new Master will do *that*?"

Sarah dropped her apron, crossed her arms in front of her chest, and gave me a brazen stare. "When we earning *wages*," she said, with a dangerous quiet to her voice, "we can take care of those things ourselves."

Never had she spoken to me in that tone before; it was as though she could barely contain a lifetime of suppressed rage. Was that what her silences had been hiding, then?

"I pray the Lord that you are right," I told her briskly, and turned my back upon her.

As soon as they had left the room, I looked to Mr. Iredell with my mouth open, but he put a finger to his lips to hush me and shut the door. Immediately explanations and apologies began pouring from him: he had meant to tell me of this Law, but he had not wished to worry me, and there had been some expectation it would be changed. Peter and Sarah had in fact entered the State, not as our slaves, but as our indentured servants for a Term of seven years, which is what the law allowed; Mr. Iredell had seen to this, because otherwise they would have been considered free at once. Even though the terms of seven years had not yet expired, the Law forbade us from bringing them back to Carolina against their will. Peter and Sarah themselves had not been aware of their true situation until quite recently—Mr. Iredell had meant to tell them as well, but seven years seemed such a long time, he had thought there was no hurry. Some weeks ago, though, Sarah had been approached in the Market by a man from the Abolition Society, who had questioned her regarding her status and informed her of the Law. So that was what she meant by "the Man," I thought.

"Of all the meddlesome busybodies!" I cried, pacing the room. "How dare people go about interfering with the property rights of others?"

"Well, as the gentleman himself saw it, I presume, he was merely informing Sarah of *her* rights under the Law."

"The Law! Then it's the Law's fault. How can Pennsylvania decide that we no longer own what we brought into the State? Could they tell us that this"—I searched the room for an object we had carried with us from Carolina—"this snuff box is no longer ours, now that we've brought it across the State line?"

Mr. Iredell chided me, saying that surely I knew the Question was far more complicated than that; he reminded me that we ourselves had deplored the institution of Slavery, so liable to be abused by unscrupulous Masters, and had agreed that someday it must end. But not now, I thought; not with Sarah. I sank into the wing chair, as fatigued as if I had climbed a steep hill—my Throat had been sore for a day or two, and now my head was aching and I was beginning to feel feverish. "In any event," I said, rubbing at my temples, "even if I had known of the Law, I should have hoped they would choose to stay with us."

Mr. Iredell put a hand on my shoulder. "As did I."

"We've always been decent Masters. Sarah herself said they had no complaints." Then I gasped a little, remembering something Mr. Iredell had written in a letter while he was on Circuit. "You left Peter behind in Jersey—you forgot him, when the Carriage left!" Mr. Iredell's hand fell from my shoulder, and I rose to face him.

Mr. Iredell sighed with apparent remorse. "I was terribly distressed when I realized what had happened, I assure you. But there was a gentleman traveling on the Stage with me, quite an impressive fellow, and we were so deeply engaged in conversation ..." He shrugged. "I do forget things sometimes, you know. That key, for instance, to the desk. Do you remember?"

"I do remember, indeed. But *Peter*—Peter is not a key!"

"No," said Mr. Iredell drily. "No more than he is a snuffbox."

This stung me; I turned my back to him, my arms crossed.

"But you cannot lay the blame on me for their wanting their freedom," he continued. "Peter spoke to me on this very Subject before we had even reached Bristol. It seemed he had been thinking about it for quite some time—he and Sarah. Ever since she met that gentleman at the Market." Mr. Iredell put his arms around me and drew me to him. "I know it is hard for you to part with her, my dear, after all this time. But think on it, imagine yourself in her situation. Would you not perhaps do the same?"

I pressed my face into his shoulder and shook my head no. In truth, I cannot understand Sarah—to leave behind all that is familiar and secure, to go off into this wilderness that is Philadelphia, with no friends, no family other than Peter—without myself and Mr. Iredell to tend to her needs. Indeed, I fear for her, and for Peter; I have seen some of these free Negroes in the Street, their clothes ragged, their faces drawn with hunger. How odd that this place, which is to me nearly a Prison, should lure Sarah with a promise of freedom; and that Carolina, which is the one place I feel myself truly free, should be to her no more than a Jail.

From Samuel Johnston to James Iredell:

Hayes Plantation, near Edenton, North Carolina, April 10, 1793

... Your friends here are very happy in the Anticipation of your return to reside among them. Everyone is inquiring for the Arguments of the Attorney Genl. and the Judges on the Georgia Case. Your Opinion is universally applauded... .

Monday, April 29, 1793

Mr. Iredell left us again this morning, to hold the Court in Delaware—then on to Maryland and Virginia, not to return until the middle of June. But what a misery of a day it is, and has been these two days past, with sheets of rain and a whipping wind. I tremble to think on the condition of the roads, with Rivers swelling and overflowing their banks—bridges being swept away, perhaps. It is this sort of weather that brings on illness; I have had a troublesome Fever these past few days, and my throat continues very sore—even though (when I have had the time) I have gargled with vinegar and water, and applied Spirits of turpentine to my neck.

I have been troubled not only by illness, but by the presence of Sarah—I cannot accustom myself to the Idea that she has decided to leave us. My first flash of anger at her has passed, but there is an awkwardness between us. Some veil has been torn aside that can never be replaced; when I look on her smooth, impassive face, when I see the set of her mouth, when I listen for words that rarely come, I cannot help but wonder if she is harboring thoughts about me that I would shudder to hear.

And yet, when I told her just yesterday evening, after discussing the matter with Mr. Iredell, that she and Peter could leave us now if they wished—that we would help them find some lodging, and give them a sum of money to tide them over until they could find employment—she refused me. She thanked me politely enough for the offer, but said she would not leave me until I had found a Servant to replace her, and certainly not when I was ill.

"You know you take such good care of everyone else, Ma'am," she added, wagging a finger at me, "but you don't know how to take care of yourself. Someone got to be here to make sure you stay in your bed when you need to." She planted her hands on her hips and cocked her head at me. "And from the way you look right now, that's just where you should be."

Perhaps my emotions have been addled by Fever, but I felt tears rise to my eyes when I heard this, and had to turn away.

From James Iredell to Hannah Iredell:

Head of Elk, Maryland, May 3, 1793

. . We arrived here a little before dark, very well but through execrable roads. Luckily it seems now likely to clear up. I am very uneasy about your disorder, fearing you will not pay proper attention to it...
I am fatigued to death, & can scarce keep my eyes open...

Thursday, May 17, 1793

Such a din in the streets today as would wake the dead! Throngs streaming by the house, bellowing French songs at the top of their lungs, waving French flags, and yelling French slogans about liberty or equality or some such. I had to leave off the girls' arithmetic lesson for a full half hour, until the Clamor had died down, and poor Helen was awakened untimely from her nap.

All this for that Citizen Genet, as they call him, the new French Minister, who arrived in this City yesterday—the Patriotic Citizens of Philadelphia, as they style themselves, are advancing in a horde upon his quarters, to present to him a congratulatory Address. The more respectable elements, of course, are keeping their distance. I have never entirely approved of the French, though their assistance to us during the War was of course exceedingly helpful. The Reports of the direction their Revolution has taken are most alarming; now that they have murdered their King and Queen, I suppose we may expect anything of them.

My health quite recovered now, I have advertised in several of the newspapers for a Servant to replace Sarah. I want to see that she and Peter are established, with someplace to live and positions with which to support themselves, before we abandon them entirely to their own devices. It will be expensive, paying a Servant and at the same time helping Peter and Sarah with some money here and there (indeed, we cannot afford to replace Peter as well), but it is the only way I can leave this City with a clear Conscience.

Diary of Hannah Gray

Boston, Massachusetts

Wednesday, May 29, 1793

I have been inspired to take up my pen because I have but today finished a thoroughly delightful novel—*Evelina, or the History of a Young Lady's Entrance into the World*, by the exceedingly clever Mrs. Burney—whose heroine, a beauty of about my own age, leaves her cloistered life in the English countryside and has a host of quite extraordinary adventures amidst London society. Not that I pretend to even a fraction of Mrs. Burney's talents, but one must start somewhere, mustn't one? Of course, I am sadly lacking in one quality that Mrs. Burney has in spades—imagination. I couldn't *possibly* invent such things as she does, not if a million years were stretched before me.

So, as powers of imagination and invention seem rather essential in a novelist, I have decided to become a diarist instead, and write the story of my own adventures. Alas! there is the other difficulty: in addition to being bereft of imagination, I am bereft of adventures! I have but a dreary, humdrum existence, surrounded by my drab little family in this drab little city. Nothing, but absolutely *nothing* ever happens in Boston! Oh, it used to, I suppose, and Mama and my Aunts and Uncles are always going on about how lucky we are to live in such a place, with such a distinguished history—the Boston Tea Party and the Boston Massacre and so on. But those things all happened twenty years since, before I was even *born*! And since then, everything has happened in Philadelphia, or in New York, leaving us isolated in the far Northern corner of the country—plagued by horrid, frozen winters, and tripping over somber and disapproving members of the Clergy at every turn.

Oh, to be anywhere but here! To be in Paris—in the midst of the most romantic and thrilling adventure this world has ever seen, fighting for freedom and equality, and casting off the dead weight of Monarchy! But, alas no, it seems I am condemned to live out my days in this drowsy place, dancing at balls with the same dull gentlemen I've known, and danced with, since I was a girl and they were boys—and half of them, in any event, being my cousins. Mama reminds me at least once a week that I am now nineteen (as if I could forget it), and of an age to think seriously of marriage, but the very *thought* of marrying any of the young men of my acquaintance nearly makes my stomach turn. Not because they are so disgusting in themselves (as *most* of them are not), but because I can see with such terrible clarity the remainder of my life: a house on Park Street, or perhaps State—in any case, close enough that Mama can stop in whenever she pleases, and tell me all that I am doing wrong; the same old balls and teas and dinner parties, with the same people I've danced with and taken tea and dinner with since I was a child; all this interrupted only by the arrival of a series of children, who will tie me to the house and wear me down and ruin my form; until, all too soon, I am not only *chided* by my mother, but indeed have *become* my mother! Oh, dear God, surely life should hold more for me than that.

And I must be on my guard: last Sunday after Church, Henry Dolbeare asked me to walk with him in the Common (*why* I agreed to do so I cannot recall, except that it was such a pleasant day for a walk, all the new buds popping), and he stammered and blushed so much I was quite *certain* that he was going to propose marriage—even though we're cousins, and have known one another since we were infants! Where he got the idea that I would be receptive to such a proposal I cannot tell. Well, I suppose I *have* flirted with him a bit, but no more so than with any of the other men of my acquaintance—and certainly I meant nothing by it. It was merely a way to wrest *some* amusement from this dreary life.

"Oh dear!" I cried, clutching at my stomach, just after he'd managed to announce he had something of importance to discuss with me. "Not today, Henry—for I have of a sudden such a pain in my bowels that I fear I must return home at once."

And when I did return home, Mama was full of such inquiries about Henry, and what had transpired during our walk, that I am convinced there has been some conspiring going on. I will not stand for this—for my future being determined by others, who think *they* know what's best for me. I shall do everything in my power to avoid being left alone with

Henry Dolbeare again. I don't know why Mama doesn't concentrate her efforts in the marital line on Sarah, for she's two years older and hasn't yet had a serious suitor—and with *her* looks, she'll certainly need Mama's assistance more than I do. And why Mama should settle on Henry Dolbeare as a husband for me I cannot fathom; I believe his fortune is far from adequate for my requirements and those of my family. Mama is always reminding us how difficult it is for a widow to keep three daughters equipped with clothing decent enough to be seen in polite society!

But what am I to set down in this diary? Surely I cannot make much of an adventure out of Henry Dolbeare's awkward pursuit of me, and my attempts to elude him. If something doesn't *happen* to me soon, I shall run out of things to say!

Wednesday, June 5, 1793

I am only writing to say that I have *nothing* to write about. All is deadly dull! Saw Henry Dolbeare approaching me on Summer Street, near Trinity Church, but pretended I hadn't and ducked into Bishop's Alley.

From the *Columbian Centinel*, Boston, Massachusetts, June 8, 1793:

Yesterday the Circuit Court of the United States opened in this town: When the Hon. Judge WILSON delivered to the Grand Jury, a Charge, replete with the purest principles of our equal Government, and highly indicative of his legal reputation. After the Charge, the Rev. Dr. THATCHER addressed the throne of Grace, in prayer.

Sunday, June 9, 1793

I now have something extraordinary to write about—at least, it *may* be extraordinary, it's too soon to tell. We were in church this morning, and Dr. Thatcher was droning on, as is his custom. I confess I had allowed my attention to wander to the feather trim on Mrs. Cooke's new hat in front of me, which was of a charming bluish green color, when of a sudden I felt an elbow in my ribs. Quit that, Sarah, I hissed, or I'll give you as good back. No, she whispered with some urgency, her hand shielding her mouth, don't you see that old gentleman there on the other side of the aisle, the one with the piggy face and the spectacles? He's been staring at you this past quarter of an hour, his mouth hanging open for all the world to see.

I glanced in the direction she indicated, with a little shift of her head, and indeed there was a gentleman—a stranger—staring at me quite boldly, although I thought Sarah's description of him unjust. He had a round face and something of a double chin, and a short, upturned nose, but he did not put me in mind of a pig in the least. Or not much, anyway.

On and on Dr. Thatcher's sermon went, and now I could feel the gentleman's eyes on me, studying me it seemed, though I'd been entirely ignorant of them before Sarah pointed him out. I dared not raise my own eyes in his direction, lest I be thought immodest, but I did manage a quick glance every now and then. I don't know what it was, exactly, about the man that so unsettled me. Perhaps it was his age, or the intensity of his gaze. In any event, I began to feel quite flustered and faint, which is not characteristic of me in the least.

I thought Thatcher would never stop—it was a full two-hour sermon, I'll warrant, and not one of his best, I could tell even from what little mind I gave it. Then there were hymns to be got through, and a closing prayer—and at last, just as I expected that we were all to be released, Dr. Thatcher cleared his throat and began to speak yet again.

"We are deeply honored this morning," he intoned, "to have with us, in our midst, joining us in reverent worship and praise, an esteemed member of the highest court of our Nation, the Honorable Judge James Wilson."

And at this, the very gentleman who had been staring at me so intently arose—revealing that he was of quite an impressive height—and bowed graciously, first to Dr. Thatcher; and then, with a quick series of little bows, to various members of the congregation; and finally, with the deepest bow of all, directly to me! I fear I blushed a deep crimson, for I could feel my face grow hot. I smiled and nodded my head back at him, as seemed only polite.

"You see?" Sarah hissed. "I *told* you!"

Then, when we were saying our farewells to Dr. Thatcher just outside the church door (and trying to sound sincere in complimenting him on his sermon), who should come up beside us but this same gentleman, Judge Wilson, smiling expectantly.

"Ah, Judge Wilson—allow me to present Mrs. Gray," Dr. Thatcher said (for it was obvious that Judge Wilson was desirous of an introduction). "And her charming daughters, the Misses Sarah, Hannah, and Lucy Gray."

Another deep bow from Judge Wilson, which we returned with curtseys. Much of the congregation was waiting behind us, so we were obliged to move on, with Judge Wilson following ("Like some sort of large sheepdog," Sarah scoffed later, continuing her ridiculous animal comparisons).

We conversed for a few minutes—or rather Mama and Judge Wilson did: innocuous chit-chat about the weather, and Judge Wilson's circuit (which he is, it appears, in the midst of), and so on. It was obvious that the Judge was originally from Scotland, as he had retained quite strongly the accents of his youth (I predicted to myself, correctly, that Sarah would have no end of fun imitating his speech later on). It was also obvious that his primary interest was not in the weather, or his circuit; for he continued to stare at me, even in the midst of conversation, which made things a trifle awkward.

At length the skies, which had been of a looming gray all morning, let loose a few drops of rain. We began to bid Judge Wilson goodbye, so as to hurry home before we were drenched, but he interrupted us.

"Can I not, Madam, offer you and your amiable family a ride home in my coach?" he said to Mama, with another bow. "It would be a great honor for me, I assure you."

"How very kind of you, Sir, " Mama said. "But surely you cannot accommodate all four of us."

"Ah, dear lady, but indeed I can!" Judge Wilson replied.

Judge Wilson then led us around the corner onto Coopers Alley, where there stood the most resplendent coach I have ever seen—of a spotless creamy white, with a bluish gray trim, and pulled by four handsome chestnut steeds. On seeing Judge Wilson approaching, the driver leapt from his perch and opened the door, revealing benches ample enough for six, covered in a deep red velvet, and the ceiling and walls upholstered in red silk.

"Oh, my heavens," I could not help but cry. "How exquisite!"

Judge Wilson smiled down at me from his lofty height and bowed yet again. "Miss Gray, if it meets with your approval, I could wish for no higher compliment."

As soon as his back was turned to us for a moment, I saw Sarah roll her eyes at Lucy. I glared at them and shook my head.

Ah! it was bliss itself to be riding the streets in that elegant vehicle, and seeing the eyes of the less fortunate, rain-dampened pedestrians (including poor Henry Dolbeare) follow us with envy; I almost imagined myself to be Evelina—for there is a most memorable scene in the novel, in which Lord Orville graciously allows Evelina and her exceedingly embarrassing relatives the use of his coach when they are all stranded at Kensington Gardens during a sudden downpour.

Once we reached the house, it seemed only proper to invite Judge Wilson inside to take dinner with us—and indeed, I confess I was becoming more and more intrigued with the gentleman. Certainly it was highly flattering to find such an eminent personage so intrigued with *me*, and on the basis of so scant an acquaintance!

I was, I confess, a little surprised that a man of such evident wealth and taste was not better acquainted with the niceties of table manners—he began eating as soon as he was served, for example, not waiting for Patience to set plates before the rest of us (and she, poor girl, scurrying madly to get the rest of us served as fast as possible, so as to lessen the awkwardness). But what are such rules of etiquette but mere conventions of society? Surely what is more important is what a man *does* with his life, what he accomplishes, the legacy he leaves behind. When history is written, will it be recorded that such-and-such a great man did not wait for all to be served before he began his dinner?

And a great man this Judge Wilson most assuredly is! I had not realized what all his accomplishments were, although his name was vaguely familiar to me—but Mama seems well acquainted with his reputation. She told us later that Mr. Wilson, even before he was made a Judge, was one of the *most* important and distinguished figures in the founding of our Republic: a signer of the Declaration of Independence, a representative to the Confederation Congress—and then, as a representative to the Convention, one of the prime authors of our Constitution!

Nor are these his only accomplishments: he has given a series of lectures on the law at the College of Philadelphia, which he mentioned were attended by all the most eminent inhabitants of the city and members of the government—even including the President and Vice President themselves! And he intimated that should the present Chief Justice resign his seat (which is quite possible, Judge Wilson said—for Judge Jay sought election to the governorship of New York last year, and is likely to do so again), he himself would be next in line, being the next most senior judge on the court except Mr. Cushing, whose health is not good. The salary of a judge must be something greater than I had imagined, if it enables Judge Wilson to purchase such a fine coach, and such well-tailored clothes as he was wearing.

He lingered until near 4 o'clock, at which time he began to excuse himself, saying that he had some reading to do in order to prepare for court tomorrow. He had, throughout his visit, addressed most of his remarks to the family as a whole, and I was beginning to wonder if he had lost that interest in me which had burned so brightly earlier in the day. I had done my best to make what I hoped were intelligent and witty remarks, but I thought that perhaps my ignorance and lack of sophistication had revealed themselves despite my best efforts—perhaps he had decided that what he had believed to be a rose in full bloom was merely a bud, not yet ready to be picked. But at the door, just before he took his leave, he turned to me—to me directly, and to no one else—and said, with a bow, that as I had been so taken with his coach, he would be most honored if I would consent to go for a ride with him into the country, when his duties at the court were finished!

"That is," he said, turning to Mama, "if such a plan meets with the approval of the young lady's Mother."

"Oh please, Mama!" I cried, clapping my hands and entirely forgetting that I wanted to appear a fine lady, and not a raw girl. "May I go? For a short ride, at least?"

"Well…" Mama hesitated, but with a smile that I knew betokened indulgence. "I cannot see the harm in a *short* ride."

Directly he had left, Sarah and Lucy burst into horrible peals of laughter, imitating Judge Wilson's Scottish burr and the way he twitched his eyebrows and peered over his spectacles when he was talking.

"And all that bowing!" Sarah cried. "Must be his idea of a gentleman's manners—for it's clear that, as far as manners go, he's in serious need of instruction."

"You would think," Lucy joined in, following Sarah's lead, "that someone as old as that would have learned the rules of etiquette by now.

Why, he must be sixty, if he's a day! I wouldn't want some old man sighing and fawning over *me*."

"As if *anyone* would ever sigh over you!" I shot back. "All skin and bones, and no bosom whatsoever."

Lucy clapped her hand to her mouth, an expression of surprise and injury on her face—as though she hadn't just been baiting me beyond endurance. "Mama!" she cried. "Did you hear what Nannie just said to me?"

"I certainly did, and I don't want to hear any more—from any of you. Now go to your rooms, and stay there until it's time for supper."

Treating us like children! But, of course, that's what Sarah and Lucy were acting like—little children, who must make fun of what they cannot have themselves. For I am certain they are only jealous, as they always have been of my looks, and the way that gentlemen admire me. It isn't *my* fault my sisters are plain—and yet they persist in acting as though it is. Oh, I must get away from this family. If I do not, and soon, I shall surely explode!

From the *Federal Gazette*, Philadelphia, Pennsylvania:

Boston, Massachusetts, June 10, 1793

Friday last the Circuit Court of the United States opened in this town.

It is said that a Charge has been delivered "replete with the happiness of equal government." This idea comes with an ill grace from a man, who parades our streets with a coach and four horses, when it is known his exorbitant salary enables him to make this flashy parade*, and the money is taken from the pockets of the industrious part of the community. Query: Where is the "equality" when an officer of government is enabled by his excessive salary, to live in a style vastly superior to any member in the society that supports him? ...*

Wednesday, June 12, 1793

What a day this has been! Here it is, ten o'clock at night, and my mind is racing in such a way that I swear I shan't sleep tonight—or perhaps ever again! I feel myself so awake, so *alive*, that it is as though I have all my life slept till now.

This morning Judge Wilson sent his man round to inquire whether I would be at liberty to ride out with him this afternoon, as the court finished its business yesterday, and I replied that I would. I spent the remainder of the morning performing my toilette—though I have *nothing* decent to wear. By the time a fashion reaches us in Boston, it is no doubt already well out of date in Paris or London! I pleaded with Sarah to dress my hair, for no one does it as well as she, and after a show of reluctance (just to tease me, I believe), she at length consented, all the while complaining that she could not see what my fuss was about. I had decided against a fichu to cover my bosom (for really, it is one of my best features), but Mama when she saw me *insisted* that I wear one, threatening to keep me at home if I did not.

Judge Wilson drove up in his splendid carriage at the appointed hour of three o'clock, and we set off. I asked him where he would like to ride, and he replied that in truth he cared not, for he was sure that whatever beauty might pass by the coach window, it surely would not rival the beauty that now lay within it. I smiled modestly and thanked him for the compliment, then suggested that we travel over the bridge to visit Cambridge, and the University—adding, however, that whatever constellation of scholarship and wisdom we might find there, it surely could not rival that which (with a little nod of my head in his direction) lay within. At this Judge Wilson threw his head back with delighted laughter (a gesture that afforded me a good view of his teeth, some of which are in excellent condition).

I suppose we did tour Cambridge; truth to tell, neither the Judge nor I spent much of our time looking out the window—we might as well have ridden round and round the Common for all the trouble we took to view the sights. Judge Wilson told me much about his early life: how he was born into a respectable family of modest means, farmers in Scotland; how the great hope of his parents, who were exceedingly devout, was that he would enter the Church; how he knew that he was not suited to such a profession, that he burned to make his mark in some more worldly manner.

Fortunately (or, perhaps I should rather say, unfortunately) Judge Wilson's father died, causing the family's circumstances to be reduced (how I can sympathize with *that*!), and Judge Wilson was obliged to withdraw from the course of studies in divinity that he had undertaken at his parents' insistence. He became a tutor to a gentleman's family, but, he said, he soon realized that a man of his modest background could never ascend far in Scotland, no matter what his talents—or at least, not far enough to satisfy his own ambitions. The idea of America seized hold of him: a land so vast, so uncharted, that there would be no boundary to what a man of intelligence and energy might achieve there.

"Oh, and what you *have* achieved!" I said, clapping my hands together beneath my chin.

"I have achieved much, it is true. But I hope to achieve even more."

"Becoming Chief Justice?"

"Not *only* that."

I could not fathom his meaning; was he aiming at the Presidency, then?

Judge Wilson took my hand in his (the which liberty, I confess, sent a little thrill through me) and began to tell me with great earnestness of the various land schemes in which he is interested. I have heard Mama speak with some distaste of "speculators," as she calls them, but I am now convinced, after listening to Judge Wilson, that in fact such endeavors are clothed with a purpose that is entirely beneficial to the public—indeed, one might say noble. The object of these schemes, as Judge Wilson described it, is to people the vast wilderness of this country with courageous, industrious men, who will till the land, and such, and generally make the nation stronger and larger. He has settlements—or rather, he intends to have settlements, for it is a very involved business: first one must purchase warrants, for a relatively modest price; then one must hire a surveyor to draw up a map (and sometimes contend with Indians or illegal white settlers who believe the land to be theirs); and *then* one must quickly raise whatever cash is necessary to complete the purchase, which often requires convincing others to invest in the scheme—or failing that, borrowing money. Only after all that can one begin to clear the land, lay it out in lots, and advertise for settlers—Judge Wilson believes many will come, like him, from Europe, and has already sent emissaries there.

Who could quarrel with such an eminently useful endeavor? And yet, I told him, it seemed an endeavor that must absorb all his energies; I was surprised that he could find the time to do his judging. At this he smiled, and said that he has associates to attend to the details—he particularly mentioned a Mr. Wallis—allowing him to fulfill (as he put it) his "judicial obligations."

150

"But," he added, "much as I love the law, and the work of the Court, it does not hold for me the excitement—the fascination, perhaps I should say—that this pursuit of land does." He inhaled deeply, as though smelling some sweet perfume, then shook his head and closed his eyes for a moment. "It is, one might say, like some elaborate game of chess, played for very high stakes. One must constantly be anticipating the moves of one's opponents—one's debtors, one's creditors, one's rivals." He smiled at me with the fondness one might show towards a clever child. "But I'm sure all of this is quite remote from the concerns of a young lady—an exceedingly young lady—like yourself."

I smiled back at him but drew myself up straighter; he seemed to think my time was spent in rolling hoops or playing at battledores! "Perhaps not as remote as you imagine," I said.

I thought briefly of a ball I had been to some weeks before, when I had to endeavor to position myself near Thomas Adams, yet try to avoid Henry Dolbeare, and keep an eye on that coquette Rachel Carey—all the while appearing smiling and unconcerned with any of it. It had been something of a game, indeed; and I believe I derived from it much the same pleasure that Judge Wilson finds in his land schemes. (Of course, pleasure is not the only benefit; Judge Wilson gave me to understand that his coach, and other luxuries, were affordable to him not by virtue of his judicial salary—as some in the press have intimated—but from the honest profits from these investments that have already come his way.)

"I believe I quite understand the attraction, Judge Wilson," I told him.

"Ah, Miss Gray." Again he took my hand, this time going so far as to press it to his lips; my heart beat faster, and I felt my cheeks flush. "You have no idea how much it means to me that you are in sympathy with these plans of mine." He paused, looked out the window—we seemed to have left Cambridge, for the countryside looked unfamiliar to me—and then returned his gaze to me. "My wife, although an excellent woman in many ways, did not entirely approve of them. She thought I was—I believe the word she used was `overreaching.' "

With some alarm, I began to withdraw my hand. "Your wife?"

"Gone to her Maker, these seven years since—God rest her soul." He sighed (as did I, secretly—with relief). "She left me with six children, the youngest but an infant when she died. Indeed, she took sick at her confinement and never recovered."

Six children! This put a rather different light on things. At my request, Judge Wilson listed them: four boys, aged about seven, fourteen, sixteen, and eighteen (Judge Wilson was surprisingly vague on their exact ages); and two girls, ages ten and twenty-one. Good heavens, I thought—he has a daughter fully two years older than myself.

"It has not been easy since Mrs. Wilson died," Judge Wilson continued, "not for any of us. She was, as I said, an excellent woman. I have often thought I should remarry, but I have not found the right … that is … I …"

Here Judge Wilson colored violently, so that for a moment I feared he had taken ill; but then he once again grasped my hand and held it between both of his own, as in a position of prayer. "Miss Gray, I scarcely feel I have the right to address such words to you as I am about to, after so short an acquaintance, but I cannot resist the urgent importunings of my heart. And as my public duties will call me from here in but a few days, I have not the luxury of biding my time."

A sense of what was about to come from the Judge's lips began to creep over me, unsettling my stomach and constricting my throat. I had not expected this—not yet, not today. And there was no escape, as there had been with Henry Dolbeare; nor was I sure I entirely *wanted* to escape.

"From the moment I first caught a glimpse of you, last Sunday in church, I have been experiencing emotions to which I thought I was long since dead. Your beauty—the delicacy of your complexion, the curve of your neck, and those eyes—so dark, so inviting, so mysterious …" He swallowed and took a deep breath; drops of sweat had appeared on his brow. Indeed, I began to fear for *his* composure more than my own. "And on further acquaintance, my admiration for you has only deepened—such easy wit, such natural charm. In short, Miss Gray, you are exquisite, and you have captured my heart. Permit me to say that I now understand what Paris must have felt, on encountering his Helen."

Never had such a speech been addressed to me before! Other men—younger men—have paid me compliments, but their efforts were clumsiness itself compared to this.

"Of course, I am no Paris," the Judge went on. "I know that my own appearance is far from the ideal, and I am, as you have surely noticed, considerably older than yourself—fifty-one, to be precise."

Aha, I thought—*not* sixty, then, as Lucy said.

"But I flatter myself that I yet possess certain attractions, for the lady who can discern them. I hold a position of some importance in this Nation, and I am a man of, shall we say, not insubstantial means." He smiled and removed a hand from mine momentarily in order again to push his spectacles up his nose. "And I dare to hope that the strong affection—no, I shall say it plain, the *love*—that I have felt for you since first I saw you may be reciprocated, at least in some measure. Indeed, I dare to hope"—he swallowed again, and tightened his hold on my hand—"I dare to hope that you will consent, like Helen, to leave your Sparta behind for my Troy. In short, I ask you to be my wife."

There was a silence, during which I tried desperately to collect my thoughts—scattered as though by a tempest—in order to make some answer: something neither overly encouraging nor overly *dis*couraging. Before I could, the coach came to a halt, and the driver rapped on the roof. "Shall we turn back here, Sir?" he called. "It's getting on to supper time."

Judge Wilson stuck his head through the window. "Yes, fine, very well," he called back impatiently, before returning his attention to me.

"Sir," I said at last, "you do me a very great honor, for which I am most grateful. That a man of such exalted stature, and such noble accomplishments—and ambitions—should form so strong an attachment to me, and in so short a time, is exceedingly gratifying. But surely you understand that I cannot give you an answer, yea or nay, at once. I must have time, you know ... to consider."

"Of course, my dear Miss Gray, of course. I would not dream of pressing you for an answer immediately. But"—his ample eyebrows rose to form two sloping lines of supplication, giving him a most pathetic aspect—"I may dare to hope? You aren't merely being coy? For I would rather know the worst now than spend days and nights dreaming and hoping in vain."

Was I being coy, I asked myself? Indeed, if truth be told, the speech I had just delivered had come merely from my brain and not my heart—an organ whose workings I had not yet had time to plumb. But now, in a few short seconds I examined my feelings as best I could: Here was a man of substance, of intelligence and vision—not a callow Boston youth like Henry Dolbeare. Why, he had already done more in one lifetime than most could accomplish in three! And, out of all the women of his wide acquaintance, he wanted me—only me. This great man, to whom so many bowed and scraped, was brought nearly to his knees by *me*. Surely there was some bond, some connection between us that he had discerned. And, I confess, I did in a flash see myself on Judge Wilson's arm, at the President's house in Philadelphia, wearing a gown of the richest material and cut to the latest fashion, commanding the admiration of all in the room.

I leaned towards him, so that our faces were but inches apart. "You may indeed hope," I said slowly, gazing into his eyes. "I give you my assurance that you may hope."

"Miss Gray," the Judge breathed, "you have just made me the happiest of men."

"I have not yet given you my answer, mind you," I warned. There were still those children to think of—all those children!

Just then, the coach hit something in the road—a stone, I imagine—and suddenly the Judge and I were thrown into one another. Somehow (I know not if this was by accident) his hand brushed against my bosom; and next I knew his lips were pressing against mine, just for a moment, until I pushed him from me. I confess that a part of me wished that he would continue, but of course I could not allow such liberties—not yet.

"Forgive me, Miss Gray," the Judge said, now bright red. "I quite forgot myself. But I must tell you this: I sincerely doubt whether I can live without you!"

There was little to say after this exchange, and we spent the remainder of the drive largely in silence. When at last the coach arrived at my door, the Judge once more grasped my hand and asked if he might call on me tomorrow. Feeling the need to digest all that had transpired, I pleaded an engagement. But as the Judge said he must depart for Newport on Monday, I consented to his coming for tea on Friday afternoon.

After he had exchanged a few pleasantries with Mama and said his goodbyes, I sank into a chair in the parlor, my head in a whirl.

"So, Nannie?" Lucy said, kneeling at my feet and gazing up at me, looking for all the world like the sweet little sister she sometimes is. "What was it like?"

"Oh, Lucy," I replied, "you have no idea. It was like—why, it was like a novel!"

From Samuel Wallis to James Wilson (addressed to Newport, Rhode Island):

Philadelphia, Pennsylvania, June 14, 1793

... I wish much to see you & to say more to you than I choose to commit to paper... The 60,000 acres entered for you on the waters of Loyal Sock &c will be totally lost unless I can find some Other way of paying for them before I leave Town ... Great Numbers of Warrants are Issued to Other people who are gone Out to execute them, which most undoubtedly will interfere with ours...

... When you return to this place, please to let me hear from you by leaving a letter at the post Office ... Notwithstanding all that has happened a good deal may yet be done ...

Diary of Hannah Iredell

Philadelphia, Pennsylvania

Saturday, June 15, 1793

Mr. Iredell returned home this evening, as well as ever I knew him, thank the Lord, though greatly fatigued from his Journey, which—owing to a recent alteration in the Law, allowing for only one Supreme Court Judge to ride a Circuit rather than the two that had formerly been required—he undertook alone. The benefit of the law is that he will likely have only one Circuit to ride each year from now on—and, God willing, none this Fall, leaving him free to undertake our removal to Edenton.

Despite his fatigue, I felt it necessary to raise with Mr. Iredell the question of allowing Peter and Sarah their freedom now, before we leave the City—for I have found a young woman, by the name of Mary Dusenbury, who I believe will serve well enough to fill Sarah's position. Mr. Iredell seemed quite pleased that I had embarked on this Plan—he is not one to balk at the expense, certainly. I shall give Peter and Sarah the news tomorrow, and help them begin to look for suitable accommodation on Monday.

What weather we have had! Nothing but chill and rain in May, and now hot and dry as a Desert. The unpleasant stench of Summer is wafting through the streets already—with flies buzzing about the rotting fish heads and horse droppings in the alleys, and as well around a dead dog that lay right outside our door for several days before we could manage to hire someone to cart it away. Edenton has its smells and its heat, to be sure, but the crowds of people (and their refuse) in this place make what we suffer infinitely worse. Ah, but a few more months, I remind myself—but a few more months!

Diary of Hannah Gray

Boston, Massachusetts

Sunday, June 16, 1793

Judge Wilson has just taken his leave of us—he will depart for Rhode Island, to hold the Court there, tomorrow morning—but I have made him go without his answer! Poor man, he seemed quite distraught, as though he truly thought I might refuse him. I felt quite remorseful, for I am indeed already exceedingly fond of him, but it will not do to accept his proposal but one week after I first made his acquaintance—even though I am certain that I *shall* accept it, in time.

Of course the Judge made a formal request to Mama for my hand. It was quite amusing, really, to see how he stammered and reddened, just as though he were some lovesick youth; I may have blushed myself, in sympathy. Mama simply told the Judge that we were all highly flattered by his attentions to me, but that of course we would need some time to come to a decision.

Mama believes it would have been indecent to give Judge Wilson an answer so precipitately—though I cannot imagine her refusing so handsome a match, in the end. She raised all sorts of objections, but I believe I have been able to beat almost all of them off: To the objection that the difference in our ages was too great, I answered that Judge Wilson's age should give her *confidence* that he would take care of me wisely and well, with all the accumulated experience of his years. Then, as I knew she would, she began going on about all those children: "You simply have no idea, Nannie, what is required to take charge of a family, particularly one of that size ... Marriage is a difficult enough proposition, without taking on six children who have lost their mother ..." Indeed, the six children were all that made me hesitate, at first; but I soon realized that most of them are scarcely children at all! One is older than myself, and one nearly the same age. There are only two that can rightly be called *children*, I argued; and I added that Judge Wilson had told me the oldest, Polly, wants nothing more than to continue acting as mother to them all—so I shall have a nursemaid right in the family! (To myself I reflected that his having all these children may even be to my advantage; for perhaps he will want no more, and I shall be spared the discomfort and danger of having any of my own.)

"In any event, I'm certain that a gentleman of Judge Wilson's considerable fortune has an experienced and competent staff of servants to manage things," I pointed out as we finished supper last night; I then glanced at the doorway to make certain that Patience wasn't nearby, and added in a loud whisper, "More experienced and competent than ours, I'll warrant!"

At this Lucy and Sarah began to laugh, and I even saw Mama smile a bit—all of us thinking of how poor Patience is always spilling the soup and dropping the roast and tripping over the carpet, especially when we have company. Encouraged by their laughter, I went on.

"He *is* quite wealthy, you know. He owns a great deal of land in the West, and intends to establish mills, and settlements, and things. And he is now engaged in constructing a house in Philadelphia that will surely be the equal of any in the elegance of its design and construction." I then repeated some details that Mr. Wilson had mentioned to me—including the eight bedchambers, all with Italian marble mantlepieces of a type that he's seen at the house of that Mr. Bingham who is said to be so wealthy; and the pale blue flowered silk wallpaper for the dining room, which he says is identical to what is in the house of the Mayor of Philadelphia.

I could see Mama turning all this over in her mind, and I decided to keep my peace for a moment. Certainly she did not need to be reminded how exceedingly advantageous it would be to have a wealthy son-in-law.

"He does seem possessed of something of a fortune," she said at last, but cautiously. "But some of these speculators, you know, appear to be more than they are. I'm sure you'll agree, my dear, that some inquiries are necessary."

"What?" I cried, gripping the edge of the table in my outrage. "Are you insinuating, Mama, that Judge Wilson has misrepresented himself to me? How *can* you be so suspicious? He is a judge—on the highest court, no less!—charged with upholding the law, and I cannot *imagine*"—

"Now, Nannie, that is quite enough," Mama replied in a voice that put an end to discussion. "I am simply saying that we must be careful—one cannot be *too* careful with a decision of this magnitude."

So that is where the matter stands now: Mama is attempting to "make inquiries," discreetly, I hope—while my poor swain dangles on the thread of uncertainty. (And he reminded me when we parted, in the most somber and portentous tones, that he "could not live" without me!) I've told no one outside the family (though I could not restrain myself from writing to my old friend Lucy Breck, who now lives in Philadelphia, that I might soon be her neighbor again), but I imagine—what with Mama's "inquiries," and the Judge and I having walked out together on the Common several times—that the news of Mr. Wilson's proposal has traveled about town. I suppose I am quite the topic of conversation in certain parlors! And envy too, I shouldn't wonder.

From James Wilson to Hannah Gray

Newport, Rhode Island, June 20, 1793

My dear Hannah,

By this tender though familiar Appellation, permit me to begin ... I mentioned that, at the Conclusion of the Court here, I would either see you in Boston, or write to you, if I could not have the Pleasure of seeing you. To this last Expedient I now see, as I then apprehended, that, in all Probability, I must be confined.

But why should I delay Writing till the <u>Conclusion</u> of the Court? Why should not my Pen sooner take up a Theme so constantly present to my Thoughts? When I find it so difficult to delay Writing, you may easily judge how much I long for an Answer. <u>Do</u> let that Answer be speedy and favorable: Let it authorize me to think and call you mine. Remember what I told you on this Subject.

Your Letter, sent by the next Post, will reach me before I leave this Place. With Emotions of the purest and warmest Attachment, I am, my dear Hannah, your affectionate,

James Wilson

From John Quincy Adams to Thomas Boylston Adams:

Boston, Massachusetts, June 23, 1793

... The most extraordinary intelligence which I have to convey is that the wise and learned Judge & Professor Wilson has fallen most lamentably in love with a young Lady in this town, under twenty, by the name of Gray. He came, he saw, and was overcome. The gentle Caledon was smitten at meeting with a first sight love—unable to contain his amorous pain, he breathed his sighs about the Streets; and even when seated on the bench of Justice, he seemed as if teeming with some woeful ballad to his mistress eye brow. He obtained an introduction to the Lady, and at the second interview proposed his lovely person and his agreeable family to her acceptance; a circumstance very favorable to the success of his pretensions, is that he came in a very handsome chariot and four.

In short his attractions were so powerful, that the Lady actually has the subject under consideration, and unless the Judge should prove as fickle as he is amorous and repent his precipitate impetuosity so far as to withdraw his proposal, you will no doubt soon behold in the persons of those well assorted lovers a new edition of January and May.

Methinks I see you stare at the perusal of this intelligence, and conclude that I am attempting to amuse you ...; no such thing, it is the plain and simple truth that I tell—and if you are in the habit of seeing the Miss Brecks as frequently as your wishes must direct you to see them, you may inform them, that their friend and mine, <u>Miss Hannah Gray</u>, has made so profound an impression upon the Heart of judge Wilson, and received in return an impression so profound upon her own, that in all probability they will soon see her at Philadelphia, the happy consort of the happy judge.

Cupid himself must laugh at his own absurdity, in producing such an Union; but he must sigh to reflect that without the soft persuasion of a deity who has supplanted him in the breast of modern beauty, he could not have succeeded to render the man ridiculous & the woman contemptible ...

From Henry Jackson (Boston Merchant) to Henry Knox (U. S. Secretary of War):

Boston, Massachusetts, June 23, 1793

... <u>Judge Wilson</u> is violently in love with Miss Gray ... She is about 18 or 19—and he it's said is 55. He saw her for the first time at Doctor Thatcher's meeting, and Cupid with his dart <u>instantly</u> struck him in the heart. He has accordingly address[ed] her on the subject of Love—which she has under consideration until his return from the Circuit Court. It is conjectured from all circumstances that this Passion will not prove <u>tragical</u>, and that the wound will be healed by the Lady's giving him her fair hand. It will be highly flattering to see one of our Boston Girls in her <u>Coach & four</u> rolling the streets of Philadelphia ...

Monday, June 24, 1793

Mama has *at last* given her consent to my marrying Judge Wilson—or James, as I suppose I should begin to call him, as he is to be my husband (it feels quite odd to be addressing someone of his age and eminence by his Christian name, but I shall have to get used to it). It will come as a great relief to him, I am sure, knowing that he will not need to terminate his existence on my account!

I don't know exactly what were the fruits of Mama's inquiries into Judge Wilson's character, but I suppose her fretting about his finances was put to rest. To be sure, there have been some men ruined by their speculations, but are there not at least as many who have been elevated by them to the highest ranks of wealth? Whose names will live in glory for generations to come, attached to new streets, cities, counties—even, perhaps, new states? And to think that my name—my name that is to be, that of *Wilson*—may well be one of those, shining through History!

But I have no time now for idle daydreams. Judge Wilson—*James*—did not mention a date for the wedding (as indeed would have been improper, the question of my marrying him not having been resolved), but judging from his impatience in this whole endeavor, I imagine he will want to get it done as soon as possible. Certainly not before the fall, though—I must assemble my trousseau, and as we haven't enough money to hire a seamstress to do all of it, we will all need to set our needles and thread flying. Mama so often complains that I neglect my needlework in order to waste my time (as she terms it) reading novels; but let her see what I can do with a needle when I have some reason to impel me!

Of course, it *is* a bit sad to think that I shall be leaving Mama and Sarah and Lucy—much as I have longed to get away from them. But as I told them, when they all began to look as though they might burst into tears, they must come and visit me in my grand new house in Philadelphia, where I shall introduce them to the President and all his Cabinet, and all the Judges of the Supreme Court!

From Hannah Iredell to Nelly Tredwell:

Philadelphia, Pennsylvania, July 22, 1793

I had the pleasure of hearing today from Capt. Carpenter that you, my dear Nelly, & all my friends were well…

We are all well, I thank God, tho' Helen is some times a good deal unwell. I was apprehensive she would be this hot season, when the Children here are generally sick. She has got within a short time 4 teeth and one eye tooth. Annie was seized with a violent Cholic—we were about six miles from town, on our way to see the old Lady, when she grew so ill we were obliged to return. Her disorder was happily soon over and in the evening she was quite well and has continued so …

One half of the blots on this letter are owing to Mr. Iredell's snuffing the candle! …

From James Wilson to Samuel Wallis:

Philadelphia, August 7, 1793

… This Letter you will receive by Mr. Parker, to whom I have advanced six hundred Pounds … To answer your future Demands for Surveying, etc. (which I hope will be as moderate as possible) Money will be lodged in the Hands of Thomas FitzSimons, Esquire. On him you will draw as your Occasions necessarily require …

From James Iredell to Nelly Tredwell:

Philadelphia, August 12, 1793

... I assure you I sincerely rejoice in the probable prospect which I now have of going with my family to Carolina in October or November next; about the middle of the former month is the time that I now fix upon, and hope then to accomplish it. The sacrifice I must personally make in being so much more absent from my family, I flatter myself, will be compensated by the greater satisfaction they will enjoy, and the money I may be enabled to save by it. With regard to the difference of society, considering how many dear friends I have in Carolina, I prefer it infinitely ...

Diary of Hannah Gray

Boston, Massachusetts

Monday, August 19, 1793

I have had a letter today—at last!—from Judge Wilson, I mean to say James, and can now state with confidence that I am to be married in just a month's time. He has managed things so that he is to ride only a portion of the Eastern Circuit this fall, which will bring him to this part of the country in any event. I must now arrange for Dr. Thatcher to perform the ceremony—as he was the serendipitous agent of our meeting on that rainy day in June, so shall he be the agent of our holy and permanent union on what will, regardless of the weather, most assuredly be a glorious day in September. Or some such language—I fear my own feeble attempts to paraphrase James' letter do little justice to his eloquence.

I only wish I had been the recipient of more of that eloquence! I do not mean to complain, but for so ardent a suitor, my intended has been oddly silent these last few weeks. Ah well, he is a highly important personage, and surely he has been occupied with his business affairs and his judging. And I imagine, as well, that he has been engaged in completing construction of the house and in making preparations for my arrival—as I, to be sure, have been engaged in my own preparations.

Mama has allowed me to order the most exquisite wedding gown, of a lustrous dove gray silk; the seamstress assured me that the color is now extremely popular in New York and Philadelphia, so that it will do me service for the parties and balls and things I shall no doubt be attending after my marriage. And since the seamstress was here anyway, I begged Mama for two other gowns as well—she had brought some charming printed cottons to show me. Mama has been clucking about us going into debt for this wedding, and so on, but even if we are, I am sure Judge Wilson will be only too happy to assist in making up the debt, once we are married; these piddling expenses are no doubt scarcely noticeable for a man of his means.

Ah, I can scarcely sleep at night for the excitement! I feel as though my real life, my true life, is on the very verge of coming into being—as though wondrous things await me just round some bend up ahead in the road, and I am straining, craning my neck to see them. No doubt I shall have many highly interesting observations to commit to this Diary after my marriage. Strange that *Evelina*, like nearly all of the other novels that I have read, comes to an end just as the heroine embarks on marriage. *All is over, my dearest Sir,* Evelina writes to her guardian on the very last page of the book, *and the fate of your Evelina is decided! This morning, with fearful joy, and trembling gratitude, she united herself for ever with the object of her dearest, her eternal affection!*

Well, perhaps for Evelina all was over at that juncture, but when Hannah Gray is united with the object of *her* eternal affection, surely all will have just begun!

Diary of Hannah Iredell

Philadelphia, Pennsylvania

Wednesday, August 21, 1793

Mary has just come from the Market in a great state of alarm, poor girl. It seems the talk there is that a number of deaths in the vicinity of Water Street, down by the docks, have been attributed to the Yellow Fever. No less an authority than Dr. Rush has pronounced it so, she said, and another Doctor has ascribed the cause to a quantity of coffee left rotting on Ball's Wharf. Some say the cause is merely the usual filth of the city; others point to the Refugees recently come from the Slave rebellion in Santo Domingo, many of whom arrived here sick as dogs and spoke of a horrible fever in their native land. And still others say it isn't the Yellow Fever at all, but merely the usual Autumnal fever, and that Dr. Rush is being irresponsible in spreading unwarranted Panic.

Panic indeed there is; I could see it in Mary's face and aspect, the way she knotted and unknotted repeatedly the strings of her bonnet as she stood in the kitchen, the basket dangling from the crook of her arm. I tried to calm her, telling her that I had lived through many a sickly Summer in Edenton, and this could be no worse.

"Oh, I don't know, ma'am," she said, her eyes blinking fast. "My Mother remembers the last time the City was struck by the Yellow Fever, some thirty years ago, and the stories she tells are something terrible: people being seized all of a sudden, their skin and the whites of their eyes turning yellow, and then they begin to vomit blood and a foul-smelling black bile. Her own Sister was struck down—only six years old she was. And hundreds of others, she says."

166

The Girl was now quite distraught, so that I felt it necessary to take the basket from her and tell her she must sit down and have some cold Cider (wild cherry tonic would have had a more soothing effect, I warrant, but I had none to hand). Now then, I told her firmly, for all we know it is merely the usual Seasonal disorder; it was too soon to draw the conclusion that Yellow Fever had struck, as the Doctors themselves seemed to disagree on the question.

"But there are some as are taking no chances." She waved a mosquito from where it was buzzing about her cap (they have been most annoyingly plentiful this Summer). "Alice Schmidt, who works for the Brecks, she told me three of the families that live near to them have already left for the countryside, and the Brecks themselves are going tomorrow to Bristol. And Alice overheard a Gentleman telling Mr. Breck that if he didn't leave soon, the roads would be clogged and all the best accommodation taken!"

For a few moments I felt myself drawn into her agitation; my heart began beating faster, my hands trembling. What to do, I thought? Run upstairs to where Mr. Iredell worked at his desk, and plead with him to flee the City at once? Gather the Children's clothes and ours into a trunk? Procure a Carriage? But then my head cleared a bit, for I could see that Second Street—aside from the stifling Heat that refuses to leave us, and the buzzing mosquitoes and flies—was much the same as usual: draymen hauling their carts laden with produce to and from the High Street, Gentleman hurrying to their business appointments, a cluster of Ladies at the corner flapping their fans and chattering gaily. None of these people appeared the least bit concerned about this supposed Yellow Fever; certainly no one seemed to be making any plans to evacuate the City. I scolded myself: I should know better than to rely on idle gossip from the Market.

As for gossip, Mr. Iredell has related to me a piece of intelligence that is surely making the rounds of Philadelphia parlors: it seems that Mr. Wilson found himself a Bride on his last Circuit in Boston—a girl of nineteen, no less! And to house her, he is (when not preoccupied with his Land schemes and business dealings) overseeing the construction of a veritable Palace at 8th and Market Streets, quite close to the President's house—so lavish and ostentatious in its design and scale that were it mine, I should be ashamed to own it.

There is to me something indecent about a match between a young Lady and a Gentleman old enough to be her Father—almost, even, her

Grandfather. Why should Youth—so shallow, so unripe—prove so irresistibly appealing to Men? As to what the Lady finds appealing, I cannot think it is Mr. Wilson's person. And while he is reputed to have a first-rate mind, I doubt that a Girl of nineteen, unless she is highly unusual, is fully capable of appreciating it. God forgive me if I suspect some more crass motive on her part, one to which I earnestly hope no Daughter of mine would ever succumb.

Sunday, August 25, 1793

It is decided: we must flee, and that as soon as possible. Mary's alarm, it seems, was quite justified, for the Situation in this City grows worse by the hour.

Yesterday we heard of a death just a few doors down the Street from us—a charming little girl about a year older than Annie and Fanny. Whether it was the result of Yellow Fever, no one can say for sure, but it seems more than likely. Major Butler came by as well yesterday, to tell us he and his Daughters are repairing to Jenkinstown, where they have been able to secure lodging; he said that he would write to us when settled, to inform us what sort of accommodation might still be available, should we decide to leave. At the time, we were still undecided; now I doubt we shall be here to receive Major Butler's Letter, when it arrives.

For this morning at Church—to which we ventured through a violent rain Storm—we chanced to meet Dr. Duffield. The poor Man was besieged by parishioners demanding to know how they should conduct themselves in the face of this pestilence. Most of these inquiries he turned aside, as he was on his way to a meeting of the College of Physicians to address this very question; but when he saw Mr. Iredell and myself, he took us aside for a moment.

"You would certainly do yourselves no harm by leaving, if you have somewhere to go," Dr. Duffield said gravely. "And you may well do yourselves and your Family a great deal of harm by staying." He looked quickly behind him, where several Ladies and Gentlemen appeared to lie in wait for him, their faces drawn in Anxiety. "But you may wait, at least, for the recommendations of the College—where I must hurry now, lest I be late for the meeting. In the meantime, gather yourself some fresh earth and strew it in a Chamber to a depth of two inches."

"Fresh earth?" I said in surprise.

"Yes, Mrs. Iredell—it is a sure preventative against Fever. Change the earth twice daily, if it be convenient. Frequent warm baths as well, followed by the Asiatic remedy of Myrrh and black pepper—five grains of each, every three hours. And now, my friends, if you will excuse me …" And with that he patted his hat snugly onto his head and hurried off into the Storm, in the direction of the State House Yard, leaving those others who had been awaiting his counsel looking after him in disappointment.

I could not bring myself to import fresh earth into the house, as Dr. Duffield counseled; for the only earth available was pure mud, which Mary and I daily strive to keep *out* of the house. I did take the precaution of soaking some rags in Vinegar, and wrapping Camphor in linen, so that when it is necessary for us to go out, we may carry a rag to put to our noses, and wear camphor about our necks. Yet all the nostrums in which I place so much Faith may be no more than pebbles hurled at a Behemoth. Flight is, most likely, the only sure preventative; but where we shall fly to I cannot say.

I know where my heart would lead me—to Edenton, without delay. But there is no time, as Mr. Iredell has admonished me—no time to wait for a ship and a favorable wind, no time to pack up all our belongings. Besides which, he says, we would most likely be no safer in Edenton than we are here, at this time of year. He has determined that we must repair to some location as close by as possible, yet free of contagion, and wait until it is safe to return to the City. God grant that it be soon!

From Dunlap's American Daily Advertiser (Philadelphia):

Tuesday, August 27, 1793

… The College of Physicians having taken into consideration the malignant and contagious fever, which now prevails in this city, have agreed to recommend to their fellow-citizens, the following means of preventing its progress.

… That all unnecessary intercourse should be avoided with such persons as are infected by it…

To place a mark upon the door or window of such houses as have any infected persons in them…

To place the persons infected in the center of large and airy rooms ... and to pay the strictest regard to cleanliness ...

To put a stop to the tolling of the bells...

To bury such persons as die of this fever in carriages, and in as private a manner as possible...

To keep the streets and wharfs of the city as clean as possible...

To avoid all fatigue of body and mind...

To avoid standing or sitting in the sun, also in a current of air, or in the evening air...

The College conceives FIRES to be very ineffectual, if not dangerous means, of checking the progress of this fever. They have reason to place more dependence upon the burning of GUN-POWDER. The benefits of VINEGAR and CAMPHOR are confined chiefly to infected rooms ...

Diary of Hannah Gray

Boston, Massachusetts

Saturday, August 31, 1793

The seamstress was here today, and I am like to scream and tear at my hair—for she has made the hem of my wedding gown too short, and the sleeves of it too loose, and in other respects it is not at all as she described it to me! I was too distressed to speak to her properly, so Mama, who was nearly as horrified as I was, explained to her that she must take it home and fix it at once, that there was no time to lose, and that she should not see a penny of payment until it was done to our satisfaction. Mama told me I must go to my chamber and rest until I had calmed myself—but *rest* I simply cannot, so disordered are my feelings and my thoughts. Mama says there is no need to worry, that surely all will be ready before Judge Wilson arrives, but the truth is we don't know exactly when he will be here, and it won't do to keep him waiting because my wedding gown is still at the seamstress! Oh, surely the seamstresses in Philadelphia are better acquainted with their trade.

There was a report that Mama showed me in the newspaper of a malignant fever in Philadelphia; but I suppose it isn't serious, or James would have written to me concerning it. The truth is, I have heard nothing from him these past two weeks, except for a brief, but very affectionate, note in which he expressed his keen impatience to see me again in the most urgent terms. I, too, am impatient—but perhaps, at this precise moment, more impatient to see the seamstress, returning with a gown that I can indeed *wear*.

From Dunlap's American Daily Advertiser (Philadelphia):

Monday, September 2, 1793

It has been remarked, that the black people *in our city have in no one instance been infected with the malignant fever which now prevails ... The only design of this remark is to suggest to our citizens the safety and propriety of employing black people to nurse and attend persons infected by this fever; also, to hint to the black people, that a noble opportunity is now put into their hands, of manifesting their gratitude to the inhabitants of that city which first planned their emancipation from slavery, and who have since afforded them so much protection and support, as to place them, in point of civil and religious privileges, upon a footing with themselves ...*

Diary of Hannah Iredell

Bethlehem, Pennsylvania

Wednesday, September 4, 1793

It is now a week since we left Philadelphia, and such a week as I would hope never to repeat. We have at last found refuge in this town of Bethlehem—and the significance of the name is not lost on us.

We waited in the City several days in hopes of receiving Major Butler's promised letter; but when, on Tuesday, it was said that two people were taken sick in a house just at the back of ours, Mr. Iredell resolved to wait no longer. We would go to the Mullers' farm, and stay with Mother; it was not a sanguine prospect, but I had no other to suggest.

Somehow—and I imagine at more expense than we could rightly afford—Mr. Iredell managed to procure a Driver who had at his disposal two scrawny horses and a small cart, into which we began to load as many of our things as we could manage. We asked Mary if she would come with us, for we have all become quite fond of her, and I was reluctant to abandon her to an uncertain Fate. She was quite torn, poor girl; in the end, she said she would stay behind in the house and keep watch over all our belongings, as all her Family was in the City, but perhaps she would come to us later on, when we were settled.

"And what of Peter and Sarah?" I said suddenly to Mr. Iredell, amidst the frenzy of packing up clothes and other Necessities. We had not seen them since the Fever began, but my thoughts had often turned to them with some Concern, as they lived near to Water Street, where the number of those afflicted was highest.

Mr. Iredell said there wasn't much time, but that he would go and find them and offer them places in the cart; it would be crowded, but we would manage. I offered to go myself, but Mr. Iredell insisted that I mustn't expose myself to such Contagion; so I equipped him with two freshly filled camphor bags and a rag dripping in Vinegar, and bid him be as careful as he could. Within fifteen minutes, he had returned—alone. He had found Peter at home, he said, but could not persuade him to leave the City.

"What!" I cried. "Is he mad? Where was Sarah, then?"

"She has found work"—Mr. Iredell paused for a moment, then shook his head—"tending the sick."

"The sick! You mean those with the Fever? She's deliberately putting herself in the way of Contagion?"

Mr. Iredell nodded and shrugged. "Someone must do it, you know—it's a mission of mercy, really, to tend to those poor Souls. And Peter and Sarah seem to believe that because they are Black they are immune to this Disease, as some have been lately maintaining."

"But that's nonsense! Those Santo Domingans were all sick, Black as well as White. Anyone with eyes in his head could see that."

I turned away from him and kept to myself the thought that if I had been the one to go, I could have persuaded Peter to leave the City—or found Sarah, and persuaded her. The thought of her—of both of them—left behind helpless and surrounded by Contagion distressed me to the point of Tears, and I wished that for their own Good at least, they were still ours to command. But there was no time now, either for command or persuasion: the Hour that we had allotted for packing and loading had passed, and the Driver had returned, looking impatient to be going. We could only take the Children from Mary and set them atop the bundles in the cart, bid her farewell, and assure her that we would write to her when we were settled.

The roads leading from the City were clogged with carriages, chaises, carts like ours—even people on foot, their backs bent under the weight of their belongings. As a result, our progress was slow, and it was near nightfall when we at last spied the Mullers' small white house, which gleamed against the darkening sky like a beacon of Hope and Comfort. True, I had not wanted to come here; but now the thought of the cozy hearth, with Mrs. Muller's cakes and tarts spread before it, was as alluring as the prospect of a freshwater well to a traveler in the desert. Our bones were rattled from the cart, and our clothes and skin and hair covered with dust from the road; the Children were complaining of hunger, and we had nearly exhausted our supply of bread and cheese.

But instead of the Welcome we had expected, we were greeted at the door by a stony and distinctly inhospitable stare from Mr. Muller.

"You must not come in," he said, in his Germanic accents. "The Fever, in the City—we do not want that here. So, you must go."

I gasped, and Mr. Iredell reddened; both of us were too stunned to speak for several moments, and Mr. Muller took advantage of our Silence by commencing to close the door.

"Now just one moment, Sir," said Mr. Iredell, pushing the door back open. "I understand your concern, but none of my Family is ill with Fever, and I assure you we pose no threat to you. Will you not allow us to take refuge here, with my Mother, until the Danger is passed—for which hospitality, of course, we are prepared to compensate you? Please, Sir—for the sake of our Children!"

How much of this Speech Mr. Muller understood was not clear, but it was clear enough that he would not allow us over his threshold—not even to pay Mother a brief visit. Nor would he allow Mother to emerge, even for a few minutes, to speak with us outside.

"I am sorry for it," he kept repeating, "but you must go."

"Very well, then," I now heard Mr. Iredell saying coldly to Mr. Muller. "Please to tell my Mother that we shall call on her as soon as … as soon as it is possible."

We then had the Driver, who had been watching and listening with an expression of some Concern, turn the cart back towards the road. But when we reached it Mr. Iredell bade him stop for a moment, so that we could resolve on a direction to go in. The sky was nearly dark, although only one or two stars had yet come up.

"Where will we go now?" Annie asked, breaking the sober silence. Her eyes were wide with Anxiety, and she looked close to tears.

The Children all gazed expectantly at me and Mr. Iredell—even little Helen, who sat on my lap. Mr. Iredell and I could only look at one another in confusion. After a moment or two, the Driver—a rough and weather-beaten but not unfriendly man—told us of a Tavern, some two miles further on, where Stages were known to stop, and where we might in any event find Lodging for the night. It was but a rough place, we found when we arrived there, and full to the gills with travelers from the City; but a Stage was to leave the next morning for Bethlehem, a town that was said to be well equipped with Inns.

We spent the night uncomfortably in the Tavern's Dining room, sleeping on our bundles on the floor as best we could, amidst the chatter of some foul-mouthed Fellows who were drinking and playing at cards; but at least we had a roof over our heads, and food in our Stomachs. Three nights we spent in that manner, along with others in the same predicament; for the Stages the next two mornings were full; when at last we boarded a Stage, it was of course exceedingly cramped.

But, thank the Lord, we have been so fortunate as to find a room in Bethlehem (though a small and rather musty one), and the inhabitants here, members of a Sect that is called Moravian, have been most kind and welcoming; they don't appear at all apprehensive about whether we have brought contagion with us. But oh, how I wish we were in Edenton instead! If only I had urged an earlier departure on Mr. Iredell, I persist in chiding myself, perhaps we might all be there now, with Sam and Nelly and Tom and all our old friends—settled in our old house, and free of these terrible anxieties.

From Dr. Benjamin Duffield to James Iredell:

Philadelphia, September 5, 1793

... I have snatched a moment to request that you will not think of returning here. It is really hazardous, although the alarm has been too much spread by timidity, ignorance, or avarice. But at our end of the city, the disease is likely to continue, and increase, from the Naval Hospital being crowded with 200 diseased Irish, who, before a guard was planted to prevent their crossing the Schuylkill, were endeavoring to slide into the city through its lower avenues, in spite of all the vigilance of the Mayor and Corporation. I have yet lost but two patients by actual disease; but if a tooth aches, such is the general trepidation, that "it is this Fever," certainly...

From Major Pierce Butler to James Iredell:

*One mile from Jenkinstown, in the Old York Road,
September 9, 1793*

... I have this moment heard that the fever becomes serious. I am uneasy for you, Mrs. Iredell, and the children. If you incline, which I

think you must, to leave town, I think I can get you accommodated near us. Suppose, my friend, you ride up and see the place yourself; and if you like it, you shall take down my caravan for Mrs. Iredell. The solicitation for lodgings in this neighborhood exceeds credibility. I cannot keep the preference longer than tomorrow ...

From Mary Dusenbury to Hannah Iredell:

Philadelphia, September 18, 1793

... The fever is all around us, and one calamity seldom comes alone; there is a set of villains that feel not for the distressed citizens, but take this opportunity of plundering the houses of those that are absent... Business of every kind is stopped, and provisions double price. I have had the furniture in the tea-room packed, but Mr. Eldridge will not take it for fear of carrying the fever with it...

I have tried every means to get to you, but can't. Give my thanks to Mr. Iredell for his kind letter...

Diary of Hannah Gray Wilson

Boston, Massachusetts

Friday, September 20, 1793

It is done, the die is cast: no longer do I write this Diary as Hannah Gray, who passed her idle maiden days in sporting with the callow local youths; for I now claim the name of Hannah Wilson—or better still, Mrs. James Wilson. And who can tell what this Mrs. James Wilson may prove to be? A new and intriguing face, about whom all in Philadelphia are bedeviled with curiosity? And within a few months, perhaps, a gracious and renowned hostess, who will rival even this Mrs. Bingham that my new husband has praised so highly? Shall she hold salons, and serve elegant teas and dinners while effortlessly dispensing remarks of breathtaking wit? Shall she be the devoted support and comfort of her eminent husband, and the cherished mother of his darling children? Ah, she may be all this and more—but as I have been her for less than twenty-four hours, I am not at all sure that the expected transformation has yet taken place! Indeed, to tell the honest truth, I feel rather disappointingly the same as before.

We were married yesterday evening, by Dr. Thatcher, and although it was a small wedding (Mama, growing more and more anxious about the amount of money we were spending, having insisted on that measure of economy), I flatter myself that it was nevertheless a celebration of suitable elegance. I have almost forgiven the seamstress, for the gray silk gown, once altered, showed me off to great advantage—and had I been in any doubt on that score, the amazed and admiring look on my bridegroom's face when he saw me in it would have served to remove it.

I confess that as our guests (mostly aunts and uncles and cousins) began to depart, I found myself hoping they would linger; for, although James and I were to spend the night in my parents' house, we were to

178

spend it as husband and wife, both of us squeezed into my own little bedchamber. Mama had explained to me what would be expected of me, as part of my wifely duty, and it caused me no little alarm; I suddenly realized that, although of course I have the greatest esteem and affection for James, we have not spent a great deal of time in one another's company. The thought of disrobing and sharing a bed with the gentleman sent quite an agitation coursing through me.

But of course, he was now my husband, and it had to be done. After the last guest had gone—indeed, but a second or two afterwards—James bowed and offered me his arm.

"It has been a long and exciting day, and I believe it is time for us to retire for the evening, Hannah," he said rather formally. "Do you not agree?"

Sarah cleared her throat at this, but I shot her a black look lest she take it any further—into laughter, as I feared.

"Why yes, my dear," I replied, forcing a bravado into my voice. "I am indeed quite fatigued."

And so we proceeded up the stairs together, the rest of the family watching us go—Mama with a look of some apprehension on her face, which I attempted to ignore. And indeed, she need not have worried, for the whole thing was not nearly as disagreeable as I had feared. In fact, I confess that there were some aspects of the experience I would not mind repeating; and I feel quite sure, judging from James's behavior, that I will soon have my opportunity. For the look of blissful gratitude on his face, from the time he closed the door of the bedchamber until at last he fell quite soundly asleep, was wondrous to behold. To think that I, Hannah Gray—no, Hannah *Wilson*—have the power to inspire that look in such a man as he!

But I must leave off now and begin my packing, for we have no time to linger here in Boston. James must hold the Court in Hartford on Wednesday morning, and so we must leave at first light on Monday. It is just as well, as it turns out, that we are to be on the road for some weeks before reaching Philadelphia, for James tells us the fever there has grown worse. (Fortunately, his family has retired safely to Reading, where they have a number of relatives on their mother's side.) Our circuit will occupy us until the middle of November at least, by which time there will most certainly have been a good frost, and the City will be safe from disease again—so we shall be able to make our triumphal entrance without fear.

Diary of Hannah Iredell

Bethlehem, Pennsylvania

Thursday, October 3, 1793

Alas, we are still here; the news from Philadelphia is every day worse—so alarming and piteous, indeed, that I can scarcely bear to listen to it. And yet at the same time I seek it out, questioning Mr. Iredell closely as to any scraps of intelligence he may have heard from those who have recently arrived, or passed through on the Stage. I have become the instrument of my own torture, inflicting on myself what I most dread, and yet I cannot stop myself: I do not wish to know, and yet I must.

We have been told that over 1400 died during the month of September, and that often, these last two weeks, there have been as many as 70 burials a day. It is almost too much to comprehend, these numbers; and indeed, what shakes me more, down to my very bowels, are the bits of news we receive concerning individuals of our acquaintance. Most distressing of all, I have just had a Letter from Mary—which I soaked in vinegar and dried before the Fire before handling, as we have done with any newspapers from the City—to tell me that a Negro man came by the House and left word that Peter had taken ill. I know no more, and I am exceedingly anxious; I can only pray that his case is mild, and that Sarah does not become afflicted as well. So much for the supposed protection afforded by their Black skin!

Not that we are all so well: no Fever has visited this place, thank the Lord, but Annie, and now James, have got very bad coughs, and as we are all in such close quarters, I fear it won't be long before the others begin coughing as well. I have done what I can, dosing the Children with

Flax-seed tea and Castor oil, but alas, the coughing has only increased, keeping us all awake through the Night.

When their health has permitted it, I have tried to keep up the Children's lessons and take them on walks by the River—especially important, I believe, considering how terribly close our room is. The weather is cooling now, at last, giving me some Hope—for they say that it won't be safe to return to the City until there have been at least two hard frosts there. At the same time, though, the cooler weather makes me anxious, for the Clothes we brought with us will scarcely do in the cold. Shall I go to the expense of having new ones made here, when perfectly good clothing sits at our house in Philadelphia?

When I have not been too distracted by the painfulness of our situation, I have been able to take some stock of my surroundings here. It is a most curious place, this Bethlehem; indeed, to my mind it makes a most edifying contrast to Philadelphia. The inhabitants are all sober, virtuous, and God-fearing; their dress is modest and plain, and their favorite amusement is to make glorious music in praise of the Lord. Some of their customs—such as housing the "Single Sisters" and "Single Brothers," as they call their unmarried citizens, in two large buildings, one for each Sex—are indeed rather odd. But others (as explained to us by a Guide provided by their Church—for many visitors come here with the express purpose of inquiring into the Moravian manner of life) make eminent sense. They place a high value on education, and have established Schools for both Boys and Girls, to which many respectable people—non-Moravians among them—entrust their Children. All of the Inhabitants, even including their leaders, are expected to engage in productive work, and the Town is a veritable beehive of industry, with various Mills, a tannery, and a waterworks in near constant operation. And one finds here none of that wasteful mania for Luxury and show that afflicts even the Quaker population of Philadelphia; for all here appear to be on much the same humble but comfortable level, and content with it.

From Hannah Iredell to Nelly Tredwell:

Bethlehem, Pennsylvania, October 20, 1793

... We should have been on our way before now had we not been driven from the City by that fatal fever. We have waited now seven weeks

in hopes of returning & sending our things to Carolina. But there seems very little probability of returning with safety till the middle of Winter, & we must either go without our things or not go at all. We have not even clothes to serve us. Much as I wish to see my friends in Carolina, it is extremely painful to see them upon such terms. I should not be so uneasy about it if I thought we should get our things from Philadelphia before the River is froze, but even that I am very doubtful of.

All my Children have had very bad coughs ... James was very ill for some days, but thank God they all keep their spirits & appetites & are getting better ... We are unfortunate, but how much more so are those miserable families who have been obliged to stay in the city.

The confusion of this letter will show you that my brain is almost disordered. Mr. Iredell talks of setting off in a few days to Carolina, but it seems to me madness almost to go without clothes & to a home without furniture. Servants we may get, I suppose, of some kind. Peter [was] ill when we heard of them last; it was their own choice to stay.

Give my love to all my friends. I hope if we do go to have the Happiness of finding you well ...

Diary of Hannah Wilson

Exeter, New Hampshire

Monday, October 28, 1793

This town has little more to recommend it than did Hartford. The ladies of this place have done their best for me in the way of hospitality, I am sure, but I confess that their efforts have only made me yearn all the more to reach Philadelphia. Indeed, even Boston appears a sophisticated and worldly city when compared to these remote villages—so starved for excitement that the arrival of Judge Wilson and myself is all too evidently an event of great moment in the lives of the inhabitants. We have been feted and celebrated as though we were the President and his Lady themselves; never did I think I would tire of having teas and dinners held in my honor, but it is no easy task to maintain pleasant and graceful intercourse with people who appear to exhaust their meager stores of conversational material within the first two minutes of acquaintance. Indeed, much of the time I feel that, far from being *entertained*, I am the one who is doing the *entertaining*.

But Jamie (as I have taken to calling my husband—"James" seemed much too formal for a relationship as intimate as I intend ours to be) tells me that I must try to understand the situation, and have patience.

"Nannie," he intones (I have instructed him to call me by that familiar appellation, for the same reason that I have chosen to call him Jamie), "you and I are the very embodiment of the government—the government made flesh and blood, if you will—and it is imperative, for the survival of our Union, that we comport ourselves with the utmost propriety and graciousness, however tiresome you may find that task to be."

All very well for him to say! He spends the entire day in court, hearing arguments and deciding cases and whatnot, while I have little choice but to sip dreadful tea, and engage in even more dreadful conversation, with the local rustics. I have tried attending at court, at Jamie's suggestion, but found that to be even duller, if such a thing can be imagined. Fortunately I happened to bring with me three novels; I have read them all but am starting to read the first one again, as there does not seem to be a bookshop anywhere in the vicinity, and I must have *some* amusement. I now begin to understand why those who write novels bring them to a close at the heroine's marriage, for certainly the tedium of *my* married days would draw few readers.

My nights, at least, offer some pleasures: my husband has been quite affectionate and attentive, still brimming over with praises of my eyes, my lips, my slender neck, and so on. We have had some little disagreements and complaints about one another, as I suppose all newly married people will (and perhaps most especially those whose acquaintance before marriage was so brief); but whatever wounds and bruises we take to bed with us are there quickly healed by tender caresses, so that we awake unblemished and unscarred as newly minted lovers.

Diary of Hannah Iredell

Bethlehem, Pennsylvania

Wednesday, October 30, 1793

Mr. Iredell has decided that we can wait no longer here, the expense and discomfort being too great; and I cannot say I disagree. And so we shall leave this place in two days time and make our way, somehow, back to Carolina—but without our clothes, without our furniture, for they say it is still too dangerous to return to Philadelphia to retrieve them, and there is no telling when it will be safe.

I am glad, now, that I decided to go to the expense of having a few warm clothes made up for us, for we shall need them on the Journey and then in Edenton—and glad as well because I would otherwise not have made the acquaintance of someone I will bid farewell to with great regret. A few weeks since, I inquired of the Innkeeper where I might find a good seamstress. He replied that the Town was well equipped with seamstresses—indeed, the Women here are renowned for their fine needlework—but that it would be best to ask at the Single Sisters' House. That I did, and was there introduced to one of its residents, Sister Anna—not only an expert needlewoman, despite her youth (she can be no more than sixteen), but as amiable and unaffected a young Lady as I could ever hope to meet. She is quite a beauty as well, with a creamy complexion and eyes of the most exquisite blue-green hue; but whereas in a place like Philadelphia, her natural endowments would no doubt be ruined by paint and other artificial enhancements, and her manner corrupted by coquetry on the order of a Mrs. Andrews, here where simplicity and modesty are prized above all else, she shines like the proverbial ungilded Lily.

Indeed, Sister Anna has been far more to us than a seamstress. The Children adore her, and she has frequently offered to take them for their walks so that I may rest or read, even teaching a little German to the older ones (for she is far more fluent in German than English, as is usual here). And for Mr. Iredell and myself, she has served as something of a guide to the ways of this Community, through the narration of the details of her own life: how she left her Parents' house at the age of twelve to live with the other Single Sisters; how she will remain there until she finds a Husband—a search in which not only she and her Family, but indeed the entire Community participates; how the ribbons on her cap will then change from pink to blue, to signify that she has passed from the single to the married state.

I asked her a few days ago whether she was happy here—as I have so often wondered if I might have been happy, had I been born to this life as she was. She raised her lovely eyes to mine with a puzzled expression.

"Happy?" she repeated (though her accent caused the word to sound like "heppy"). "To tell truth, Madam, I do not know, for I have never given any thought to the question."

"Ah, well then," I declared, taking her small hand in mine, "you are happy indeed; for it is a question that is asked only by those who are discontented. The mark of a truly happy person is never to have asked oneself if one is happy or not."

She smiled at me then with such an expression of sweet guilelessness that I was very nearly moved to tears; I realized at that moment that we were leaving quite soon, and that I would certainly never see Sister Anna again. I was seized with the notion that I should give her something to remember me by—some small trinket or ornament. Of course I had left most of what would have been suitable behind in Philadelphia, but I remembered that I had with me a small and rather modest silver brooch, set with a few pearls, that had been given to me by my sister Jean. I found it in a box at the bottom of my trunk and presented it to Anna. At first she exclaimed and protested that she could not accept it, as any polite young lady would do; but after I insisted enough to convince her that I was in earnest, and that I would be quite disappointed if she refused, she at last relented.

"Oh, Madam, I thank you," she breathed, gazing at the brooch as though it were made of diamonds and rubies from India. "I have had nothing like this, ever."

I reflected that this was quite possibly true, as the Women's dress in Bethlehem, though beautifully stitched, was quite devoid of jewelry and ornament.

"I shall keep this, always," Anna continued, "and when I look upon it, I shall think of you and Mr. Iredell and the Children, and pray for your health—and your happiness."

I thanked her and kissed her on the top of her head, and assured her that where we were going we were certain to be happy—for it was, in a way, our own Bethlehem, a place where we had many dear Friends, and where we need never feel ourselves alone or abandoned. And as I spoke these words of reassurance to her, I already felt myself—for the first time in many weeks—entirely happy, and at peace.

From Samuel Wallis to James Wilson (addressed No. 19 Maiden Lane, New York City):

New York, New York, November 17, 1793

... I have waited at this place 3 or 4 days in hopes of seeing you here, but as I can't be informed of any particular time of your coming shall return to Philadelphia this afternoon. I want to see you exceedingly. Both your Interest & mine make it Necessary—I have done a good deal since I saw you, but much more remains to be done which I can't do ... without first seeing you—and unless I see you very shortly ... both you & I will be foreclosed.

Be assured that it is your Interest to hasten to Philadelphia as expeditiously as you possibly can.

Diary of Hannah Wilson

New York, New York

Saturday, November 30, 1793

Oh, the frustration! We have only *just* arrived here in New York (only yesterday evening, to be precise), a destination I have been awaiting with the most exquisite anticipation, and my husband has now announced that we must leave tomorrow morning. What a wedding trip this has been: two weeks, or thereabouts, in towns where all amusement was exhausted in two *days*—followed by a mere twenty-four hours in *this* City, where I could easily pass a month! Jamie has a large acquaintance here, or so he has told me, and I was particularly looking forward to a round of teas and dinners and levees—a small reward for all the deadening counterparts of those gatherings that I have had to put up with in the provinces these past two months. Indeed, from what little I have glimpsed on the streets, there is no lack of fashion and elegance in these parts. I saw the most charming bonnet on a lady walking on the street they call the Broadway—it was adorned with blue feathers and creamy white silk flowers—and I had resolved to have one just like it made up for me before we left.

But, alas, it is not to be. This morning our landlady brought us a letter she said she had been keeping for "his Excellency" for some time—a letter from Jamie's friend Mr. Wallis, who had apparently been waiting in New York for our arrival. We were delayed, as the courts required more time than Jamie had expected, and Mr. Wallis eventually returned to Philadelphia to attend to some pressing business. I don't know exactly what was in the letter, as Jamie chose not to show it to me, but evidently it urged him to repair to Philadelphia as quickly as possible, to attend to some sort of land purchase. Why it is all so urgent I cannot tell, for it seems as if Jamie has plenty of land already, but he clearly wants this particular parcel of land very much.

"November 17th!" Jamie exclaimed to the landlady when he saw the date of the letter. "Good God, woman—why did you not show this to me as soon as we arrived?"

The poor landlady grew quite flustered and sputtered excuses—it had slipped her mind, she had not realized its importance—as Jamie towered over her, all red in the face, shaking his letter in one hand.

"Now, now then, sir," I interjected, for it seemed that he was quite forgetting his manners, "I'm sure it makes no difference. The horses needed a rest in any event—as did we—so we could not have left any earlier, even if you'd known of the letter yesterday."

Jamie merely turned from the woman, growling and muttering to himself, so I took it upon myself to thank her for her services and dismiss her from the room. Jamie then demanded, with ill humor, why I had sent her away, as we needed to tell her to get our horses ready and alert the driver to our imminent departure.

"Oh, surely not, my dear," I protested, and pointed out that we had already accepted an invitation to dine with the Jays this afternoon, and it would not do to disappoint the Chief Justice. (I myself was eager to meet not only Mr. Jay but his lady, who comes of one of the Nation's finest families, and who is renowned for her beauty and elegance; but I did not think it necessary to mention this consideration.)

"Besides," I continued, "tomorrow is Sunday, and the land office, or whatever it is called, will surely be closed, so that you will gain no advantage by going today. We can set out first thing in the morning, and most likely you'll arrive before the close of business on Monday."

At length he agreed, although he remained agitated and distracted throughout the day, even while we dined at the Jays. I hope his bad spirits were not too noticeable to others, although I fear they must have occasioned some private comment: there was more than one occasion when some pleasantry was offered, and the entire company joined in laughter—all except my husband, who remained staring into the distance with a scowl fixed on his face. I did what I could to compensate for his deficiencies, and I flatter myself that I made a favorable impression. Indeed, Mrs. Jay—who is in every way as estimable as her reputation—seemed quite charmed by me, and genuinely disappointed to hear that we would be leaving the city so soon.

"My dear Mrs. Wilson, you must *promise* me," she said, inclining her slender neck towards me as we sat in the tea room after dinner, "that you will *return* here as soon as you are able, and we shall spend a morning in each other's *company*. I will show you *all* the best shops; I'm afraid that the goods available in Philadelphia are quite *inferior*."

Mrs. Jay has the most charming way of giving emphasis to certain words, not so as to sound eager, but with a sort of languor that is quite thrilling. I am certain that I could learn to speak that way, if I were to practice a little—indeed, I hereby resolve that I *shall* learn to speak that way. If I set my mind to it, I could most likely learn to do it even before our first important social engagement in Philadelphia; and the inhabitants of that city, not yet being acquainted with me or my habits, would assume that such was my *natural* manner of speaking; and soon enough it *shall* be.

Philadelphia, Pennsylvania

Tuesday, December 10, 1793

I believe I have scarcely slept since last I wrote: there have been so many novelties to contemplate and consider that the hours usually allotted to wakefulness are rendered inadequate.

About our journey here the less said the better, as it was most unpleasant: a violent snowstorm overtook us nearly as soon as we left New York, so that we were forced to remain at a town called Elizabeth, in Jersey, for several days—Jamie all the while pacing and moaning about how he must get to the land office. He even went so far as to blame me for our predicament, saying that if only we'd left before our dinner with the Jays, all would have been well!

When at last we reached Philadelphia (our journey, once resumed, still being slowed by the residue of snow on the roads), it was well after noon on Saturday—too late for Jamie and Mr. Wallis to transact their precious business at the land office—and neither of us was in a particularly good humor. I, at least, was soon distracted by my first sight of the city: the neat, straight streets with their well-tended brick houses, and glimpses here and there of something grander, such as the spire-topped building Jamie grudgingly pointed out as the State House. Many of the houses we passed had black ribbons on their doors, which Jamie said meant one or more of the inhabitants had been victims of the recent fever. Indeed, Jamie observed that the streets were noticeably quieter than usual, either because the population has been decimated by illness (they say several thousands have died), or because many have not yet returned from their places of refuge.

At length the coach came to a stop before our own house, and I peered eagerly out the window. It is certainly an elegant and commodious house, but on our way through the city we had passed another house—which Jamie pointed out as belonging to the Binghams—that was more in the line of what I had expected. Perhaps I revealed some slight disappointment, for Jamie quickly explained that the house was not yet finished; the arrival of the fever had made it difficult to obtain workmen, and many little ornamentations remained to be done.

"That is just as well," I told him, "for if I can have a hand in finishing the place, I shall consider it more truly my own."

The children gathered quickly in the parlor for their introductions to me; I know not who was the more anxious, them or myself. And Jamie (still out of sorts, I believe, over missing the land office) conducted the whole thing in a rather severe and gruff manner.

"Children!" he said, raising his chin slightly and peering down at them through his spectacles. "This is your new mother." He took my hand and drew me to his side, for I had, without realizing it, been standing to the rear of him, I suppose in a vain attempt to hide. "I trust you will treat her with the respect and affection she deserves, for which she will reward you with a mother's care and regard. Each of you will now come forward, as I call your name, and salute her in an appropriate manner. Polly, as you are the oldest, we shall begin with you."

I knew that Polly was two years my senior, and now, as she stepped forward, I could not ignore the fact that she was several inches taller; she also bore a marked resemblance to her father, which in her case was unfortunate. (There are certain features which sit well enough on a man, but do nothing for a woman.) She made a respectable curtsy and said in a voice so soft as to be barely audible, "Very pleased to make your acquaintance, madam."

I thought this decent enough for a first introduction, but Jamie was clearly displeased. "Polly!" he barked. "You will please embrace her as a daughter would a mother—and call her "Mother.""

Polly reddened slightly but complied, putting her arms about me stiffly and placing a small dry kiss on my cheek—scarcely more than a brush. "Pleased to make your acquaintance, Mother," she said.

I began to giggle at the absurdity of this sentence—it was my nerves, I warrant. But as no one else seemed inclined to laughter, I quickly stifled my own and placed a hand over the telltale upward-turned corners of my mouth; as I did so, I caught the eye of the younger girl—Emily—who is ten or eleven years old, and saw that she was smiling rather mischievously as well.

"William!" Jamie was saying. "But—where *is* William?"

William, I remembered, was the eldest son (being about my own age), but apparently something of a disappointment to his father; every time Jamie had mentioned him, it was to make some disparaging remark. Polly explained that was still in Reading, having decided to look after some iron works in which Jamie apparently has an interest.

"Without consulting me?" Jamie sputtered. "What does *he* know about producing iron? He must be summoned home at once, before he causes any further damage." He then turned to a pale, dark-haired boy standing next to Polly—tall like Jamie, but far thinner. "Very well, then—Bird, come and greet your mother."

Bird's white skin flushed even redder than Polly's as he shuffled forward, then stood stiffly before me.

"Go on, then," Jamie said, with a hint of tenderness in his voice that had been absent until now, "give her a kiss. She doesn't bite, you know."

Poor Bird leaned quickly forward, tapped the cheek I offered lightly with his lips, and then recoiled as if burnt. "Mother," he mumbled, before stepping back to the place he had formerly occupied.

"He may not look it at the moment," Jamie said confidentially to me—although in a voice that I warrant was audible to the rest, "but he's quite a promising lad. Good head on his shoulders, that one has. Best of the lot. And only sixteen, you know."

"Seventeen next month, Father," Bird interjected, confirming that he had heard every word.

We then proceeded through the rest: James, Jr.—called Jem—a year or two younger than Bird, who proffered his kiss without incident; Emily, a pretty, dark-haired child (she must favor her mother—her *real* mother, that is), who flounced toward me with what seemed genuine enthusiasm; and lastly, little Charles, only eight years old, who refused to come forward at all, and instead ran to his sister Polly and hid his face in her skirts.

"Charles!" Jamie cried. "Come here at once."

Charles only buried his face deeper; Polly patted his head, but seemed torn as to whether to offer him comfort or instruct him to obey his father.

"Oh please, my dear," I said to Jamie, "I am so tired at present, and Charles and I have a good deal of time in which to become acquainted. Won't you show me to my room now, so that I may have a little rest before supper? And will you not rest yourself?"

This succeeded in distracting him, for I believe he was eager to show me our bedchamber (indeed, it is an exceedingly comfortable and well appointed room); and as we passed by Polly, I saw Charles steal a glance at me, his face puffy and tear-streaked. I gave him a little smile, but received none in return. It is now Tuesday—three days have passed—and he has still not said a word to me, nor come anywhere near me.

Indeed, the only one of the children who has shown much interest in me is Emily, who is curious about my gowns and my hair combs and ribbons and such like—it seems that her sister Polly has little interest in fashion, so my trousseau is something of a novelty. I confess that Emily's inquiries would verge on the tiresome, were it not for the fact that no one else in this house is paying much attention to me. I believe Bird would do so if he were not so timid; I've caught him gazing at me once or twice, though as soon as I meet his eye he reddens and turns away.

We have three servants: a woman named Elizabeth Nice, who as far as I can tell lives up to her name—the children seem quite fond of her; Ezekiel, the driver, who tends primarily to the horses and the coach; and a Negro boy named Thomas, who says very little and has skin of the darkest hue I have ever seen. There are of course some Negroes in Boston, but not nearly as many as I have already observed here.

The only visitor we have had thus far is Jamie's friend and business associate Mr. Wallis, who called on Monday morning in order to accompany Jamie—at last—to the land office. (I gather that they were successful in transacting whatever the business was, for Jamie's mood was much improved on their return.) Mr. Wallis seems quite an amiable gentleman although—as he lives on a farm somewhere in the West—rather rustic in his manners. As he and Jamie hurriedly left the house, he paused to say to me, "He's a visionary, is your husband—no man has greater plans for this country, or is better equipped to carry them out." This remark afforded me some compensation for my abandonment, as I considered that in permitting their hasty departure I was serving both my husband—the visionary!—and my country.

If I were inclined to moping I might consider myself lonely, with so little company in my own household; but fortunately I am of a sturdier temperament. If I cannot find amusement within the walls of my own house, I shall seek it farther afield. Yesterday I called at the house of my old Boston friends, the Brecks, and passed an hour with Hannah and Lucy, whom I had not seen since they moved here some two years ago.

They were quite delighted to find me on their doorstep, having heard of my marriage and daily expecting some word of me. We are engaged to dine there on Thursday, and I am in hopes that Jamie will soon find the time to introduce me to others in society here; if not, however, I am sure my friends the Misses Breck will see to that, as it appears that they know all the most important people.

Diary of Hannah Iredell

Hayes, Near Edenton, North Carolina

Thursday, December 12, 1793

I write this in my old bedroom at Hayes. Through the panes of the window I can see the fields, now lying brown and dormant; the waters of the Bay, gray-green and roiling today under a dull winter sky; and beyond, at last, the huddled buildings and soaring spires of Edenton. My own small house awaits me there, I know—just beyond the spire of the Courthouse—although I cannot make it out from this distance. The whole Tableau has a dream-like aspect, rippled and wavering, on account of the irregularities in the window glass; but it is all blessedly real—as real as the chill wet wind that greeted me when I stepped outside this morning, as real as the damp Earth I sifted through my fingers as I walked through the fields, as real as the soft, familiar voices and beloved faces all about me.

How foolish I was to vex myself so with questions of clothing and furniture! For from the moment the spire of the Edenton Courthouse was visible on the horizon, as we sailed up the Sound, such a Peace settled over me that I felt I had sunk myself into a bed of feathers after a long forced march. I only pray that Nelly will, in time, become herself again, and that we will be able to resume our former intimacy. There is a Caution about her now, a sadness at her core that Sam says has been with her since Betsey's death; and as well, a distance and a wariness in her dealings with me that have caused me some distress. But she is with Child again, the birth expected in the Spring. I earnestly hope that, if all goes well, the anticipated happy event will erase, or at least soften, those painful memories that now stand between us.

I discovered shortly after our arrival that Sarah's daughter Mamie died of a severe Chill last winter, and no one thought to send word to us in Philadelphia. Perhaps it is just as well that Peter and Sarah don't know, for it would be a sore blow to them indeed. As for Sukey, she is well, and as sassy as ever. When last I saw Sarah, I promised that I should look after her girls as best I could, and I have already approached Sam about taking Sukey with us when we remove to our own House a few days hence; as I expected, he has no objection. The wench was quite out of sorts to find her parents not returned with us, and I could not make her understand the reason. Perhaps, in truth, I kept my explanation rather vague, for I was loath to raise any hopes or Expectations in her that are unlikely to be satisfied. Nor did she seem over pleased to hear that she would be returning with us to Edenton (Sam says that she has lately been keeping company with Marcellus, one of his field Negroes), but I told her it was her Mother's wish, and she appeared to accept it.

Yesterday evening, as we all sat by the fire after supper, our faces tinged golden from the firelight—Mr. Iredell and I and the Children, Mr. Iredell's brother Tom, Nelly and Mr. Tredwell, Mr. and Mrs. McKenzie, and Sam and Mrs. Johnston with their brood—I knew to a certainty that all my Happiness lies right here, in this little corner of the world, and that I shall never stray from these parts again. And if a part of me yet suspects that Mr. Iredell's true Happiness lies elsewhere—in Philadelphia perhaps, and with a different Lady at his side—well, I shall endeavor to put that from my mind. As long as he appears genuinely to care for me here, while he is in Edenton, I shall not think on what transpires beyond its boundaries; for Edenton is all the World I need, or care for.

Diary of Hannah Wilson

Philadelphia, Pennsylvania

Wednesday, December 18, 1793

Such a stream of people coming and going through this house! Rustic land surveyors in buckskin, dandies from New York and Philadelphia with cuffs trimmed in the finest lace, Frenchmen and Germans and Dutchmen. Alas, though, not a one of them is coming to see me: they give me a quick doff of the hat, or, if I'm lucky, a bow and a peck on the hand, and then they go off and closet themselves in Jamie's office, discussing surveys and warrants and titles and terms of loans and rates of interest and such like.

I have asked Jamie to tell me something of what he *does* for all those hours in that room; but he answers only that it is exceedingly complicated, and that he hasn't the time necessary to explain it—nor, he assures me, would I have the patience to listen. It concerns purchases of land, he tells me (as though I could not figure *that* much out for myself), and it will make our fortune, and that is all I need to know, is it not? Perhaps it would be, if Jamie did not expend nearly all his time and energies on these endeavors, leaving precious little for myself, or his children, or nearly anything else. We have received many invitations (I flatter myself that some of these are due to an interest in making the acquaintance of this new bride Judge Wilson has brought back from Boston!), but he scarcely wants to accept a one, and it is all I can do to convince him to do so. He was even loath to accept one of the most coveted invitations in this City—to one of Mrs. Bingham's salons, on Christmas Eve—but fortunately Mr. Bingham extended him a large loan some months back, and Jamie at last decided that it would be ungracious to decline. Most days, I visit with Lucy and Hannah Breck, or entertain them here, and they have introduced me to a good number of their acquaintance; Lucy was kind enough to accompany me to Mrs. Washington's yesterday evening, as Jamie declined to go.

I do not mean to complain; I know that my husband has many important and pressing matters to attend to, and that I cannot expect to be always foremost in his thoughts. I have thought back to the days last summer when he *did* talk to me, and eagerly: how he explained to me that a warrant was no guarantee of ownership in land, how his eyes gleamed merrily when he described what an intricate game it was to secure title before one's rivals. And it has occurred to me that I am, to him, not so different from a choice parcel of land: when all he had was a warrant to me, I was nearly the center of his universe, crowding all other thoughts and pursuits from his mind. Now that he has undisputed title, he has moved on.

Tuesday, December 24, 1793

At last something has turned Jamie's attention from his land schemes, at least temporarily: the return of William from Reading. Alas, it is hardly a pleasant diversion. At first I believed that Jamie must have been too harsh on the lad—that some unfortunate rift had developed between them—and I flattered myself that I might be the agent of their reconciliation. But after a most unpleasant private interview between William and myself yesterday afternoon, during which he displayed a shocking insolence, I have come to believe that Jamie's exasperation with his eldest son is well justified.

I was in the tea-room reading when he sauntered in; it was the first the two of us had been alone (and, if I have any say in the matter, the last as well). I put aside my book and rose to greet him with a smile, hoping that he and I, at least, could conduct ourselves in a civil, perhaps even affectionate, manner, as befitting a mother and son. He returned the smile, but as soon as he began to speak, I recognized that his was not so much a smile as a sneer.

"Ah, my ... *mother*," he said, with an exaggerated bow. "Forgive me if I have difficulty with the word, Madam, but it is in my mind forever linked with one whose memory is for me eternally hallowed—a lady of noble character, possessed of a disposition of exquisite sweetness and generosity, and with a modesty and simplicity about her person that is all too rarely seen in these days of luxury and ostentation."

While it is natural, indeed commendable, for a son to revere the memory of his deceased mother, I thought this speech a trifle impolitic as an opening foray into conversation with one who was to be her replacement; indeed, from the look he gave my attire (a light green and white striped cotton gown over a pink petticoat, trimmed with a broad blue silk ribbon—not even the latest fashion, as the waist is far too low), one might conclude he had intended his last remark as a direct criticism of myself. I reflected, however, that I might be mistaken about his intention; and that in the interest of domestic harmony, it would be best to give him the benefit of the doubt.

"From what I have heard of my husband's late wife," I said, "she was indeed a lady deserving of the utmost respect, and I shall do my best to be worthy of taking her place in this household."

"Taking her place?" William's eyebrows wiggled upwards in the manner of his father's; indeed, he looked much like a youthful version of Jamie: tall and fair, leaner but with the same fleshy face and snub nose. "I hope, Madam, you are not laboring under the illusion that you have been brought here in order to fulfill so impossible a mission. In any event, Polly has been filling the role of mother quite capably—indeed, she's the only mother poor Charles has ever known."

William paused to idly examine a small inlaid wooden box, which Jamie had bought me as a wedding present in Hartford. To my dismay and irritation, I began to feel tears threatening. True, I hadn't particularly *wanted* to be anyone's mother, but to be told that I could not, and in this rude and dismissive fashion, was extremely vexing.

"It's possible my father hoped that by marrying you he might free Polly up to enter into a strategic marriage of her own," he continued, seemingly oblivious to my distress. "Someone with a bit of cash in the family would come in quite handy, from his perspective. But Polly isn't likely to go along with that sort of scheme, and I imagine even my father understands that." He had moved to the fireplace as he spoke, and now turned to face me, warming his backside at the fire. "No, I'm sure my father had his reasons for marrying you, my dear madam"—and here he directed a brazen look at my bosom—"but I don't believe they were the result of any kind of calculation."

"Sir!" I was trembling now, and was far from sure I could hold back the gathering flood of tears any longer. "I will take my leave of you now. And I shall thank you never to speak to me in that manner again."

William then proffered me another bow, and I imagine his lips were curled into a sneer when he arose from it, but I didn't linger to find out. I spent the remainder of the afternoon pacing in my room, unable to sleep or write or even read—reading I could not even attempt, as I had left my book in the tea-room and was unwilling to risk another encounter with William in order to retrieve it. How could William say such things to me? Were the others—Polly and Bird, at least—thinking the same, but being too polite to voice them? And what of the wider world—was I a laughing-stock to others, a subject of titters and gossip in the parlors of Philadelphia? Ah, there she goes, the old man's plaything, his legal whore! And worst of all: was it true? Was I no more to Jamie than a comely body, with which he could take his pleasure when he pleased?

After half an hour of weeping, however, I felt my resolve rising: I would *not* accept William's assessment of the situation. How dare he imply that I could never be mother to these children, never be a helpmeet to my husband, never be anything more in this household than a voluptuous ornament—like the gilt mirror over the mantle in the parlor! No; I would show William, show them all, that I was no mere bauble. I began that very evening at supper, for which William fortunately had gone out, when I exerted myself in engaging the children in conversation. My great triumph was managing to coax a smile from Charles, and a promise that he would play quoits with me in the garden tomorrow.

Later, at night, when I had Jamie's full attention, I confided to him what had transpired between William and myself. At first he leapt up from the bed and railed at William, denouncing him as a villain and a scoundrel, and declaring that the boy would not spend another night under his roof. I said little to this; it seemed harsh, but perhaps it would be for the best.

At length, after his fury was somewhat spent, I asked quietly, "But is it true?"

"True?" Jamie turned to me, puzzled. "Is what true?"

"What William said. About your reasons for marrying me."

"Nannie!" He returned to the bed, took my hand between both of his own, and pressed it to his lips. "How can you think that? You are to me all that a woman can be."

I waited for a moment, but he did not elaborate. "All that a woman can be? And what is that, then?"

"Why … You are possessed of such beauty as can take my breath away—you know that, for have I not told you a thousand times? Your eyes, your neck, your lips"—

"But what *else*? I thank you for the compliments to my person, but is there nothing more about me that draws you?"

Jamie looked flustered; his eyebrows danced like two fat caterpillars engaged in a ritual of greeting. "Of course, of course. Your … sweet nature. Your quick wit. And your—well, your ease in company, the way you always seem to know what question to pose, or what answer to make. How to venture a pleasantry without causing offense, how to express interest in another without overstepping the bounds." He looked away from me, as though studying the counterpane, and his voice dropped to a mumble. "I haven't that gift, you know. And so, when I see how naturally such things come to you, I cannot help but marvel at it."

As he said this, I could for a moment see him as the youth he must once have been: shy and awkward and earnest. I smiled and pulled him close to me. "If you admire me so," I whispered in his ear, "promise me that you will show it more often."

"I will, I will," he murmured, until his words were lost in a shower of kisses.

Today, alas, I have not seen any marked change in Jamie's behavior towards me; but he did call William into his office and (as Jamie told me) berate him for his impudence. William then agreed to return to his uncle in Reading on Friday, and I doubt any of us will be regretful at parting. Perhaps the ironworks at Reading will suffer from William's presence, but I warrant that I, and the rest of the family, will benefit from his absence.

Sunday, December 29, 1793

I made the most extraordinary and alarming discovery today on the way home from church. There not being room for all of us in the carriage, Bird volunteered to walk the half mile home, and—it being a fine day, and this appearing to me as an opportunity to become better acquainted with my son—I said I should be glad of the exercise as well. Bird colored a bit at this, but said only that of course he should be pleased to have my company. Jamie said very well, but we shouldn't dawdle, as he was already growing hungry and did not want dinner delayed on our account.

Accordingly, we walked briskly up Third Street, a route I suggested as it would take us past the Binghams' house at Third and Spruce. As Bird said he had never seen the interior, I described it to him as it had looked a few evenings ago, when Jamie and I attended Mrs. Bingham's salon: the drawing room chairs from London, the backs in the shape of a lyre, with festoons of yellow and crimson silk; the rich red carpet of an intricate and evidently expensive pattern; the paper on the walls (as another guest told me) styled after that at the Vatican in Rome; and what was not papered covered in mirrors, the glass reflecting the glittering light of the numerous candles in gilt sconces and chandeliers—and the no less glittering jewels worn by many of the ladies in attendance. (I had but a necklace set with pearls and a few small garnets, but Jamie has promised me something better—rubies, I am hoping—before our next engagement.) And of course the brilliant conversation—much of it concerning a rather scandalous book on "the rights of woman," by an English lady called Mrs. Wollstonecraft; as I had never heard of book or author, and did not wish to appear ignorant, I had said little on the subject.

Bird listened to all of this politely but without, it seemed to me, a great deal of enthusiasm. And so, when we turned up Chestnut Street and I caught sight of the spire of the State House, I took up politics as my theme, thinking that he would perhaps find that subject more engaging.

"Ah, to live in the shadow of that great building," I remarked, "the birthplace of our independence! For you, I suppose, it is quite commonplace, but for one newly arrived here like myself, every glimpse of it stirs recollections of the bravery of the men who gathered there—including, of course, your own Papa. To think that without their efforts, we might still be living as slaves to a foreign power, instead of the free and self-governing people we are today."

"Indeed," said Bird in his quiet voice. "And yet some in this nation are slaves yet."

"Yes, to our eternal shame! It is quite disgraceful that enlightened men such as your father were unable to prevail against the Southern interests. But that, I suppose, is politics. At least there are no slaves in *this* state—to sully, as it were, this hallowed ground."

"On the contrary … M-m-mother," Bird said, revealing a slight stutter that I had not noted before, "there is yet slavery in these parts. There have indeed been vigorous efforts to abolish it in this state, but the best that could be achieved was a gradual outlawing of the practice. One who was born a child of slaves before the year 1780 may still be owned as a slave until he attains the age of twenty-eight."

I was pleased to have prodded Bird to speech at last—this was the most he had yet said to me—but greatly disturbed by what he imparted. "Dear Lord! Why, Bird, are you quite sure of this? I had no idea. In this very state, in this city—one man owning another, as though he were a head of livestock or a piece of furniture? Cannot something be done about this? Your father has many connections in the government of this state, does he not? I shall speak to him as soon as we arrive home about correcting this sorry circumstance."

Bird chewed his lip for a moment and tucked an errant curl of dark hair behind his ear. "Your sentiments, madam, are certainly commendable, and I could not agree with you more. But you should know, before you bring this suit to my father, that he owns a slave himself."

I stopped stock still at this, causing a gentleman walking behind us to tread upon the hem of my dress before he managed to maneuver around me. We were now directly in front of the State House, the very spot where my husband had inscribed his name, near twenty years before, to a document declaring all men to be free and equal.

"A slave?" I said slowly, staring at Bird in disbelief. "Do you mean … Thomas?"

"Yes, Thomas. He is but twenty, and so can remain a slave for eight more years." There was a moment's silence before Bird said anxiously, "If you don't mind, I think we should resume our walking—we don't want to keep my father waiting for his dinner."

"No, of course not," I said, now recovering from my shock. "And he will have more than dinner on his plate, once I arrive home."

I once again set a brisk pace, as I was now burning to deliver the indignant speech already taking shape in my mind. When we reached the corner of Seventh and Market Streets, Bird spoke again.

"I should warn you, Mother, that it won't do any good—speaking to him about it, I mean. I've tried myself, several times." He sighed. "It's not that he's in favor of slavery, mind you. Quite the contrary, I assure you. But he received Thomas in payment of a debt, and he says he simply cannot afford, at this juncture, to give him his freedom—and to sell him to some stranger would be even crueler than keeping him in his present situation, where he is at least well cared for."

"Bird, my dear boy," I told him, "you must leave this to me."

By the time we reached our own doorstep at the end of the block, my temper had cooled somewhat—enough to allow me to realize that railing at Jamie before the entire family, assembled for Sunday dinner, would most likely do little good. I have learned that my husband is a man who is generally loath to admit error, and it appears he is even more unwilling to do so in front of his children—as though such an admission would cause his family to doubt his authority in all things. I therefore determined to wait until bedtime, when we should be alone, before raising the subject of Thomas. No doubt Bird was puzzled, for he kept throwing expectant looks in my direction throughout dinner and the long afternoon that followed.

When at last the hour arrived, I began by telling Jamie how greatly I admired his brave and noble efforts to bring freedom to the people of this nation—how I knew he must cherish the ideal of freedom for all people, as he had been willing to risk even his own life for it—and how it must pain him excessively to think that so many citizens of this country were yet cruelly denied their natural rights.

As I continued with this speech, I observed Jamie's expression slowly turn from satisfaction to apprehension. "What's this about then?" he said sharply when I paused. "Is it to do with that book they were talking about at Mrs. Bingham's, the one about women? I knew we should never have gone to that ridiculous 'salon,' or whatever she calls it. All this talk of rights has grown entirely out of hand."

"Mrs. Wollstonecraft's book? Ah no, my dear, nothing to do with that, I assure you." His features relaxed, but only momentarily; he again turned wary, and waited for me to continue. "I refer, not to the ladies of this country, but to the Negro race—to the many who live out the entirety of their wretched lives as chattel owned by their fellow man."

I had hoped to see some softening at this, some recognition of the justice of my remarks; but Jamie's eyebrows were drawn nearly together in the center of his forehead and his arms crossed before his chest. I swallowed and took a breath. "I speak," I said softly, "of poor Thomas."

"Poor Thomas!" Jamie cried, unloosing his arms and beginning to stride about the room. "Nannie, you haven't any idea what you're talking about. Why, the best thing that ever happened to him was his being given to me. You ask him if he isn't happier here than on that plantation he came from."

"But my dear," I said, endeavoring to coat my words with honey, "should we not rather ask him if he would be yet happier living in freedom?"

Jamie continued to scoff, telling me that I simply did not understand—that Thomas would be free in a few years anyway—that slavery was a complicated and difficult question—that, in any event, he could not afford to relinquish Thomas at this juncture. And so on and on.

I continued my efforts to make him see how unnatural, how barbaric and selfish his position was. But, as honey was not having the desired effect, I soon resorted to gall; within a very few minutes, we were in the throes of an extremely heated argument, and I feared our voices would carry to other rooms and alarm the children.

"Very well, then," I hissed at him, opening the door to the hall. "If you are determined to remain a slave-owner, you may find somewhere else to sleep. For I will never share my bed with one who traffics in human flesh."

His face was now nearly as red as the interior of his carriage. "I don't *traffic* in … I merely …" he sputtered.

"Hush now, sir, and be gone," I whispered. "But be assured that as soon as you have divested yourself of your human chattel, your wife will be awaiting you in the marriage bed, as obedient as ever."

He appeared too angry to speak, and stalked off in the direction of William's vacant room. I shut the door after him and then leant against it, trembling. I have lain awake now for some hours, shedding more than a few tears, and fearing that I have permanently alienated my husband's affections, that he will never forgive me for my audacity. And yet, despite all, I do not doubt that I have done right in pleading for Thomas's freedom. And I remain hopeful that within a few days, the nobler elements of Jamie's nature (assisted, perhaps, by more fleshly considerations) will prevail, and I shall in good conscience be able to admit him to my bed once more.

Manumission Executed by James Wilson:

The Bearer Thomas Pursel has been emancipated by me.
James Wilson   2ⁿᵈ January 1794
[on verso]

Manumission
James Wilson to
Negro Thomas Pursall
Recorded in the Pennsylvania abolition society Book B page 45
Benj. Johnson

Friday, February 14, 1794

The Supreme Court has been sitting these ten days past (excepting the Sunday, of course), and I must say it is quite thrilling to behold my own husband seated up there on that raised platform in his robe and wig, three massive arched windows shedding their light from behind him, and many of the finest people in Philadelphia assembled in the audience observing the proceedings. I have seen him about his work before, of course, when we were riding Circuit; but it is an altogether different thing to see him here, in the very seat of government, flanked by his distinguished colleagues. There is one judge missing, a Mr. Iredell, of North Carolina, who sent word that he was taken sick on the road and obliged to turn back. Jamie expressed great concern for the gentleman, saying he was a most amiable, obliging fellow, and that he should have liked me to meet him. Ah well—I shall have to wait for the next session, in August.

Jamie is more pressed than ever, conducting meetings and going over papers in his office early in the morning, before the Court convenes, and then again late into the evening. I'm sure that he takes his judicial labors quite seriously, but he does seem anxious for the session to be finished—it comes at quite an inconvenient time, he says, as he has plans afoot to build factories and houses on some of his land in the Western part of the state. It is all quite thrilling; he calls the settlement "Wilsonville"! Perhaps someday we shall travel to see it, once there is suitable accommodation there.

Jamie has been grumbling about a great many things lately—I suppose because he has been so oppressed with business, and so short of sleep. Why, he even complained about being invited to the President's house for dinner last week, shortly after the Court opened! Imagine complaining about such a thing. It was not, I admit, quite as amusing as I had expected it would be—not nearly as amusing as Mrs. Bingham's—on account of the strict observance of etiquette, and protocol, and such. (Jamie was a bit cross with me afterwards, as he said I talked rather too much—but how is it possible to observe as much silence as the President does at dinner?)

I was glad that I had a new gown to wear—a rose-colored silk, well cut by a Philadelphia seamstress—and that I had managed to convince Jamie to purchase that ruby necklace for me but the day before. He had insisted that if he emancipated Thomas, he would never be able to afford the necklace—that I should have to agree to give it up in exchange for Thomas's freedom. I did agree, of course, but I suspected that it was merely a ploy, that he only insisted on this condition to exact some concession from me. Surely a man who buys and sells hundreds and hundreds of acres can afford one ruby necklace! (He even hired a serving boy to replace Thomas, when I pointed out to him how much we needed one.) And indeed, after but a little coaxing and grumbling, he relented.

Jamie had Ezekiel collect us in the coach, though it was scarcely any distance to our house, thinking it would make a better impression—as I'm sure it did. Ah, to be riding away from the President's house in a coach and four, with a ruby necklace at my throat, and one of the most distinguished Gentlemen in the country at my side! I was in a state of utter bliss.

Wednesday, February 26, 1794

Emily and I today went to Mr. Ricketts' Circus at Twelfth and Market Streets, in the company of Hannah and Lucy Breck and Mr. Thomas Adams and some others, and it was splendid beyond words! I had heard much about it, but until now was unable to see it, as Mr. Ricketts has not been here since last summer, before the yellow fever struck—indeed, Mr. Adams told me that the enormous circus building was for a short time used to house unfortunate victims of the fever who had no other refuge. That such a gruesome business had transpired there was difficult to credit in the midst of a cheering crowd of near seven hundred people, all gasping in unison at the amazing feats unfolding before them: gentlemen balancing on the thinnest of wires suspended above us; others pretending to fall from high swings and such, but catching or righting themselves at the last possible moment; and most amazing of all, the equestrian feats performed by Mr. Ricketts himself: riding around the ring with a boy on his shoulder, in the attitude of the winged Mercury; dancing a hornpipe in the saddle, gay as you please; even springing over a pack of ten horses in one buoyant leap. Emily and I were fairly clutching one another in our excitement.

And then, who should Emily and I encounter in the course of our return from Ricketts' Circus but our old servant Thomas! It was Emily who spied him; indeed, I'm not at all sure I would have recognized him myself, as he was considerably thinner and all spotted in mire and muck. He was pulling a cart full of the most malodorous refuse from the market, which I gather is how he earns his living now. We bade farewell to the rest of our company so that we might speak with him, and I asked how he was enjoying his freedom. He replied that he was liking it well enough, thank you.

"And would you not like to return to your native country, now that you are free?" I asked.

He looked at me blankly for a moment. "You mean Virginia, ma'am?"

"Why no, I mean where your people come from—Africa, of course."

He set down the cart and scratched his neck. "Well, ma'am, I don't know about that. I don't have no friends there or nothing. And it's a good distance away. I don't know how I'd get there."

I smiled at the boy's ignorance; the idea of returning to Africa seemed never to have occurred to him! "Why, Thomas, it's an entire continent of people just like yourself, and I'm sure you would find friends there very quickly. As for getting there, you must go and inquire at the Abolition Society. They would be able to tell you of schemes for providing transport to Africa for boys such as yourself."

He assured me he would make some inquiries, and then excused himself because, he said, he needed to empty the cart and return to the market soon, or he'd be risking a beating. Emily and I told him goodbye, relieved to be upwind of the cart at last (Emily had been wrinkling her nose and coughing throughout the conversation). I commended Emily on her sharp eyes; for if she had not realized the lad was Thomas, I would not have been able to communicate to him intelligence that will surely alter the course of his life for the better.

Saturday, April 19, 1794

Such excitement as we had this evening! I at last succeeded in convincing Jamie to allow me a dinner party; as I have now been here going on six months, it seemed high time for me to make my debut as a hostess. I have been asking him these three months past, but he kept putting me off with the excuse that he was too busy to be bothered with such a thing—if I would just wait a few more weeks, his business affairs would be in a more regular state, etc. etc. Well, it seemed that the day of "regularity" would *never* come; and indeed, I began to suspect that the real difficulty was not business but a secret anxiety about playing the role of host; I have not forgotten what Jamie confided to me, months ago, about feeling ill at ease in company. Accordingly, I endeavored to assure him that he could leave it all to me—that I should smooth the conversational path, and relieve him of any awkward responsibilities in that line. It was clear to me that I had adopted the right tack, for his resistance began almost immediately to waver. (When he at last gave his assent, I reflected that, for all that he is such a great man—judge of the highest court, proprietor of an empire of wilderness that will someday be filled with houses and cloth mills and such—in my hands he is sometimes no more than a large and temperamental *piano-forte*, which my experienced fingers may direct to play nearly any tune I wish.)

I was lucky enough to snare not only Mr. Randolph, the Secretary of State (I have learned the names of all the Cabinet officials, or most of them, and have taken to reading the newspapers to follow their doings), but also Mr. and Mrs. Bingham, the Powels, the Cadwalladers, and the Chews. (I very much regretted not being able to invite Hannah and Lucy Breck, as they have been so kind to me—and especially as it was through their offices that I obtained introductions to the Powels and the Chews—but our dining table will only hold so many, and the Brecks are not *quite* at the top rung of society; I shall have another, more informal dinner at a later date, to which I will certainly invite them.) Mr. Jay, who was holding the Circuit Court in this city, had said he would come if he could, but that the press of business was such that he could not promise it. And indeed, in the end, it was not Court business that kept him, but matters perhaps even more pressing—his appointment as our envoy to Great Britain, to conduct the negotiations for a treaty!

Indeed, that was the talk on everyone's lips, for the Senate only just confirmed Mr. Jay's nomination earlier today—he sent word that he would be unable to join us, as he was greatly fatigued and needed to expend his remaining energies on reviewing certain documents related to his mission. It was a great disappointment to me, of course, not to have the Man of the Hour with us at table; but considering what transpired just when we were all sitting down to our first course, perhaps it was just as well.

We heard a great commotion in the street and, thinking that some accident had occurred, we all rushed to the windows that gave out onto Market Street. There we saw approaching a crowd of perhaps a hundred rather rough-looking fellows, those at the head marching with some sort of figure, and the whole company chanting slogans I could not make out. As they drew closer, I could see that the figure was made out of straw and was dressed as a man. Closer still, I was startled to see that about its neck it wore a placard bearing the scrawled word "Jay."

"Dear Lord!" I cried. "It's meant to be an effigy of Mr. Jay."

"Ah yes," said Mr. Randolph, whose height is such that he could easily see out over my head. "This sort of thing is to be expected. Jacobins, I presume, or at least French sympathizers, most likely on their way to the President's house."

The crowd was now passing only inches from the open window, and I was able to make out some of what they were saying: "Death to the Anglomen!" I heard, and "No Treaty with the British Tyrant!" Two or three of the men passing closest to us scowled and shook their fists in our direction.

"I suggest," Jamie broke in, "that we close the window on that rabble and return to our dinner. They're like naughty children, that lot—they only want attention, and we should certainly not be in the position of obliging them."

"Oh yes, of course my dear," I said quickly. In the excitement, I realized, I had quite forgotten my duties as a hostess. "Please, ladies and gentlemen, let us return to our seats before the soup gets stone cold."

There was then some lively discussion of the difficulties lying ahead for poor Mr. Jay, who has been charged with convincing the British to cease doing the disgraceful things they have lately been engaged in (such as capturing American ships, and leaving the sailors stranded on some desolate island)—and who is already encountering such violent opposition from the baser quarters of the populace, without yet having done a thing. Mrs. Bingham said she must remember to give Mr. Jay a letter of introduction to a particular friend of hers in London, the Duke of Something-or-Other, who would at least ensure that he has some amusement to divert him from his labors.

"Is that not the gentleman who is so enormously fat?" said Mrs. Powel (who is, I discovered, Mrs. Bingham's aunt). "Really, one cannot help feeling sorry for him."

"Ah," replied Mrs. Bingham, with a wicked little laugh, "but it is the *Duchess* who should have our sympathy!"

It took me a moment to understand that Mrs. Bingham was referring to matters of the bedroom, and when I did I could not help but blush; but as the rest of the company, including Jamie, was laughing heartily, I joined right in. Certainly in Boston one would never hear such a remark at a polite table—and even here in Philadelphia I have heard Mrs. Bingham and her circle criticized as being rather too free in their speech, perhaps as a consequence of their associating with too many of those titled refugees from France. But in truth, it *was* amusing, and I have decided I see nothing wrong in it.

In any event, the evening was a complete success, and I believe that Mrs. Bingham's wit and skill at conversation was a great asset—although I suppose I must allow myself some credit as well. Indeed, at the end of the meal, Mr. Randolph proposed a toast to the hostess, and there I was, at the head of my own elegant table, with the cream of Philadelphia society raising their glasses to me and crying, "To Mrs. Wilson!" Wouldn't Mama and Sarah and Lucy have been proud to see me praised and feted in this fashion! I know my husband was: he is not one, as I have learned, to lavish compliments on anyone (excepting during periods of courtship!); but he did kiss me tenderly and say, after we had bid the company farewell, "Good work, my lass, good work."

Ah, surely I made no mistake in marrying Jamie (not that I should ever allow my thoughts to run in that direction); for how else should I have found myself so thrillingly situated in the absolute dead *center* of things? My entire body is a-tingle; I don't think I shall sleep a wink tonight.

From the *Daily Advertiser* (New York), July 3, 1794:

NEWPORT, June 27—Last Thursday arrived in town the Hon. Judge Wilson, his Lady and Daughter, from New-York. The same day the Circuit Court of the United States for Rhode Island District met in this town, and adjourned until next day 11 o'clock A.M.

Thursday, July 3, 1794

Really, *why* Jamie insisted on taking Polly along to Newport I cannot fathom—well, I can, to be truthful. William was right: he does have hopes of arranging an advantageous marriage for her, and Newport is known to have its share of wealthy families. But the young lady has to cooperate at least a bit—Polly's no beauty, so she must try and offer at least a modicum of wit and gaiety. But no, she was as glum as a beagle and silent as a mouse the entire time, except to fret to me over how Charles and Emily were faring in her absence—and when I tried to console her by assuring her that Mrs. Nice would be able to manage them quite well without her, all she did was look daggers at me. I believe she's still smarting from what happened when we left Philadelphia: Charles clung tight to Polly, of course, but Emily lavished all her attention on me, and fairly ignored her sister. Well, it's not my fault if the girl prefers me, is it?

Really, Polly is quite impossible. I have done my *utmost*, my very utmost, to bring myself into her good graces, and my efforts have been repaid with little but iciness. I've thought of complaining to Jamie, but I fear it might only make things worse—he can't very well banish her from the house, as he did with William, but I fear he'll take some blunderbuss tack with the girl that will only make her dislike me all the more. And he's been so distracted with his land schemes of late that I am loath to add to his burdens. It was quite inconvenient for him to be in Newport for a week at this juncture; I don't know all the details, but I believe he is in a situation of great delicacy. There are questions of warrants to be obtained, and titles to be guaranteed, and of course the construction of the machinery and the buildings at Wilsonville—sixty-four looms in one factory, and machinery to saw thousands of feet of timber in another!

213

It's really too much for one man to attend to—even one as energetic and capable as I know my husband to be—and I've told him, several times now, that he really *ought* to resign this seat on the Supreme Court, as it interferes so much with his other activities. But he absolutely will not hear of it—*insists* that he can perform his judicial duties and still have ample time available for his more lucrative endeavors—that it is a public service, and he owes it to his country to give them the benefit of his talents and accumulated knowledge and such.

In truth, I believe he is hoping to be appointed Chief Justice soon; there is speculation that Mr. Jay will resign his post on his return from England, and Jamie has hinted on more than one occasion that he believes the President would turn next to him. And I must admit, that *would* be a step up—not just the wife of a judge, but the consort of the Chief Justice of the United States! I believe, now that I've had a bit of polishing, I might cut even as fine a figure as Mrs. Jay—why, I suppose I would have my own "evening," just as I'm told she did when the government was in New York. So perhaps it is worth it for Jamie to spread himself so thin, as such a reward may be in the offing.

From Henry Hubbell, Land Agent, to James Wilson:

July 21, 1794

... I have done all towards surveying our Land I can git done till I git the warrants, for the surveyor will not sign the Returns till the warrants are in his hands ...

If you will send these warrants with the money to pay the surveys & expenses it will strengthen our business; if not I can do no more. But Pray sir, don't fail. It is your Interest much more than mine ...

Saturday, July 26, 1794

We have just had the most alarming—and yet, I confess, thrilling—news. It seems that a rebellion has broken out in the Western part of the state, in some counties by the name of Allegheny and Washington (what irony that a county named in honor of our Nation's leader should take up arms against him!). Something to do with

214

opposition to an excise tax on whiskey —though it is generally believed that the populace in the West are so rough and unruly that they will seize near anything to rebel against. Certainly Jamie's surveyors have had their troubles with them! In any event, a mob has attacked the house of the government's tax collector, in a scene that sounds reminiscent of the worst barbarities being perpetrated by the French. Indeed, some believe it is the French who are behind this attack, or that the Western rebels have at least had some encouragement from their admirers here—the Jacobins and the like. Others say the British are behind it, still hoping to blow apart our Union.

But the thrilling part is this: the President has asked Jamie—my own Jamie!—to certify that the militia must be sent in to put down the rebellion; apparently a certification by a Judge of the Supreme Court is required by the law. He is, as I write this, shut into his office with the papers that have been sent over from the President's house, and just sent word that he would need to have them "authenticated." According to Bird, who has been very kindly explaining all this to me, that means he must see some evidence that the rebels have used force, such that the courts and the law wouldn't be able to put a stop to all this. Oh, I do hope he doesn't keep the President waiting too long a time! It certainly sounds to *me* like the militia is necessary. And it surely won't advance Jamie's chances of becoming Chief Justice if he denies the President so important a request as this.

From James Iredell to Hannah Iredell:

Philadelphia, Pennsylvania, August 3, 1794

... I arrived here yesterday, extremely well, though greatly fatigued ... The city was never known to be healthier ... All of your friends express a great desire to see you back again ...

I sent to Peter, and he came to me last night. He will wait on me while I am in town. Poor fellow! he looks very thin, and gets his living by cutting wood every day ...

I am going to take a family dinner with Judge Wilson ... The papers will give an account of a very melancholy resistance to the Excise-law in this State, which has already cost some lives ...

I have at last had the pleasure of making the acquaintance of the great Judge Iredell, who I have been eager to meet not only because Jamie has spoken of him in such warm terms. I also understand that last year he, alone of all the Judges of the Supreme Court, reached the *correct* conclusion as to whether a state might be sued in a federal court! Congress some time ago proposed an amendment to the Constitution to overturn that Georgia case, and Jamie has grumbled about it quite a bit. During one bout of such grumbling, I managed to pry from him the intelligence that one of the Judges had indeed favored the result Congress now desires—and it was none other than this Mr. Iredell. (Jamie, of course, maintains that the *Court*, not Congress reached the correct conclusion; but, I ask, whose view shall prevail in the end?)

Mr. Iredell came to us yesterday for a simple dinner and proved himself a thoroughly charming gentleman. I apologized for the meanness of the repast, for I had not had time to command provisions of any great delicacy, but Mr. Iredell assured me in the most sincere manner that he was more than well satisfied with the fare. Indeed, he added—most prettily—that the elegance of the surroundings and the beauty of the hostess would render even a plate of beans as delectable as the finest pheasant!

Mr. Iredell seems the sort of gentleman who is generally attentive to the ladies (even to Polly, who seemed to fairly glow when he put a comment or question to her), and equipped with a nimble tongue and an easy wit. When he spoke of his travels on circuit (which appear to have been even more extensive than Jamie's), he often mentioned what charming and beautiful women he had encountered in this town or that; and I shouldn't be surprised if those ladies found Mr. Iredell most attractive as well. Although he is short of stature and possessed of a head of hair that appears to have a mind of its own, there is a gentleness to his manner and a kindness to his eye that is most appealing. He also has a lisp to his speech, which might render some gentlemen ridiculous; but because Mr. Iredell appears so untroubled by it, it soon becomes part of his particular charm. And when he looks upon a lady (or at least when he looked upon *me*!), he has a most beguiling way of making her feel that she is the most delightful creature he has ever laid eyes on. Would that my husband might borrow a few pages from Judge Iredell's book!

I believe Mr. Iredell did have some influence on Jamie yesterday for which I am most grateful: he urged him to send that certification to the President, in connection with the rebellion in the West (which Jamie had *still* under his consideration!). Mr. Iredell pointed out that sworn affidavits and such were all very nice in the usual course of things, but that this was a time of crisis, the danger of secession looming and so on, and not a moment to be lost. To my great relief, I heard Jamie accede to Mr. Iredell's argument, and declare that he should send off the certification that evening.

Jamie then said something to the effect that, since he had done Mr. Iredell this favor, perhaps Mr. Iredell would be so good as to return it: Jamie expects that he will be assigned the Southern Circuit for the fall, as he alone of the Judges (other than Mr. Jay, who is still in England) has never ridden it. But it would come at an awkward time, he said, as many of his business affairs were at a delicate juncture. Would Mr. Iredell take it in his stead? (I was rather put out to hear Jamie make this request, as I thought it would be rather diverting to journey through the South.)

Mr. Iredell, who had looked eager at the first mention of a "favor," appeared more and more uneasy as the nature of that favor was revealed. "My dear Wilson," he began, "you know that it would give me the greatest pleasure to do anything in my power to oblige you"—

"Good, good then—it's settled," said Jamie. Either he was oblivious to Mr. Iredell's discomfort, or he chose to ignore it. "I knew I could rely on you, my friend."

I expected Mr. Iredell to offer some demurral to this, as it seemed evident to me that he had been about to put forward some reason why he could *not* oblige Jamie. But he merely grew rather pink in the face, fell silent, and began to fiddle with the lace of his cuff (which, I couldn't help but notice, looked a bit dingy and threadbare).

Mr. Iredell then, to my regret, announced that he must take his leave, for he said he had recently received some melancholy news that he was obliged to communicate to his wife. Someone Mrs. Iredell had been very fond of, he said—someone she left behind in Philadelphia with great reluctance—had passed away, and it was his duty to inform her of this unfortunate event.

"A dear friend, was it?" I said with sympathy.

"Someone who was dear to her, yes," he replied. "A Negro woman who came here with us from Carolina—we were obliged to give her her freedom here, under the operation of the laws of this state, and so she remained behind when we left, nursing the victims of the fever. Alas, as my wife feared, she herself eventually succumbed to that illness. Mrs. Iredell, I know, will take her death very hard, as they were babes together, and remained together all their lives—until a year ago, that is."

I scarcely knew what to say to this speech. To engage in the barbarity of owning another human creature—to free that human creature only because obliged to by the law—and then to be greatly affected by that creature's death? It made no sense to me at all.

"Indeed," I said at length, as it was necessary to say *something*, "that is unfortunate. I hope Mrs. Iredell will not be too … too distraught."

Mr. Iredell thanked me and rose from the table, saying that he must also take some rest in order to prepare himself for court tomorrow. At the door he turned to me and made a graceful bow, lifting the hat he had just put on his head. "My dear Mrs. Wilson, words can scarcely express the delight I have taken in making your acquaintance. My friend Judge Wilson has proven that he can exercise, in matters of the heart, quite as excellent a judgment and discernment as in matters of law and of business—not that I ever doubted he could." He smiled and dipped his head towards Jamie before returning his attention to me. "I fervently hope, my dear madam, that this is only the first of many meetings between us, and that the warmest of friendships will arise therefrom."

This was so well-crafted a speech that I thought it impossible to answer it in kind, but I resolved to try. "Any friend of my husband's is of course a friend of mine—but to you, Mr. Iredell, I would gladly pledge my friendship even if you and Mr. Wilson were strangers to one another. Indeed, although we have just met, I have already conceived such an admiration for you that I feel as though we have known one another for many years."

Jamie yawned loudly at this. "Yes, well," he said briskly, opening the front door, "Court opening tomorrow, as you said, sir. See you in the morning, eh?"

"You were right," I said to Jamie after Mr. Iredell had left, and we still stood in the front hall. "Your friend is indeed a most amiable gentleman."

"Iredell? Oh yes—excellent man, excellent. And he seems quite sensible to *your* charms, my dear." Jamie smiled at me slyly, and (as the children and servants had all left us), took me in his arms and began to plant kisses all over my person; it seems that the sight of another man admiring me had served to inspire in him some amorous intentions.

"Now, now, Jamie," I whispered, playfully pushing him away. "There will be time enough for that later. I believe you said you were obliged to attend to that certification for the President this evening?"

He gave an exaggerated sigh and pinched my cheek before disappearing into his office. "Ah, Nannie, you are a hard taskmaster," he called over his shoulder.

But really, it was Mr. Iredell who at last spurred Jamie to complete this task—and to give the President the result he seeks. I do hope we have the pleasure of Mr. Iredell's company frequently when he is in Philadelphia, for rarely have I met a gentleman to whom I have felt myself so drawn.

From James Wilson to President George Washington:

Philadelphia, Pennsylvania, August 4, 1794

... From Evidence, which has been laid before me, I hereby notify to you that, in the counties of Washington and Allegheny in Pennsylvania, laws of the United States are opposed, and the Execution thereof obstructed by Combinations too powerful to be suppressed by the ordinary Course of judicial Proceeding, or by the Powers vested in the Marshal of that District...

From James Iredell to James Wilson:

Philadelphia, Pennsylvania, August 5, 1794

... As few things can be more painful to me than not to find it in my power to comply with any request you can make, I am anxious to convince you that my reasons for declining that as to the Southern Circuit are no trivial ones, but such as when I state them I am persuaded must meet with your approbation...

... There is ... depending against [me] in the [North Carolina] Court a very important suit in Equity now ready for decision. A further delay ... occasioned by my attending that Court as a Judge would occasion the most heavy [and] just discontent. Indeed I was really

ashamed to appear there at the last Term lest some illiberal minds might suspect I had used artifices to attend there to delay a decision.

... When I add that I have attended (sometimes with inconceivable distress, anxiety & inconvenience) the same Circuit 5 times in 4 years—that owing to the shortness of my stay on my return lately I was obliged to leave my Family in a very sickly part of the Country, where they unfortunately had been all sick and some of them repeatedly—that my undertaking to go this Circuit again would allow me a very short time to be at home with them in the course of 6 months, and might compel me to quit them in a situation either of ... sickness or danger ... I am sure you will strongly sympathize with reasons [which must] powerfully affect every generous mind...

James Iredell to Hannah Iredell:

Philadelphia, Pennsylvania, August 8, 1794

... [T]he Eastern Circuit was assigned to Judge Cushing, the middle to Judge Blair, and the Southern to Judge Wilson, so that I am at liberty to go home ...

... Judge Wilson is to carry to the Southward with him his Wife ...

Tuesday, August 12, 1794

I must say I'm very disappointed in the President for not doing a single thing, as yet, with Jamie's certification that the militia needed to be called out for the West. Why, he only issued a proclamation ordering the rebels to disperse! What was the point of obtaining the certification if he's simply going to let things go on as before? Jamie says it's all very complicated, and that I don't understand it—it has to do with the Governor of the State, and such. The President will act when the time is right, Jamie says, and in any event he certainly knows what he's about better than I do. Well, perhaps that's true, but I must say, I don't believe I'm going to invest quite so much time and energy in reading the newspapers in the future if *this* is all that it gets me—I don't seem to understand much more than I did before.

I very much regret that we must bid farewell to Judge Iredell—he has been round several times for tea and such, and he alone among all of Jamie's friends pays as much attention to me as he does to Jamie. On his last visit he told us all about his mother, who resides with a farmer and his wife, near Germantown—a very amiable lady, it seems, who has suffered a string of misfortunes but nevertheless has managed to keep her good cheer. I observed to Mr. Iredell that it was unfortunate that he should be separated from his mother by such a great distance; he allowed that indeed it was, but that she was so very happy with this farming couple that he was loath to separate her from them, and had determined to content himself with seeing her but two or three times a year. Such a considerate, self-sacrificing gentleman, Mr. Iredell is!

The conversation put me in mind of my own mother—and my sisters as well. They have written several times now, inquiring when it might be convenient for them to visit. I should like them to come, of course, but the time never seems quite right; and now, as we shall soon be embarking on the Southern Circuit (Mr. Iredell having eventually declined to take it, and setting forth his reasons most convincingly), the fall is out of the question. Perhaps in the spring; and perhaps by that time, I shall be able to greet them as the wife of the Chief Justice! Mr. Jay has not yet returned from his mission to England, but I heard at Mrs. Powel's the other day that some gentlemen in New York have already put his name forward as a candidate for governor of that state. If he were elected he would of course be obliged to resign from the court—with Jamie, as all know, the most likely candidate to replace him.

Thursday, September 25, 1794

At last—after weeks of dithering and shilly-shallying—the President has used the authority Jamie gave him nearly two months ago, and has called out the militia to march on the rebels in the West. Not a moment too soon, either, from what I've heard; at Mrs. Knox's the other day it was said that the rebellion has begun to spread not only elsewhere in this state, but to Maryland and Virginia as well.

I certainly hope the matter is resolved quickly, for Jamie and I leave next week to ride the Southern Circuit; and I don't relish the thought of traveling miles along deserted roads with rebels on the loose—especially in the company of the very Judge who certified that force might be used against them!

From James Iredell to James Wilson:

Edenton, North Carolina, November 24, 1794

... It was a great satisfaction to me to hear that you and Mrs. Wilson had got safe so far on your way as Fayetteville. I anxiously hope this letter will find you both perfectly well at Wake, and less dissatisfied with your Journey, troublesome as I know it must have been, than perhaps you expected. I have suffered, almost ever since my return home, from a continual scene of distress, and anxiety. <u>All</u> of my family have been sick; some of them repeatedly. I thank God, however, they have all been preserved, and are now in good health.

... I warmly congratulate you on the great success of the Western expedition. I am persuaded it has added strength and dignity to the Government. We have many discontented people among us, but I think Federalism is in a state of convalescence; and if Mr. Jay's mission should be successful, it will keep under the little barkings of ill-humor which are now perpetually assailing our ears.

It would give Mrs. I. and myself great pleasure if you and Mrs. Wilson could spare the time to see this part of the country before your return. In that case we hope you would be so good as to accept during your stay here an apartment under our humble roof, where, with no elegance, you would meet with a most sincere welcome...

Edenton, North Carolina

We now find ourselves, Jamie and I, exhausted and bedraggled from our two months on the road, fetched up in this rather dull and wretched place called Edenton. Thank God Charleston was our first stop on the Circuit, as I can't imagine I would have had sufficient energy for the dinners and teas and balls that greeted us there if that stop had been our last. It has, indeed, been rather downhill from there. Augusta, in Georgia, might have appeared pleasant enough had it not suffered so in contrast to Charleston; and Wake, in North Carolina, was barely a town at all—just a courthouse in the midst of nothing. And as for the roads and taverns and houses in between, the less said about them the better. At least we had no fears of rebels accosting us on the roads, for we received news in Charleston that the militia was able to rout the scoundrels in short order.

To be fair to Edenton, it's something of an improvement over Wake, but little more, I fear. Of course, it has as a distinct attraction Mr. Iredell himself, but I really think I should have been willing to give up the pleasure of seeing him in order to return home directly. And I was very much surprised that Jamie accepted Mr. Iredell's invitation to sojourn here, as it was *he* who was complaining about how long the Southern Circuit would keep him from home—now here he is, extending the absence! In truth I believe what brought him here was not so much a desire to see his friend as to investigate the possibilities of purchasing lands in this vicinity. One would think Jamie had quite enough land in Pennsylvania, but he seems to have become convinced that the South is now where the real bargains lie—the only conversations that appear to have truly engaged his interest on this journey are those having to do with land, and he has initiated them at every opportunity. All sorts of tiresome details come pouring forth from otherwise quite charming

223

gentlemen: the quality of the soil of a particular tract, the nature of the vegetation, the prospects for improvement—and of course the price.

There is a neighborhood to the north of this place that goes by the extremely uninviting name of the Dismal Swamp, and Jamie appears determined to have a look at it—although no one seems particularly anxious to take him, the local inhabitants apparently all doing their utmost to avoid the place. But where others see only a dismal swamp, my Jamie sees houses and farms and factories! That, indeed, must be his gift. So eager is he to investigate this swamp that he has sent for Bird to meet us here—for Jamie is clearly cultivating Bird as his associate in these land dealings, having given up entirely on William. I must say, it seems like a terribly long way for poor Bird to travel, just to see a swamp, but I shall be extremely glad of his company; we expect his arrival daily.

Not that we lack for company here, at least after a fashion. There is Mr. Iredell of course—and Mrs. Iredell, who is something of a mystery to me. Or perhaps I should say it is the marriage itself that is a mystery. Mr. Iredell is at all times so gracious and well-spoken, and so much at ease in company that, though he makes his home in this modest village, he would be not at all out of place in the most fashionable parlors in Philadelphia or New York—or even London, I dare say. While *Mrs.* Iredell—well, rarely have I seen a couple so mismatched. One spots the physical differences immediately, of course: she tall and thin to his rather short and round—and clearly not a beauty, even in her youth; she now appears a good ten years older than her husband. More than that, I have scarcely heard her open her mouth the whole time we have been here, nor even smile. Certainly I can see what attracted her to *him*, but what drew him to *her* is a puzzle indeed. Perhaps money had something to do with it—for her family, many of whom reside here, clearly hold a high position in the society of this state, and her brother's plantation, just across a small creek from town, is obviously a prosperous one. But, judging from the character of the house and general household economy, few if any monetary advantages seem to have accrued to Mr. Iredell from this marriage.

Mr. Iredell mentioned to me once that his wife generally displays an unfortunate timidity with strangers; and yet I have the distinct impression that there is in her manner some particular hostility towards myself. Several times now I have noticed that her frown has deepened when Mr. Iredell and I have engaged in some particularly animated conversation; and yesterday evening, when Mr. Iredell very kindly helped to arrange my shawl about my shoulders because I felt a chill, I happened to glance in her direction and saw in her eyes a look I can only describe as murderous—indeed, I felt a far greater chill after I saw that look than I had before! It is evident to me that she is the type of wife who is inclined to jealousy, and I suspect that she sees in the innocent friendship that has grown between Mr. Iredell and myself something of a darker and more improper hue. Indeed, given the disparity between them in their persons and general dispositions, it wouldn't surprise me if perhaps Mr. Iredell *has* given her some cause for jealousy from time to time.

In any event, I should prefer to avoid her; but that is impossible, as we are lodged with the family, and they have but a small house. In addition to ourselves and Mr. and Mrs. Iredell, there are three rather noisy children and several black servants—slaves, of course. The poor wretched creatures stay mostly in the kitchen, which is a separate building at the back, but the house feels quite full enough without them; and there has been a steady stream of visitors, all eager to meet and pay their respects to Jamie. That, at least, has served as some diversion from Mrs. Iredell's unfriendly silences. Fortunately, I shall most likely never see the lady again after I leave this place, since she has no more intention of returning to Philadelphia than I to Edenton. One of the few things I *have* heard her say is that she greatly prefers Edenton to Philadelphia—proof positive, if I needed any, that we are worlds apart in our tastes, and cannot possibly have anything in common.

Diary of Hannah Iredell

Tuesday, December 30, 1794

It has been over a year since I have had the inclination to take up my pen and set down my thoughts in this Book; indeed, I had believed that, once at home in Edenton and surrounded by my friends, I should never feel the need of it again. And in truth, life here has been smooth enough, though we all of us suffered a great deal from the intermittent Fever this past Summer. And Nelly, alas, has remained rather cooler towards me than I had hoped; I had expected that with the passage of time, and the addition of little Peggy to her family, we might by now have resumed our former intimacy. But though I have had some measure of distress and disappointment, I have experienced nothing like that terrible panic and Melancholy, that near disorder of the mind, that afflicted me when away from home, and which more often than not was what spurred me to set down my frantic thoughts on paper.

Now, however, it seems to me that my own dear home, my humble little Haven, has suffered a veritable invasion from Philadelphia, causing in me a resurgence of those painful sensations I had hoped I had left behind there forever. The invading army numbers no more than three—it is merely Mr. Wilson and his Lady, recently joined by his son Bird—but their effect on me has been as devastating as that of the Militia upon those rebels in Pennsylvania. In truth, though I bear no great fondness for Mr. Wilson, it is this *Mrs.* Wilson whose presence is nearly intolerable to me. For she is one of those brazen coquettes one finds in the large cities—like that Mrs. Andrews, whose memory I had nearly managed to obliterate from my mind: her lips and cheeks painted, her bosom immodestly exposed, her conversation livelier and more abundant than comports with polite behavior. And she is forever tossing off names—her "great friend" Mrs. Bingham, or Mrs. Powel, or Mrs. Jay—as though attempting to arm herself with the spirits of more established and substantial Ladies. For really, she is herself little more than a Girl.

But an artful, even a dangerous Girl, for she seems already skilled in flattering and cajoling and—I shall say it—even *seducing* Gentlemen. One would think that Mr. Wilson would pull the reins in on her behavior, for it can only serve to confirm what all the world suspects, that she married him only for his fortune; but no indeed, he merely looks on benignly while she works her wiles on other Men, almost as though it actually reflected credit on him to have so flirtatious a Wife. (That is, when he notices at all, for much of the time he is off making inquiries about the purchase of Lands in this vicinity; he appears to have his eye on the Dismal Swamp, among other places, which I feel certain can lead to no good.) Why, she even flirts with her own Son—or what is called her Son, though he is younger than her by only a year or two—while he gazes back at her with the mute adoration of a love-struck swain. Truly a most improper spectacle!

But most shocking of all, she appears to reserve her most determined coquetry for none other than my own Husband. Several times now I have heard her say (the most recent instance being only this morning) that she feels some particular connection exists between the two of them, that they are so very much alike in certain ways, and so on and on. This morning she actually adverted to the ridiculous belief of certain Heathens that the dead return to life rather than ascending to Heaven (or descending to Hell), and suggested teasingly (her fan poised at her little pointed chin in mock contemplation) that perhaps she and Mr. Iredell had known one another in some former Life! What shocking nonsense—Mr. Iredell is no more like her than an owl is like a peacock! And the audacity of suggesting such a thing, in my presence—indeed, in my own house.

Mr. Iredell has insisted that she means nothing by what she says—that she simply has an excess of what he calls enthusiasm, and is naturally possessed of a warm and friendly Disposition. If so, I have seen little of that pointed in *my* direction! Whether Mr. Iredell understands it or not, she almost certainly has designs on him; and to my dismay, *he* seems to find her thoroughly delightful and charming. I have bitten my tongue over and over again these past two weeks, but today I could no longer restrain myself: I begged Mr. Iredell to tell me whether there was anything between them of an improper nature. He sighed wearily (just as he did when I asked him about Mrs. Andrews), and set me down on the bed (for we were in our chamber), and stroked my cheek. I mustn't allow such wild fantasies to plague me, he said, for his heart was entirely mine, and always would be; there was no Woman he placed above me.

I found some comfort in his words; indeed, I wanted nothing more than to relinquish my fears, and believe in them implicitly. Yet I found that, try as I might, I could not. Ah, I shall be glad to see the last of this Mrs. Wilson. Thank the Lord they intend to leave next week, as Mr. Wilson has affairs to attend to in the City; I pray for the strength to continue to perform my duties as hostess with that graciousness and courtesy that befits a Southern Lady. For I flatter myself that, despite Mrs. Wilson's outrageous behavior, I have dissembled so successfully that she has not the least suspicion of my true feelings towards her.

Diary of Hannah Wilson

Philadelphia, Pennsylvania

Thursday, March 12, 1795

Mr. Jay's treaty with the British has arrived—though Mr. Jay himself has not, as yet, fearing the rigors of an Atlantic crossing in winter—but the terms of it are a closely guarded secret, not to be revealed until the Senate convenes in June, and perhaps not even then. Of course, that has not prevented certain factions from denouncing it anyway, as they have done even before the thing arrived—most likely, even before it was concluded. I am quite sure that once the contents of the treaty are revealed, it will be recognized by all sensible parties that Mr. Jay has struck us an excellent bargain, and the Jacobins and the Republicans and such will be consigned to the oblivion they deserve. What a pity the terms must remain confidential for so long!

As for secrets, I have one of my own to keep now, at least for a while—an exceedingly distressing one, in fact. For several days since, I have been experiencing peculiar sensations such as I have never felt before. At first I thought I had contracted some illness, and therefore asked Mrs. Nice to prepare me an infusion of penny-royal, such as my mother used to give me when I had a complaint of the stomach. The penny-royal seemed to have some beneficial effect, but two nights ago Mrs. Nice gave me an odd look, and remarked that perhaps I should have no more of it, as it would not be the best remedy for a lady in "a certain condition." For a moment I hadn't the slightest idea what she was talking about, but once her meaning became clear to me I felt myself all a-tremble and had trouble catching my breath, and so repaired to my room at once.

Of course, I realized, it was perfectly possible that I was with child—surely many women in my position, married near a year and a half, would have come to that realization earlier. And I don't deny that the subject has entered my mind, on occasion, but—as with most unpleasant subjects—I simply could not see the point in dwelling on it. Nor has Jamie mentioned it more than once or twice, and then only in passing. I suppose some husbands would be quite anxious for an heir, but as my own is already well supplied in that regard, and has his hands so full with business affairs and such, he seems not to have concerned himself with it any more than I have. No, I cannot see that my bearing a child would do either of us much good, and of course it could do me a good deal of harm—indeed, could quite possibly be the end of me, as it has been for so many women!

I was still in hopes, however, that my trouble was no more than an odd sort of indigestion, and so yesterday I consulted Mrs. Bingham—she being the only married woman I know in this city in whom I felt I could confide. When I described my complaints in a private interview in her bedchamber, she gave me a tender smile and clasped my hand in hers.

"Yes, my dear!" she cried exultantly. "I think there can be no mistaking it. Now, you must be at pains to take care of yourself, for I should say you are at a delicate juncture. Take moderate exercise, do not over-indulge in food or drink, and use olive oil regularly as a purgative—that is what I have always done, and I only ever had one disappointment. Still and all, it's always wise to be cautious and restrained in one's emotions, difficult as that may be, for misfortunes do often occur—especially the first time, you know. I should *certainly* take no more penny-royal—indeed, one hears stories of fallen, depraved women who take it deliberately, in order to get *rid* of a child. Use charcoal instead. It's quite as effective for nausea, and perfectly safe."

It took all my strength to keep from weeping during the course of this speech, and at the end of it I rose to excuse myself, saying that I felt rather faint.

"Of course, of course, my dear," Mrs. Bingham said, helping me to rise. "Indeed, you've gone quite pale—you must go straight home now and take your rest." She then pressed me gently to her bosom, and when she released me I could see that her eyes were moist. "Promise me that you will have Dr. Shippen attend you at your confinement—he's quite the best physician for this sort of thing. Oh, I am so pleased for you, my dear!"

I remained quite distraught for the rest of the day, although I did my best to conceal it. Bird might have had his suspicions that something was amiss, but Jamie has been so busy with his plans for the factories at Wilsonville, and his inquiries into lands in the South, that I'm quite sure he paid me no notice. It was not only the prospect of childbearing, with all its attendant discomforts and dangers, that so disturbed my thoughts; but also the knowledge that I am so very unlike other women in being so fearful of it. Why, there was nothing but joy in Mrs. Bingham's countenance when she discerned my condition—and quite clearly, she expected that I should feel nothing but joy as well; or that if I did feel fear, it would be fear of the pregnancy's untimely termination—a "disappointment," as she put it—which in fact is an event that would bring me the greatest relief.

Am I a monster, then? A sniveling, selfish coward? Or can it be that all these other women are, as it seems to me, endowed with the courage of warriors and the self-denial of martyrs? I shall never forget attending with Mama at my aunt's confinement when I was but thirteen. Aunt Lucy was much younger than Mama, and such a pretty, lively, high-spirited creature that I could not help but adore her—indeed, I used to imagine that she was the older sister that by rights I should have had, so much more to my liking than the one Fate had delivered to me. This was to be her second child, and as the first birth had proceeded uneventfully, I suppose Mama saw no harm in bringing me with her to the house. But once we arrived and I heard my beloved Aunt Lucy's plaintive moaning, I knew I could not bear to listen to it and slipped away from the women attending her in the bedroom. Within an hour or two, it was evident that something had gone badly wrong: the soft moans had turned to ghastly screaming, then back to whimpering, and finally—most alarming of all—a hushed silence. The doctor was called, the women scurried to and fro fetching things, my uncle paced the rooms and tore at his hair and clothes. I was left forgotten in a corner of the parlor where I huddled, whimpering and chewing at my fist, until many hours later, when Mama, her face grey and tear-streaked and inexpressibly sad, came to collect me. Aunt Lucy had gone to Heaven, she told me, along with her baby.

I suppose it was from that moment that I began to pray I should never find myself with child. But women suffering beyond measure, and even dying, in childbirth is so common an occurrence that I cannot think my experience unique; indeed, I have known many others who have failed to rise from the birthing bed, or have risen in a greatly changed and broken condition. What is it that enables other women to go so cheerfully to what they know may be their doom? Certainly the great majority of them are in other respects ordinary and unremarkable. I should not object to their being awarded honors and prizes for what they endure—but that *I* should be condemned (as I surely would) for what appears to me as quite a reasonable desire to preserve my own life strikes me as harsh and unjust.

Perhaps it is that the prospect of motherhood appears to other women as a prize of irresistible allure, for which they are prepared to endure all manner of peril—whereas for me, motherhood *itself* appears as a peril. I cannot imagine a worse fate than to be tied to some ever-wailing, helpless creature—like those Iredell children, with their laughs and shouts and insistent cries of "Mama!" Am I expected to willingly risk my life for *that*? Emily and Charles are quite enough for me in the way of children; they have reached the age where they generally can be trusted to comport themselves as they should—but I confess that even they try my patience sorely on occasion.

When I think on what lies ahead for me, a cold terror overtakes me—I believe I have never been more frightened of anything in my life. I stare down at my stomach in horror and disbelief, imagining it swelling to monstrous proportions—ever greater and ever more threatening, day by day. *There must be some way out of this*, is the thought that pounds at my mind over and over; but my brain is so disordered, I cannot imagine what it may be.

Friday, March 13, 1795

Last night I had a most alarming dream: I was astride a horse that was galloping wildly, madly towards a sheer cliff. I had no reins, no means to try to stop the horse or divert it from its fatal course—and to throw myself from its back would mean certain death. So I had no choice but to cling to its neck and shut my eyes tight, awaiting the horse's leap into the ether, and then a long, sickening fall to the ground. I awoke with a start, gasping and sweating, and feeling that my body had indeed just hurtled down from a great height. I sat straight up in bed, relieved to find myself in one piece.

I could not find my way back to slumber, for all manner of agitated thoughts concerning my present condition were coursing through my mind. But at length a plan began to form, or the possibility of a plan, that might provide the solution to my difficulty, and I began to feel a measure of calm descend upon me. I know not yet whether I shall indeed follow through with this plan; but it is a comfort to think that at least I have some choice in this matter—that I am not in fact unwillingly strapped to a runaway horse bent on its own destruction, and mine.

Saturday, March 21, 1795

It has now been some five days since I suffered what Mrs. Bingham would surely term my "disappointment," and I am, I think, nearly recovered—at least, in body. Everyone has been most kind to me—including Jamie, despite the business affairs that I know are pressing on him daily. He was so good as to buy me a pair of pearl and ruby earrings that I admired in a shop window two weeks ago, in hopes that they would cheer my spirits. And Bird has been such a dear boy, popping his head into my bedroom nearly every hour to ask if there is something I require, and generally treating me as delicately as if I were made of brittle porcelain.

Poor Mrs. Nice came and tried to apologize to me—said tearfully that she was sure it must have been the penny-royal that did it, and that she should have guessed at my condition sooner and warned me off of it at once. I assured her that I did not hold her responsible in the least, for was there not nearly a week between the last dose of penny-royal that she gave me and the day of my disappointment? She went away comforted by that, I think. It appears that neither Mrs. Nice nor anyone else suspects the truth, for I was careful to procure my own stock of penny-royal, at a shop where I was certain I should not be recognized, so as not to deplete Mrs. Nice's own supply. Then I waited till the dead of night to prepare the infusion; thank God we don't have so small a house that the servants must bed down in the kitchen.

It's a great relief to me, of course, that it's over and done with; and yet I cannot rid myself of a fit of melancholy that descended upon me shortly after it happened. I hadn't realized there would be so much blood, I suppose—I have never had a strong stomach for bleedings, and the quantities of it gave me quite a turn. I suppose it's just as well that I exhibit such distress now, as it seems to be expected of someone in my position; and yet it comes as quite a surprise to *me*. It's as though my emotions have developed a will and a mind of their own, so that I haven't the faintest idea what they will do next.

This morning, for example, Mr. Iredell called on us—he must leave soon for the Eastern Circuit, poor man, and wanted to pay his respects to us before he went. I hadn't been downstairs since ... well, since the event occurred, but I insisted to Mrs. Nice that I felt strong enough to dress and to receive Mr. Iredell, for I was certain that a visit with him would be a tonic for me. And indeed it was, at first, for we chatted about all manner of subjects: what is being said in the coffee houses about Mr. Jay's treaty; whether he would be elected governor of New York (I was heartened to hear that Mr. Iredell agreed with me that Jamie is likely to succeed him as Chief Justice); what might happen at the trial of those who were arrested for their part in the rebellion in the West. I could talk politics all day with Mr. Iredell, for he has the knack of making it quite as interesting as gossip! And he never waves away my questions, as Jamie sometimes does; indeed, he often compliments me for having asked what he says is an excellent one.

But then the talk turned to his impending Circuit, and his sorrow at not being able to return to his family until after the Supreme Court's August sitting—a full eight months, at least, he must spend away from them, and to include the summer, which is a dangerously unhealthy season in that part of the country. He began to tell me of the presents he had recently sent home to his children: handkerchiefs, beads, ribbon; a locket for his elder daughter; a drum for his son (to be used only out of doors, he said); and a set of painted blocks for the youngest, Helen.

"She's an unusual child—seems to dwell in her own little world, sometimes," he said with a fond note to his voice. "But she can be exquisitely sweet as well—like all children, I suppose."

At this I suddenly felt tears begin to well up at my eyes, and within a moment or two I was sobbing quite helplessly. Jamie and Mr. Iredell were immediately at my side, attempting to comfort me—Mr. Iredell, of course, blaming himself for his blunder in bringing up the subject of children.

"My dear Mrs. Wilson," he said, his brow furrowed in concern, and his own usually merry brown eyes moist with sympathetic tears, "I assure you, you'll yet have children of your own, for you're still very young. Mrs. Iredell and I were married for twelve years, you know, before we were blessed with a healthy child—we had nearly lost all hope, and you see our situation now. So I beg of you, do not despair!"

Mr. Iredell's well-meaning prediction that I would find myself with child once again—as certainly seems more than likely—only served to unloose a fresh flood of sobs; for I could not bear the thought of going through once more what I had just suffered—no more than I could bear the thought of allowing another pregnancy to continue to its natural conclusion. I felt, and still do feel myself, quite caught—like an animal with its foot in a trap, able to choose only between accepting its fate and dying where it lies, or else tearing its ensnared limb from its body and limping off elsewhere to meet its bloody end.

Ah, such morbid thoughts as now haunt my mind! I feel quite unlike myself. I even find myself wondering, with a grim remorse, what it might have been if it had lived: girl or boy. If I had *allowed* it to live. I must leave off writing now, for it is certainly doing nothing to cheer me.

Saturday, June 6, 1795

It has been quite a while since I have taken up my pen to write in this journal—over two months. But I hadn't the spirits to write, nor the energy; and I shouldn't have had a thing to set down, other than an examination of my own melancholy—which would only have had the effect of increasing it, I'm sure. I have, truth to tell, been rather a recluse these past two months. I have scarcely left the house, seen practically no one, turned down nearly every invitation that has come our way—though Mrs. Bingham and Lucy Breck have been exceedingly kind to me, calling on me faithfully and bringing me the latest intelligence and gossip in an effort to cheer me. And Jamie, as well, has been most attentive and affectionate, offering me various pretty trinkets that he thought might bring a smile to my lips; I now have quite a treasure hoard of jewelry to choose from, when I am again in spirits to reenter society: an emerald ring, a bracelet of pearls, a locket fitted with a diamond on the outside and containing a miniature of Jamie within.

The first week or so, Jamie would sometimes sit and read to me. He even began *Charlotte, a tale of truth*, though I know he considers novels a miserable waste of time (I requested it, as it seemed absolutely *everyone* in the city was reading it, and I hoped its rather sensational plot would take my mind from my own troubles). It was wonderfully kind of him, but I could see him glancing nervously at his watch now and then when he thought I wouldn't notice. At length I insisted he return to his office, for so many schemes and endeavors awaited his attention there. The construction at Wilsonville is proceeding apace, I gather, and an associate of Jamie's by the name of Farmar has been dispatched to take up residence there and convey a full report. And Jamie has become quite passionate about buying up lands in the South—he has written to gentlemen whose acquaintance we made during our Circuit there, asking for additional intelligence about tracts that have caught his fancy. New associates and prospective partners have begun to turn up at our door: a Mr. Allison and a Mr. Blount have come rather frequently (both of them tall and red-haired, so that I continually confused them) and spent hours closeted with Jamie in his office, poring over maps and debating terms of sale.

But all has been much quieter these past few weeks, as Jamie has been away on Circuit—or part of a Circuit, holding courts in Maryland and then Virginia. It was difficult to part with him at such a time as this, and I was very much hoping to receive at least a few letters from him, to assure me of his health if nothing else—but he has written only to Bird, to keep him apprized of intelligence concerning Southern lands.

The benefit of Jamie's being away is that Bird has had so much more time at his disposal, for Jamie would keep him at work for hours, copying documents and locating tracts on maps—and of course studying the law, for it has been decided that Bird will take up his father's profession. Being a diligent boy, Bird has kept up with his studies, but that still leaves him a good part of the day free, and he chooses to spend much of it with me. The entire family has been very good to me during my recent fit of melancholy—even Polly, who I may perhaps have misjudged—but Bird has certainly been the best of all. His concern for me seems to have at last trumped his native shyness, and we have spent many hours conversing: first in the parlor, then—as he insisted that fresh air and exercise were essential to my recovery—during rides in the carriage, and at last, when my strength had returned sufficiently, on long walks.

Certainly I have never met so earnest and good-hearted a young man. So intent has he been on lifting my spirits that I began to feel I must recover them for *his* sake, if not for my own. At first, assuming that I had simply been the victim of capricious misfortune, he discoursed on the mysterious ways of God, and how we must trust in His wisdom—that disappointments and reversals are all part of his grand plan, which we mere mortals cannot fully grasp—and so on. I smiled and nodded, not so much because I found comfort in the words themselves—for indeed, they were no more than what I had been hearing in Sunday sermons all my life, and seemed to have little to do with my actual situation—but because I was so moved and flattered by Bird's strenuous efforts to cheer me. And yet at the same time I could not help but consider that so moral and upright a person as Bird would surely shrink from me in horror if he could but discern the true blackness of my character; the more he exhibited his own goodness and decency, the more painfully conscious I became of my own position on the opposite end of the spectrum of virtue. And so all his efforts, and my own, were in vain: melancholy clung to me, thick and stubborn as tar.

At length, on Wednesday last, I put to him a question that was couched (I hoped) in such philosophical and impersonal language that he would not be led to think it had any direct relation to myself: I had heard from a friend, I said, that there were certain women who were so depraved, so removed from the natural course of human emotions, that—impossible as this might be to imagine—they actually took steps to *cause* such misfortunes to befall them. What view, I wondered, did he think God would take of such sinners? Was it possible that such a crime might ever be divinely pardoned?

Bird looked not at me, but at the cloud-flecked blue sky (for it was a fine day, and we were out walking near the outskirts of the city), as though searching for a heavenly answer; I was relieved that he had not shot me a suspicious glance, and yet I was still all a-tremble in fearful anticipation of his answer. I confess that it was not so much God's forgiveness I sought—although indeed that was a part of it—as Bird's. How would I be able to live with myself—with *him*—if he were to issue some iron, unbending condemnation? How might I ever consider myself worthy to be called his mother?

"Indeed," he said at length, "I have heard of such things." He drew himself up a bit, and assumed an air of *gravitas*—as though to say, I'm not so innocent as you believe. "I would never have mentioned such a possibility to you myself, of course, as I feared it would cause you too much pain to contemplate. But as you have invited my opinion, I shall be glad to give it, for it presents a highly interesting question."

I nodded encouragingly. At another time, I would certainly have been flattered by the tone in his voice, for it suggested that he and I were colleagues, of a sort, in the search for knowledge. But at that moment my mind was too filled with apprehension to admit of any other emotions.

237

"I should think it would depend on the state of mind of the sinner," he continued. "That is, whether she continued to go about her life without any real consciousness of the monstrous sin she had committed—or whether, indeed, she was filled with guilt and remorse at what she had done."

"Oh, but she"—I started to cry, but quickly stopped myself. "But suppose that she is quite *consumed* by remorse. What then?"

"Well, in that case, if she threw herself upon God's mercy, and earnestly resolved to follow the path of righteousness from then on—if she were quite sincere about these things—then I'm sure that God would forgive even so great a sin as the one you have described. For He is not a vengeful God, but seeks to bring even the worst of sinners into His fold, and sustain them with His love."

This was a doctrine rather more forgiving than I had heard in the sermons of my childhood; and to hear it from Bird's lips was infinitely comforting. Something heavy and shroud-like lifted from my chest, and I breathed deeply of the clean spring air. We were in the area near the Schuylkill River, a section of town where streets have been laid out, trees cleared, but few buildings have as yet been erected: suddenly I was aware of birds soaring overhead, rabbits scampering through the fields, the warm breeze tickling my face. I felt more at peace than I had in months—certainly since the dreadful event had occurred. I had an impulse to throw my arms about Bird, but contented myself instead with giving his arm a little squeeze.

"Why Bird," I said, "you speak quite as well and as wisely as the finest of preachers."

He reddened slightly and looked away in embarrassment, but I saw a smile of pleasure spread across his face. "Indeed," he said, kicking a pebble, suddenly a boy again, "a preacher is what I should like to be, if Papa would allow it. But he has his heart set on the law for me."

"Ah then, never mind," I told him, "I'm sure you shall be the finest of lawyers, and most likely will have far more amusement in life. Ladies never flirt with preachers, you know!"

His face grew even redder at this, poor thing.

"Now, as you have helped me so greatly these past weeks, my dear Bird, I shall repay the favor by helping you: I shall give you instruction in flirting—for it's a skill that every gentleman should possess. And it's quite diverting as well, once you know how to do it."

I confess that Bird appeared less than enthusiastic concerning this proposal, but that's only his being timid again—and he did say that if it would amuse *me* to instruct him, then he should be glad to oblige me. So we have commenced our little school of flirting: I give lessons each afternoon while we take our walk. I point out this young lady and that, as we pass them, until Bird at last admits that he finds one of them to be pretty, and then I tell him to imagine that I am her. We converse as though we are strangers who have just met—or rather, *I* do most of the conversing, as Bird has not proven as apt a pupil in this subject as I'm sure he is in all others.

And so, thanks largely to Bird, my spirits are much brighter now; indeed, I feel nearly myself again. And I have had other news to cheer me as well: the returns from New York have been coming in, according to the newspapers, and Mr. Jay's election as governor seems almost assured. We expect Jamie's return from Virginia any day now, and I do hope that he will be here, with me, when the final result is known, for I should so relish seeing the glow of satisfaction and expectation on his face!

From John Rutledge, Chief Justice of the South Carolina Court of Common Pleas, to George Washington:

Charleston, South Carolina, June 12, 1795

... Finding that Mr. Jay is elected Governor of New-York, & presuming that he will accept the Office, I take the Liberty of intimating to you, <u>privately</u>, that if he shall, I have no Objection to take the place which he holds, if you think me as fit as any other person, & have not made Choice of one to succeed him ...

Several of my Friends were displeased at my accepting the Office of an Associate Judge ... of the Supreme Court of the United States, conceiving (as I thought, very justly) that my Pretensions to the Office of Chief-Justice were at least equal to Mr. Jay's, in point of Law-Knowledge, with the Additional Weight of much longer Experience, & much greater Practice ...

I [have] never solicited a Place, nor do I mean this Letter as an Application—it is intended merely to apprize you of what I would do, if elected ...

What an outrage—the Senate ended their session yesterday without appointing a replacement for Mr. Jay! Mr. Bingham came by yesterday evening, straight from attending there, and told Jamie it was no fault of his or the other Senators—that Mr. Jay had not yet submitted his resignation as Chief Justice, so what could they do? And yet the gentleman is set to be sworn in as governor of New York in a mere four days time. I cannot fathom his reasons for behaving in so selfish and negligent a manner; indeed, I have nearly lost all respect for the man.

Jamie was quite put out as well. He said it was owing to the fact that the Court must now continue in its reduced state, short one member, as has been the case since Mr. Jay departed for England last year; for surely, he said, there would now be no replacement before the fall Circuits, as Congress would not return until December. Mr. Bingham remarked that under the Constitution, the President had the power to fill the vacancy during the recess. Then Jamie bellowed that he knew what was in the Constitution, of course, for hadn't he written the damned thing?—but what self-respecting gentleman would accept a commission that could later be withdrawn by the Senate?

Jamie was quite red and agitated by this time, and I fear poor Mr. Bingham did not take this fit of temper kindly, for he declined my offer of tea and excused himself rather hastily. After he'd gone, I rubbed Jamie at the back of his neck, just at the spot where he likes it, and once I felt his muscles begin to relax I spoke to him soothingly—even though I was still seething myself.

"Now, now, my dearest," I said. "It's terribly unfair, I know, but you must only wait a few months longer, and surely the office will be yours."

He reached up and patted my arm absently. "Ah, Nannie my lass, you mustn't be so certain of things. There are all sorts of rumors circulating. You've no idea what it's like when there's a vacancy of this sort. I'm sure the President's desk is cluttered with letters from hopeful office-seekers and their friends, urging their qualifications and their merits. I've heard Mr. Randolph's name mentioned, and Mr. Chase—and also Mr. John Rutledge. He was on our Court years ago—when you were just a child in Boston. He lasted but a year before he resigned his commission. Only rode a circuit or two—never even attended a sitting of the Court. But it's said that Washington holds him in high esteem, for some reason."

Jamie removed his glasses and rubbed the middle of his forehead, as though to supplement my rubbing at his back. "Of course, I imagine the President will feel obliged to offer the post first to Judge Cushing. You know that his commission is dated three days earlier than my own, giving him the advantage of seniority."

"The *advantage* of seniority?" I settled myself on Jamie's lap and curled my arms about his neck. "Why, Mr. Cushing has so great a measure of *seniority* that he can scarcely stir from his bed!"

This brought a small chuckle, so I pressed on.

"Indeed, we should be glad of the delay in nominating Mr. Jay's replacement, for by the time the Senate returns Mr. Cushing will be even older and more decrepit than he is now! Perhaps"—I leaned close and whispered in his ear—"*perhaps* he will even have gone to his well-deserved resting place with the angels."

"Ah, Nannie, you *are* a wicked lass!" Jamie pushed me away, but with a smile, then drew me close and kissed me on the lips.

From George Washington to John Rutledge:

Philadelphia, Pennsylvania, July 1, 1795

... Your private letter of the 18th ult. and Mr. Jay's resignation of the office of Chief Justice of the U.S. both came to my hands yesterday.

The former gave me much pleasure, and without hesitating a moment, after knowing you would accept the latter, I directed the Secretary of State to make you an official offer of this honorable appointment—to express to you my wish that it may be convenient & agreeable to you to accept it—to intimate, in that case, my desire & the advantages that would attend your being in this city the first Monday in August (at which time the next session of the supreme Court will commence)—and to inform you that your Commission as Chief Justice will take date on this day July the first ...

From James Iredell to Hannah Iredell:

New York, New York, July 2, 1795

... I am perfectly well, but extremely mortified to find that the Senate have broke up without a Chief Justice being appointed, as I have too much reason to fear that owing to that circumstance it will be unavoidable for me to have some Circuit duty to perform this fall ... I will at all events go home from the Supreme Court if I can stay but a fortnight—but how distressing is this situation? It almost distracts me. Were you & our dear Children anywhere in this part of the Country I should not regard it in the least—But as it is, it affects me beyond all expression.

The state of our business is now such that I am persuaded it will be very seldom that any Judge can stay at home a whole Circuit, so that I must either resign or we must have in view some residence near Philadelphia, I don't care how retired, or how cheap it is. The account of your long continued ill health has given me great pain, and I am very apprehensive you will suffer relapses during the Summer. My anxiety about you and the Children embitters every enjoyment of life. Tho' I receive the greatest possible distinction and kindness everywhere, and experience marks of approbation of my public conduct highly flattering, yet I constantly tremble at the danger you and our dear Children may be in without my knowing it in a climate I have so much reason to dread...

Tuesday, July 7, 1795

Well, I *am* cross! This past week the streets have been plagued with angry roving mobs bearing torches and effigies and threatening mayhem and destruction—one takes one's life in one's hands merely to visit one's acquaintance, or make purchases in the shops. And all on account of Mr. Jay's Treaty, which the Senate has approved at last and which (now that the *Aurora* has seen fit to publish the terms, which are still officially confidential) has occasioned the most violent disagreements. Most of my friends believe that Mr. Jay did the best he could, that the British drove him a hard bargain, and I'm sure they're quite right. But certain elements (the rougher ones—Jacobins and French-lovers) have taken it into their heads that Mr. Jay deliberately betrayed the country, and go around shouting insults about "Anglomen" and such. Last week a mob actually attacked the Binghams' house, I suppose because Mr. Bingham had taken a leading part in securing approval of the Treaty in the Senate; but fortunately, thanks to the protection of the tall and very well-built fence that surrounds the property, no serious damage was done.

And as if all that weren't enough, William has come from Reading and plans to stay with us for at least a week. I suppose I shouldn't complain, as he hasn't bothered us with his company for the past year and a half, but his very presence gives me quite a case of nerves. He has done or said nothing truly objectionable as yet (other than wearing a constant supercilious sneer), but I am ever on my guard that he may, and careful not to allow him to catch me alone. Neither Jamie nor Bird are available to offer me much protection, as they are spending nearly every waking minute going over papers in Jamie's office, or meeting with land agents or surveyors—all to do with Wilsonville, or swamps in the South, and such.

My only consolation is that Mr. Iredell has recently returned from riding the Eastern Circuit and has already come to take tea with us twice. Poor man—he left home in January, when he was obliged to come North to attend the Supreme Court's February session, and will not be able to return until after the Court has concluded its session in August; and he fears that, unless the President appoints a Chief Justice soon, he will be assigned a fall Circuit as well, and the Lord knows when he will see his family again. That is, he *expresses* great distress over this state of affairs; and yet he is in such demand for dinners and parties and such that I cannot imagine he is suffering too terribly. Indeed, when I saw him at Mr. Bradford's house the other evening, he looked to be enjoying himself quite well, deeply engaged in conversation with a very attractive lady whose name I did not catch. And alas, when I invited him for dinner here this evening, he told me he was already engaged to dine at Major Butler's! But I managed to snare him for tomorrow evening, and I expect that, despite the pall cast by the presence of William, I shall have as amusing a time as I always do in his company.

From Robert Farmar to James Wilson:

July 16, 1795

... At your request [I] shall endeavor to give as full and ample description of the Lands at and adjoining Wilsonville as lies in my power from my residence there. At the upper and lower Falls there is Twenty two Houses & Shops, some of which are finished in a very neat manner. The End of the Factory that is erected is 8 feet Long, 42 feet wide—4 stories high ... The distance from the Factory to the Saw Mill at the upper Falls is one and a quarter mile...

[T]here is now every year upwards of 400 Tons cut of excellent Timothy at the Settlement, which is from 4 to 7 miles above the Factory—where there is Twenty-two Families settled, a number of whom have erected good frame houses & Large Barns ...

Thursday, July 16, 1795

Mr. Bradford came to the door this morning to see Jamie, and I was certain it was to inform him that the President had determined to nominate him as Chief Justice; and yet, in retrospect, his manner was so subdued that I suppose I should never have allowed my hopes to be raised in that fashion. And of course, once they emerged from Jamie's office, I could tell at once that whatever intelligence Mr. Bradford had come to communicate was far from welcome; Jamie's face was grim and set, his eyebrows drawn downwards towards the top of his nose. Mr. Bradford, for his part, looked eager to be on his way.

"I sincerely hope, Sir," I heard Mr. Bradford say as he took his leave, "that the President may nevertheless rely on the continuance of your invaluable service on the Court for many years to come."

Once the door was shut, and Jamie's back to me, I saw his shoulders suddenly sag in the most alarming way; and when at length he turned towards me I scanned his face for some clue as to what had transpired. He paused and glanced at me for a moment, his head shaking slightly.

"It's Rutledge," he said shortly, before retreating once more to his office and shutting the door. "If he chooses to accept the post, that is."

244

Since then he has let no one in and has refused to come out, not even for dinner; it is now going on five o'clock, and I begin to grow quite alarmed. I thought perhaps to send for Mr. Iredell, for surely he—being both a colleague and a loyal friend—would know what to say or do to offer Jamie some comfort; but then I considered that Jamie is more the sort of person who prefers to keep his disappointments to himself—even, alas, from me! Oh, how I wish he would allow me to go to him and rub his neck and kiss his cheek. I know what I would tell him: that surely he is far more deserving and qualified to be Chief Justice than this Mr. Rutledge; and that if the President is so unappreciative of his talents that he has seen fit to pass over him in this insulting manner, perhaps it is high time to resign his post as Associate Judge. For I believe it brings in precious little income—certainly far less than what Jamie can gain from his land dealings; and he is continually complaining that his judicial duties—the circuit riding and such—make it difficult for him to attend to his business affairs as he should.

The more I think about what the President has done, the more livid I become. I suppose that if Mr. Rutledge turns down the post, it will then be offered to Jamie; but he absolutely *must* not accept, not after the cavalier way he has been treated.

From William Bradford, Attorney General of the United States, to Samuel Bayard, Clerk of the United States Supreme Court (currently residing in England):

Philadelphia, Pennsylvania, July 16, 1795

... No appointment of Chief Justice is yet made—but Mr. Rutledge (Ch. Jus. of S. Carolina) will be the man if he inclines to accept it. Mr. Blair talks of resigning his seat—and I suspect Mr. Wilson will not continue long on the bench...

Saturday, July 18, 1795

Jamie appears to have made his peace with this insult to him, for better or for worse. When at last he came out of his office Thursday evening, he appeared entirely composed; and yesterday, when I asked him if he intended to resign, he replied that he had indeed considered such a step but decided against it. I began to protest, but he told me his mind was entirely made up: he had devoted his life to the law; and for all that he complained about the demands made on his time, there was no other post he would prefer to occupy. He even allowed that if Mr. Rutledge should decline the post of Chief Justice, and it were offered to him instead, he would accept it! He says I mustn't fret about his having sufficient time to attend to his business affairs, that he is quite capable of managing everything. Well, I suppose he is right, there; most men couldn't do half of what my husband does, nor do it half so well.

But William—oh, horrid William! He caught me in the tea room yesterday when I was alone there—so absorbed in reading *Ethelinde*, by Mrs. Smith, that I failed at first to notice him—and for reasons best known to himself decided to strike up a conversation. I would have found some excuse to leave, but the subject he chose was one so interesting to me that I could not tear myself away.

"All this gloom and doom," he exclaimed, stretching his long frame out in the wing chair, his hands clasped behind his head, "about a decision that I'm sure came as no surprise to most in this city."

I put down my book and drew myself up straight on the settee. "And to what do you refer, William?" I asked—though I had a pretty clear idea of the answer.

"Why, Rutledge's being preferred over Papa, of course. From what I've heard, Papa was never under serious consideration for that post."

I was stunned by his audacity, but within a moment collected myself sufficiently to tell him that he obviously had no idea what he was speaking of; that his father, being one of the most learned and eminent jurists in the country, and nearly the most senior of the Associate Judges, had every right to expect the appointment as Chief Justice.

William hesitated a moment before replying, resting his brow in his hand as though considering how to proceed. He then went to close the door to the parlor. I nearly protested, but was paralyzed by the fear that he was about to tell me something truly dire.

"I suppose," he said at last, "being so much in his thrall, it is well nigh impossible for you to imagine how others see your husband: rash, intemperate, self-important, consumed by greed and grandiose ambitions."

"How dare you say such things?" I sputtered. "My husband has many friends—many!—who hold him in the highest esteem, and"—

"But he has a number of enemies as well—you wouldn't know them, of course, as most of them don't call at the house and tip their hats to you and kiss your hand. But certainly the President, and those in his administration, are aware of them. And aware, as well, of how precarious my father's financial situation is, how dangerously he has overextended himself in his mad pursuit of land and more land."

William had risen from the chair and now strolled casually to the fireplace. There he rested an elbow on the mantlepiece, so that he loomed lazily over me as I sat on the settee, frozen in apprehension. "Perhaps, dear lady, you are unacquainted with the details of these transactions. You see, for some fraction of the purchase price, my father obtains a warrant for a tract of land and commences to have it surveyed, with the understanding that once the survey is done he will produce the balance of the money and buy the tract outright."

"Yes, he has told me"— I began defiantly, before William interrupted.

"But, before that first transaction has come to a close, some other alluring tract catches his eye. He must have it! He then buys the warrant for this second tract, perhaps borrowing the money and hoping that the proceeds from the first tract will pay the full cost of the second, when it comes due. But of course, all then depends on the first transaction proceeding swiftly and successfully. If it does not, the success of both is endangered—unless he borrows yet more."

William sighed as though contemplating the foibles of an incorrigible school boy. "Over and over again this pantomime repeats itself! Thousands upon thousands of acres—not only in this state, where his holdings already extend to near half a million acres, but now also in Virginia and North Carolina and God knows where else. And to finance it all, he's in debt well above his ears, to people all over the country—people who, like you, don't understand the true nature of his situation, and think to make their own fortunes by charging him ridiculous rates of interest. It's to the point where he's borrowing money to pay interest on other borrowed money. Do you really think a man who conducts himself in this manner is likely to be elevated to the highest judicial office in the land?"

I forced myself to repel these words, and the fears they engendered. I reminded myself that what William described was completely at odds with the picture Jamie has given me of his land dealings; when he tells me of them, which I admit is not often, he talks of "great opportunities," and "abundant success," and the time being ripe for action and such. Who was I to believe, then: this jealous scoundrel, or my own husband?

"You know nothing of his true situation!" I cried. "Why, there are many respectable gentlemen who invest in land as does your father. And it is owing to them—men like your father—that the country will become great, that our wildernesses will be populated and productive. Jamie has plans, schemes for settlement. He is"—I suddenly remembered Mr. Wallis's words to me—"a visionary!"

William let out a guffaw. "Believe that if you like, Madam. Oh, I know he has schemes—pamphlets being distributed in Holland and England, seeking investors and settlers, describing in vivid detail the fertile paradise that awaits those who cross the Atlantic. Milk and honey! Coal lying on the surface of the land for the picking! Apples dropping from the trees! If there are any in Europe so gullible as to believe such claptrap, just wait until they arrive and find themselves in swampland, or perhaps on some barren mountain-side, at the mercy of wild beasts and savage Indians who have no respect for a piece of paper purporting to establish title. As soon as word gets back about *that*, you can be sure there'll be no more boatloads of settlers arriving."

"But all this is mere invention on your part. How can you know the details of your father's business affairs?" There was little need for me to point out that the two hardly speak.

"Oh, Bird has provided me with the occasional tidbit. But much of this is common knowledge, my dear lady—the talk of the coffee houses." He smiled at me, almost kindly. "You appear alarmed—understandably, of course. You believed you were marrying one of the wealthiest men in the country, did you not? Take my advice and return to your family in Boston, before this house of cards comes crashing down on your head as well as his. It's not too late to repent of your mistake." His voice suddenly grew serious, and low. "Save yourself, madam."

I saw the ruse now: all this was merely an elaborate tale concocted to evict me from the house, and from the family. No doubt Polly was behind this, too, for she had never truly accepted me as her mother. To her and to William, I was still a presumptuous interloper—and the implication that I had married for mercenary reasons made my blood seethe.

"I have made no mistake," I spat at him. "It is *you* who are mistaken, sir. Not only do I dearly love my husband, but I believe in him with all my heart, and in his vision for this country. It is not I who should leave this house but *you*—for how, in good conscience, can you continue to help yourself to his food and lounge in his comfortable quarters when you hold him in such low esteem? No gentleman would be capable of such behavior."

I had thought to cut William to the quick with this, but he merely shrugged. "Remain blind then, if you insist, but never say you weren't warned." He then bowed and took his leave.

I have told myself repeatedly that most likely William is simply being malicious; no doubt he understands that it is through my doing that he was sent away. But it is an unfortunate coincidence that at the moment William sauntered into the tea-room I was engaged in reading a most affecting scene in *Ethelinde* set in a debtor's prison, and as a result my mind has busied itself in conjuring up all manner of horrors. In any event, I have resolved that the proper course of action, and the one most likely to provide me assurance, is to go to Jamie with William's accusations, and ask him directly if there is any truth to them.

From Edmund Randolph, Secretary of State, to George Washington:

Philadelphia, Pennsylvania, July 25, 1795

... The proposed nomination of Mr. Rutledge, tho' mentioned without reserve, is not known to have excited much, if any sensation, among his colleagues. But it is very seriously whispered that within these two months he is believed in Charleston to be deranged in his mind...

Tuesday, July 28, 1795

The newspapers *today* are certainly worth perusing! For—in the very same number that makes public the news of Mr. Rutledge's nomination—there is an account of a most extraordinary speech made by Mr. Rutledge in Charleston some ten days ago, denouncing Mr. Jay's treaty in the most intemperate language imaginable. The man actually had the temerity to say that he had rather the President would die than that he should sign that treaty! One might expect to hear such railing from the mobs in the streets, or even from some of the more vehement opponents of the treaty in Congress; but from the man whom the President has just nominated as his Chief Justice? He has surely bitten clean through the hand that would feed him; and, I should think, grievously injured his own reputation and prospects as well. For this intelligence will be taken as proof that the reports that have circulated in this city recently—whispers that Mr. Rutledge has become insane, and overly fond of his bottle—are far more than idle gossip.

"Well," I said to Jamie and Bird, as we all three leaned over *Dunlap's Daily Advertiser*, our mouths agape, "I imagine the President regrets his choice now!"

"Indeed," said Bird, stroking at his chin, "perhaps he will withdraw the nomination. For it would be a great embarrassment to allow it to go through."

"Yes, perhaps," remarked Jamie, straightening up and crossing his arms before his chest in a manner that bespoke satisfaction. "But if it be too late for that, the Senate will surely refuse to approve it, when they return. Either way, I'm afraid old Rutledge is dead in the water."

"Ah, so you're *afraid*, are you?" I cried, poking him playfully in the ribs—for his voice betrayed anything but fear. "*Afraid? Afraid* that you might be called upon to take his place?"

"Now, Nannie!" Jamie gaily fended off my pokes, and I allowed him to wrestle me into an embrace. "Don't you start counting your chickens, my lass."

"But it's *your* chickens I'm counting, dearest, and I'm quite certain they'll all hatch," I teased, and kissed him smartly on the lips.

I fear we embarrassed Bird with our high spirits, for when I turned to ask him his opinion, he had gone quite red in the face and left us, saying that he had some urgent business to attend to. Really, he can be a bit of a prude sometimes.

Well, no matter—nothing can dampen my spirits today. For not only is it certain that Mr. Rutledge will be sent packing, but William took his leave of us today as well. I at last mustered the courage to speak to Jamie about what William had said of his finances, several days after that awful conversation, and I'm extremely pleased that I did. For Jamie explained it all to me quite clearly, and I am now entirely reassured: he said that of course he was in debt to some extent, that anyone embarking on a land scheme of a decent size was required to go into debt, but that the eventual profits will certainly far exceed what he has borrowed. It was merely a question of time, and patience, and—most importantly,

Jamie said—of not losing one's nerve. When others are panicking and beginning to sell off their lands (as it seems some other investors are commencing to do)—that is when the wise investor snaps up bargains, even if he is obliged to borrow a great deal of money to do so.

And when I confessed to him that my fevered brain had entertained alarming visions of debtor's prison, he threw back his head and laughed, and said it would never come to *that*, for he knew how to manage his affairs. And even if some creditor were to prove unreasonable (for he says the law concerning debt is in a sorry state, and much in need of reform), there is still no cause for anxiety; for, being a judge, he is accorded a privilege against that sort of arrest. Well, that *was* a relief to me. And now that I understand, I'm of course entirely opposed to his giving up his seat on the court—especially now that it once again looks likely he will become Chief Justice.

Of course Jamie was quite vexed with William for worrying me needlessly—and for casting such aspersions on his own father's character. Jamie gave the lad a good talking-to, and I flatter myself we won't be burdened with his company again for quite some time.

From Edmund Randolph, Secretary of State, to George Washington:

Philadelphia, Pennsylvania, July 29, 1795

... The newspapers present all the intelligence which has reached me relative to the treaty. Dunlap's of yesterday morning conveys the proceedings of Charleston. The conduct of the intended Chief Justice is so extraordinary, that Mr. Wolcott and Col. Pickering conceive it to be proof of the imputation of insanity...

From William Bradford, Jr., Attorney General, to Alexander Hamilton:

Philadelphia, Pennsylvania, August 4, 1795

... The crazy speech of Mr. Rutledge, joined to certain information that he is daily sinking into debility of mind & body, will probably

prevent him [from] receiving the appointment I mentioned to you. But should he come to Philadelphia for that purpose, as he has been invited to do—& especially if he should resign his present Office, the embarrassment of the President will be extreme. But if he is disordered in mind in the manner that I am informed he is, there can be but one course of procedure…

Wednesday, August 12, 1795

So—Mr. Rutledge has at last found the nerve to take his seat as Chief Justice, a full ten days after the Supreme Court's session officially began! Were I the subject of so much drawing-room gossip, and round condemnation in the highest offices of government, I should certainly have kept my distance from the Capital. I attended at the Court today and found it quite crowded with the curious, hoping for a look at the man who has occasioned so much scandal; but Mr. Rutledge appeared quite unperturbed by the gazes and whispers. Either he is a gentleman of uncommon fortitude, or else just as mad as the rumors would have it, and entirely oblivious of the controversy that swirls about him.

In any event, it is generally agreed that once the Senate returns—which, alas, is a full four months from now—they will waste little time in giving the negative to his nomination. The only advantage I can see from this delay is that Mr. Rutledge will most likely be assigned a circuit to ride this fall—or so Mr. Iredell hopes. He paid us a call this evening, and expects that, thanks to Mr. Rutledge's appointment, he will be able to return to Edenton as soon as the Court adjourns and then spend several months at home with his family. Ah, but their gain is indeed my loss! The more I see the gentleman, the fonder I grow of him.

Monday, September 28, 1795

Alas, alas, I know not what to do—I am in hopes that if I set down my disordered thoughts on paper, it will bring me some relief from the unceasing agitation of my brain.

In short, it has happened again—I am with child. I am quite sure this time, for I distinctly recall the peculiar sensation in the belly that attended me when last I found myself in this condition. There is nothing else quite like it. Still, I have been for some time able to delude myself that it was nothing, to convince myself that what I felt was no more than the product of a morbid imagination. But now that a month has passed without nature taking its usual course, I can no longer keep up this game of pretend. It is real, it is true: a child is growing in my belly, and if I do nothing to interfere I will most likely find myself brought to bed of it seven or eight months from now.

Seven or eight months!—it sounds so long a time. And yet, if I am to act, I must do so speedily. I know that to delay is dangerous in cases of this kind. But when I think on last time—the penny royal, the river of blood flowing from my body, the unbearable feelings that followed—I lose all resolve.

No, no—I must go through with it, I have no choice, even if I go to my death as a result. I shall pray daily to God to spare me—Bird will help me to pray, I am sure. I am but twenty-one, surely He will have mercy on me. But alas, my Aunt Lucy was not much older than that when she died in childbirth. I wonder—would it be sinful to pray for a disappointment to occur—by accident, of course? Ah, silly me, of course it would, I mustn't think that way. But perhaps it will happen all the same.

Saturday, October 31, 1795

Jamie returned from holding court in Delaware yesterday afternoon, and we made our announcement about the expected child last night at supper. Emily clapped her hands and bobbed in her chair and promised to help look after it; Polly showed the sweet side of her nature, rising to give each of us a kiss on the cheek and wishing us joy; Charles echoed her wish without much enthusiasm and then asked if he might be excused from finishing his boiled potatoes.

Only Bird seemed rather subdued; was there some muted melancholy to his expressions of congratulation, or did I merely imagine it? I have tried my best to maintain a certain coolness towards him, and to treat him more as a parent than as a friend. But really, it is nearly impossible—especially these past few weeks, when Jamie has been away or occupied with his land schemes (Mr. Thomas, who is Jamie's lawyer in these matters, has been here frequently), and Mr. Iredell no longer here to amuse me. I have been to visit Lucy Breck and Mrs. Bingham and all my other friends, and really endeavored to keep myself out of Bird's way. But here he is, right in the house, and apparently eager for my company; and I *am* so fond of him.

What I must do, really, is to find some young lady who might become the appropriate object of his interest and affections. I shall keep my eyes open at all the balls and teas and such, for a likely candidate. That is, if this wretched pregnancy will allow me to go out in society—for alas, I have felt rather unwell of late.

From George Meade, Philadelphia Merchant, to Theophilus Cazenove, General Agent of the Holland Land Company:

Philadelphia, Pennsylvania, November 20, 1795

... [T]he present is on the Subject of the 110,000 Acres of Land I bought ... James Wilson, Esq., has done everything in the business that a man of honor ought not to have done ...

I do not mean to give you the Smallest offense, but I shall ever have my opinion of Judge Wilson ...

Wednesday, December 16, 1795

Hurrah! Mr. Bingham has just come by to tell us that the Senate have at last voted down Mr. Rutledge's nomination. Why they were so long about it I don't know, for they've already been in session a full week.

My health has improved, and I seem to have passed unscathed through what the doctor says is the most uncertain time for a pregnancy. He says I must expect a May birth. I have confessed my apprehensions to Bird—indeed, he is the only one who knows the full extent of them, for he has a way of drawing me out by saying little and looking quietly sympathetic—and he has been exceedingly good to me, praying and talking with me nearly every day. Really, I don't know what I should do without him, now that Jamie has grown even more distracted by his business affairs. It's most vexing: I've been forced to attend quite a few social events alone, because he refused to be pried out of his office; and last week he insisted that I put off a dinner party that I had planned, saying he simply couldn't take the time. Indeed, he's looked so grim of late that I was put in mind of those things that William said, and asked

Jamie whether there was any cause to worry; but he assured me that all was in order, and that it was merely a question of obtaining some short-term credit—or some such, I forget the exact phrase.

So I shall let Jamie concern himself with his finances, as he tells me I ought, for I have other matters to preoccupy me. Indeed, I have been a little melancholy since yesterday, when Lucy Breck came to call. Not that she did anything deliberately to cause me grief—dear girl, I cannot imagine she would ever do *that*; but only that she spoke of Boston, and Mama and my sisters, in such affectionate terms that it made me quite nostalgic for them.

"And I suppose, my dear, that your mother will be coming to attend at your confinement?" she said, her brown eyes serious and wide. "And Sarah and Lucy as well, perhaps? Oh, it will be such a joy for me to see them again."

Well, of course I had written to them concerning the pregnancy, but I had said nothing of their coming; and I was suddenly seized with such an overpowering desire to see them that I nearly threw poor Lucy out of the house in order to get at my pen and paper. Oh, I do pray that Mama, at least, will be able to come! I sometimes think that should the worst befall me in childbirth, I would never see their faces again. I have neglected them terribly, writing only the odd letter here and there, and putting off all their inquiries about visits. I don't know why—perhaps I felt that if they were to come here, my old life would in some manner invade the new, and I should be reduced to a child again instead of the mistress of my own fine and elegant household. I wonder if something like that may be the reason Jamie generally refuses even to speak of his family in Scotland—as though to do so would strip from him all the layers of learning and accomplishment that he has piled upon himself in this country, and reveal underneath—like the humble, wrinkled pit at the center of a plump, ripe fruit—the modest farm boy he once was.

From G.K. Taylor, Richmond Merchant, to James Wilson:

Richmond, Virginia, January 30, 1796

... Some weeks have elapsed since I received the mortifying notification that the bill drawn on you for one thousand dollars was protested for non-payment...

When I was last in Philadelphia, I delivered to you a list of the lands purchased in the Dismal swamp under our contract, and received your assurance that exertions should be made to meet the demands. On my return I made similar assurances to the seller, by which they have been hitherto kept in a state of discontented inaction. But the blow can be no longer averted—a whole tempest of Law is ready to burst on my head, and will overwhelm my fortune and my reputation unless you exert yourself to shelter me from the storm...

You will recollect, sir, that when we were about entering into this business, the question was frequently propounded to you, "Are you certain that your funds will enable you to go through with this contract?" The answer was invariably, positively, & with confidence, in the affirmative... I know that your resources are immense, and that you are able at any time to exonerate yourself from a breach of contract, and us from disgrace...

In fine, Sir, I shall be in Philadelphia about the twentieth of the next month, from whence I must not venture to return unless this business be beneficially adjusted. I trust that by that time you will so have arranged it as to satisfy yourself and us ...

From the *Aurora* (Philadelphia, Pennsylvania):

February 3, 1796

Letter from an Anonymous Correspondent in Charleston, South Carolina, January 9, 1796:

"About ten days since Judge RUTLEDGE attempted to drown himself. I was at the spot when he was taken from the water. Two Negroes saw him jump in and ran to his assistance. He damned them for rescuing him. I believe he was a little insane. *About a week afterwards we heard of his appointment being negatived by the Senate"* ...

Thursday, February 18, 1796

I have of late been experiencing a discomforting degree of uneasiness and melancholy, such that it has interfered with my slumber.

256

Indeed, I have on several occasions resorted to a few teaspoonfuls of laudanum, which I purchased at the apothecary's, and have found it most helpful (although Mrs. Nice *will* cluck her tongue at me, and mutter about how it contains opium, and I should be careful not to become too fond of it—really, she has become quite brazen about expressing her opinions). Even the presence of Mr. Iredell, who is in the city this month to attend the Supreme Court, hasn't been enough to lift my spirits.

I suppose the inexorable approach of my confinement has much to do with my difficulties—only three more months until what may be the end of my sojourn on this earth! There are times when I look about me, studying the faces of Jamie and Bird and the children, gazing at the objects in my bedroom—my ruby earrings and necklace, my pale blue silk gown that lies in the clothes press—and think on how I may not be here, among all that I love, four months from now. And I cannot be sure that I will ever see my dear Mama again, for she has written to say that—although of course she very much wants to be with me at my confinement—her health has suffered a great deal this winter and she cannot promise that she will be strong enough to come.

But that is not all that troubles me, for we still have heard nothing from the President concerning Jamie's appointment as Chief Justice. Of course he was obliged to offer the post first to Mr. Cushing, the most senior Judge; but the old man turned it down a good two weeks ago, as all expected, and still the President has made no move to propose a replacement.

And, though I have tried my hardest to follow Jamie's instructions and not concern myself about his land schemes and his finances, I cannot help but worry—especially after what Bird told me yesterday. That lawyer, Mr. Thomas, and a number of others have been here so frequently, and Jamie has been so distracted and irritable, that yesterday, unable to bear it any more, I asked Bird if anything was amiss.

Bird at first said nothing—merely reddened slightly and tugged at the hair at the back of his head, which he is apt to do when he is nervous. He said that his Papa had forbidden him to discuss these matters with anyone—including myself!—but at last he revealed to me that certain creditors have become quite troublesome of late. One in particular—a Mr. Taylor of Richmond, who is expected to arrive in the city within the next few days—has threatened public denunciation, and perhaps worse, if Jamie did not satisfy his demand. Such has been the cause of Jamie's meetings, and hurried comings and goings: despite being much occupied with Court business, he has been attempting to raise sufficient money to appease Mr. Taylor.

"But please don't upset yourself over this—I'm sure Papa will manage to patch it all together at the last minute," Bird finished earnestly. "He always does, somehow."

I suspected that the dear boy was saying this only because he wanted to relieve my anxieties. I suppose he could tell that I still had my doubts, because he immediately added that Jamie had just gone out to see Mr. Allison and Mr. Blount. Bird told me something I had not known, that they are Jamie's partners in this Dismal Swamp scheme of which I have heard mention—a plan that seems, indeed, to have taken quite a dismal turn.

"These men," Bird said as he pressed my hand reassuringly, "Blount and Allison—they are in a position to avail themselves of certain funds, and I'm quite certain they will assist Papa. For if they do not, their own reputations and credit will be endangered as well."

This did serve to provide me some reassurance, for men's self-interest is ever to be better trusted than their generosity. I kissed Bird's cheek and assured him that my anxiety was greatly assuaged (and as well, of course, that I would breathe a word to no one of what he had revealed to me). Indeed, for a time I did feel much calmer; but last night—alone in bed, with Jamie still bent over the desk in his office, toiling over the Lord knows what—I found again I could not sleep.

From Samuel Johnston to James Iredell:

Williamston, North Carolina, February 27, 1796

... I am sorry that Mr. Cushing refused the office of Chief Justice, as I don't know whether a less exceptionable character can be obtained without passing over Mr. Wilson, which would perhaps be a measure which could not be easily reconciled to strict propriety ...

From James Iredell to Hannah Iredell:

Philadelphia, Pennsylvania, March 4, 1796

... I this moment have read in a News-Paper, <u>that Mr. Ellsworth is nominated our Chief Justice</u>, in consequence of which I think it not

unlikely that <u>Wilson</u> will resign. But this is only my own conjecture, and therefore I wish you not to mention it.

Friday, March 4, 1796

I am thoroughly shocked, and poor Jamie is shut up once again in his study: Senator Oliver Ellsworth, says the newspaper, is to be nominated Chief Justice!

I almost pleaded again with Jamie to resign from the Court—but stopped myself, remembering what he had told me about being privileged from arrest for debt. Not that it will ever come to that, of course, but still, one doesn't like to take a risk. And I cannot help but wonder whether vicious rumors about Jamie's speculations have played some part in the President's passing over him, twice now. Is Jamie—are *we*—being whispered about in drawing rooms and coffee houses? I am grateful, for once, that my present condition has limited my excursions into society, for I shouldn't like to be stared at.

Well, never mind, I tell myself: when Jamie's schemes have all borne fruit, surely his name will be on everyone's lips for quite different reasons. Wilsonville alone is growing rapidly, Jamie tells me, and there are plans afoot for new houses, and new mills; he has even installed, in the cloth mill, an ingenious machine that will print patterns on fabric. Let them scoff; someday, years from now, Wilsonville will be a city to rival Philadelphia—and Mr. Ellsworth will be but a marginal note in the history books.

From John Adams to Abigail Adams:

Philadelphia, Pennsylvania, March 5, 1796

...Yesterday Mr. Ellsworth's Nomination was consented to as Chief Justice...It will give a Stability to the Government ...to place a Man of his Courage, Constancy, fortitude, and Capacity in that situation...Mr. Wilson's ardent Speculations had given offense to some ...

Friday, March 25, 1793

I have been anxiously looking for Mama these past two weeks, for when she last wrote she said she felt well enough to come, and thought to arrive in the middle of March, so as to have ample time to help prepare me for my confinement. And so yesterday afternoon, when Emily came running up the stairs to tell me that a carriage had stopped outside our door, and a lady was descending from it, I at once began conjuring before me that kind and anxious face, whereon expressions of happiness and concern for my condition should be jostling for primacy. When at last I heard footsteps and voices approaching, the smile of welcome was already at my lips, the tears of joy brimming at my eyelids.

But there before me, when at last the door was opened, was not Mama at all, but Sarah—her face pale, her eyes wide, looking about her as though calculating the cost of the damask drapery and the Oriental carpet.

"Mama is not here," Sarah said flatly, no doubt in response to the disappointment she discerned in my expression. "She wished very much to come, but her health was still too uncertain—I told her she mustn't think of making such a journey. So she sent me in her stead."

I began to weep; Sarah looked pained, and brought her little finger to her teeth (aha, I thought through my distress, so she still bites at her nails); Polly, who had accompanied her up the stairs, said something about attending to Charles and fled the room.

"I'm sorry, Nannie," Sarah said, sitting at the edge of the bed. "I know I'm not the one you wished for. But really, Mama is in no condition for such a journey—the roads are quite abominable, and the accommodation even worse. Lucy is still too young to travel on her own, and Mama needed one of us to stay at home. So it was me or no one."

I swallowed hard and wiped at my wet cheeks with the sleeve of my dressing gown. "Of course I'm glad to see you, my dear. It's just that … I had *expected* Mama. And she knows—well, things that you don't—about bearing children and such."

"Ah, no need to worry about that." Sarah's sharp features relaxed somewhat. "Mama wrote down instructions for me." She began fumbling in a small satchel that she had carried into the room and brought out a piece of paper bearing a familiar script. "Let's see, I'm to rub your skin with olive oil … administer castor oil as a cathartic … *cheerful* conversation only"—she looked up and gave me the briefest of smiles—"rub the infant with lard and then rinse with lukewarm water and old soap." She caught sight of the bottle of laudanum on the table next to my bed and frowned. "And it says *no* ardent spirits, tinctures, or essences."

Now I was beginning to feel cross—just as it used to be at home, with Sarah ordering me about—or trying to. I regretted ever having asked for any of them to attend at my confinement. "Really, Sarah, I'm sure there's no need for all that. I'm under the care of a doctor—Dr. Shippen, who has been recommended to me by my friend Mrs. Bingham—Mrs. William Bingham, that is, I imagine you've heard of her. Dr. Shippen attends all the finest ladies in Philadelphia and employs the most modern methods, and he has said nothing to me of olive oil, or lard, or such—are you sure that was not a *recipe* that Mama gave you?"

"Well, all right then." Her lips pressed together, she rose from the bed, folded the paper, and began to return it to her satchel. "It was *you* who brought up the subject, not I. If this Dr. Shippen has more *fashionable* ideas, I'm sure I won't presume to contradict him. But I'll leave you now—you must be tired, and I'm sure I am. Polly said she would show me the room where I'm to stay—she seems an amiable young lady." She turned to go, and I did nothing to stop her.

Ah well, I shall try to make the best of it; Sarah is better than no one, I suppose. I have been a little lonely, of late, what with Jamie so busy—first with Court business and now that the session is over, with his business affairs. And he has kept Bird occupied nearly every waking hour as well.

I know—I shall have a small dinner party tomorrow night, in Sarah's honor, with Lucy and Hannah Breck—and Mr. Iredell, if he is free; for he will be leaving for Carolina, now that the Court is over, not to return until it meets again in August. And who can tell—with "the happy event" looming before me—whether I shall still be on this earth then, to greet him?

Tuesday, April 12, 1796

I know not whether to be alarmed at what has just transpired. A man by the name of Mr. Leiper has been by to "look at" the house, apparently with a view to buying it! Not that we will be forced to move out, fortunately; the plan is that he will then rent it back to us. Jamie presented it all as though it were nothing out of the ordinary: Mr. Leiper simply finds himself with excess cash, he said, and is searching for a suitable investment; whilst Jamie is in need of cash at the moment, and will use the money he gets from the sale of the house to pay off certain debts and complete certain purchases of land. Eventually, when Jamie's

261

various investments bear fruit, we will simply purchase the house back from Mr. Leiper—or perhaps buy an even grander one.

Well, it does sound simple enough, when Jamie explains it; and yet it was awkward to have Mr. Leiper here, tapping at the walls and trying the windows, while Sarah was looking on. At last I suggested that we take a ride in the coach, in order to get away from the man—who was quite an unappealing creature, with a protruding stomach and rolls of fat under the chin, despite the expensive lace at his cuffs. He must have satisfied himself that the place was a sound investment, for by the time we returned the business had all been concluded, and Jamie said he'd obtained quite a decent amount. Still, I shall rest easier when we've bought it back.

All seems so uncertain, despite Jamie's assurances, that I wonder what sense it makes to bring another child into this family. And Jamie, despite his protestations of happiness when I first told him the news, seems nearly to have forgotten that he is to become a father again. Ah, why do I endanger my own life to produce a child that no one appears to want, that may only be an additional burden? I should have found the courage to remedy the situation while it was still possible. But there is no turning back now, of course: I am astride that runaway horse, as in that dream I had long ago, galloping madly towards the cliff that stands but a few feet ahead.

Thursday, May 26, 1796

So—I have not been dashed lifeless on the cliff, though my body is as bruised and aching as though I had been. The child was born two weeks since, on May the 12th—a boy, whom we have called Henry, though he has not yet been christened. He is a red-faced, scrawny infant who spends most of his waking hours crying in the most alarming manner. I have told the wet nurse, Susannah, to keep him as far from my room as possible, for I must have my rest; and yet his cries are audible throughout the house. Jamie professes to be delighted to have another son, but I notice that he spends as little time as possible at home these days. I do not know, in truth, what I feel for the child, for the sensation that overwhelms me is one of relief—relief that I am yet alive, and (so the doctor tells me) likely to enjoy a complete recovery.

"Ah, Mrs. Wilson," Dr. Shippen said jovially at his last visit, "your constitution is sound enough, and your bones so arranged, that you may easily have ten more children with no ill effect."

Good Lord! I thought (though I only smiled at him politely), I should do away with myself this instant if I thought I were to bear ten more. For, despite the doctor's assurances that my delivery was an easy and uneventful one, it is an experience of which I dread any repetition. Even to recall it now makes me cringe: unbearable pain, massive quantities of blood, such screams escaping me that I afterwards was hoarse for days. And through it all, such fear and terror that I was nearly out of my mind; I believe (although the memory is hazy) that I clutched at my sister, who stood by the head of my bed, and begged her over and over again to assure me that all would be well. And this she did, with a tenderness that I had not heard in her voice before—nor, indeed, since.

Though she has been her usual chilly self towards me of late, she has exhibited great affection towards her new nephew. Between Sarah and Polly, who also appears charmed by the child, he does not lack for attention. Just as I cannot understand their delight in him, they appear not to understand my own aversion. Polly is too polite, or perhaps too timid, to say anything to me directly on the subject, but I see her disapproval in the glances she sends my way when the child is offered to me—bawling and kicking—and I decline to hold him. And Sarah, of course, has felt free to chide me, even going so far as to accuse me of being "unnatural." Sarah will be leaving for home in a few weeks' time, and—although at times her presence has been a comfort, and she has made herself useful writing letters to announce the birth and such—I shall not be entirely sorry to see her go.

Only Emily—Emily, who clapped her hands with joy at the announcement that a child was to be born—appears to have feelings in sympathy with my own.

"He isn't at all what I thought he would be," she said to me a few days ago, while she perched on the edge of my bed and brushed out my hair. "He doesn't really do anything but cry."

She looked at me guiltily, as though she expected a reprimand for such a remark—for Polly or Mrs. Nice surely would have administered one. I said nothing, but she seemed to take my silence itself as a rebuke, or at least an invitation to soften her words.

"Still," she added without great conviction, "I expect he will get better, in time."

Indeed, I hope he will, for—despite what Sarah believes—I am no monster. I should *like* to be a good mother to him, if I can. The truth is, he frightens me. I had not thought a mother could be frightened of her own child, but there it is; I cannot help it.

From James Iredell to Sarah Gray:

Richmond, Virginia, June [7], 1796

... You really conferred upon me a very great and pleasing obligation by attending so kindly to my anxiety for the fate of your sister as to inform me of the birth of her son, and that they were in such good health. I sincerely rejoice in an event which must make the whole family and all her friends so happy. I offer my warmest congratulations.

The only abatement of satisfaction I felt in reading the letter you did me the honor to write arose from the information that you were so soon to go to Boston, so that I fear it may be a long time before I shall again have the pleasure of seeing you. It is one of the painful circumstances attending the life I lead that I form many agreeable acquaintances whose society is dear to me, and from whom I part with an uncertainty of ever seeing them again. My disposition is not such that I can feel such a situation with indifference...

Thursday, July 21, 1796

There has been such horrid commotion in this house of late that I almost cannot bear it. Yesterday Mr. Wallis came by—I was glad to see him, as he had not been here in some months, but I could tell almost immediately that something was amiss. For though he was polite to me as always, there was a darkness to his brow that was not usually in evidence. And then, after he went into Jamie's office, I heard such terrible shouting and swearing. It was quite distressing, for Jamie and Mr. Wallis have always been such good friends. After about ten minutes he emerged and—scarcely saying goodbye, and not even inquiring after Henry—strode quickly out the door.

I later learned that Jamie owes Mr. Wallis a good deal of money, and Mr. Wallis—even though he is aware of the difficult financial situation in which Jamie now finds himself, and the near impossibility of his obtaining further credit or even raising cash through the sale of lands—says he will wait no longer for satisfaction. Other gentlemen have been here in recent days as well, some of whom I recognize and some of whom I don't, and I have heard other angry voices from behind the closed door of Jamie's office. Often Mr. Thomas, the lawyer, is here to meet with them, and raises his own voice on Jamie's behalf.

It seems that Mr. Thomas has taken Mr. Wallis's place in Jamie's affections; Jamie speaks very highly of his character, and his legal skills, and certainly Mrs. Thomas, whom I have met on several occasions, is an amiable lady. But there is something about the man I find unsettling—his eyes, when he is speaking to me, rarely meet my own, but seem to dart about the room; and they slope downward at the outer edges, so that he ever appears simultaneously fatigued and anxious. There is a guardedness, a watchfulness to him, as though only one part of his mind is fixed on the conversation, and the other off who knows where. Perhaps that is what makes a good lawyer, being able to run one's mind on two entirely separate paths, but indeed it does not make for pleasant social intercourse.

We have been forced to make some economies these past few weeks. The elegant carriage with the red interior—the one in which Jamie squired me about Boston so long ago—has had to be sold, and we are making do with a simple chaise with but two horses. I was exceedingly sorry to see the carriage go (although I told Jamie that it made no difference), but it could not be helped—we were already two months behind in paying the rent to Mr. Leiper. And I would so like a new gown—I saw a pattern-book from London at Mrs. Bingham's that contained the most charming styles—but Jamie says that I must be patient and wait until we can afford it. Ah, well—now that so many people are experiencing difficulties, we receive fewer invitations, and so I have less call for fashionable gowns. At least I still have my ruby necklace and earrings, even if at present I haven't anyplace to wear them.

I must add a few words about Henry, to whom I have become—to my great surprise, and perhaps that of some others—quite attached. He is now over two months of age, cries very little, and has the most enchanting smile—which he bestows on me more than anyone else! He somehow seems to understand that I (and not Susannah, the wet nurse) am his mother, and he often looks upon me with an expression of wondering adoration in his round brown eyes. Indeed, he has grown to look remarkably like his father, and at times when he gazes upon me in that way, I am reminded of how Jamie once gazed upon me, almost as worshipfully—before he grew so distracted by warrants and titles and suits in ejectment and such. When I feel anxious about the shouts from Jamie's office, I need only cradle Henry in my arms, and bask in his sweet glow, and I am warmed by a mantle of innocence and calm. Until he begins to cry, of course, and then I send for Susannah to come and take him.

Monday, August 1, 1796

This morning the Supreme Court opened, and yesterday afternoon Mr. Iredell joined us for tea. He made a great fuss over Henry, when Susannah brought him into the parlor (I can see that he must be a doting father), and was considerate enough to say nothing about our financial situation, although I warrant he has heard the gossip. Nor did he remark on the disappearance of the mahogany side table in the dining room, or the gilt looking-glass in the front hall, or any of the other items Jamie has determined we must sell. He is far too kind a gentleman to bring up such unpleasant matters, and certainly too kind to take any glee in them—which is more than I can say for others in this city.

Oh, it is all too terrible! When I enter a parlor or tea room these days, I am keenly aware of a hush falling, and meaningful glances exchanged. I certainly shall not show my face at the Supreme Court this session—bad enough that Jamie must sit so conspicuously on the bench. Three days ago I called at Mrs. Bingham's and was told that she was not at home—though I'm *quite* sure I saw her face at an upstairs window. Why, *her* situation would not be so different from my own, had her elder daughter not recently made an exceedingly advantageous marriage to Alexander Baring, of the London banking family. (Ah Polly, why could you not have been the sort that would attract, and accept, a wealthy husband in order to please your Papa?) Only the Brecks—Lucy and Hannah, my childhood playmates—have continued to receive me with what appears to be sincere hospitality and genuine warmth. How I regret that I never was able to extend them an invitation to a really grand dinner; now—or at least, for the moment—it is impossible.

Edward Burd, Philadelphia Lawyer, to his Brother-in-Law, Jasper Yeates, Associate Justice of the Pennsylvania Supreme Court:

Philadelphia, Pennsylvania, August 4, 1796

... Ruin is staring in the faces of most of the Land Speculators. The Day of reckoning is at hand, and no prospect of disposing of their Lands. There are a great number of Judgements against your friend Wilson lately confessed by him. People speak very freely as to the Situation he is likely to be in very shortly...

James Iredell to James Wilson:

Richmond, Virginia, August 20, 1796

... I never expect to hear in a letter from you how you or your Family are—but I assure you I shall always be solicitous to know, and shall feel real satisfaction in hearing favorable accounts, whenever I have an opportunity of knowing. You will oblige me in presenting my very respectful Compliments to Mrs. Wilson, Miss Emily, and your Sons ... The youngest has my wishes ... for his happiness, as he possesses no small share of my admiration...

Wednesday, September 21, 1796

Things are no better—I daily expect some disaster to befall us. Elsewhere they may talk of the election—for the President has rebuffed all efforts to convince him to stay in office for a third term, and I suppose Mr. Adams will succeed him—but I have no patience for such matters any more. I haven't even attempted to read a newspaper in weeks. It all seems so trivial, so remote from all that is important in my own life. Perhaps that is selfish of me, but when one is poised at the brink of a yawning abyss, I suppose selfishness is a natural consequence.

What has most distressed me is Henry—for we have had to let Susannah go. She insisted on staying on for a few days with no wages, in order to try to wean the child; she kept shaking her head and saying, poor babe, not even five months and taken off the breast. We tried fresh new milk, mixed with a little stale bread, but he would have none of it, refusing both a tea-spoon and a bottle rigged with a heifer's teat. At last she said she must go, that she had obtained another position—and that perhaps in any event he would be more willing when she was out of his sight, for as long as he saw her he naturally expected to nurse. She left us tearfully, and with many instructions as to Henry's future nourishment.

But he went a full day—a long, seemingly endless day of tears and failed experiments—refusing all that I offered, only issuing wails and screams that, much to my alarm, grew increasingly weaker. Polly and Emily and Mrs. Nice tried to be of help, but yesterday morning I shooed them all from the nursery, thinking that I might get on better with Henry if it were only the two of us. I held him close, and he ceased his crying to look up at me, his wet, uncomprehending eyes an accusation: why do you starve me so? I whispered to him that he *must* eat or drink, that Susannah was gone and not returning—but of course he only began wailing again within a few seconds.

Then, in desperation, I unbuttoned my own bosom—oh, I knew better than to expect milk to flow from my breasts, of course, but I could not think what else to do, and I hoped to provide the child with some comfort, if not nourishment. He stared at me in surprise for a moment, then—when I held him to my breast—began to suck with great eagerness and desperation. It was an odd sensation, part pleasurable and part painful, but I had not much time to consider it, for Henry very shortly realized that my breast was but dry and barren and useless. And then such a wail escaped his tiny mouth as to dwarf all that had come before, his face bright red and his whole body appearing to be consumed by disappointment and anguish. And I wept as well, for my utter inability to give him what he needed so urgently—the one thing a mother should, by the grace of nature, be able to provide. Dr. Shippen advised me to nurse the babe myself, but of course—then, in the state that I was in—I paid him no mind. And now it is too late, too late.

Polly came running after Henry's ferocious cry, to see what was the matter, and found us both in tears, my bosom uncovered. She immediately understood the situation, and, to my surprise, embraced me and told me gently that I mustn't blame myself, that we must call the doctor—babies were weaned every day without incident, and Henry would be too. I clung to her and said, through my sobs, that we hadn't any money to pay the doctor.

"I have something I could sell, that should fetch a pretty sum," she said quietly. "A ring, that I got from my mother."

This only made me weep the more. "Oh, no, Polly, you mustn't!" I cried. "If anyone is to sell jewelry, it should be me."

Polly said there would be time to arrange all that later, that the doctor would come without asking for payment in advance. Indeed, when Dr. Mease came he was good enough to look unconcerned when we told him we would have to send his payment on later, although I imagine he had his doubts. He gave Henry three drops of laudanum, for he said that the child was in too nervous a state to be cajoled into embracing the bottle; and, in the drowsy stupor that then ensued, Henry did at last allow himself to be coaxed into sucking at the heifer's teat for a few minutes before he fell asleep, exhausted.

So grateful and relieved was I that, tears coursing down my cheeks, I ran to fetch my ruby earrings from the trunk in my bedroom, and pressed them on Dr. Mease—but he refused, saying they were certainly worth far more than any payment he was entitled to, and that he would send his bill in a few days. He seemed rather alarmed at my own condition, for he prescribed fifteen drops of laudanum for myself; he said we might give Henry more of it as well, but only if it proved necessary to induce him to take nourishment.

When Henry woke this morning he took the bottle after only a little protest, but he did not take much from it—and then he brought up most or all of what he had taken. Mrs. Nice said we mustn't worry, that he will adjust in time. But he still looks so frighteningly weak and pale.

Jamie knows there was something amiss, but not the extent of it—he was out when the doctor came, and I thought it wasn't necessary to tell him, for he has more than adequate troubles at present. Just as he often chooses not to burden me with the details of *his* difficulties, so I shall not burden him with mine.

Thursday, September 29, 1796

What I have feared so long for Jamie has happened—and is now past—and I pray the Lord that no one has heard anything of it, for it all came about and was done with so quickly.

He went out after dinner three days ago, on his way to a meeting at Mr. Thomas's, and when he had not returned by dusk I began to grow rather anxious. Bird insisted there was no reason to worry—that most likely the meeting had been a long one, or had adjourned to a tavern—but I could discern some alarm in his voice as well. At last, when we were all at supper (or rather, the others were; I was pacing the room with Henry, for he continues rather out of sorts), a knock came at the door. Bird ran to answer it, the rest of us watching from the hall.

It was a ragged young fellow holding a paper of some sort. "Wait there," I heard Bird say after he took the paper. He then closed the door and turned to us. His face, always pale, now was nearly the color of flour. He swallowed hard before speaking.

"He's in Prune Street jail," he said. "He writes that he was arrested, at the behest of a creditor he does not name, as he was making his way up Market Street, not two minutes from home."

"Oh, dear God!" I cried. I must have clutched Henry too tightly without realizing it, for he began to wail, and Polly took him from me; perhaps she thought I was in danger of dropping him. Indeed, I suppose I might have been, for the room began to sway before my eyes, and when I took a step forward I began to stumble. Bird rushed to catch me and, holding me steady, told me I mustn't worry, it was all a mistake, and we could easily obtain Jamie's release because of his judicial position. Bird then went into the office, found a pen, and scribbled something on the back of the paper. He found the urchin still waiting outside the front door.

"Be quick about it now," he said, handing the boy the paper along with a coin.

He told us he must go immediately to the jail, to bring his Papa some money to obtain a room there, and some supper; for though criminals are housed and fed at public expense, those in jail for debt must pay their own way (I don't understand the reason for this, as debtors are generally imprisoned because they lack money in the first place, but it is the law). I asked if I might go with him, but he said he thought it best if he went alone—that Prune Street was no place for a lady. He then swore us all to strict secrecy, for he said that as soon as it is known that one creditor has taken legal action, all the rest become anxious about the security of their debts and follow suit.

We all nodded solemnly, and watched weakly as Bird opened a drawer in Jamie's desk, withdrew a handful of bills and left the house. He was gone for over an hour, during which time we sat in the parlor, barely speaking, taking turns holding Henry. It was a pleasing diversion to jiggle him and give him his bottle and coo at him until he grew calm; and

I think we were all a bit disappointed when at last he closed his eyes, opened his small pink mouth into a yawn, and went to sleep.

When Bird returned he seemed surprised to find us all downstairs, awaiting him, and told us we must go to bed. His Papa was well and in reasonably good spirits, under the circumstances; he now had a decent room, which he was sharing with his friend Mr. Allison. On his way home, Bird had called on Mr. Thomas, who assured him that all would be arranged the next morning.

I scarcely slept that night—was even glad of it when Henry awoke and wanted his bottle—and by noon the next day I was nearly beside myself. Bird had left directly after breakfast, saying he must go with Mr. Thomas to arrange for his Papa's release, and we had heard nothing from him since.

At last, just before supper time, the door opened, and Bird appeared, with Jamie just behind him. Never was I happier to see anyone come through a door, though a terrible stench clung to his clothes—from the prison, he said. I shudder to think what horrors that stench may betoken; perhaps some day I shall ask Jamie, but I'm sure he doesn't want to talk of it now. I had him take off the clothes immediately, of course, and instructed Mrs. Nice to wash them thoroughly—I was quite desperate about it, as though to eradicate the smell would eradicate the memory of the place as well. I believe they will be nearly as good as new.

I wish I could say the same of Jamie; he has not been quite himself since he returned—there is an unfamiliar quietness to him, almost an absence, as though he left the confident, energetic part of himself in that hole on Prune Street.

Monday, November 7, 1796

I went this morning and sold my ruby earrings—oh! would that Dr. Mease had taken them when I unthinkingly begged him to, for it would have been much easier to part with them in the passionate generosity of that moment than it was in the clear, cold light of deliberate reason—a light that made them sparkle more alluringly than ever, as though they were winking me a plea to once again attach themselves to my ears.

But Dr. Mease's bill and many others have been lying unpaid in the parlor for some weeks now—including one for the rent, so that we daily expect Mr. Leiper to come pounding at our door (as he has now done on

271

two occasions). Jamie insists that we need not trouble ourselves over these bills, that those who have issued them must simply bide their time until the situation is improved—which, he says, is likely to be the case in but a few more weeks. Perhaps he is right—I certainly pray that he is—but it is difficult, knowing that the bills are lying there—crouching, I sometimes think, like beasts in the forest, waiting to spring on us all unawares.

Polly has been worried as well, and even Bird—though he is so loyal to his Papa, and loath to doubt him. Yesterday evening, after Emily and Charles had gone upstairs to bed, Polly said we must do something about the bills now, while Jamie was away from home—for he left us on Saturday for Maryland, where he was to open the circuit court today.

"We could sell something, something he wouldn't realize was missing," Polly said, as the three of us sat at table, the crumbs of our meager supper of bread and cheese still unswept. "And then simply pay the bills ourselves with the proceeds. He wouldn't notice whether they'd been paid or not, for he's far more concerned with those who are demanding his land."

She spoke briskly, with no apparent hesitation—which was surprising, for she's generally such a mousy thing.

I looked about the room. "But what could we sell, that he wouldn't notice?"

Polly clasped her hands in front of her and straightened her back, as though about to recite a poem. "It must be something small, of course, but also valuable. For there's no point in doing it unless it yields enough to pay the bills, or the better part of them." She paused. "I have a ring, a diamond set with pearls"—

"Not Mother's ring!" Bird interrupted. "You couldn't—it's almost all we have of her."

I was momentarily confused, for I am so used to thinking of *myself* as their mother; but in an instant I recollected what Polly had said about a ring when Henry was ill, and we decided to call in Dr. Mease.

"I never wear it," Polly was saying, "and I'm sure that if Mother were here, she would rather that we have something decent to eat, and a place to live, and that we are able to hold up our heads in this city."

I hesitated only a moment (well, perhaps *two* moments) before I said, "You *do* have a mother here, and she will provide for you. I will sell something of my own."

272

I was trembling slightly, but then Bird took my hand and kissed it, and when I saw the expression of gratitude and admiration on his face I felt a calming strength come over me; indeed, I felt rather proud of myself, not only for what I had said, but also for the phrasing of it.

"That is exceedingly good of you," said Polly, still brisk and business-like. "I know of an establishment that is discreet and, I believe, honest. You can go tomorrow morning."

"Tomorrow? So soon?"

"My father could return at any time. Perhaps there is very little on the Maryland docket. You know he's not going on to Virginia—and what the consequences of that will be, we cannot tell."

This is yet another worry; for Jamie was adamant in his refusal to set foot in that state, apparently on account of that Mr. Taylor in Richmond, and unsuccessful in persuading any of his colleagues to take his place. And Delaware as well—he was supposed to have gone there to hold the court at the end of last month, but decided not to at the very last moment, because some creditor there had made threats. The court must have failed, for there was no time to alert another judge. And what will the government do if Jamie continues to neglect the duties of his post?

"Very well, then," I said to Polly. "Tomorrow. But you must come with me."

Polly then added up the amounts owing and determined that we would need to raise at least three hundred dollars, which would enable us both to pay the debts and to retain a little cash for current expenses. I thought the earrings would be sufficient—for I'm certain the necklace is worth far more than three hundred—but when we went this morning, the jeweler wanted to give us only two hundred fifty for them. It's a good thing Polly was there, for I suppose I should have simply accepted that amount—loath as I was to part with the earrings, I was all a-fluster, and could not reason clearly. But Polly said no, we would not accept such a piddling sum, that the earrings were worth three-fifty if they were worth a penny, and that we could certainly take them elsewhere if the gentleman didn't recognize their worth. The jeweler hemmed and hawed, and went on about times being hard for all of us, but in the end he agreed to meet our price.

My gaze lingered on the earrings until the man put them in a pouch and shut them up in a drawer, and Polly then pulled me out onto the street. To my surprise, as soon as we had turned the corner from the jeweler's house and were safely out of sight, she stopped and clasped my hands.

"We did it!" she whispered urgently, her plain face alight with triumph and glee.

I embraced her, so that she might not see the selfish regret that I feared stamped my own features. "*You* did it," I whispered back. "You were magnificent."

Thursday, December 3, 1796

All the money from the earrings is long gone, and poor Henry is ill and needs the doctor, as well as some medicine—he has a troublesome cough and a fever; Mrs. Nice says it is on account of his teething in the cold weather. And so this morning I asked Polly to come with me, back to the gentleman who bought the earrings. I took the necklace—my beautiful ruby necklace, red as a field of poppies, that I thought to wear to scores of grand balls and parties—and bid it farewell.

I got four hundred dollars for it. Polly tried to bargain for more, but the man said it wasn't like last time—now that the distress is so general, there are few takers for ruby necklaces and such—we wouldn't find a better price elsewhere, and that was God's truth. And we knew that he was right.

There are now many others who have gone to Prune Street jail for debt—respectable men among them, though none, I think, so respectable as Jamie. Indeed, there are probably more than I know of, for I should think that those who can keep it a secret do so. But it is growing ever more difficult to keep a secret in this city. I have heard that even Mr. Morris and Mr. Nicholson—who thought to make such a fortune from buying up all the land in the Federal City that is to be constructed on the banks of the Potomac—are in great distress, their notes selling for fifteen cents on the dollar. Or perhaps Bird said twenty, or ten—I have a poor head for numbers.

And Jamie, poor Jamie. He has never fully recovered from that terrible episode of imprisonment, brief as it was. He who once flew from one endeavor to the next now spends his days in idleness, as there is no business for him to conduct: no one who has money to invest in land schemes, no one willing to lend him capital, nothing with which to finance the printed descriptions of his proposed settlements. I know not what is the situation at Wilsonville, for he refuses to speak of it, but I fear that much of the machinery there has been seized by creditors, and what the unfortunate settlers will do now I cannot tell. Perhaps we shall never see the place, after all—I don't know that I would want to see it at present.

Jamie will not leave the house, nor answer the door, for fear of having a process server's hand clapped on him again (the law being that he is protected from arrest while in his own house). He exists in a kind of daze, and fails to notice much that is going on beneath his nose—I don't believe he realizes that Henry is ill, although I haven't tried to hide it from him. This even though he sits in the parlor much of the day, no longer retreating into his office as was his habit—I suppose it makes him anxious to be there at present, surrounded by all those letters and documents and deeds, poised in piles upon his desk like paper mountains threatening to collapse upon his head. He will stare vacantly at the wall in the parlor, or sometimes at the fire, lost in his thoughts for hours on end.

Yesterday, even though I was extremely anxious over Henry's cough, I sat across from him in the parlor and did my best to engage him in some genuine conversation. I fear that I babbled a great deal of nonsense—and got little or no response for my efforts. At length I inquired whether he would not like to read something. He shrugged and said he supposed he could try, and I hurried off to his library to retrieve a selection of books.

I returned with some that he once perused over and over: Aristotle's *Politics*, both volumes of Russell's *History of Ancient Europe*, Cicero's *Orations*, and the first book of Vattel's *Law of Nations*, for this was all I could easily carry. These I lay at his feet, and crept off to see to Henry. But when I returned an hour later, I saw that though he had the Cicero open on his lap, his eyes were yet fixed in the same vacant stare.

"My dear," I said, "are these books not to your liking, then? Shall I try to find you something else?"

He brought his gaze to my face, startled as though interrupted in a dream. "Something else, yes. I cannot read these, my mind cannot attend …" His great eyebrows now drew together upwards in an anxious inverted "V," pitiful to behold.

"What can I get you? Only tell me, as I don't want to bring you the wrong ones again."

"Bring me … bring me a *tale* of some kind. One of those books *you* like to read."

"A novel?" He could not mean that, I thought; Jamie has always scoffed at my reading novels—silly women's drivel, he calls them. "You want to read a novel?"

His face drew up in a kind of pout, causing him to look remarkably like Henry. "Yes, I believe I would," he said in a small voice.

I flew up the stairs to my bedroom and quickly chose *Charlotte, a tale of truth*, by Mrs. Rowson—the very novel that he had begun to read to me over a year ago, when my own spirits were so low. If ever there were a tale to take one's mind off one's troubles, I thought, this would be the one: an innocent girl enticed from her governess by a young officer, who brings her to America; the marriage ceremony not forgotten, but postponed; the girl dying a martyr to the inconstancy of her lover and the treachery of his friend. A dramatic tale, indeed, and very life-like in the telling. And yet, I wondered—would Jamie, his mind honed to so sharp an edge by his readings in philosophy, and history, and the law of nations and such—would he not consider these situations trivial and beneath his concern?

I found my answer but half an hour later when, passing by the parlor, I saw that he was wholly engrossed in the book—no longer dazed and staring and mumbling at the wall, but turning pages with great avidity. He stayed up well past supper reading, and had to be coaxed to bed, then took it up again directly after breakfast this morning. At this rate he shall soon tear through my entire collection of volumes!

From Chauncey Goodrich, U.S. Representative from Connecticut, to Oliver Wolcott, Secretary of the Treasury:

Philadelphia, Pennsylvania, December 13, 1796

... This place furnishes indication of great depravity; bankruptcies are frequently happening. Mr. Morris is greatly embarrassed. 'Tis said that Nicholson has fled to England; that Judge Wilson has been to gaol and is out on bail; but there are so many rumors I vouch for the credit of neither...

From the Commonplace Book of Benjamin Rush, Philadelphia Physician:

December, 1796

... This month great distress pervaded our city from failures, &c. One hundred fifty, it is said, occurred in 6 weeks, and 67 people went to jail ... in two weeks. [The notes of] Morris and Nicholson, said to amount to 10 millions of dollars, were currently sold for 2/6 in the pound. Thirty percent per annum was given for money. Hundreds drew their money in from Banks and common interest to lend it by the hands of Brokers at that usurious interest, all of whom suffered more or less by the failures...

Judge Wilson deeply distressed; his resource was reading novels constantly.

From George Peter, Auctioneer, to James Wilson:

[Philadelphia, Pennsylvania,] December 29, 1796

... Please to take Notice that the Lands you have conveyed to me as a Security for the Debt, will be sold on Wednesday the 4th January 1797 at 7 o'clock in the Evening, agreeable to the advertisement Inclosed, which will inform you of the different Tracts, Unless you pay the Amount due before the Day of Sale...

Thursday, January 12, 1797

I know not how to write this, nor why I should even attempt it—for all seems useless, hopeless now. My child, my only child—my Henry—is gone, carried off by the measles. It has been, I suppose, a week now, but it seems an eternity. For every day that has dawned since then has been a crushing burden, and I know not how I shall go on.

The fever he had some weeks ago seemed rather ordinary—indeed, it went away almost entirely. But I suppose it weakened his system, and there was much disease about. Even Dr. Mease was stricken, and so could not come when the fever returned. We thought to wait until the doctor was recovered, but when the fever grew worse and the spots appeared, we knew it was something more than just another chill. Dr. Mease was still unwell, and so we sent for another doctor—this one well along in years, and I now wonder if perhaps he was not as well acquainted with modern methods of physic as he should have been.

The doctor recommended milk-punch, which seemed to reduce the spots; but the cough and the fever only grew worse—poor babe, he was burning to the touch, and his tiny body convulsed by the violent coughing. He became weaker and weaker—I could feel him slipping from me, leaving me. I thought of how he had not been the same since he'd been deprived of Susannah's milk; and how it was my own fault that I was not able to give him that vital nourishment myself.

And yet, to the end, he looked at me with such tender, innocent affection in his reddened eyes—wanted only me to hold him, and would cry if Polly or Mrs. Nice attempted to take him, to give me some rest. But I had no desire to rest, I only wanted my child, wanted to sing to him and kiss his hot cheeks and stroke his few strands of corn-silk hair—and watch for signs that the terrible fever was releasing its hold on him, that he was regaining some strength. I watched and watched until my eyes burned and ached and were like to fall from my head, but still I watched. And saw only what I dreaded most.

And then at last I allowed myself to be convinced; sleep, you must sleep, they repeated, or you will do yourself some injury. And so I slept a few hours; until I awoke with a start, and a sickening feeling that some disaster had occurred. When I came to the door of the nursery and saw Jamie there, I knew I was right, for he would not have come unless the end was near. But oh, the end was past already—all over, over forever. He went peacefully, they told me, a little lamb returned to his Maker. It was meant to comfort me, surely, but I would not be comforted; I sobbed and sobbed, crying out that I should have been by him, I should have stayed.

Rivers of tears, oceans of tears have been shed in this house—to think that so small a being could produce such waterfalls of tears. He was the one thing that truly linked us all to each other, me to them, the one blood tie. And now we are linked in grief, I suppose, forever. But no—for they have other siblings, and Jamie has other children. But I have nothing, nothing that will take his place—nothing shall *ever* take his place. He took my heart and soul to the grave with him. I shall not laugh again, I shall not smile.

"It is God's will," Bird intoned in his best preacher's voice, though he wept as much as any of us. I suppose he meant the words as a comfort, but to my mind—heavy with secret guilt—it was nothing less than the passing of a divine sentence upon me: I did away with a child I did not love, and now God has done away with a child I held dearer than anything else. Dear God, if you have judged me unfit to be a mother, I will accept that judgment—but do not, I pray you, subject me once again to this torture. Rather have some mercy on me, and let me never be with child again. Oh, how shocked Doctor Thatcher back in Boston would be to hear such a prayer—for he always held up the goodness of my namesake Hannah in the Bible, and how she prayed so fervently to *be* with child. But God allowed that Hannah's child to live, and He has taken mine. Unworthy as I am, did I truly deserve such cruelty?

Saturday, January 21, 1797

Polly tried to take away the cradle today, but I would not let her. It must stay by my bed, where I can extend a hand in the middle of the night and touch it, as I used to. I used to feel his hair, and stroke his cheek, when he was sleeping, and listen to the tiny flutter of his breathing. Polly says that it is time, that it only encourages mournful thoughts to leave it there. I told her I saw nothing wrong with mournful thoughts, under the circumstances.

Jamie has taken no notice that the cradle is still there, nor I suppose would he have noticed if Polly had taken it. He takes so little notice of anything, these days. I don't know what I would do without Polly and Bird—Bird especially. He has insisted that I take some exercise, and accompanies me on walks every day that the weather permits, and I believe it is doing me some good. He tells me it was not my fault, none of it—that it was not my leaving Henry, or hiring a wet nurse, that caused his death. Dear Bird; he could not be more solicitous of me were the child his own, and I his wife.

Monday, February 6, 1797

A most salutary change has come over Jamie, I think. The Supreme Court opened today, and we were all apprehensive that Jamie might refuse to attend, for fear of being arrested again—or simply because he lacked the spirits. But on Friday, after talking with Mr. Thomas—who assured him that he would be safe while actually engaged in the business of judging—he resolved that he would go, and immediately threw aside the novel he was reading (*Camille*, which I obtained for him from a lending library, and which I am most eager to read myself) and took up some law texts. And then today he looked as well as ever on the bench—for Polly and Bird convinced me to attend, though I was most reluctant to go abroad. I have scarcely gone anywhere since Henry died. Nor have I had a new gown in quite some time, for we owe quite a bit to Mr. McIlhenny; but I found an old one that looked decent enough.

The stares and the whispers in the courtroom were much as I anticipated, but I found they bothered me less than I had expected; for I carry about with me such a wall of inner misery that very little—good or bad—can penetrate it. And yet there was one encounter, just as we were leaving, that left me feeling rather uneasy. We were just inside the door of the City Hall, waiting on Jamie, when we saw Mr. Iredell coming down from the courtroom, in the company of two other gentlemen. When he saw us, Mr. Iredell's expression immediately shifted from polite joviality to tender concern; he withdrew slightly from his companions, clasped my hands and told me, in few but heartfelt words, how sorry he was for our loss. I have on other occasions found myself recoiling from such expressions of sympathy; but the connection that has formed between myself and Mr. Iredell is such that I was greatly affected, as was he. We stood and merely gazed upon one another for a few moments, our eyes speaking far more than what our voices could have rendered. But then Mr. Iredell abruptly looked away and introduced his companions: Major Butler and his associate, a Mr. Gibson, who had just been sworn in at the bar.

Major Butler I had of course encountered before, at dinners and such. He is a tall man, sharp-eyed and aristocratic in his bearing—and the sort of aristocrat who has the money to carry off the part. This Mr. Gibson was far shorter, with rather thick lips that hung slightly open. Within a moment or two, Jamie appeared, carefully making his way down the stairs so as not to trip on his robe; when he saw Major Butler, he looked surprised, then dismayed, and his step slowed further. I then recalled that Jamie has on occasion expressed a dislike of Major Butler; apparently there was once some argument between them.

"Judge Wilson," said Major Butler with a slight bow. "I have just had the pleasure of making the acquaintance of your charming wife and daughter, and this fine young man, your son."

Jamie, now having joined our party, returned the bow but did not smile.

"You remember Mr. Gibson, Sir, who took his oath before you this morning?" Major Butler continued. "You may encounter him again, for I have retained him to look after my legal affairs in this city—I leave for Charleston in a few days, and shall be there for some weeks."

Jamie's eyes narrowed. "Will Mr. Gibson be representing you in some business before the Court, then?"

Major Butler seemed to find this amusing; he tilted his head and gave Jamie a small, chilly smile. "No, not that sort of thing. It seems that some paper of yours has come into my possession—some notes for a goodly sum, that you gave to William Blount and David Allison a year since. Those gentlemen borrowed money of *me* some time ago, and as part payment they have signed over to me the notes that you gave to *them*, to secure the loan. You recall those notes, of course."

"I do." Jamie's face had gone quite red, and his voice was quiet but furious. "But this is neither the time nor the place to discuss business affairs, sir."

"Perhaps not. I shouldn't have brought up the matter now, you know, but you have been … *scarce* of late. And I only thought to take the opportunity to introduce Mr. Gibson, as he will soon need to discuss with you the matter of interest coming due on one of your notes."

Jamie nodded curtly at Mr. Gibson. "Pleased to make your acquaintance, sir. And now, if you'll excuse us, we must be getting home. Our dinner awaits us."

Jamie turned to the door, and Bird and Polly made to follow; I stayed behind only a moment, to tell Mr. Iredell he must come to us, this evening or tomorrow, and he said that he would. Jamie kept up a brisk pace all the way home, saying nothing, his robe trailing behind him.

We all sat in near silence through dinner, for Jamie's demeanor was still forbidding. When we were done, he ordered Bird to come in to his study. Jamie hasn't yet said a thing to me of what they discussed, but Bird told us later—Polly and me, that is—that he is to go tomorrow morning to a Mr. Coxe (apparently a very wealthy gentleman) and offer a large tract of Jamie's lands in Pennsylvania as security for a substantial loan. I was exceedingly relieved to hear this, of course, because I imagine it will enable Jamie to pay off that money Major Butler was speaking of (I did not like the tone he took, it was quite alarming), with perhaps some left over to pay the rent, and order some new clothes from Mr. McIlhenny, and give Mrs. Nice and Hansel—Jamie's office boy—some of their overdue salary. And Jamie will still have other lands, of course; Bird says there are thousands upon thousands of acres, surely Jamie cannot need them all.

I must leave off writing now; I think it's best if I retire to bed early this evening. I confess it is not mere fatigue: I worry that Jamie, having recovered some of his vigor, may seek to assert his rights as a husband. We have not, these last few months, lived as husband and wife—not in the physical sense—for we have both been distracted by our separate tribulations. We have not discussed it, as the situation seemed to arise naturally, by mutual and tacit consent. But it cannot continue like this forever—and I cannot yet tell what I want. A part of me yearns for the comfort of his touch—and to lose myself, and my grief, in the pleasures of the marriage bed. But would it not be wicked, and unfeeling, to experience pleasure so soon after so terrible a loss? More than that, I cannot bear the thought of another child, and the risk of losing it. I therefore intend to feign slumber, in the hope that it will discourage any advances.

From James Iredell to Hannah Iredell:

Philadelphia, Pennsylvania, February 24, 1797

... The misfortunes of Judge Wilson throw an unfortunate gloom over his house, though I have been there two or three times, and have experienced all their former kindness...

I inquired for Camille *for you, but could not get a copy in the city. It is printing by subscription, and I will get one as soon as it can be had...*

Saturday, March 11, 1797

I have had a letter from home today, bearing the news that my sister Lucy is to be married next month, to a Dr. William Dobel—I recall the family, but not the particular gentleman. My first thought was that Lucy is still too young to be married, but then I realized that nearly four years have passed since last we were together—so that she is now almost two years older then I myself was when I married! I imagine her excitement, her anticipation, the feeling that her true life—which she has been awaiting so patiently—is about to be unfurled before her in all its splendor. I think I shall not tell her what I now understand—that marriage is a dark and shadowy path, leading us into unknown terrain where we must stumble and find our way as best we can—for surely it would be cruel to cast so melancholy a pall over the happiest hour of a young woman's life. Let her be happy, then, for now; perhaps in her case, the happiness will endure.

Jamie, at least, is still in good spirits, though Mr. Thomas is here daily, always—I believe—with news of more creditors and judgments against us. The details are generally kept from me, but there are certain names that reach my ears again and again: Major Butler, and Messrs. Allison and Blount, and of course Mr. Coxe—who has so far resisted Jamie's efforts to procure money from him. I know not who is at fault any more, Jamie or these hounds that are nipping at his heels. Jamie says—as he always has—that they must simply be patient; that his lands, if kept intact or nearly so, will one day bring far more than what they could at present, while they are still largely wilderness, and prices are so low. He has even resolved to send Charles off to Mr. Drake's school, at Pottstown, near Reading, where Jem now is. He says that surely Mr. Drake will exercise forbearance with regard to the tuition, for it will be worth something to him to have two of Judge Wilson's sons among his pupils.

How I wish I could adopt some of Jamie's confidence, but his assurances that all will be well in time no longer comfort me; I feel a terrible foreboding and helplessness—rather like what I felt in that dream I used to have, about being on the back of a galloping horse headed towards a cliff. But there is one thing in my life that has improved. I spoke to Jamie about my fear of being again with child, and to my surprise he listened with sympathy. He told me that he too would prefer not to bring another child into the world, at least at present, and he acquainted me with certain practices that he says will ensure that no child can be conceived. This intelligence has greatly eased my mind, and we are now able to enjoy the full benefits of marriage with as much pleasure as formerly—or nearly so. It is, alas, the only pleasure allowed to me in these trying times.

From James Gibson, Philadelphia Lawyer, to Major Pierce Butler:

Philadelphia, Pennsylvania, March 22, 1797

... *I have requested the payment [for a] year's interest from Mr. Wilson on the bond dated in Feby. 1796 for 58,110 Dollars and shall on the first of April make a similar demand for the rest; notice of the unpayment has been given to Mr. Blount and Mr. Allison...*

... *[Mr. Wilson's affairs], tho' much depressed, are not so desperate as represented to you; the report I fancy is founded in an assignment made by him of Georgia Lands, in trust, to pay off the Judgements obtained against him last September amounting to 70,000 Dollars—his person at that period was in custody under an execution and actually within the Prison; he continued there a short time as the Creditor came to terms... The prospect before him is very gloomy; it is impossible at present to foretell the final issue...*

Wednesday, May 3, 1797

I ventured out today, which I rarely do any more, in search of some articles for Charles to take with him to school—he is in desperate need of trousers, and as we cannot afford to have them made by Mr. McIlhenny, I thought to buy a few yards of cassimere—if Mrs. Nice and Polly and I all put our hands to it, perhaps we can manufacture something he would not be ashamed to wear. I had a few dollars left from the proceeds of a locket I sold some weeks ago, and it seemed to me it would be sufficient. The poor child will have enough to worry over without his companions taunting him because he is in rags.

I went to a shop on Front Street, for I saw in the newspaper that it had new supplies of cassimere in stock. There I was waited on by a young Negro man, very polite and well-spoken, though it seemed that he regarded me strangely. At length he said, "Do you not recognize me then, Mrs. Wilson?"

I looked at him more closely. "Why—is it Thomas?"

He smiled broadly back at me and assented that indeed it was. I remarked that he seemed to be doing well for himself—certainly far better than when I had last seen him, pulling that foul-smelling cart from the market. His clothes were neat and well-made, and he had obviously been eating well.

"I owe you some thanks, ma'am," he said, "for it was good advice you gave me."

"Did I?" I could not recall what I had said to him that might prompt this remark.

"Yes ma'am. You told me to go to the Abolition Society."

Now I remembered. "Yes, but—you did not go to Africa, it seems."

"No, ma'am, I didn't. But there was a kind lady at the Abolition Society, a Quaker lady, who told me she could teach me how to read and write, so that I could get a better position. I'm sure Africa is a very nice place, ma'am, but I decided that I'd rather stay here and learn my letters. So I did, and here I am. This shop is owned by the Quaker lady's husband, and they've both been very good to me indeed."

I congratulated him on his success, and we then proceeded to the business at hand, him showing me some bolts of very fine cassimere in different colors. I settled on black as being the most practical choice; but when I inquired the price I was unpleasantly surprised. I examined my purse and saw that it would not stretch so far as the yardage required for a pair of trousers.

"It's very nice," I said to Thomas, with what I hoped was a careless smile, "but I am not yet entirely decided. Perhaps I shall come back another day."

Thomas nodded and began to fold up the cloth, then hesitated and excused himself for a moment. I saw him engaged in conversation with an older gentleman, who I took to be the owner of the shop.

"I was mistaken as to the price, ma'am," he said when he returned. "In truth, it's only half what I told you. I'm still learning the trade, you see, and sometimes I forget how much things cost."

I felt the gathering of tears behind my eyes, for I suspected what he had done, and I was deeply grateful—but at the same time, embarrassed and filled with self-pity. What must he have heard concerning our situation? But I collected myself and said, with as much dignity as I could muster, that in that case I would take two yards. He cut it expertly and wrapped it, then handed it to me with a flourish.

"I wish you well, ma'am," he called to me as I departed.

I smiled back at him, but did not trust the steadiness of my voice sufficiently to wish him the same.

285

Reading, Pennsylvania

I have had a most unhappy surprise: Jamie has just told me that his plan, after leaving Charles at school here, is not to return to Philadelphia at all—at least, not at present—but to retreat to some secluded place where he can, as he says, arrange his affairs from afar, without interference from his creditors. He intends to direct Bird and Mr. Thomas by letter in the satisfying of certain judgments against him that are now outstanding, and will return only when he is certain it is safe to do so. I suspect affairs have reached a point where he fears that some other creditor will have him arrested and hauled to Prune Street, the law notwithstanding.

Alas, I don't know what to do. Jamie says I may return to the city if I choose, but he has made it plain that he would much rather I remain with him; indeed, I have rarely seen him in the sway of such emotion as he was this evening.

"I know, Nannie," he said, "that our manner of life, of late, has not been what you expected when you agreed to marry me—what you had every right to expect. You have no idea, my dear, how it pains me to see you in this situation—fending off creditors who clamor at the door, selling your pretty trinkets, wearing clothes that have been mended more often than they should, going without meat day after day."

Here he paused, and took a breath; he rubbed an eye as though a mote of dust had flown into it. So he did know all that I was suffering—that *we* were suffering, all of us.

"Such a creature as you should be living as a queen, with every luxury at your command—and I promise that you will, in time. But you must know"—and here he took my hand and pressed it hard to his lips, momentarily—"that you are even now, and always, the queen of my heart."

286

He then dropped my hand and turned from me, and I suspect a tear or two escaped his eye. I quickly put my arms about him and assured him that I loved him still, and then we lay on the bed together, me stroking his head, until at last he fell asleep. He is sleeping now, as I write, here in the room we have been given in the house of a local family—friends of Jamie's from many years ago, who have shown us the most generous hospitality.

When he wakes I must tell him my decision. What I most want, if I am to be truly candid, is not to return to the children and all our troubles, but to fly away to Boston, to see Mama once more—and Lucy and her new husband—and even Sarah. To be a child again, and a sister, and no more a mother or a wife, to be coddled and cared for—at least for a while.

But Jamie seems to need me so. And his face, when he is sleeping, is so child-like and soft and helpless—so very like my own sweet Henry. Indeed, Jamie is all I have left of Henry, now.

From James Iredell to Hannah Iredell:

Richmond, Virginia, May 25, 1797

... There is such an immensity of business to do here that I cannot even conjecture when I can get away. For a great deal of it I am to thank Judge Wilson, who suffered the Court last Term to be entirely lost by his non-attendance ...

From James Wilson to Bird Wilson:

Morris Tavern, Bethlehem, Pennsylvania, June 9, 1797

... Notwithstanding all the pains taken, the Stage last Evening was full. I have engaged one to hire from Bethlehem tomorrow Evening, and to return on Sunday. I wish to see you here tomorrow: leave as early as you can. Do not disappoint me. Remember me to the Family ...

P.S. [**in the hand of Hannah Wilson**] *Bird, if you can conveniently, I wish you would bring your papa's black cassimere coat that hangs up in my chamber closet next to the windows.*

Bethlehem, Pennsylvania

Monday, June 12, 1797

We have had an arduous time of it, wandering hither and yon through the state of Pennsylvania, but we have been here, in this town called Bethlehem, for over a week now, and Jamie appears to have settled on it as being convenient to Philadelphia—but not so convenient that he is likely to encounter anyone he doesn't wish to. What he wants is for Bird to be able to come and go easily, and bring him papers and such, and receive instructions to bring back to Mr. Thomas. Indeed, Bird came to us on Saturday, and I wept to see him; his visit was all too brief, as he was obliged to depart the next day, in order to attend to Jamie's affairs.

We managed to slip away for half an hour from the musty, airless room in the inn where Jamie and I have found a room (not the nicest inn in this place, by far, but all that we could afford at present)—just Bird and myself, leaving Jamie to review some papers—and take a promenade by the river. There has of late been a damp chill in the air here—indeed, I had Bird bring his Papa's old coat with him, for Jamie has had a cough, and I feared it might worsen. But Saturday was a lovely day, with a gentle breeze and a few soft clouds above, and it put me in mind of those walks Bird and I used to take in Philadelphia, so long ago, when we had nothing more serious to occupy our time than my attempts to give poor reluctant Bird an education in flirtation. I cannot see that my efforts have borne much fruit—for I asked him whether there was anyone in Philadelphia who had claimed his heart, and all he did was blush and deny it and quicken his pace.

I considered that this, perhaps, was a subject best left untouched; as Bird no doubt had far more serious matters weighing on him. "Tell me then, how are you all bearing up?" I asked, catching up with him. "Has Mr. Leiper come around again?"

Of course he had, several times—but Bird said they'd all pretended no one was home. He said that he was in hopes of having some income soon, as Mr. Thomas had promised to send him some legal work. To my dismay, he added that Polly and Emily have begun to take in needlework, and that Jem (who has left school, as Mr. Drake said he couldn't keep both boys on credit) has talked of finding employment in a shop.

"Oh, Bird, must they?" I said, feeling tears coming on. "What will people say?"

Bird shrugged. "They cannot say much worse than they have already, I'm afraid. And we must have money to buy food, and clothing. Poor Jem—or James, as he now wants to be called—hasn't had any new shirts or trousers for some time, I've had to lend him some of mine. And Emily's gowns and petticoats are growing far too small on her."

I now began to weep in earnest, and Bird put his arms about me, kissing the top of my head—I suppose I should have stepped away, but I was sorely in need of comfort. When I had quieted some, he told me we must go back now to the inn, for Jamie would be expecting him. I told him he must go ahead, that I should walk a ways more and compose myself.

"Very well," Bird said, "but please, not a word of this to Papa. It would only distress him, and I suspect he should try to forbid them from attempting to earn some cash."

He then kissed me once more on the cheek and was gone; we did not see one another alone again before he left for the city. How I shall miss him! But perhaps this separation won't continue much longer. If he and Mr. Thomas are successful in their endeavors, Jamie and I may return to Philadelphia within a week or two, and all will be as it once was.

From Bird Wilson to James Wilson:

Philadelphia, Pennsylvania, June 20, 1797

... Mr. Thomas has not informed me what progress he has made in the settlement of the judgments. As a letter from him accompanies this, I did not think it necessary to press him upon that subject. He has not yet had a conference with Mr. Allison, but he has received from him word that he will see him in a day or two...

I will receive your salary when due; if it will not be inconvenient to you, I hope you will give me leave to discharge Mr. McIlhenny's bill, as we are in great want of clothes...

Friday, June 23, 1797

How the weeks drag on here. Alas, we have not seen Bird since that first visit, two weeks ago; perhaps he will come again soon, for Jamie often says there are matters he should like to discuss with him. Well, to tell truth, he says it rather differently—calls him a dull-witted rascal, which I know he does not mean, and says he needs a good talking to. I think Jamie is only growing impatient with how long it is taking to resolve matters (for all that he tells *me* I must be patient), and finds it convenient to direct his anger at poor Bird.

There is so little to do here, and so few people to converse with—only the other lodgers at the inn, most of them men of the rougher sort, so that I keep my distance. I have gone walking a great deal, for the countryside is lovely in these parts, and the weather generally mild. Certainly it is far preferable to remaining in that dank and tiny room with Jamie, who scribbles away at letter after letter—offering lands for sale, I suppose, or drafting proposals to his creditors—I know not. I know only that the sound of his scratching pen, hour after hour, is something I cannot bear. Listening to it, I imagine we are buried in some deep hole in the earth, and that Jamie is attempting to dig us out of it with his little goose quill, one grain of dirt at a time.

And so I walk, finding some comfort in the sweetness of birdsong in the morning, and the way the setting sun causes the hills to glow at dusk. Indeed, I have walked so much that I have entirely worn out a pair of slippers, and have had to find someone here to make me new ones. When I asked Jamie for the necessary money yesterday, he railed a bit at first, and asked if I intended to girdle the earth with my footsteps—could I not merely sit and watch the river flow? Did I not know what expense we were put to, staying here? Whereupon I chided *him*, and told him that it would do him a deal of good to quit the room and take some exercise, that his health would likely suffer from his sedentary habits. And as for the expense of staying here, I said, it wasn't anything of *my* doing that prevented us from returning home. And so we sat in hostile and uneasy silence for a while—each of us, I think, torn between anger and remorse. At length Jamie said, very well, then, but I must order the slippers on credit, to be paid when his salary comes; and not to accept the first price that was given, but to bargain a little—a thing I have never been able to do, but I assured him this time I would.

When I inquired this morning of the innkeeper where I might obtain slippers, he directed me to a shop in the Market Street, directly across from the very odd-looking cemetery they have here—all the gravestones square and laid flat upon the ground, like stepping stones. The door was answered by a young woman—quite pretty, with lovely blue-green eyes—who said that her husband was away at the tannery, but that she could measure me for a pair of slippers.

"Tell me," I said, as she traced the outline of my foot, "why do the gravestones in that cemetery not stand upright, as normal gravestones do?"

"Ach, madam," she said, in the German-flavored English that most of these people employ, "that is because of our belief that we are all of us the same—equal—in death, as we are in life."

"Well, I can see the truth of that in death, to be sure," I said, offering her my other foot. "But in life? Equal in certain respects, I suppose—natural rights, and such. But some are cleverer than others, some more pleasing to the eye." I glanced at her, to see if she might apply this last remark to herself, but she continued calmly with her tracing. "And there's wealth, of course. Some have a good deal more money than others."

"Not among us, madam. Some have a little more, of course, but all of us have our labors, even our leader, our Bishop. His daughter makes wafers, which are sold in the cities—in New York, and in Philadelphia—and he makes the wafer boxes."

"Really! It isn't like that in Philadelphia, where I live—not at all. You'd never find, say, the daughter of the mayor of Philadelphia making wafers, and him making the boxes." I laughed at the thought. "My own husband is a judge—a very important man in the government, you know—and we ..." I remembered Polly and Emily and the needlework. "People such as ourselves are generally not accustomed to having our daughters employed."

The woman smiled but said nothing for a moment, as she gathered up the papers with my foot tracings. "I met another lady from Philadelphia—her husband, too, was a judge, I think," she said. "It was years ago, before I was married. They were here—her family—because of the fever in the city. So kind, she was. She gave me a pretty thing, I will show you." She ran to a cupboard and extracted a rather unremarkable silver brooch, set with a few small pearls, which she exhibited gingerly, as though it were a precious treasure. She then immediately returned it to its hiding place. "I cannot wear it, of course, because it is not our way, but I often take it out and look upon it. I cannot remember the name of this lady, but perhaps you know her?"

"I doubt it. There are a great many people in Philadelphia." The woman probably believed that Philadelphia was on the order of Bethlehem, and that everyone was acquainted.

"*She* did not like Philadelphia. She said that our life here was much more pleasing to her, much simpler—like in a big family." The woman smiled again, dreamily, as though enjoying a private memory; I could not help but notice how it increased her loveliness. What a beauty she would be, I thought, with a decent dress and something more elegant on her head than that tight cloth cap—and perhaps a bit of rouge on her cheeks.

"Oh, but life in Philadelphia can be very amusing," I said. "Perhaps she simply didn't know the right people." I knew I should be on my way—after all, the woman had taken the measurements, and I am not accustomed to engaging in lengthy conversations with shop girls. But it had been so long since I'd spoken with anyone other than Jamie, and I was in no hurry to return to the inn. "There are a great many teas, and dinner parties, and balls to go to, so that one is rarely dull. Why, some days, I've had to change my gown three times before supper."

The woman's eyes were wide, and her mouth slightly open. "It is hard to picture," she said.

"Well yes, I suppose it would be, living here." I looked out the window, at the nearly silent street and the cemetery beyond it—and beyond that, the massive buildings made of greyish-brown stone, which I have heard serve as schools or common living quarters of some kind. "It seems very far away, even to me—almost like something I once dreamt."

"Ach, but you will return there soon, yes? And it will be so … *amusing* for you. That is the word, yes?"

"Yes, yes—that is the word," I replied. I then told her briskly that I must go, hoping that she would not discern the emotion that had overcome me.

"But would you like me to embroider you some flowers on the slippers?" she asked.

Some flowers would be pretty, I thought, but I hesitated. I had entirely forgotten to bargain. "What would it cost?"

"Oh, it will cost you nothing—I like to make embroidery, for me it is … *amusing*."

Just then, the front door opened and a man's deep voice called out, "Anna?"

The woman called back something in German, then said to me, "It is my husband. I will give him the tracings, and he will make for you the slippers. You will come back in two days, please madam?"

I thanked the woman and hastened away, sweeping past the bearish-looking man who had just entered the room. Tears were beginning to fall from my eyes, and so rather than take the Market Street, and subject myself to the stares of those I passed, I ventured into the cemetery—that community of indisputable equality, a monotonous and dreary sight. How dull, I thought, to spend one's *life* on a plain as level as this plot of ground, with no pinnacles to climb or aspire to. But shall I ever ascend those heights again? Would it not perhaps have been better to stay on level ground, and never run the risk of tumbling downwards?

As I stood in the cemetery, the gravestones stretched out before my feet—flat and gray and square, the modest markers of lives modestly lived—and I saw them again as stepping stones, a kind of path laid out for me. But to where, I asked them silently, as I let my tears envelop me—to where?

From James Wilson to Bird Wilson:

[Bethlehem, Pennsylvania], June 27, 1797

... On considering the many important Affairs, concerning which I wish to communicate with you in the Absence of Mr. Thomas from Philadelphia, ... it will be proper you should come here by the Stage, which will leave Philadelphia for this Place, on the Wednesday of next Week. Secure immediately a seat in it.

In the mean Time you can receive my Salary on Saturday next. Pay a Quarter's Rent to Mr. Leiper, and Mr. McIlhenny's Account; leave enough with the Family till your Return; and bring the Balance up with you, and I will settle Matters as to the Disposition of it. Write to me by the Return of the present Stage ... and send the Newspapers, and all

News. Inform Mr. Thomas, if you have an Opportunity, that I have made Contracts for the Settlement of all the Lands beyond the Allegheny River, except the seventy Tracts purchased from Mr. Adlum. Bring here with you the Contract and all the Papers and Certificates relating to the Contract with Mr. Allison; and all the Certificates you can find respecting the Lands in Glynn County in Georgia. I think there is a Bundle of them lying on the Right Hand as you go into the Library, on the Books in one of the Shelves. Remember me to all the Family ...

Friday, July 7, 1797

Bird has come to us again, and gone. Glad as I was to see him, it was not what I should describe as a pleasant visit. There were certain papers he was supposed to bring with him, which he did not—he could not find them anywhere, he told Jamie, who called poor Bird all sorts of ugly names in his rage. At length I could not bear it any longer, and told Jamie that I needed Bird to accompany me on a walk, for I thought a few minutes solitude might cool the fires of Jamie's anger.

We walked slowly along the river promenade and said nothing for a while; I could see Bird was greatly distressed, and thought it best to leave him be for a few minutes.

"You must save yourself," he said at length, his voice soft but urgent.

A chill ran through me; I was reminded of something, I could not think what—and then I knew: it was what William had said to me so long ago. I asked Bird what he meant.

He sat heavily on a bench placed by the side of the path, and I sat beside him. "Go home, I beg you," he said in a pleading tone. "To Boston, to your mother. There is no telling where all this may end, and what you may suffer because of it."

His words then came spilling out: he had tried to bring some order to his father's affairs, but all was in hopeless disarray—papers lost and jumbled, creditors at every turn, lands so encumbered with mortgages that they could never be sold. The only solution, Bird said, was for his Papa to turn over control of his affairs to a committee composed of his creditors—to act as trustees, he said; they might then divide all his lands up among themselves as they saw fit, and perhaps be satisfied. But when he had tried to broach such a proposal to Jamie, he was met only with a furious refusal.

"We shall never make any progress like this," he said, his voice breaking in frustration, "not with him hiding himself away out here and trying to settle it all from a distance. And if he returns without an arrangement such as I've described, he will at this juncture most likely be clapped into prison again. And it may not be so easy to obtain his release next time; Mr. Thomas now says that the point of law—the judge's privilege from arrest—is not quite as settled as we had believed. But he *must* return in August, for the sitting of the Supreme Court—his neglect of his judicial duties has already occasioned a good deal of comment." His voice dropped to a whisper. "I hear there has even been talk of impeachment."

I was alarmed, of course, at what Bird was telling me; but equally alarmed at his angry despair, the deadness in his eyes. It was evident that he, who had so worshiped his father, had now lost all faith in him. And if Bird, who knew so much more of his father's affairs than I did, thought I should return to Boston, who was I to argue? The thought had of course crossed my own mind more than once these last weeks. And yet—to return home, in disgrace rather than in triumph; to leave Jamie here, bereft and alone.

Bird's voice, hesitant now, intruded on my thoughts. "I have thought, perhaps, that if *you* appealed to him …"

"Me? But you know that he has never looked to *me* for advice on his business affairs—he scarcely tells me anything about them."

"But you have some power of persuasion over him that no one else has. I've seen it. I remember what you did for Thomas, obtaining him his freedom within a few days, after I'd wasted months in futile argument."

"Oh, *that*." I blushed to recall the manner of persuasion I had exercised on that occasion. "I am not sure that I still wield such power."

"You are too modest—and I must say, I have never known you to suffer from that particular flaw." He smiled and kissed my hand, as if to reassure me that he meant the remark but fondly. But then his expression grew anxious and hopeful. "But will you try, at least? I shouldn't ask you, you know, but I see no other way. If things continue as they are …"

"Of course, my dearest Bird, of course." It was not so much that he was asking, after all. "I shall try, I promise you."

He kissed my hand again, this time with great feeling. "May God be with you—may God be with you always. But if you should not succeed in this, you must return to Boston. At least for a while, until the situation has—somehow—been settled."

I began to protest, to say that my place was with my husband and children; but then a vision of home floated before my eyes—of peace, of calm, of an end to this constant anxiety.

Monday, July 10, 1797

It has come to naught—I have failed Bird, failed them all.

"My dearest," I said to Jamie last night, as he began to kiss my neck and shoulders, "I should so like to leave this place, and return home with you."

"Just a little more time, Nannie," he said absently, between kisses. "I am seeing to it all."

His kisses were having their effect; I nearly surrendered to the drowsy, languid warmth that was stealing over me. But I forced myself to continue, for I felt my moment of opportunity slipping away. "But I have heard that some gentlemen, who have found themselves in difficulties such as yours, have been able to achieve a very satisfactory resolution, by having their creditors form a sort of committee, and then"—

He jerked his head up of a sudden, and I saw his eyes burning at me through the darkness. "You have *heard*? What have you heard? Who has put you up to this?"

"Nothing—no one—it is just common wisdom, is it not, that when someone is—well—very much indebted to his creditors, and wants to avoid the prison"—

"Common wisdom, indeed!" He had climbed off the bed now, and was pacing the room—so agitated that he did not think to put on his dressing gown. "It was Bird that put you up to this, wasn't it? I know what he thinks I should do, but he simply doesn't understand the situation—and you, Nannie, *you* certainly have no means of grasping it. You know nothing whatsoever about these things, and"—his face was red, and I could see the flush extending down his throat, to his chest. He began to sputter. "The *audacity*, trying to meddle in my affairs—and at a moment such as this, when a man should be free to enjoy the benefits of marriage without having his wife tell him what he should do with his money!"

I tried to calm him, to soothe him, but none of my usual wiles were adequate to the task; I had, I see now, made a grave miscalculation in raising the matter at the particular time that I did. At length he returned to bed—there being no alternative, other than the floor—and we lay at opposite edges of the mattress with our backs turned to one another. I was unable to sleep for several hours, and I believe Jamie was as well—for he generally snores, and I heard nothing from him. As I lay there, I turned over and over in my mind what Bird had said, and considered with some agitation what my next step must be. Could I do again what I had done when Jamie and I quarreled over Thomas? Aside from any other consideration, I did not have the same fire, the same certainty; I couldn't entirely satisfy myself that Jamie was indeed in the wrong. Perhaps Bird was simply losing his nerve—for all that I love him, he is at bottom a timid soul. And yet, did he not see things more clearly, sometimes, than his father?

At length my head began to ache, and I wept as silently as I was able, hoping that Jamie wouldn't hear. Shortly before I at last drifted off to sleep, I came to the decision that I would take Bird's advice and, at the next opportunity, make my way back to Boston. I don't remember what I dreamt, but I know that when I awoke this morning it was with a deep calm, a sense that I was safe and cared for. I arose quickly and went walking, and when I returned I found Jamie dressed and sitting at his desk.

I had thought he might apologize for his behavior of last night, that he might even be willing to discuss the question of his creditors calmly and reasonably, but he only regarded me coldly. I told him of my decision, presenting it as a visit only—to see my mother, for the first time in four years, and my sister, whose husband I have never met. To my surprise he made no arguments against the journey, and even said that I might as well remain in Boston into the fall, as he expected to go the Southern Circuit then and should not return until late in December, or possibly even January.

"Very well, then," I said, striving to sound calm. "I shall inquire of the innkeeper if he knows of anyone traveling towards Boston, for I shouldn't like to travel unaccompanied."

"Of course. You mustn't go alone."

What to make of his tone, so level and unfeeling? Was he indifferent to my presence, eager to be rid of me? Or perhaps only attempting to conceal strong emotion? Certainly I was endeavoring to hide my own distress. Perhaps, it occurred to me, he was feigning unconcern in order to make it easier for me to go—out of consideration for me, and the conviction that I should be happier at home, at least for now. I could not tell. I used to think I could play him like a piano-forte, but he no longer responds as he once did. I'm no better than a pianist attempting the fiddle or the flute—the effects I produce not at all what I expect, and all my years of practice for naught.

Boston, Massachusetts

Friday, July 21, 1797

I am home at last—although I cannot say for certain where my *true* home is at present. I had to wait only four days in Bethlehem before a respectable couple passed through, on their way from Philadelphia to Boston in a hired carriage, and glad to find someone to share the expense.

Jamie had remained rather cool towards me since the night of our quarrel; but on the morning of my departure, just as I was bidding him farewell, his manner suddenly changed.

"Promise me that you will come back to me," he charged me, holding my face in his hands. There was something frightening in his expression; I was unable to find my voice.

"Promise me," he repeated. "I shall not have the strength to go on, to do the many things yet remaining to be done, unless I can rely on your return. I cannot say what may happen to me, to the family, unless you promise me this."

I reached up to take his hands from my cheeks; for he was now gripping them so tightly that I could not move my mouth. But even then, I hesitated. How could I deny him what he so wanted to hear? But in truth I was—and still am—entirely uncertain whether I should or should not return. Then I saw what I thought might be an opportunity. "If I make such a promise," I said, "will you promise *me* something in exchange?"

He eyed me suspiciously. "And what would that be?"

"*You* know—that you will allow the committee, the one made up of creditors"—

"No!" he cried—so loud that I feared we should attract attention, for we were in the inn's sitting room, and there were others about. "No," he then said more quietly, "I must have absolute freedom to conduct my affairs as I see fit. If I cede control, then all will surely be lost; if I can only gain a little more time, and obtain certain additional sums"—

"More money? You want to borrow *more* money? Now?"

He closed his eyes, as though his patience were being sorely tried, and took a breath before opening them. "*Now* is when the opportunities are presenting themselves. There are lands in the South—rich lands, ripe for settlement, and going cheap—that no one is buying, because they haven't the courage, the determination. If I can only raise the cash, if Bird and Mr. Thomas would only assist me in that, then"—

At that moment, the driver of the carriage called out that it was time to board and I ran from the room, relieved to have an excuse to terminate the conversation. A few minutes later, just as the driver took his whip to the horses, I remembered to look out the window for Jamie. There he stood, his face red and brow furrowed.

"Promise!" he called.

The horses clopped forward, and the carriage began its rattling progress. I looked back as Jamie's figure receded into the distance.

"You did not promise!" he bellowed.

It was too late to call anything back to him; nor did I know what to call. So I only waved my hand; but he didn't wave in reply, only stood there with an expression that was part anguish, part accusation.

My traveling companions regarded me curiously, but fortunately asked me nothing concerning what they had just witnessed. I sat there, bouncing uncomfortably on the wooden bench, and pretending to contemplate the countryside, but in fact imagining, upon every boulder and every tree, Jamie's face as he stood by the inn, awaiting the promise I had not given him.

As the journey went on, though, and we drew closer to Boston, my spirits began to lift; the terrain and the houses began to look more familiar—the towns in Connecticut are remarkably similar to those in Massachusetts. By the time we reached Providence, I felt almost my old self again. Indeed, here in Boston all is much as it was when last I saw it—except that Mama has more lines in her face, and greyer hair, and a slower gait. And Lucy, of course, no longer lives at home, but her house is not far off. Her husband, Dr. Dobel, is a most amiable gentleman, with quite the kindest smile I have ever seen—there is a certain sadness to it; I believe it is because his eyes are narrow and nearly close shut as his lips curl up, but the smile is all the sweeter for it. He has been very attentive to me, and quite interested in hearing of my life in Philadelphia—as have they all.

I have had to be careful, of course, in what I tell the family. There was an awkward incident when I first arrived, for I hadn't enough money left in my purse to pay for my share of the carriage. I tried to make light of it, and chastised myself for what I called my neglect in not bringing with me sufficient funds—but of course, I had brought all that Jamie could spare me. I had to look to Mama for the rest, and she was very obliging and asked me no questions. But I think they suspect nothing, for I have regaled them with my tales of dinners at the President's House, and the salons at Mrs. Bingham's. It has been a great tonic to me, to relive those times; I can almost forget all that has transpired this past year. Indeed, in some ways I have traveled even farther back into the past, to before my marriage—before I lost Henry, before all my troubles began. Sleeping in my former room, taking meals in our old dining room with my mother and sisters, calling on my old friends, I feel almost a girl again—and I wonder now why I was then so extremely eager to leave all this behind.

And yet at night, when all is quiet and I am alone in bed, I am frequently plagued by anxious thoughts; for my mind will turn to Jamie and Bird and Polly and the rest. I have had no letters from anyone, though Jamie promised to write, and I wrote to Bird before I left Bethlehem, to tell him of my plans. The Supreme Court will meet soon, I know, for the August session always begins the first Monday of the month. I hope to God that Jamie will be there, to take his place among his colleagues.

From James Iredell to Hannah Iredell:

Philadelphia, Pennsylvania, August 11, 1797

...All the Judges here but Wilson who unfortunately is in a manner absconding from his creditors—his Wife with him—the rest of the Family here! What a situation! It is supposed his object is to wait until he can make a more favorable adjustment of his affairs than he could in a state of arrest ...

Sunday, August 13, 1797

Well, the truth has come out, or some of it. I still have not told them about Jamie's arrest last year, for that is something I think I could never bear to tell anyone. But they began to notice things—the tears in some of

301

my gowns, which I have tried to mend myself; the fact that I hadn't brought any cash with me; the absence of most of my jewelry. Mama asked me yesterday evening, with a kind of studied ease that was laden with suspicion, what had become of the locket she had given me at my marriage, and I began to offer up some story about having unfortunately left it behind in Philadelphia. But then my voice began to break and I had to stop, and I must have looked fairly stricken because Mama was immediately at my side, on the settee in the parlor, with her arm about me.

"What is it, child?" she asked.

To be called "child"—to be thought my mother's child again—was somehow too much for me: all the tears I had kept in check for the past few weeks now came bursting forth, and I had to bury my head in her shoulder. It was some time before I could calm myself sufficiently to answer her question. As the story came out, in bits and pieces, she clucked and cooed and generally made mother hen noises that were somewhere between sympathy and disapproval. I should have preferred to tell her, and only her, but as we were in the parlor, and Sarah and Lucy and Dr. Dobel were there as well (for it was in the evening, and we had been playing at cards), the whole family witnessed the scene. When I had finished, or said enough that they could imagine most of the rest, Sarah began to speak.

"I could see it coming, you know, when I came down there for your confinement," she said peevishly. "The extravagance, the opulence"—

"Hush now, Sarah!" Mama commanded; then, in her former tender tone, she said to me, "You poor dear, what you've been through! It must have been terrible for you."

Lucy and Dr. Dobel murmured their agreement. I nodded assent, and the sympathy of my family (or most of it) unloosed in me a fresh little torrent of tears.

"But now you're home with us, Nannie," Mama continued, "and you mustn't think about all of that. You must simply rest and recover your health and your spirits. You haven't been yourself since you arrived, you know."

I glanced around at them—their faces nodding, full of concern. Even Sarah's. And here I thought I had been in such high spirits! And so they were, at least compared to the state I had been in before.

Lucy leaned forward in the settee she shared with her husband, the sweet oval of her face drawn with anxiety. "You used to laugh so,

Nannie—such a gay laugh, I used to envy it, for no one who heard it could resist joining in. But now, you know, you scarcely laugh at all. And when you do, there's some ... *sadness* underlying it—almost as though you were laughing in a minor key."

At this I did laugh—ruefully, I suppose. I then addressed myself to Lucy's husband—who had been regarding me with as much concern as the rest, but who, perhaps out of deference to my blood relations, had so far kept his silence. "Well, Dr. Dobel, what would you prescribe for someone suffering from my complaint? Severe constriction of the purse, would you call it?"

"Brought on by unchecked laxity of expenditure," Sarah muttered. I shot her a quick glare, but otherwise chose to ignore this remark.

"Well, sister," Dr. Dobel said, "for you I should prescribe plenty of rest—as did your mother—and a reliance on the love and comfort of your family here. And patience. I know you must be exceedingly anxious about your family in Pennsylvania, but the fact is that there is little you can do for them; you must trust to your husband and your son to arrange these matters, and bide your time."

This was delivered with such gentle authority that I could not help but feel reassured by it; Dr. Dobel must be very successful in his profession, for in truth I think nine-tenths of it is merely providing reassurance, and so many doctors are ill equipped for that role. I began to feel a great weight lifted from me, and we passed the remainder of the evening in quiet conviviality—indeed, Mama called for tea and cakes (the latter rather leaden, as Patience's cakes are wont to be, but to me tasting deliciously of my childhood). I am indeed quite relieved to have the truth come out, or most of it; for the strain of keeping all these troubles a secret has been almost as wearing as the troubles themselves.

Writ Sworn Out by Simon Gratz in the New Jersey Superior Court:

Burlington, New Jersey, August 23, 1797

... The Judges of the Inferior Court of Common Pleas in and for the County of Burlington do certify to the Justices of the Supreme Court of Judicature of the State of New Jersey that ... James Wilson, in the annexed writ named, was taken and arrested by virtue of a writ of the said State, commonly called a Capias ad respondendum, returnable ...

303

on the first Tuesday in November to answer Simon Gratz ... of a plea of Debt, & this is the cause of the Caption and Detention of the said James Wilson.

From the Diary of Thomas Shippen, Philadelphia Lawyer:

Philadelphia, Pennsylvania, September 3, 1797

... My father had been taken away from our family card table last night by a message from ... his new patient at Bristol who conceived herself very ill ... He did not return till this morning when ... [h]e told us ... of Judge Wilson's being confined in Burlington Gaol. What shall we come to? One of the highest Court in the United States, one of the 6 Judges in a Jersey Gaol!

James Wilson to Bird Wilson:

Burlington, New Jersey, September 6, 1797

... An Express from Mr. Wallis gives me an Opportunity of expressing my extreme Astonishment at your not coming here before this Time. At all Events set out as soon as you possibly can upon receiving this Letter; tomorrow Morning at latest. Another process has been executed, which will require about 300 Dollars, or Bail to the Amount of 600 Dollars, to discharge it. Mention this to Mr. Thomas. Bring with you some Shirts and Stockings—I want them exceedingly—as also Money, as much as possible, without which I cannot leave this Place...

Thursday, September 14, 1797

I have had not a line from Jamie since I arrived here, and I don't know whether to be cross or anxious. I did today receive a letter from Bird at last (I have written to him several times, asking for news) telling me that Jamie was unable to attend the Supreme Court in August because he was detained by urgent business in New Jersey. Well, I suppose if the business was truly urgent, those in the government will overlook the lapse, provided that Jamie does not trespass on its good will any further. Bird mentioned that Jamie has been assigned the Southern Circuit for the fall, as he wanted; I think he *must* go, or else resign his seat. And yet I fear he only wants to return to the South in order to scout for more land.

Bird's letter was exceedingly vague, so that I really have no idea whether Jamie has come to terms with his creditors yet or not. He did relay one piece of intelligence that rather alarmed me: there have been reports of yellow fever in the city, and he tells me I must under no circumstances consider returning until the cold weather sets in, at which point he hopes to be able to come north to escort me home himself. He added that at present the cases are confined to an area at the south of the city, far from our house, but he assured me that if there appeared to be any danger, the family would find a way to leave immediately.

I have in fact been rather unnerved by this letter, for it sparked such a flood of anxious questions in my mind. Here I have been, I scolded myself, doing nothing more than attempting to amuse myself at teas and dinners and the occasional ball (and these, in the main, far less amusing than what I was used to in Philadelphia)—when poor Bird and Polly and Jem and Emily have been struggling to obtain the necessities of life! I, whom they call Mother, have abandoned them in what is surely their hour of need, taking refuge in playing the role of daughter.

And, indeed, it is a role that begins to pall. Being coddled and clucked over and taken care of has its price, and it is one I am not sure I am willing to pay. Several times now Mama has scolded me for staying out till what she believes is an improper hour, or conversing too spiritedly with gentlemen at parties. And Sarah continues to carp and cavil over what she calls my extravagance. Extravagance! Two new gowns and a petticoat, which—considering that what I brought with me was little better than rags—I certainly required. And the people here, so stodgy and staid—they are polite enough to my face, but I'm certain the whispering begins the moment my back is turned. On Sunday I happened to meet Henry Dolbeare at church, in the company of the mousey little lady he has persuaded to marry him, and he had the temerity to put on a solemn face and tell me how concerned he was for me, that he had heard something of poor Mr. Wilson's "difficulties." Judging from his air of smug self-satisfaction, I'm sure he was sorely tempted to add something about how I must now be consumed with regret that I hadn't chosen to marry him instead. I now recall vividly why I was so anxious to leave home in the first place!

But am I anxious to leave now? It is no longer so simple as it was, for I now have a far clearer idea of what awaits me. Today Lucy came to call and found me alone, as Mama and Sarah both happened to be out, and in the midst of perusing Bird's letter for the second time. I told her something of what he had written, and my anxiety on his behalf and the others'; and also of Bird's proposal that he escort me home, and my uncertainty about whether to return.

"But what of your husband?" she said at length. "Do you still *love* him?" There was a hint of impatience in her voice. "I should think that would settle the question."

I sighed, remembering—remembering so much: our quarrels and our love-making; his cold silences and tender entreaties; those terrible, desperate last words of his to me—"You did not promise!" It seemed that too much had passed between us to be encompassed by any one word, be it "love" or something else.

"I used to think I knew what love was," I said at last.

"Well, *I* know what love is!" she burst out, with spirit.

I smiled at her fondly, my dear little sister. "Perhaps," I said, "that is only because you haven't been married long enough to know better."

Sunday, October 1, 1797

All these weeks I've been distressing myself over the yellow fever in Philadelphia, which the papers say has grown worse, yet it is here in Boston that disaster—terrible, incomprehensible—has struck. Two nights ago Dr. Dobel was taken from us by a virulent fever that came upon him less than a week ago; I am not certain what it was, he himself thought perhaps the influenza. But what does it matter? He is gone, that gentle, kindly spirit; I had grown remarkably attached to him these past two months. We are all distraught, but of course Lucy is truly beside herself, nearly out of her mind with agony and grief. She never left his side these past few days, once we saw that it was serious, taking little sleep and less food. I fear for her, as her constitution is considerably weakened from the ordeal, and she has been so much exposed to sickness. And what is more, she discovered only two weeks ago that she was with child.

Poor girl, she has been saying her life is over, that she no longer wishes to go on; I suppose widows are wont to say such things—particularly when their marriage has been so cruelly terminated after not six months' duration. She is young, she will no doubt go on to marry again; but it is too soon to tell her such things, of course. What I do tell her is that she must live, for her child—hers and William's—that she is now responsible not only for her own life but for that of another, a poor innocent who will need its only parent desperately.

Watching over her, stroking her wispy hair, wiping away her tears, coaxing her to drink some broth, I cannot help but wonder how I should feel in her situation. Jamie, as far as I am aware, is in fine health, of course—indeed, he should be leaving soon to begin the Southern Circuit in Charleston—but so was Dr. Dobel not two weeks ago. His death is a reminder, if any we should need, of the fragility of all health, of all life; the end may come at any time, sudden and capricious. And when I imagine myself in Lucy's place—Jamie laid out pale and cold—I feel such a sudden stab as takes my breath away—a silent inner scream of "No!" Is this, then, the answer to Lucy's question? Is my horror at the thought of Jamie's death the proof that I still love him?

I cannot tell; all I know is that the thought that I might never see him again is unbearable to me. Never again to hear him call me "lass," to feel his rough hand under my chin, holding my face up to the morning light. When I think on these things, my whole body yearns for him, for his voice and his touch. I know now that I must make my way back to Philadelphia, as soon as it is safe, and await his return.

James Wilson's Proposals for Selling or Mortgaging Some of His Lands:

[Philadelphia, Pennsylvania,] October 4, 1797

I propose to sell Lands in Pennsylvania to the Amount of twelve hundred thousand Dollars. The Purchase Money is to be applied, in the first Place, to the Discharge of any Incumbrance on the Land purchased; and to the Completion of the Titles...

My Son Bird Wilson has Powers to transact this Business for me; and will shew a Schedule of the Lands to be sold or mortgaged according to the Contract...

I have had a letter from Jamie at last, written in Philadelphia before he left for his Circuit; he apologized if his long silence had caused me anxiety, and assured me that progress was being made in the resolution of his financial affairs, but said little else. I was greatly relieved to get it, and not terribly surprised at its lack of substance, for that is Jamie's way; I must take it on faith that he yearns for me as I yearn for him, for if I waited for him to volunteer that information I should surely die unsatisfied.

What is more troubling than Jamie's reticence is that I still have had no answer from Bird, though I wrote to him near three weeks ago; I believe the fever is over by now, and it must be safe for me to return. I tell myself that Bird must be greatly occupied—perhaps he has at last acquired some clients, and is engaged in handling their cases. But at times I fear some misfortune—some further misfortune, I should say—has befallen the family. Even if he cannot afford the time or expense to come for me, I hope he will at least be able to send the money for my fare home; I wouldn't like to be obliged to ask Mama for that, as she persists in telling me that I am far better off here with her, and that I am courting disaster by returning to my husband at so uncertain a juncture.

She says a great many other things against Jamie as well, and moans that she always knew the man was not to be trusted, with his showy coach-and-four and fancy lace cuffs; but her every imprecation against him makes me fiercer in his defense. I tell her that he is only one of many who have exerted themselves industriously in trying to make something of this country, and whatever profits he came by were no more than his due; and that the unfortunate situation in which he now finds himself is not of his own making, but rather a general misfortune that has affected many others—the respected Mr. Morris and Mr. Nicholson among them. And now Jamie says, in his letter, that matters are improving. So he was right, then, it was only a matter of time.

From Hannah Wilson to Bird Wilson:

Boston, Massachusetts, November 3, 1797

... I wish very much to hear from you my dear Bird, to know whether it will be in your power to come on for me, or to send me my money. It will give us all great pleasure to see you, but if it will not be convenient to you do not propose it to anyone else; if you cannot come I will run the chance of getting home, as there will be many opportunities. Write me as soon as possible.

Have you not heard from your papa, Bird? I am very anxious to hear. I think he will write from Charleston, or rather I hope he will. I see by the papers that the fever is very much abated [in Philadelphia], and that many families are returning...

I am sure my dear Bird you sympathized with us for the death of Dr. Dobel. Next to Lucy I do not know of anyone who will feel his loss more severely than myself. I felt the affection of a sister for him, and I think [even] if I had been in Philadelphia nothing should have kept me from him. His death is one of the mysteries of Providence; there is nothing to be said but that whatever is, is right—which seems to me a very hard doctrine. Do not let anybody see this, as I should not be as open to everyone as I am to you...

I shall write to Polly Saturday or Sunday... Write soon ...

Your affectionate Mother,

H. Wilson

Philadelphia, Pennsylvania

Thursday, November 23, 1797

I should not want to say that I am sorry to have returned; but indeed, it has been a shock. Things are no better, despite what Jamie said in his letter; they are, if anything, yet worse: the parlor turned into a sewing room, with embroidered pillows and crocheted reticules displayed for sale as though it were a shop, and ladies who used to be our social equals—or inferiors—now coming in for fittings; Mrs. Nice here only twice a week; the house bare and cold, and the larder nearly empty. Poor Polly looks thin and pinched, years older than when I saw her last, some six months ago. And Emily, too—she is but fifteen, so that her looking older is only to be expected, but all the youthful joy is gone from her, and she seems frayed and limp as an old blanket. I tried to hide my dismay, for the family did their best to welcome me with what cheer they could provide; but coming from my mother's house, I felt as though a lofty featherbed had been whisked from under me and replaced with a bare wooden pallet. For a moment—just a moment—I wished that I had heeded Mama and remained in Boston.

I now know what Bird was keeping from me, and why he could not come to collect me or send me any money for the journey; in the end I had to beg from Mama yet again. I found a family to travel with, but it was an unpleasant voyage, the icy wind blasting through the flimsy walls of the carriage, and some of the inns where we stayed crowded with rascals who played at cards and such late into the night, drinking and swearing and rendering sleep impossible. But at least, during the voyage, I allowed myself to imagine that when I arrived I should find some vestiges of my old life here, and my hopes quickened with every mile that we drew closer.

Needless to say, Jamie has still not come to terms with his creditors—it was only by dint of luck that he managed to escape prison again. Bird says that he and Mr. Thomas are engaged in attending to these matters, in an effort to arrange things before Jamie's return from the South, but it is clear that he believes there is little hope.

There was a letter from Jamie awaiting my arrival—sent from Charleston near three weeks ago—that has caused me no small degree of concern. He went on at some length about the excellent opportunities he had encountered in the South, and how so much might be done with a little cash, and instructed me to tell Bird that he must immediately send a letter concerning the state of his negotiations with the creditors; for he says he has been greatly hampered in his activities by the lack of such intelligence. He also desires Bird to meet him at Edenton next month, after he has done with the Southern Circuit, in order to bring him funds and assist him in arranging for detailed surveys of his lands in that part of the country. And he suggested that I accompany Bird, but that had something of the ring of an afterthought.

When I showed the letter to Bird, his only response was a bitter laugh. He has no intention of going, that is clear enough; and I cannot imagine how I might undertake such a journey alone. Besides, if it's business that Jamie wants to transact, it's clear he has more use for Bird than for me—or thinks he has. I believe he still thinks of Bird as the adoring lad who eagerly copied out his briefs and papers and stood ever ready to do his bidding—the lad I found when I arrived here, five years since, basking in his father's praise.

Bird has become great friends, in my absence, with Dr. White, the rector of Christ Church—I had met the gentleman before, of course, as he is an old friend of Jamie's. We took tea with him and his family a few days ago, and he seems a very generous and kindly man, tall and ruddy with hair gone entirely white, so that his appearance matches his name. It is obvious that Bird admires Dr. White greatly, and has found much consolation in discussing with him matters of theology as well as the particulars of his own difficulties. I am glad for him, and yet it baffles me that as Bird's misfortunes increase, his faith in God should be strengthened. For me it is quite the opposite, and so I told Bird; why is it that a benevolent Creator would so arrange things that Henry should die, or Dr. Dobel? And, though I fear it sounds selfish, I cannot understand why our own poor family should be brought so low, when we have done nothing to deserve it. Bird and I had a lively discussion of the question, as we have before, neither of us convincing the other.

Ah, how I have missed Bird, for there truly is no one else with whom I can be so candid, so much my true self. Even now, we can still amuse one another, and manage to forget, if only for a few minutes, the cares that so weigh us down. It is for that reason, I suppose, that we have talked mostly of anything *but* the matters that urgently confront us; for what is there to say? I must take up my needle and do my best to help Polly and Emily; Bird must bring in what he can from what legal work Mr. Thomas is able to send him; Jem will continue to try to find some employment. Charles is still at Mr. Drake's, for the time being, but I fear that soon a demand for tuition will be made, and perhaps that will be the end of his education as well. And William—William is in the city, or so Polly tells me, but has kept his distance from the family, which is as it should be in my opinion. All of us are waiting, suspended, trapped like flies dangling in a spider's web—and the one who has spun it, and spins it still I fear, is Jamie.

Tuesday, December 5, 1797

We have had no word from Jamie since the letter that greeted me on my arrival. I believe he is at Raleigh now, in Carolina, for the court was to begin there on the 30th of last month. As I had expected, Bird has announced he will not go to Edenton, he wants no part of any further transactions in lands. He has discussed the matter fully with Dr. White, who agrees with him that he can best help the family by remaining here and attempting to build his law practice. Perhaps so, but I fear that Jamie will be exceedingly irked at Bird's refusal to go; I imagine Bird fears the same, and it is for that reason that he has not yet written an answer to Jamie's letter.

Such tedium is my life these days! Bending over embroidery and crewel work and seams and hems until my eyes burn—well into dusk, but no later, as we can't afford to burn the candles. Polly and Emily have been very patient with me, but I'm afraid I'm rather hopeless as a seamstress, and half the time they're obliged to undo my work and start again. Even Emily, who once came to me for help with her needlework, has far surpassed my meager skills. I sometimes think of that woman in Bethlehem—the shoemaker's wife, Anna. I showed Polly those slippers I had made up, with their lovely pattern of vines and flowers, and she was quite amazed at the quality of the embroidery. How I wish I could work such magic with my own needle, which will only make uneven stitches, or ones that are far too large; and which sometimes even stabs its poor owner, who then ruins the cotton with the stain left by her blood.

This morning we had what is now the rare diversion of a visitor—although it was only Mr. Thomas, and he had news of a most distressing nature to communicate. I asked him (though I suspected the answer) whether there had been any progress with Jamie's creditors, and he shook his head no. He then said that he had written to Jamie and advised him not to return to Philadelphia at present—not even for the sitting of the Supreme Court in February—for in his opinion the risk of arrest was too great. I was greatly alarmed to hear this, for it can only lead to more talk of impeachment. But of course Jamie mustn't run the risk of another arrest—to be thrown in that horrid jail again, suffer that humiliation, be thrown into another black pit of despair. I fear it might even be the end of him.

I suppose Mr. Thomas, being Jamie's lawyer, does know best (and he mentioned that he has authorized Jamie to draw on him for several hundred dollars, to cover his expenses in the South, which is certainly most generous). And yet, secretly, I cannot help but entertain some hope that Jamie will return—that he will do whatever is necessary to satisfy these wretched creditors, even relinquish his lands and his dreams of vast settlements, so that he might once more be with me, and with the children. I feel sure that I could endure the endless seams and hems—and the moldy potatoes and pigs' heads we are reduced to eating—if only he were here to take me in his arms and kiss me now and then, and call me his lass.

Thursday, December 14, 1797

I was so unfortunate as to meet Mrs. Bingham at the corner of Third and Spruce this morning, while on my way to the New Market. I have spied her before, of course—for she is tall and always dressed so regally; today she wore a lovely rose-colored bonnet with a gray feather the length of my arm protruding from it at a jaunty angle. But in the past I have been able to avoid her (and others of my acquaintance as well) by darting into an alley or even, if necessary, turning suddenly and returning the way that I had come. Today, venturing so close to her house, I should have been on my guard, but I was so lost in my private melancholy that I failed to see her until I was practically upon her. We had no choice but to greet one another with great enthusiasm, although I'm quite certain she was no more eager for the encounter than I was. Then, at the point when most conversations turn to inquiries about how one has been faring, there was an awkward pause; for both of us knew that she has been faring a good deal better than I. There was no way to conceal the wicker basket that I carried, a tell-tale sign that I was out on a servant's errand.

Mrs. Bingham's thin-lipped smile began to take on a frozen look, and at length proceeded to melt gradually into an expression of sympathy and concern.

"My dear," she said, placing a kid-gloved hand upon my arm, "I am so very sorry for your recent … adversities. We were quite appalled to hear what befell Judge Wilson at Burlington. In August, was it not? Or September?"

I hadn't the faintest idea what she was talking about. August, September: I had been in Boston, Jamie in Bethlehem and then here. Burlington is in Jersey—but had not Bird said something concerning urgent business that had detained Jamie in Jersey?

"Some of these creditors," Mrs. Bingham continued, tut-tutting and shaking her head so that the gray feather swooped above our heads like a circling vulture, "they'll stop at nothing. Really, to have a sitting judge of the Supreme Court arrested and thrown into prison! I'm sure it was quite unnecessary. But so good of his son to have arranged so quickly for his release. It must have been a great relief to the family. Has Mr. Wilson returned yet, from his travels to the southward?"

I managed to mumble that he was not yet back, but everything—Mrs. Bingham's voice, the clatter of wheels and horses' hooves on the cobblestones, the cries of vendors at the market—suddenly seemed at a great distance. I half-heard Mrs. Bingham's excuses about having an appointment to keep, and smiled, nodded, watched as she and her feather went on their way—soaring back across the chasm that now separated her life from mine, the chasm that our conversation had not so much bridged as widened.

I flew back to the house, my errands at the market forgotten, and immediately went to Jamie's office to confront Bird with what I had learned. Bird ran his fingers through his hair and guiltily avoided my eyes while I spoke. He agreed that he should have told me, and said that he was very sorry, sorrier than I knew. It had been worse than the Prune Street incident, for the New Jersey judges viewed Jamie's claim of privilege from arrest rather skeptically; but in the end they had released him on the bail that Bird had managed to scrape together, with the legal question to be taken up by the New Jersey Supreme Court in a few months' time. His Papa had been in jail for a good two weeks this time,

Bird said, and it had taken its toll on him; he had given Bird strict instructions to breathe not a word of it to me, as it would only upset me and there was nothing I could have done to help him.

I was about to scold him, and tell him that he should never keep such information from me in the future, when I saw his face begin to fold in upon itself with anguish, and he quickly turned from me.

"What a mess he's made of things!" he cried, his voice containing the hint of a sob. "To drive us into ruin—humiliate us in the eyes of society—run from his creditors and leave me with the impossible task of trying to placate them! And worst of all, to force me to deceive you—you, a person so dear to me that I ...I ..." He now bowed his head and covered it with his hands. "He is not worthy of you, not worthy."

"Oh, Bird, my dear Bird!" I moved to where he sat behind the desk, turned him to me, and pressed his head to my bosom; he sobbed there like a child, and I leaned my head on his silky curls. At that moment I felt he truly *was* my child, as much as Henry was (or nearly), and I wanted more than anything to comfort him. "What you must do is apply yourself to your legal work, and provide for the others as best you can. I shall attend to your Papa—and to myself. If he does not come back in February, I shall go to Edenton alone and try to make him see reason."

"No, you mustn't go to him!" Bird cried. He lifted his head from my bosom and rose now, and placed his hands on my face almost exactly as Jamie had in Bethlehem, that day when I last saw him. "He will only drag you down with him, as he is trying to drag us all down."

And then Bird did a thing which I'm certain he would never have done had he not been so agitated that he was scarcely himself: he kissed me full on the mouth—not, I fear, in a filial manner at all, but with passion. Not the same sort of passion with which Jamie kisses me, but a gentle passion, muted by tenderness. It is awful to contemplate, a son kissing his mother in that way; and yet I confess that, in the first few seconds, my body could not help but respond. There was such sweetness to his kiss, and something within me began to turn molten.

But then I came to my senses and suddenly pushed him away. He gasped and turned from me, sobbing once more. "Forgive me," I heard him say. "Forgive me."

"It is forgiven, and forgotten," I managed to say, though my voice was far from steady. "We are both in a state, and not responsible for our actions."

Indeed, I believe it is already forgotten by both of us, or nearly so. For when Bird and I encountered one another at dinner it was much the same as ever, except that we avoided one another's eyes; I'm sure Polly and Emily and Jem observed nothing amiss. But I shall certainly have to be on my guard with Bird in future; the thing to do is to find him a young lady—an unmarried young lady—and if she be an heiress, so much the better!

From James Wilson to Bird Wilson:

Raleigh, North Carolina, December 17, 1797

... It is indeed surprising that you have not written to me. A single Reflection must have suggested to you that anything I could write to you ... concerning Mr. Butler ... must have depended very much on the Result of your Interview with Mr. Coxe; and your promise to write to me <u>as soon as possible</u> afterwards. And yet to this Day I have not heard a single Syllable from you.

I expect that, immediately on the Receipt of this, you will set out to meet me at Edenton. To Mrs. Wilson I refer you on this Point. I need not tell you to bring with you all the Money that shall be possible. I have many Things to say to you, which cannot be communicated by Letter...

From James Wilson to Joseph Thomas:

Raleigh, North Carolina, December 17, 1797

... In your letter of the 24th of October last ... you promised to write me fully by the next Post. But that next Post has not yet arrived. Agreeably to what you authorize me to do, I have drawn on you two bills payable at sight—one for fifty, the other for one hundred dollars. In a few days I shall probably draw for somewhat more.

... I cannot now give you a particular account of the Purchases I made in this State and in Georgia so far as I have received information concerning them. I can only say, in general, that the information hitherto has been favorable in a degree much exceeding my most sanguine hopes. In this State I am now procuring the most minute account of the

Situation, title & quality of every particular tract which I purchased. To prosecute this object is essential both here and in Georgia. But in order to prosecute it I must pass the winter in those States. This I have determined to do.

But in order to accomplish & secure every object, money as well as information is necessary. You can have no conception of what importance it is to me to have some funds. Twenty thousand dollars would I believe secure everything; Ten thousand would secure a great deal. Even the <u>Whole</u> of those sums would not be necessary to be transmitted here in Cash or Bankbills. One third part would suffice ... How much, & whether anything can be done in this matter, you can best tell. I can only repeat you can have no conception of what importance it would be. Without funds much <u>must</u> be lost. Remember me in the best Manner to Mrs. Thomas. Write to me fully by Bird...

From Richard Drake, Schoolmaster, to Bird Wilson:

Pottstown, Pennsylvania, January 13, 1798

... I take the Liberty of sending you your Accounts for the Tuition & Board of your Brother Charles, and shall be much obliged to You to honor my Draft for the Balance due ...

I am happy to inform you your Brother is in perfect Health. He desires me to acquaint you, he wants a pair of Trousers; shall I give Orders for a pair? ...

From James Wilson to Bird Wilson:

Edenton, North Carolina, January 17, 1798

... To what Cause shall I assign your total Silence? A full Month ago, I wrote to you from Raleigh on Subjects of much Importance; and directed you to meet me at this Place, and to send a Letter on before you. Here I have been near two Weeks, and have neither seen you nor received any Letter. I hope you will be able to account for all of this.

Situated as I now am, you cannot expect that I have any Thing new to impart to you. The Winter is passing fast; and all my Business of immense Magnitude in the Southern States is totally suspended. You may easily conceive what my Feelings are. I write this by Mr. Iredell, thinking that he may possibly meet Mrs. Wilson and you on the Road...

Friday, February 2, 1798

Mr. Iredell has just come to us—I believe he came almost as soon as he arrived in the city, the dear man. I was so pleased to see his amiable, kindly face—the lines etched at the sides of his mouth both the remnant and reminder of his easy smile—that I did not at once grasp the meaning of his appearance at our door.

"My dear Mr. Iredell!" I cried. Then, recognizing some discomfort, some awkwardness about his expression, I paused. If he is here, I thought, then Jamie should be here as well, for the court opens on Monday—they should have ridden up together from Edenton. I peered behind him, out to the street, searching. Perhaps Jamie was alighting from a carriage, retrieving his baggage from the driver. But there was no carriage, no driver; no Jamie at all.

Mr. Iredell shook his head. "He is not come," he said gently, softly, as though setting down some fragile china doll so that it should not break.

I had not realized how all my hopes had gathered around this moment, how I had been daily waiting for the sight of his face, the sound of his voice. Of course, he had not written to say he was coming—indeed, his letters seemed to indicate quite the opposite. And yet some foolish part of me expected that he would simply appear, at our door, as he had before: vigorous despite his long journey, full of plans, ready to take his seat upon the bench, and resolved to make a clean slate of his business affairs and begin anew. He would draw me to him and kiss me on the forehead and say with his gruff tenderness, "Ah, you were right, my lass, you were right all along." So I had imagined, lying alone in my bed on these cold winter nights.

"Not ... not ... ?" I could say no more; weeping engulfed me, try as I might to retain my composure. Mr. Iredell stepped forward, a hand outstretched to comfort me; suddenly light-headed, I felt my legs begin to tremble. Next I knew I was falling upon him heavily, sobbing into his chest.

"We must bring her into the parlor," I heard Bird say. "Here, lay her down on the settee."

I was lifted, carried, lowered; Mr. Iredell's face, then Bird's, hovered over me. Polly brought me a cordial, from the one bottle we have left, and helped me lift my head to sip it. The liquid trickled through my body, a little running brook of warmth.

"Thank you, thank you," I said, sitting up, and recovered enough to be rather chagrined. "I'm all right now, I promise you. Please. Mr. Iredell, won't you sit down?"

"It pains me beyond expressing that I should be the bearer of such unwelcome tidings," said Mr. Iredell, as he sat heavily on a spindly wooden chair. "He would not come—indeed, he seemed to expect *your* arrival daily, Mr. Wilson, in the company of Mrs. Wilson. He gave me this to give to you"—he retrieved a folded letter from his waistcoat and handed it to Bird. "He believed I might encounter the two of you on the road."

"Are you quite sure he is not coming?" I asked, and I was conscious of a note of pleading in my voice. "The court, you know, he must take his place on …"

I stopped. Mr. Iredell's expression, ever transparent, was now visibly pained. "My dear Mrs. Wilson, I cannot offer you much encouragement there. I'm afraid Judge Wilson is not well."

"Not well?" I set down my cordial glass and tried to stand, but felt my head begin to spin once more. "What do you mean? Is he ill?" Of course, this was the very excuse we had been giving out to creditors and bill collectors—that Jamie was indisposed; but I hadn't thought it to be true.

Mr. Iredell looked around at all of us—James and Emily had entered the room by now—and hesitated before continuing. "Not ill, exactly. But very … agitated in his mind. Anxious, extremely anxious." He made a small grimace, half frown and half smile, and sighed. "I doubt that he should be able to take up his seat, at present, even if he were here. I imagine it would be difficult for him to attend to the arguments of counsel."

"But what … what shall we do?" I looked to Bird, but he would not meet my eyes. "Mr. Iredell, you have seen him more recently than any of us. And I know that you are his friend—a true and loyal friend, indeed. If he will not come here … tell us, please, what we can do for him."

Mr. Iredell nervously tapped two fingers on the top of his hat, which rested on his lap. "He's a hard man to do things for, as I'm sure you know. He seems to know his own mind, and wants to keep his own counsel. But … he is very much alone. He stayed in our house for but a few days, and then—well, we are rather crowded, as the house is not large. And someone is always ill. In any event, he insisted that he could not impose on us longer and moved into Horniblow's—a tavern, with rooms for travelers, that is by the courthouse. And there he spends much of his time, rarely leaving his room, rarely speaking to anyone. When I call on him, I find him at the desk, in the midst of writing … *something*, I know not what. He has gone through all the quills he brought with him, you know—I made him a present of some very fine ones I had obtained from Halifax.

"But, what I meant to say was—and I hope I do not overstep the bounds, for I shouldn't want to intrude on private matters—but I do believe it would give him some comfort to have some member of his family by him. Someone whom he might allow to care for him, and perhaps bring some quiet to his mind."

There was a silence. Again I looked at Bird; he now returned my glance, but only frowned and shook his head.

"Well." Mr. Iredell stood and took up his cloak from where it lay unceremoniously on the floor, forgotten in the general agitation. "I fear I must take my leave now, for I'm greatly fatigued from my journey."

We thanked him for all the trouble he had taken on our behalf, and I was strong enough now to see him to the door. "Come see us again in a few days time," I urged him as he bent to kiss my hand.

For I know what I must do—I knew, indeed, as soon as Mr. Iredell revealed that Jamie was ill, and in need of caring for. Whether I can talk sense into him or not, my place is by his side; for we are bound to one another, not only by our marriage vows but as well by whatever it is that pulls me towards him, as irresistibly as the sea pulls a wave back from the sand—call it love, call it duty, call it what you will. I should have given him my promise, back in Bethlehem those months ago; it pains me to think he may now be in doubt concerning my intentions. But no matter—when he sees me, he will know that the promise was as good as given. It only remains to explain it all to Bird.

From James Iredell to Hannah Iredell:

Philadelphia, Pennsylvania, February 5, 1798

... I arrived here perfectly well, though much fatigued, on Friday last. Our Court is to begin today, but we have barely a quorum ... I was very unexpectedly prevented by business from going to see my Mother yesterday, after preparing for it, but I sent & found she was perfectly well—so much so as to have been at Church. Peter escaped the yellow fever, and attends me...

I alighted out of the stage to inquire for Mrs. Wilson, and found her and all his family at his house in Market-street. She was very well, but extremely affected in seeing me; and finding Mr. Wilson was not coming, she burst into tears...

From James Iredell to Hannah Iredell:

Philadelphia, Pennsylvania, February 8, 1798

... Our Court has been very busily employed since Monday, being in Court every day from ten till three... The ... Butlers are all well. Mrs. Wilson at present thinks of returning with me, which I suppose will be soon after the rising of this Court, for I take it for granted I shall go the Southern Circuit...

Monday, February 12, 1798

I have made most of my preparations for departure, such as they are (the advantage of having fewer possessions is that it is easier to select those to pack), and only await Mr. Iredell's word that the Court has adjourned its session. It is an odd state to be in, this prolonged balancing on the brink of the unknown. I am reminded of something that happened when I was a girl, and went riding out into the country with my family to a spot renowned for its beauty—the edge of a steep cliff that overlooked a green, cloud-dappled valley, all the fields and forests stretching out before us. I drew nearer and nearer, until the toes of my slippers touched the very border of the precipice, seized by a desire to plunge myself downward—and a simultaneous horror that I might do that very thing. I

321

stood there for some long moments, my arms outspread, transfixed by these strange and warring impulses, until Mama spied me and snatched me back to safety.

It is like that now—I think of Jamie constantly, for I feel sure that he is looking for me daily and fearing that I have abandoned him; I want more than anything to join him, even if it means a plunge into some abyss. And yet the thought of it at the same time fills me with terror: to return to that damp, dull town, where I know practically no one, with no money—and with no idea when I shall be able to leave it. And to join a man I have not seen in over six months, a man to whom I am bound by ties of both duty and affection, but who may be greatly changed—almost a stranger to me. I look about this house that has become my refuge—still elegant and capacious in spite of its peeling paint and soiled draperies and the bare spots where a silk-upholstered chair or inlaid table once stood—and ask myself when I shall set eyes on it again.

But I have made my decision, and I shall not look back. Mr. Thomas came by yesterday, and expressed approval and admiration when I told him of my plan.

"There is no tonic like the loyalty and love of a devoted wife," he pronounced, patting my hand in what I'm sure was meant to be a paternal manner. I don't know why, but I recoiled from it—I could not stop myself. It's really quite shameful of me; Mr. Thomas has so generously devoted himself to Jamie's interests, and has been most kind in referring bits of law business to Bird, and yet I cannot bring myself to like the man.

And he did something, while he was here, that has made me rather uneasy: he insisted that he must have some papers—something to do with the possible sale of some of Jamie's lands—that were locked away in Jamie's desk. We told him that we hadn't got the key, and that Jamie was most particular about people going into his desk—which, of course, was why he'd brought the key away with him. But Mr. Thomas was quite adamant, and at last, with some misgivings, we sent to the locksmith and had him break open the lock—for Mr. Thomas said that Jamie might stand to profit greatly if the papers could be got at, and lose a great deal otherwise. So I suppose it was for the best; but we all agreed that we should have to find the money to have the lock repaired, and not breathe a word of the incident to Jamie.

Mr. Thomas found the papers he wanted in the desk, but there as well were three bunches of lovely white feathers, bundled together like arrows.

"Quills!" I cried, delighted at the sight. "Why, just what your Papa needs. Remember? Mr. Iredell said he had gone through all he brought with him." I began to pick them up. "I can bring these with me, as a present for him. Most likely he's forgotten all about them—won't he be surprised?"

But Polly said with alarm that no, I mustn't—for wouldn't her Papa know where they'd been taken from, and that his desk had been opened? Of course, she's right; I'm always forgetting such things. What a shame, though, not to be able to present Jamie with a gift he would so much appreciate!

Thursday, February 15, 1798

Mr. Iredell came by this evening to say that the Supreme Court adjourned its session today, and that he is now free to return home—and I to accompany him, if (as he said) that is still my plan. I assured him that it was, and that my trunk had been packed for several days in anticipation of our departure; I could leave tomorrow if that was his wish. He replied that it was indeed his heartfelt wish, but that he was engaged for dinner at Major Butler's tomorrow, and so we must wait until Saturday.

"Major Butler?" I said. The very name sent little prickles of alarm down my spine. I have seen him in passing once or twice since my return from Boston, and he has asked—in a way that one would think friendly if one did not know better—whether my husband was in town, and when he was expected back. And his emissary, that thick-lipped Mr. Gibson, has been here to see Bird more than once, to remind him of Jamie's debt, and the interest on it that is continuing to accrue—as though we might forget. I had an impulse to ask Mr. Iredell not to mention Jamie's exact whereabouts to Major Butler, if he should inquire, but could not bring myself to say the words. It seemed too sordid, as though Jamie were some sort of criminal in hiding. And so all I said was, "Please give Major Butler my compliments."

"Indeed I shall, Mrs. Wilson," he said, rising from the settee. "And now, if you'll excuse me, I must retire to my lodgings and rest." His face caught the light from the fire for a moment, and I could see deep shadows under his eyes; the poor man, he looked exhausted. "I would advise you to take a good deal of rest yourself before Saturday. It's not an easy journey, as you may recall. And this time of year, with the waterways often still iced over, it's likely we shall have to go almost entirely by land."

I winced inwardly, recalling the stagecoaches' hard wooden benches, their bumping and bouncing over stones and ruts. But I only smiled at Mr. Iredell and offered him my hand. "With you as my traveling companion, Sir," I said, as he bent to kiss it, "I am certain that, whatever the discomforts, I shall take a great deal of pleasure in the voyage."

And indeed, this was no mere flattery; for, much as I dread the journey, and fear what I shall discover at its terminus, I am glad to be taking it in the company of Mr. Iredell. Such a kind and generous, so honest and trustworthy a gentleman! I grow fonder and fonder of him; and somehow—though I know this is no more than foolishness—I feel that no harm can befall me as long as he is by me.

From Thomas Blount, Representative from North Carolina and brother of William Blount, to his brother John Gray Blount, North Carolina merchant and landowner:

Philadelphia, Pennsylvania, February 16, 1798

... Major Butler, who holds Judge Wilson's paper to a very considerable amount ..., has determined to sue his Judgeship in Carolina & hold his body in custody, if he can get hold on it, at all hazards until he gives him satisfactory security—and he has upon my advice, which I found it impossible to avoid giving, determined to empower William Slade, of Edenton, where he understands the Judge now is, to commence & carry on the suit...

Mr. Butler's power of Attorney to Mr. Slade & the papers on which suit is to be brought will go from me, under cover to Capt. Collins ...tomorrow by Judge Iredell. This mode of conveyance is adopted for the sake of secrecy, which in the opinion of Major B. is highly necessary ...

Tomorrow morning I depart for Edenton; and today has been so fatiguing that I fear I lack the strength for the journey. Every member of the family has taken me aside for some parting words, or a message to their Papa. Emily has instructed me to tell him how industrious she has been, and given me a small embroidered pillow to bring as a gift and a sample of her work. James put on his most manly demeanor, and told me I mustn't worry, that he will find regular employment somewhere and provide for the family. And Polly, dear girl, took me aside and told me almost tearfully (quite uncharacteristic of her) that she had an apology to make: she had thought the worst of me when I first came here, she said, and believed I had married her Papa only for his wealth and position. (Well, I had suspected as much.) But now, she went on, she knew she had done me a terrible injustice; for I could easily have stayed at home in Boston with Mama and abandoned them all to their fates. The final proof of my devotion to her Papa, she said—if any be needed—was that I was undertaking this arduous winter journey, to a place where I knew not what would await me, simply in order to be by his side at his time of need.

"I suppose you understand this by now," she finished, "but we have come to admire and to love you—all of us."

The simplicity of this was more moving to me than any flowery effusion, and I reached my arms to her and held her in a lengthy embrace. In truth, I have lately been dreaming of what might have been had I chosen to stay in Boston with Mama—or even (dare I confess this?) if I hadn't married Jamie at all. And were Polly's first suspicions of me so wide of the mark? Though I wouldn't say I married for money, exactly, surely part of Jamie's attraction for me was the gay and glittering life I believed he would provide me. But Polly's praise of me, the image she held before me of my finest self, was so beautiful that I confess I felt tears at the mere contemplation of it; and I resolved, at that moment, truly to *be* the woman that Polly so admired.

As for Bird—alas, I don't think he will ever understand or approve my decision to go to Edenton. He's been quite out of sorts since I told him of it and barely says a word to me; but as I couldn't bear the thought of leaving him on such terms, I suggested we go for a short walk, as we used to—in hopes that we might recapture some of our old ease and happiness. Silly of me, I suppose, for Bird strode along with a glum purposefulness that was hardly conducive to pleasant conversation. Then, at the corner of Sixth and Market, we encountered a very pretty young woman with yellow curls peeking from beneath her bonnet and lovely eyes of a bluish-gray color. She greeted Bird by name and smiled invitingly, but all he did was mumble something that must have been "Good day to you, Miss," and keep on walking. So much for my tutelage in the art of flirting! I peppered him with questions about who she was and how he had made her acquaintance, but he professed not to remember her name or where he had met her.

Ah well, perhaps he will take more interest in such things once I am gone. It pains me, just a little, to think so; but I suppose that's how it must be. And yet, I do wish he were coming with us. To have both Bird *and* Mr. Iredell at my side—would that not be lovely!

From Harrison Gray Otis, Representative from Massachusetts and cousin of Hannah Wilson, to his wife, Sally Otis:

Philadelphia, Pennsylvania, February 18, 1798

... Mrs. Wilson left this place yesterday for North Carolina in quest of her unfortunate Husband, who is I am told greatly dejected and afraid to make his appearance here. She was accompanied by Judge Iredell ...

New Castle, Delaware

Tuesday, February 20, 1798

We were so fortunate as to reach this place before nightfall yesterday, but the weather turned so foul overnight that Mr. Iredell thought it best to remain here until it clears, and then catch another stage bound for the South. To travel in winter is indeed a trial, and I fear our journey will be greatly slowed by the vagaries of nature.

I have been rather gloomy company, wracked with doubts about whether I have chosen the right course of action—one minute regretting that I did not stay in Philadelphia, the next wishing for the comforts of Boston. But Mr. Iredell has been so exceedingly good as not to notice it, or pretend not to. He has scrupulously avoided any topics that ring of unpleasantness (which, alas, excludes virtually all the circumstances of my life at present), and instead has set as his task my entertainment and diversion, as though he were my own personal jester. And—though I daresay no jester has confronted so difficult an audience since Charles I stood on the brink of his execution—he has succeeded admirably.

Never did I think that tales from the annals of the Supreme Court could be so amusing; certainly I have never found them so when Jamie recounts them, which is not very often. But Mr. Iredell has such a talent for mimicry, and such a keen eye for spotting the humor in any situation, that he could recite even the Court minutes and have me in his thrall. His impersonation of Judge Chase, complete with double chins and vociferous indignation, brought tears of laughter to my eyes. Fortunately there was only one other passenger in the stage, an elderly gentleman who appeared to be quite deaf, so that we had no worries about being overheard. It is quite different being virtually alone with Mr. Iredell, instead of in our parlor surrounded by the family; I already feel that we are on intimate terms.

There has only been one incident that gave me pause. When we arrived last night and set to unpacking our things, I heard some rather shocking exclamations coming from Mr. Iredell's room, which was adjacent to my own. Thinking that something untoward had befallen him, I knocked at his door, and was surprised to find the room in a complete state of disarray, nearly the entire contents of his trunk strewn across the floor.

"Oh!" he said, reddening at the sight of me. "I do apologize if I disturbed you—I know you don't approve of swearing, my dear Mrs. Wilson—but I seem to have misplaced something very important, very important indeed."

I offered to assist in the search, and he explained that he was searching for some papers addressed to his friend Captain Collins, a merchant in Edenton, from a Mr. Blount in Philadelphia. I began to pick through the debris on the bed, hoping for a glimpse of paper, when it struck me that this must be the same Mr. Blount—Mr. Allison's associate—through whom Jamie had become indebted to Major Butler. I was even more alarmed when Mr. Iredell began muttering that he was carrying these papers as a favor to Major Butler.

"Do you happen to know," I inquired carefully, "what these papers contain?"

"No, not really," he puffed, rising from the floor, where he'd been peering under the bed. "Letters of some sort, I suppose. I only know that they're exceedingly important. Major Butler and Mr. Blount were most emphatic on the point of my delivering them personally to Captain Collins, as soon as I could after my arrival."

"Mr. Blount …" I said lightly. "Would that by any chance be Mr. William Blount? I believe Mr. Wilson is acquainted with him."

"Not William," he said, now examining the empty trunk in case the papers had somehow lodged there. "Mr. Thomas Blount, his brother. There are several brothers—it's a well known family in Carolina, cousins of Captain Collins, and I've been acquainted with them all for many years. Thomas Blount was a guest at Major Butler's when I was there for dinner last week." He stood up and crossed his arms before his chest, his hair more askew than usual. "Damn! Where could they be?"

Just then his face, ruddy from the search, registered a puzzled expression, and he began patting at his waistcoat. He inserted a hand and withdrew a rumpled but intact sheaf of papers, which had evidently been folded several times.

"Well, I'll be damned," he said wonderingly. "I must have put them there for safekeeping."

We both laughed, Mr. Iredell apologized for compounding his sins by continuing to swear, and I bade him a good night. I was greatly relieved to discover that the papers, whatever they were, apparently had nothing to do with William Blount, or Major Butler, or that troublesome debt.

From James Wilson to Bird Wilson:

Edenton, North Carolina, February 24, 1798

... With Mrs. Wilson's Letter of the eighth of this month I was favored the Day before Yesterday. I do not write her in Answer to it, because I think it highly probable that before this Letter shall arrive at Philadelphia, she will be on her Journey to this Place.

... [I]n the long Lapse of near five Months, I have not learnt from [Mr. Thomas] nor from you a single Iota of Intelligence concerning the Situation in which Affairs stand or are likely to stand with Regard to those Persons who have ... Demands against me. Is it too much for a Friend or for a Parent to solicit an immediate Communication on a Subject so very interesting? Address to me at this Place. Remember me to the Family...

Havre de Grace, Maryland

Saturday, February 24, 1798

A most distressing mishap befell our traveling party yesterday morning; and, partly as a result, I have committed a serious indiscretion, one that I must now put from my mind forever.

Our stage—containing eight of us, including myself and Mr. Iredell—had come across Delaware and Maryland, through Head of Elk, when we arrived at the broad gray expanse of the Susquehanna River. The river, it seems, is always icy at this time of year, but the ice may at some times be cut and ferried through, and at others be solid enough that one may cross over it. On Friday, when we arrived at the river's edge, we were informed that the ice would neither bear, nor could it be easily cut; and so we spent the night at an inn in hopes that the morning would bring a change in the situation.

Shortly before dawn, we were awakened with the news that the ice had been tried, and it would bear a wagon and horses. We all hurried to the river with our baggage, which was loaded onto a sleigh, racing against the sun and its melting warmth. This sleigh, pulled by two Negroes, went ahead, and the passengers followed two abreast, separating ourselves by approximately ten feet on all sides, as we were instructed by the driver. I tried to put on a brave face, but was in truth terrified nearly out of my wits, imagining the ice cracking under my foot with every step, and myself being sucked into the frigid deep. Mr. Iredell must have discerned this, for he assured me he had made this very crossing many times before without encountering any accidents.

It was bitter cold, with a sharp wind, and I could hear the child in front of me—a girl of about ten, traveling with her parents, complaining that her face and fingers were nearly frozen. Her mother—and her father, who was walking before her—repeatedly told her that she must be patient, that it would be but a little longer. And indeed, the opposite shore—which, upon our setting out, appeared as distant as the coast of

330

Europe itself—gradually grew nearer, the landscape no longer a mass of browns and greens, but separating itself into bare oaks and maples and needle-covered evergreens.

"You see?" the mother, whose name is Mrs. Baldwin, said to the daughter. "It's growing warmer now. The sun is up."

Just then I heard a cracking noise, followed by a man's scream; the mother cried out, and the girl wailed "Papa!" I could then see that Mr. Baldwin, a tall man possessed of an ample girth, had fallen through a hole that had opened in the ice and was struggling to hoist himself out. Fortunately, he had carried with him a boat hook, which he managed to attach to the ice and which seemed to be preventing his sinking.

Mr. Iredell began to move quickly forward, calling back to me, "Take Mrs. Baldwin and the child to shore—go around the hole at a safe distance." It was left to me to discern what a safe distance might be, and it was all I could do to restrain Mrs. Baldwin and her daughter from rushing towards Mr. Baldwin. Fortunately, we were no more than a hundred yards from shore. I herded them over some ice to the left of the hole, which appeared to me to have a thicker cast to it, but for all I knew we were all three in danger of finding ourselves under water in short order.

"Keep a safe distance from one another!" I called out repeatedly. I could hear shouts and splashing from the direction of the hole, but kept my eyes on the ice under my feet and those of my charges. At length, after what seemed an eternity, we reached land—dark, frozen earth, wonderfully firm and reliable. As soon as we were all safely ashore, we turned back to the scene on the ice: Mr. Iredell and one of the Negroes were still endeavoring to hoist Mr. Baldwin from the river, while the driver and the other Negro stood at about 10 feet distant, in case they should be needed. The male passengers, other than Mr. Iredell, were either heading towards shore or had already reached it—including a pale Frenchman who must have run all the way, and who paced back and forth near us on the shore, muttering *"Mon Dieu!* and *"Quelle horreur!"* Mrs. Baldwin had gone deathly pale, but busied herself in comforting her weeping daughter.

Mr. Iredell appeared to have hold of Mr. Baldwin's legs—I later learned that he had tied them up with a leather strap, which he commandeered from the sleigh—and the Negro held Mr. Baldwin's fur coat, weighted by its soaking, by the back of the neck. Within a minute or two of our reaching shore, they had managed, through what must have been a massive exertion, to lift him out. They then carried him to the sleigh, which the Negroes drew ashore. Again I had to restrain Mrs. Baldwin and her daughter from running across the ice to him, fearing another break and a further disaster.

It was only when they reached the shore that I discovered Mr. Iredell had himself fallen in while attempting the rescue; although he was not as badly chilled as Mr. Baldwin, he was certainly in some danger. The two of them were carried to this inn where we now lodge, rubbed dry, and put to bed in the front room between several blankets. Mrs. Baldwin rubbed her husband's head with brandy, while I did the same for Mr. Iredell, and within a short time they began to perspire, which in the circumstances was a sign of health. Afterwards they took a little burnt brandy and some tea, and Mr. Iredell was able to move to a chamber on the second floor.

It was there, after settling him onto the bed, that I began to weep; I had not yet done so, for my entire body had been too tightly bound with anxiety. Now, knowing that he was safe and well—and that he had risked his own life for the sake of another's—I was overcome with all the emotions I had held in check.

"Now, now," he said, his voice still weakened from his ordeal, "all is well. I'm none the worse for it, and I warrant Mr. Baldwin will be nearly as good as new by tomorrow."

"But you could have drowned!" I cried.

"Well, it seemed safe enough, once I thought of the leather strap. And I had no choice, really. It was my duty to try to save the man."

These words Mr. Iredell spoke—"no choice ... my duty"—rang as an echo of the words I had myself used with Bird, when defending my decision to undertake this journey. The thought of my own situation, mingled with my recent alarm over Mr. Iredell, set my emotions to overflowing. I could not help but throw myself upon Mr. Iredell's chest and begin to sob in earnest. I imagine he was surprised by this, but he seemed to understand that I needed comforting. He began gently to pat my back and allowed me to lie there and weep; perhaps he still felt a chill, and the warmth of my body did him some good. I confess that the warmth of *his* body acted as a tonic to me; as my sobs began to subside, I could not bring myself to lift my head, but stayed there for some minutes. It had been so long, many months, since I had lain with my head on a man's chest; sensations long unfamiliar to me began to stir. I was in a state now, indeed—uncertain of where I was or with whom, my anxiety for Mr. Iredell so mingled with my fears for Jamie that in my mind I may have confused the two.

But I shall not make excuses for myself—except to say that I did not plan what occurred next, nor do I think I was entirely aware, at first, of what was transpiring. It was certainly most improper, and I cannot bear to think of the scandal, should anyone ever hear of it. But no one ever shall—ever. I know that I may trust in Mr. Iredell's discretion. What an admirable gentleman he is! We have agreed to speak of it no more—and for my part, I shall try not to think on it, ever again.

But I must go now, for the driver has declared that the stage is to leave momentarily. What later transpired between us must await another day.

From John Rutledge, Jr., U.S. Representative from South Carolina, to his brother Edward Rutledge:

Philadelphia, Pennsylvania, February 25, 1798

... Judge Wilson has not returned yet from his southern circuit—heretofore it has been supposed by his Creditors that he was not tangible during the sitting of the Court, but this doctrine is over-ruled, & he has not been able to make his appearance at the Court this month. His poor Wife gives it out that he is sick in Carolina, & I am often asked if my Letters say whether Wilson is getting better. His family, which is large, are supported by the needle work of his wife & daughters, & the practice of his Son, which, I understand, is not extensive ...

From Thomas Blount, U.S. Representative from North Carolina, to his brother John Gray Blount:

Philadelphia, Pennsylvania, February 26, 1798

... What I now write to you is intended for your own eye only. Major Butler on Saturday last sent Judge Wilson's Bond for 174,000 Dollars, which he received of Dr. Allison & William Blount in part payment for the Salvadore Tract, to Edenton with a power of Attorney to William Slade to bring suit upon it in North Carolina. I have promised

Major Butler to engage your influence with Mr. Slade to induce him to undertake the Business, & hope I have not promised what I cannot perform—especially as the money which he may get upon this Bond from Judge Wilson is to go to William Blount's credit in the payment of the heaviest & most disagreeable debt he owes in the world.

If the Judge should be sued, as he certainly will if Mr. Slade acts as Major B. has directed him, I beseech you not to be his security, even for his appearance on the next day, on any account whatever, for his son & his lawyer have both told Major B. that he has no real Estate anywhere that is not encumbered with at least one Mortgage, & if you rely on his honor, or trust him in any thing, he will certainly deceive you. Let him go to gaol ...

Aboard The Eagle, Albemarle Sound, N.C.

Saturday, March 10, 1798

The spires of Edenton are in sight, and this is the first the ship has been calm enough, and my stomach settled enough, for me to take pen in hand. I was quite pleased when Mr. Iredell came upon this ship in the harbor at Baltimore, bound for Carolina, for I was covered with bruises from being bounced about in that stage; but the rigors of this sea voyage have been almost sufficient to make me long for its end.

And yet, though I would not remain on the water, I am far from eager to make land, fearing what I shall find when I arrive there. Just now, up on deck, Mr. Iredell offered me the spyglass through which he had been peering, but I hadn't the stomach to take it. I would have preferred a glass that would have let me look backwards rather than forwards, to these past few weeks that we have spent together.

I have, I confess, allowed my rueful fantasies to wander to what life might have been like had I linked my fortunes to Mr. Iredell, or someone like him. For he is possessed of such gentleness and sympathy that I find I can speak to him almost as freely as I do to Bird, and yet his conversation is infinitely more adept and charming; and of course, he is no mere boy, but a man of substance and experience, just as Jamie is. Perhaps he has not driven himself as hard as Jamie has, and certainly he has not endeavored to amass a great fortune—but only look at the circumstances to which Jamie's ambitions have brought him!

Indeed, it has entered my mind that Mr. Iredell combines in his character the qualities I most admire in the two other men who are dearest to me, with none of their defects. And—though it is difficult with a gentleman of such delicate manners to distinguish mere courtesy from genuine admiration—I flatter myself that Mr. Iredell has grown fond of me as well. We would have made a handsome couple, I have mused,

335

presiding over dinner tables positively crackling with wit and gaiety; and surely I would never have forced him to banish himself to a backwater like Edenton, so far from all that is amusing and important. Thus have I allowed my secret imaginings to roam!

As we stood there, on the deck—the sailors bustling about their duties behind us, and the few other passengers several yards away—Mr. Iredell withdrew his eye from the glass and turned to me, his demeanor suddenly serious. "My dear Mrs. Wilson, I would just ask you…" he began in a low voice. I felt my heart begin to beat faster. "About what occurred in Havre de Grace …"

"Yes?" I said, trembling, my hand resting on the sleeve of his coat.

He reddened visibly. "About the ice, I mean—the accident I met with. If you would be so kind as to refrain from ever mentioning it to Mrs. Iredell, as she is already inclined to great anxiety whenever I am on the road."

"Oh, of course." I could feel the flush rising to my cheeks, though I tried to affect an air of carelessness. "She shall never hear of it from me."

He returned to his spyglass, and I saw a smile play about his lips.

"Just an hour more now, Mrs. Wilson," he cried. "No more than that, I warrant. I must agree with Cicero—there is no place more delightful than home!"

It was suddenly evident to me that, though we stood on the same deck and contemplated the same horizon, there was no harmony in our moods; for while I had been lost in a reverie of nostalgia for what we were about to leave behind, Mr. Iredell had apparently been bathed in the glow of anticipated domesticity. I immediately made some excuse to go below, where I now intend to remain until the shouts of the crew alert me to the necessity of disembarking. In the meantime, I shall try to concentrate my thoughts on my unfortunate husband, who surely needs me and yearns for me—at least as much as Mr. Iredell is apparently yearning for that sour old wife of his. Can it be he truly loves the woman?

Diary of Hannah Iredell

Edenton, North Carolina

Monday, March 12, 1798

I am moved to take up my pen again, after the passage of so much Time, because the Quietude of my life has recently been seriously disturbed. I do not mean to say my existence has been Dull these last four years, for we have had our share of Excitement—all the share of it I care to have, in any case.

James is a strapping nine-year-old and shows great Promise of matching his Papa in intellect; he is quite the cynosure of Mr. Brooks's modest School here, which I fear he will soon outgrow. Annie, at twelve, is nearly a young Lady, inclined to be somewhat too quiet and Retiring—like her Mother—but possessed of a keen mind. If our James is an Iredell through and through, then Annie is most decidedly a Johnston: she has taken a great interest in the Garden, where she performs little Experiments of grafting and whatnot, under the enthusiastic tutelage of her Uncle Sam; and she and I have spent many hours reading to one another, an Occupation that I am delighted to say pleases her as much as it does myself. Our Family is enlarged by the presence not only of my dear niece Fanny, as in Philadelphia, but now also by her sister Helen, for reasons respecting both their Education (for I have undertaken to instruct them along with my own Daughters) and their Mother's health (Mrs. Johnston's nervous Complaints having increased with the years). Our House is crowded but jolly.

Of course, we have had our share of Difficulties as well, as who among God's Children does not—most distressing have been our repeated bouts of Illness, with all of our lives having been in danger from the Ague and Fever at one time or another. And Sarah's daughter Sukey has, as I feared, proved troublesome at times, rather brazenly shirking her duties and lapsing into sullen Silences that put me in mind of her poor Mother—for whose death I feel in some measure responsible. Alas, my former intimacy with Nelly has never been entirely restored; though she has borne two fine, healthy Daughters, I believe that even now, when she is with me, she is reminded of poor Betsey, and that night she left the Child in my care. Though I, with time and the help of Prayer, have contrived somehow to forgive myself for what occurred, it may be that Nelly will never see her way to doing the same—a hard thing to live with, but it cannot be helped.

And then there is our Helen—a lively child, and in good health, thanks be to the Lord; and yet (it must be said) an odd one as well. She is given to what might be called fits, or visions perhaps—I know not what they are, and the Doctor has been puzzled as well. She will start of a sudden, as though hearing a sound that no one else can discern; or sometimes even carry on an entire conversation with what appears to us to be the parlor wall, or the elm tree in the garden—but which to her is a Girl with a pink bonnet and a green dress, or a Man with no teeth who carries a lighted torch—or so, at least, she insists. What is worse are the times she is seized with such deep fear that she clings to me or her Papa as though for dear Life, and for no reason that any of us can discern, or that she can name; and nothing will calm her but that I stroke her hair and sing to her for hours and hours. The Doctor has counseled patience, as she is but recently turned six and of an age where such things may yet be outgrown; and yet I cannot help but remember those vile words uttered by her Grandmother when the Child was not yet born, and wonder if my poor innocent Darling is not doomed to live out her life under a curse. Grief and pain, the old Lady said the Child would cause me; but she has brought me as much joy as either of my other two Children, and I love her just as dearly, for all my anxiety.

These worries, though they plague me, I have lived with these past four years; they are familiar companions, I have made my Peace with them. What has now befallen me, though, is something of a different order: the arrival of that Woman, Mrs. Wilson, from Philadelphia, in the company of my Husband. There was no lack of warmth in his Greeting of us, to be sure; and yet his solicitude of her, the Intimacy that seemed to subsist between them, was as painful for me to witness as though he had snubbed me entirely. He would not even come to the house (for the Children and I had hastened down to the Harbor as soon as the sail had been spotted, in hopes that it signaled Mr. Iredell's arrival), but insisted

338

on escorting Mrs. Wilson to her Husband's lodgings—though she herself appeared in no hurry to find him.

Mr. Iredell had written to me that she was of a mind to accompany him here, but I was certain she would think better of it. It is indeed a Mystery to me why she has come at all. Mr. Wilson is certainly no longer the man of Wealth and Reputation that she married. In other circumstances one might conclude that Affection, sympathy, and a sense of wifely Duty had combined to induce the Woman to sacrifice all in order to remain by an ailing and disgraced Husband's side. But in this case, the Gentleman is hardly one to inspire, nor does the Lady appear capable of performing, such an act of Virtue and selflessness. No, there is something more—or perhaps less—here than meets the eye, either something she is desperate to escape in Philadelphia or Boston; or else something here in Edenton, other than her Husband, to which she is desperate to cling. I know little of what she may be running *from*, but I have seen enough to cause me to Suspect that what she is running *to* is none other than my own Husband—her own having proven so spectacularly disappointing.

I feel it again now, that breathlessness and Panic that I used to feel in the North, like an Illness, emotions that seem to overwhelm my intellect and drown out all Reason. I believed that I should never feel that way again—although I have once before since we moved back Home, when the Wilsons came to visit that December, over three years ago now. The way Mr. Iredell would gaze admiringly upon her, and hang upon her every silly Pleasantry, and hasten to arrange her shawl about her shoulders when she cunningly hinted that she felt a chill—it all spoke to me of a Connection that I could not bear to contemplate. When I look at her, I see all that my Husband admires, and all that I am not.

And now she is here, not merely for a brief Sojourn, but for—who knows how long? For, judging from what Mr. Iredell has told me, Mr. Wilson will not, or perhaps cannot, leave; quite aside from the Question of his health, he will not venture home while there is a risk of Jail—of which, Mr. Iredell says, he appears to have a morbid Fear. For all I know, the Wilsons will remain here among us for months, perhaps even years. My sweet sanctuary, my Edenton, once again invaded and occupied, as surely as if the British had carried out their threats during the War. Dear God, how shall I bear it?

Diary of Hannah Wilson

Tuesday, March 13, 1798

It is both better and worse here than I had feared. Better, in that he is so grateful I have come—I had thought he would be, but his letters were so cold and formal, it was impossible to be sure. But he is ever thus, in writing; it is no reflection of his true feelings, which he will not allow to flow along with his ink—lest he appear weak, I suppose. So different from Mr. Iredell, whose feelings are so generally in evidence; I'm quite sure that *he* could never write a cold letter, even if he tried.

Mr. Iredell insisted on bringing me to Jamie's room at this tavern—Horniblow's it is called, and the name sounds far cheerier than the place in fact appears. Indeed, the only horn one might be induced to blow here is an appeal for rescue, so grim and dreary are the rooms. But Mr. Horniblow seems a decent fellow, greeting Mr. Iredell and myself with great enthusiasm and hastily abandoning his customers in the taproom in order to lead us upstairs to Jamie, a Negro lad following us with my trunk.

"I know he'll be greatly pleased to see you, madam," Mr. Horniblow said to me over his shoulder, "for he has been feeling rather poorly these past few weeks."

When Jamie came to answer the door, I immediately burst into tears: his eyes were bleary, his clothing soiled and disheveled, his hair in need of cutting and his face unshaven. This was not the husband I knew, not at all. Jamie, I believe, took my tears for tears of joy, and I saw his own chin begin to tremble. But as long as Mr. Iredell was with us, he exhibited a measure of restraint, even formality. Mr. Iredell soon excused himself, however, saying that he must not neglect his family, who had been awaiting him at the dock. I was loath to see him go, and thanked him for his kindness to me at great length; for I felt that once that door had closed behind him, and he was in his own house and I alone in this forlorn room with Jamie, we should be condemned once more to live our true lives.

When at last I could delay Mr. Iredell no longer, Jamie sat heavily on the lumpy mattress, his head in his hands. "I was so afraid you would not come," he said softly after a while, lifting his head to me.

It was then that I saw it—that look in his eyes, helpless and joyous and nearly awe-struck—the same look I used to see in Henry's eyes, my poor sweet babe. And I felt it all at once—love, I suppose it was—but a feeling, at any rate, so powerful it was as though a mighty waterfall had engulfed me and was now hurtling me down towards him, beyond any volition of my own. I rushed to him, all my apprehensions slipping away, and put my arms about him, tears once more beginning to stream from my eyes.

When at length we released our embrace, I could see that his cheeks were also moist with tears. He put his hand to my face, then kissed my lips. "This is the face I see when I close my eyes at night," he whispered to me. But then his features began to harden, and he added, in a flat voice, "Bird did not come, then."

"No, I told you in my letter—the girls need him in Philadelphia, you know, for James hasn't yet found regular employment, and they make so little money from their needlework." His expression was now darkening into a sort of weak scowl, but it seemed best to keep rattling on. "But it's lovely work they do, you know—Emily sent you a sample of it, shall I find it for you now?" I rose and began to undo the fastening on my trunk. "I'm afraid it may be at the bottom—silly me, I really should have kept it on top, but"—

"He has his own views, doesn't he? He's siding with them, with the creditors—that's why he hasn't answered my letters, isn't it?" His fists were clenched, almost as though they encircled poor Bird's throat; but the expression on his face spoke more of pain than fury, and now his tone softened to melancholy. "I always loved him best, you know—he was the one I took into my counsel, the one I relied on. Even when he was just a wee boy, I used to allow him to bring books and papers to me in my office—only him, not the others." His eyes closed tight, then opened again. "Why should he repay me in this cruel fashion?"

"Oh, Jamie, no, it isn't like that!" I searched desperately for some words of reassurance or comfort, though it was difficult to draw them from the truth of the situation. "Bird loves you dearly, and respects you as a son should a father, but ... well, I think he is rather confused. It's

341

been very difficult for him, of course, and I think he hasn't written only because he has no good news to impart to you."

"Nonsense!" Some of Jamie's old fire was reemerging—although I wasn't sure whether this was cause for rejoicing or alarm. "If the boy had some gumption, some determination, he would have settled all of this long ago. Mr. Thomas, now, I imagine *he* is pursuing my cause with some vigor—he hasn't sent me much in the way of information, but at least he's sent me a bit of cash now and then, and he seems to grasp my arguments. It's in the creditors' own interest to allow me the freedom to arrange things myself—any fool should understand that to turn matters over to them would only allow them to squabble like a pack of wild dogs, with the strongest carrying away the best of the kill, and the others left with nothing but bone and gristle. It is for *them* that I insist on control, not for myself."

"Yes, but ..." I hesitated, remembering that our last conversation on this subject had ended so badly. "The creditors have apparently been quite obstinate, you know, and it seems that the only way"—

"Enough!" he barked, his sallow skin now glowing with barely suppressed rage. "I don't need to hear this nonsense from you, my own wife—the one person whose loyalty I should be able to rely upon. The one person who ..." Here his voice began to break. "The one person who cared sufficiently about me, about my health—which has not been good of late, I must tell you—to journey down here to see me, to help me ... If you turn against me as well ... I couldn't ..." He closed his eyes, and again covered his face with his hands.

"Rest now, my dear," I said, pulling back the bedclothes so that he might lie between them. I could see it would do no good to lay out my arguments before him, at least not at present.

He lay back obediently, and allowed me to tuck him in like a small child; within minutes he was snoring, and I began quietly to unpack my things, or some of them—for there is scarcely room to put things away here.

Since that first day—three days ago now—he has continued so weak, and so agitated, that I have thought it best not to attempt to raise the subject of his finances again, and so I have held my tongue and tended to his needs. I have brought the barber round to shave him and cut his hair, and have arranged for him to bathe; I have also seen to his diet, which I fear was too heavy for a man in his weakened condition. I have washed and mended what clothing I can, but much of it is beyond repair, and there is of course no money to purchase anything new. Indeed, how we shall pay for our board and lodging I haven't the faintest idea.

I believe I shall start walking in the country again, as I did in Bethlehem. The countryside about here is rather flat and monotonous, and the air heavy with moisture, but it is surely more salutary for me to be out of this room than in it. Indeed, I hope to convince Jamie to come walking with me as soon as his health is somewhat recovered. And Mr. Iredell has invited us to come for dinner as soon as Jamie is better, which I am very much looking forward to—I had worried, indeed, that he might shun me, once we arrived here; I had thought he would perhaps fear my being in proximity to Mrs. Iredell. But I had too little faith in him, in his goodness and his loyalty. We will be great friends, just as before, just as always.

It is indeed a comfort, the only one I can find at present, knowing that Mr. Iredell is near; somehow I feel that he will help us to find a way out of this morass—this swamp that is surely as dismal as the real one that lies but a few miles away—or at least prevent us from sinking further. Yes—just as he did with Mr. Baldwin in the Susquehanna, he will tie some great leather strap about us, lift us out, and deposit us safely on dry land!

Diary of Hannah Iredell

Thursday, March 22, 1798

We have had today, at Mr. Iredell's insistence, a Dinner party at which the guests of Honor were Judge Wilson and his Wife. I was rather reluctant to undertake it, as we are soon to be deprived of Mr. Iredell's company yet again; for he must leave for the Southern Circuit in a week's time, and our few remaining days with him are so Precious to the Children and myself that I am not inclined to share him with Strangers—particularly a Stranger who seems so intent on claiming his every second for herself, and drawing him into her own frivolous Banter.

Although I was loath to spend more on the provisions than was necessary, I felt it best to surround myself as much as possible with my Friends, for I knew her presence would have a most unsettling effect on me; and so I invited Nelly and Mr. Tredwell and Tom Iredell. Mr. Iredell commended me for including so extensive a Company—even seven is something of a crowd in our modest Dining room—believing that my intent was to introduce Mrs. Wilson to a portion of Edenton society; I saw no reason to disabuse him of his Mistake.

I had not seen Mr. Wilson for some weeks, even though Horniblow's is so near to us that we can see its roof quite plainly from our upper Floor, and I was rather shocked at his condition. His Skin has an unhealthy yellowish cast, and his eyes are rheumy and sometimes appear unfocused; his Clothes, which were rather shabby when he arrived, are sadly in need of repair—a patch on the sleeve of his coat had been rather clumsily sewn by, I presume, Mrs. Wilson. When they arrived, she appeared to be leading him, holding his hand and walking a step or two before him; an image of a lumbering trained Bear came into my mind, such as I had once seen perform in Philadelphia, dragged along by its dainty Owner. But alas, this Bear seemed to have forgotten all its Tricks; Mr. Wilson spent the entire time looking forlorn, and saying practically Nothing.

The Owner in this case was the performing half of the Duo; I should almost have felt sorry for the Woman—shut up in a damp Tavern room with such a miserable Specimen of a man—had she not engaged in such a brazen Flirtation with my Husband, in my very own House. Of course Mr. Iredell *would* so arrange it that Mrs. Wilson sat at his right, with Mr. Wilson and myself banished to our gloom at the opposite end of the Table. But even from that distance, I saw all too clearly the way her Eyes sparkled and danced; the way she cocked her head downwards and smiled up at Mr. Iredell, making her dimples show; the way she rested her hand on his arm when making a remark—quite as though *she* were the Wife, and I merely some distant relation. Indeed, she even scolded him for swearing—surely the province of a Wife (though, alas, none of *my* reprimands have had any effect).

At last Mr. Wilson pushed his chair from the Table and announced that he was greatly fatigued, and in need of returning to his room at Horniblow's. Nothing could have delighted me more than to have this torturous Dinner reach its conclusion, but Mrs. Wilson seemed quite distressed at the thought of parting from Mr. Iredell.

"Are you sure, my dear?" she pleaded with her Husband. "Would you not perhaps be revived by a little Coffee, or a cup of Tea?"

I was relieved to hear Mr. Wilson dismiss this suggestion, and insist that nothing would do for him but his own Bed. There followed a small flurry of thank-you's and farewells, and Mrs. Wilson remembering, just as she reached the door, that she had nearly forgotten to ask whether I had any Books she might borrow—a Novel or two, if I could spare them? I hastened to the shelves and grabbed the first two that came to hand. Whilst I was thus engaged, Mr. Iredell happened to mention that he should be leaving for his Circuit soon, which occasioned many expressions of dismay from Mrs. Wilson. For once, I feel he may be safer on the Road than here in Edenton, at least as far as his Character and Morals are concerned.

Nearly as soon as the Wilsons had taken their leave, Mr. Iredell grabbed up his hat and cloak and excused himself, saying that he had just remembered certain Papers he had been entrusted with delivering to Captain Collins. In truth, I was not sorry to see him go, for it gave me an Opportunity to assess what the others had thought of Mrs. Wilson's behavior. Alas, I was soon disappointed, for although there was general dismay at Mr. Wilson's ill health ("The poor man is even worse off than I am!" Tom exclaimed jovially, somewhat in his cups), the gentlemen spontaneously began expressing their admiration for Mrs. Wilson. Such a brave Lady, and so young to find herself in such a position—so lovely—so charming—and on and on. When Nelly and I were at last alone in the parlor—the Gentlemen taking Brandy at the table—I turned to her expectantly and asked what she had thought of Mrs. Wilson.

I was heartened to see her head shaking in disapproval. "The audacity!" she said. I was about to voice my agreement, when she added, "Did you *see* the way she looked at Sukey, when she came in to serve?"

"Sukey?" I hadn't any idea what Nelly was talking about.

"Why yes! She looked at the girl with so ridiculous an expression of Pity, it was quite comical—as though she fully expected our Negroes to walk around in shackles and leg irons! She's obviously one of those Northerners who believe we're all Barbarians, or worse, simply because we keep a few Slaves!"

I told Nelly I hadn't remarked upon this effrontery, and decided to keep my own thoughts to myself.

Diary of Hannah Wilson

Friday, March 23, 1798

I don't know that I ever fully grasped the meaning of the word "dreary" until these past two weeks: this room, these four grime-covered walls and one dusty window giving out on a patch of gray sky and grayer water—these endless expanses of time with nothing to do, no one to talk to but Jamie—and *he* can only harp on the subject of his own situation, about which I have discovered I had best keep my thoughts to myself. And I considered our stay in Bethlehem to be a hardship! Why, it was Paradise itself compared to this.

We had one brief respite from this tedium yesterday, when we went to take dinner at Mr. Iredell's house. I confess I felt quite as much excitement in anticipating this excursion as when I first received an invitation to Mrs. Bingham's in Philadelphia, years ago—a sign, indeed, of how low my life has sunk, for the Iredells' house is barely more than a cottage, and the company (excepting Mr. Iredell himself, of course) couldn't hold a candle to what one might find at even a modest tea party in Philadelphia. Yet I took great care to dress as well as I could, given the paltry materials I had to work with, and tried to make Jamie look presentable. It's fortunate that I brought my sewing basket, for the sleeve of his coat had a large gash that I managed to patch up in such a way that it was scarcely noticeable.

But while I may have managed to make Jamie *look* presentable, there isn't much I can do to make him behave that way; he was glum and silent—although I suppose that was better than hysterical and raving, which is his only other mood at present. He and Mrs. Iredell, at the opposite end of the table from Mr. Iredell and myself, made a fitting pair, for she was as sour and taciturn as ever—nearly glaring at me at times. Mrs. Iredell's niece, Mrs. Tredwell, though at first friendly and gracious towards me, after some little while grew quite unaccountably cold—though I cannot recall having said anything to offend her. The gentlemen I liked somewhat better. Mr. Tredwell is a Northerner—and not only that, but originally from Long Island, quite close to New York City, so we were able to engage in some lively conversation concerning our impressions of that place. And Mr. Iredell's brother is, I warrant, capable of being nearly as charming as Mr. Iredell himself; unfortunately, as became increasingly evident throughout the meal, he's a bit too fond of his dram.

The food was simple, but fresh and well-prepared—certainly better than what I am used to here at Horniblow's. But the pleasure of it was, for me, distinctly diminished by its being served by one of those unfortunate enslaved Negroes that are everywhere about us in these parts; it nearly brings tears to my eyes every time I look upon them, and contemplate their situation. Indeed, when I reflect upon *their* circumstances in comparison to my own, I begin to feel almost free of self-pity! The one I saw at the Iredells was a young woman, about twenty-five I should guess, and rather good-looking for someone of her race: smooth brown skin, high cheekbones, almond-shaped eyes with curling lashes. There was indeed something about her—the tilt of her head, the clear unblinking way she met my gaze when she served me—that set her apart from the others I have seen here. She appears to have retained some spirit, despite the figurative chains that hang about her. What a pity that she is condemned to waste her life in miserable bondage!

Despite the shadow cast by her presence, I managed to have quite a gay time. I should have liked it to go on much longer, but Jamie insisted that he was fatigued—and then, of course, when we got back to our room, he took, not to his bed, but to his writing desk, scribbling away as usual at something he will not let me read. I believe it's some grand plan he intends to put forward to his creditors, but he won't discuss it with me, of course.

I believe I should be able to bear this exile better if I could see some way for it to end, and end happily, but alas I cannot. I have received one brief letter from Bird, saying very little of substance—which was just as well, as Jamie insisted on perusing it. Bird—or Mr. Thomas—is supposed to be sending us some money, drawn from Jamie's salary—I pray that it will soon arrive, for we are in desperate need of cash. Fortunately Mr. Horniblow has been willing to extend us credit, but I cannot imagine that will continue much longer. I fear every day that he will appear at our door and announce in regretful tones that he can wait no longer—we must pay our bill or vacate the premises. And then where shall we be?

And Mr. Iredell is to leave in a week for the Southern Circuit! Though others here have been kind enough, I cannot rid myself of the fear that once he is gone, we shall be friendless and unprotected, at the mercy of strangers who may turn on us at any moment. I carry with me a sense of foreboding that I cannot shake off, like this gray sky overhead that always seems to be threatening torrents of rain. I suppose it comes from spending all my time in Jamie's company, for that is how he sees the world now, full of unseen perils and scheming enemies; and for all I know, he may be right.

But I shall lose myself in a novel now, one of those Mrs. Iredell was kind enough to lend me (I believe she would have given me her entire library in order to hasten our departure). I shall offer to read one to Jamie, when he wakes from his nap, or perhaps we can take turns reading to one another; as our own conversation is now so difficult, it may be that we should have more success with vicarious conversation, taking on the guise of fictional personages.

I remember how, when I was in Boston, I used to lose myself so eagerly in novels and wish that my life were as exciting as the stories they spun. Now I wish my life were a novel for quite a different reason—that I might close its pages and be done with it, as I would with any novel that had taken so dismal and hopeless a turn.

From James Iredell to Hannah Iredell:

"Hermitage," Martin County, North Carolina, April 5, 1798

I inclose letters for Mrs. Tredwell and the Children, besides Letters to you and Judge Wilson ... Presenting best respects to the Judge and Mrs. Wilson. I shall be very anxious to hear about them ...

Writ in Debt Issued by the Edenton District Superior Court:

Edenton, April 10, 1798
STATE of NORTH CAROLINA.
To the Sheriff of Chowan County, Greeting:
YOU are hereby commanded to take the body of The Honorable James Wilson, Esquire, if to be found in your bailiwick, and him safely keep, so

349

that you have him before the Judges of the Superior Court of Law to be held for the district of Edenton, at the Court-House in Edenton, on the sixth day of October next, then and there to answer unto Pierce Butler, assignee of David Allison, Of a plea that he render to him one hundred and seventy four thousand three hundred and thirty two Dollars, of the value of eighty seven thousand one hundred & sixty six pounds ... which to him he owes and from him unjustly abstains to his damage one hundred pounds as 'tis said.

Herein fail not, and have you then and there this writ ...

Diary of Hannah Iredell

Wednesday, April 11, 1798

These Wilsons, the pair of them, are nothing but trouble. This morning—perhaps an hour or two after sunup—Mr. Horniblow's Negro, Augustus, came to the door, all flustered and out of breath, apparently having run all the short distance from the Tavern. He said he had an urgent message from Judge Wilson to Mr. Iredell, and would I please get him at once.

"Heavens, boy," I told him, "Mr. Iredell is more than halfway to Savannah at the moment, with any luck. So how am I to get him for you?"

"Well, I don't know, Ma'am," Augustus panted, "but Judge Wilson, he said it was very important." He looked around and lowered his voice. "The *Sheriff* is there, Mrs. Iredell. I reckon he got the Judge under arrest."

So it had happened at last, what we had all feared—Judge Wilson more than any of us: one of his numerous Creditors had caught up with him and was set to haul him off to jail. No more than he probably deserves, was my first thought; if he believed that Edenton was some sort of debtors' Haven where the ordinary rules of Law and Morality were in suspension, he was now roundly disabused. And yet—what good would it do for a sick and broken Man, already living in an unhealthy self-imposed Confinement, to be removed into one that was yet sicklier, and enforced? And how might it tarnish the authority of the Supreme Court to have one of its Judges imprisoned—albeit the Judge who had already sadly besmirched that Authority by his own misdeeds?

"Very well, then," I told Augustus. "I'll go to him myself."

Odd, I thought, as I tied the ribbon on my bonnet, that Mrs. Wilson had not remembered that Mr. Iredell was out of town—Judge Wilson, in the general fog where he now seems to reside, might be expected to forget such a thing, but surely Mrs. Wilson was keenly aware of Mr.

351

Iredell's absence. The Mystery of this was solved when I arrived at the room and discovered that despite the crowd—not only Judge Wilson and the Sheriff, but also that rather pompous lawyer Mr. Slade—Mrs. Wilson was nowhere in evidence. I later learned that it is her custom to go out walking for an hour or two in the morning—certainly a commendable Habit, and one that her Husband would benefit from as well.

The Gentlemen all seemed surprised to see me at the door, having been awaiting my Husband; indeed, Mr. Wilson, when I had explained the situation, scowled and looked out of sorts.

"Mrs. Iredell," said Judge Wilson, his eyes wild and his voice strained and high-pitched, "would you kindly explain to these Gentlemen that if your Husband were here, he would certainly vouch for my Character and agree to act as my Security? They have a notion to cart me off to Jail!"

"Indeed!" I said, feigning surprise. "And at whose behest?"

The Sheriff, a short man whose right eye was twitching nervously, cleared his throat. "I have a Writ here issued in the name of Mr. Pierce Butler."

"Major Butler!" Now I was surprised in earnest: that one of our friends should be trying to arrest and imprison another! Surely, I thought, there must be some misunderstanding. But then I paused, remembering that awful Dinner party years ago, and the words exchanged between Mr. Wilson and Major Butler. What bad blood might now exist between the two of them?

"Mrs. Iredell," began Mr. Slade with an air of self-importance, "I have here a Power of attorney from Major Butler, commanding me in no uncertain terms to bring the full Operation of the Law to bear on Judge Wilson, who stands in debt to Major Butler to the amount of"—he paused to consult the Paper in his hands—"one hundred and seventy four thousand"—

"That Debt is none of mine!" Mr. Wilson bellowed, with more Strength than I thought was left to him. "Let him go after those who contracted the Debt, not me."

Mr. Slade took a weary breath and hooked his thumbs in his waistcoat. "As I've said more than once—and I should think that you of all people, Judge Wilson, should not need the Law explained to you—the Security that Mr. Blount and Mr. Allison gave to Major Butler was *your* Paper, with your signature, which was by its own Terms fully transferable"—

"Yes, yes," Mr. Wilson interrupted impatiently, "but I have it on good authority that they gave him other Security as well, so there's no need to hound me in this manner. For some reason Major Butler has resolved to wage this personal Vendetta against me, at a time when I must be at Liberty to put my affairs in order, so that my Creditors may benefit"—

"Judge Wilson," said Mr. Slade sternly, "with all due respect, it's common knowledge that you've done everything within your power to frustrate and evade your Creditors, including attempting to secrete yourself in this Town, and Major Butler regretfully feels he has no choice but to"—

"That, Sir, is an outrageous Calumny!" Mr. Wilson had gone quite red in the face, and a vein was throbbing at his temple. "I will not stand here and be insulted by a one-horse Lawyer who barely knows a *satisfaciendum* from a *respondendum.*"

I could see that this Interview, left to find its own course, would soon produce even uglier exchanges; Mr. Wilson may be a fine Judge, but he certainly was doing himself no service by acting as his own Advocate. "Gentlemen," I forced myself to say, "if I might withdraw for a few moments to have a word with Mr. Slade and the Sheriff? If you would excuse us, Mr. Wilson?"

Mr. Wilson waved an angry hand and turned to the dusty window, showing us his back. The other two men followed me out into the Hall and down the stairs to the small front room of the Tavern, which was fortunately empty. We seated ourselves around a Table still marked with the remains of last night's Spirits, where they regarded me with Curiosity and expectation. The Sheriff's eye continued to twitch, and to this he now added a vigorous rubbing at his nose; as his Business usually ran to nothing more momentous than arresting some Lout whose public drunkenness could no longer be ignored, it must have been rather Overwhelming for him to begin his day with the arrest of a recalcitrant Judge of the Supreme Court. I felt quite as anxious as the Sheriff looked, but I swallowed hard and found my voice.

"Mr. Slade," I began, "surely you see the wretched Condition that Judge Wilson now finds himself in—his health, his Mind, are not what they once were. What purpose could it possibly serve to confine him to a dank Cell, where he will surely only deteriorate further, perhaps even expire? Can you not find it in your heart"—

"My heart, Madam, has nothing to do with it." His face was hard, his voice clipped. I could see he was still smarting from Mr. Wilson's gibe about a one-horse Lawyer. "My orders from my Client, Major Butler, are clear and leave no room for my Discretion, or my pity: he is to be confined to Jail until the Superior Court meets to hear the case in October. You have no idea, my dear Mrs. Iredell, what Judge Wilson is capable of. Mr. Blount, whose Brother has direct knowledge of the facts that have given rise to this lawsuit, has given me the most shocking particulars of the man's recent Behavior. I would warn you and Mr. Iredell, as a friend, to resist any of his efforts to enlist you as his Security, for it will surely be to your detriment if you accede to them."

I was flustered for a moment; for all my aversion to Mr. Wilson, I was not accustomed to hearing any Judge spoken of in this way. I was tempted to insist that Mr. Iredell and I would be honored to act as his Security, simply to defy Mr. Slade's characterization, but given the amount of the Debt, I knew we were in no position to make this Gesture. I began to despair: great measures of Tact and diplomacy seemed to be the only hope of keeping Mr. Wilson out of jail, and I have never been much skilled at such things. But I resolved to try my best.

"Mr. Slade," I began, "you know that Mr. Iredell has always reposed the greatest Confidence in you, in your abilities at the Law and in your good judgment. And I'm sure that you would agree with him that there are Occasions when a skilled Lawyer such as yourself, being in possession of certain Intelligence unknown to his client, must exercise his own good judgment independently, even when it appears to contradict his Client's wishes."

Mr. Slade regarded me skeptically, but as he said nothing I felt emboldened to continue. "Knowing Major Butler as I do—as Mr. Iredell and I both do—I can assure you that if he were here, able to observe with his own eyes Mr. Wilson's unfortunate Situation, he would without hesitation agree to allow him to remain in his room here, in hopes that such modest comfort as it provides would preserve what remains of his Health. Mr. Wilson, I am certain, will be happy to give you his word that he will not leave this Town, if you will forbear confining him to the Jail. Surely Major Butler—a Gentleman the kindness of whose heart I can vouch for, from my own experience—would ask for no more. Indeed, I am certain that when he is in full possession of the Facts, he will heartily applaud your exercise of Mercy."

Mr. Slade now rubbed his Chin and gazed at a spot above the mantle; I glanced at the Sheriff, who seemed to wink at me—perhaps it was only another twitch, but I took some further encouragement from it. "I shall, of course, consider it my Duty to write to Major Butler, if you persist in this course of action. He will not, I assure you, much relish being known as the Man responsible for Judge Wilson's Demise."

Mr. Slade pursed his lips for a moment, then blew a small gust of air through them, in what seemed an acknowledgment of defeat. "But he must—*absolutely*—give his Word that he will not set one foot beyond the town limits," Mr. Slade said wearily.

Just then I heard footsteps coming down the stairs and Mr. Wilson's voice, muttering to himself. He peered in at the doorway. "Mrs. Wilson will be returning soon, I fear," he began, "and we must have this Matter resolved before she does. Now, I have a proposal"—

"It's all been arranged, Mr. Wilson," I told him, rising from my Chair. "There will be no need for you to go to Jail."

"No—no need … ?"

"No, Sir. Let me help you back to your room, and I shall explain the Arrangement to you." I then escorted Mr. Wilson up the stairs, which he managed with some difficulty. He nodded eagerly as I told him what we had agreed, and swore that he would under no circumstances leave the Town limits before the return date on the Writ, not even to indulge in an innocent ramble. "As my Wife would tell you," he said with a wan smile, "I am not much for Exercise, in any event."

When at last I was at the door, about to take my leave, Mr. Wilson called to me, "Please, Mrs. Iredell, I would ask you one Favor. I beg you, don't breathe a word of this to Mrs. Wilson. I fear it would cause her great Distress, and would serve no purpose."

I hesitated, for it seemed that a Wife was entitled to know that her Husband had been placed under arrest; and indeed, I had expected to enlist her aid in ensuring that Mr. Wilson would keep his word. But the Gentleman's expression was so piteous that I could only reply, "Of course. I shall say nothing."

He then walked unsteadily across the room to me, took my hand, and gave it a courtly kiss. "I thank you, dear Lady, for all that you have done. I promise you I will give you no cause to regret this; indeed, I am eternally in your Debt."

I felt myself soften towards him, just a bit. "I sincerely hope not, Judge Wilson," I said, "for you certainly seem to have enough other Creditors to contend with."

I hesitated, fearing that this feeble jest might have offended him. But he only smiled and said, "*Touché*, Madam, *touché*."

He then began to cough and totter on his feet, so that I was obliged to help him into his bed, where he sighed deeply and closed his eyes; poor Man, the morning's events had no doubt quite depleted his meager Energies.

But I must now write to Mr. Iredell, wherever he may be in his travels (I shall have to calculate as best I can); for surely he will wish to know that two of his dearest friends are locked in so bitter a dispute.

From James Wilson to Bird Wilson:

Edenton, North Carolina, April 21, 1798

... A Suit by Major Butler has been brought against me here. This will necessarily detain me till it can be arranged; though I believe it important that I should return to the Northward as soon as possible... I have since I came to the Southward been informed that Major Butler probably has from Gov. Blount, Mr. Allison, or both, other Security for this Debt, which you know was originally none of mine. If this be the Case, I think it would be Nothing more than reasonable that he should by proper Instruments give me the Benefit of that other Security upon my paying this Debt... Will you make this Proposal to him? Upon this Subject I shall write farther by next Post ...

Do not omit to write to me. Remember me to the Family and to Mr. and Mrs. Thomas...

Diary of Hannah Wilson

I have at last found myself some occupation, other than rereading my novels and walking in the country, and I am convinced it is a worthy one—though one that must unfortunately be kept clandestine. Last week, as I was returning from one of my walks along what is called the Perquimans Road, I happened to pass a Negro woman who seemed familiar to me; I caught her eye and realized it was the servant from Mr. Iredell's house. I believe she recognized me as well, but when I spoke to her, she merely gave me a quick curtsy and stood aside, waiting for me to pass. I did not pass, of course, but inquired whether she were not employed by the Iredell family.

"Yes, ma'am," she said, looking down towards the muddy ground, "it's them that owns me."

"Owns you, indeed!" I cried. "As though any human being has the right to own another of his kind!"

The woman now cast a quick startled glance at me, then looked nervously about her, though the road we were on was quite deserted. She adjusted against her hip the large basket that she carried, which was laden with clothing of some kind. "Excuse me, Ma'am," she said, "but I got to bring this basket over to Mrs. Tredwell's."

I realized that what I said must have come as a great shock to her; most likely she had never heard a white person express such a view. Perhaps she thought I was a spy of some sort, only trying to goad her into revealing thoughts for which she might be punished.

"Stay but a minute, I beg you," I said. "Come, bring your basket behind these trees, and we can talk for a moment without being seen." She did as I asked, although her expression still betrayed reluctance and suspicion. "Believe me, I only want to help you—but what's your name?"

"Sukey, Ma'am."

"Sukey, then. My name is Mrs. Wilson. I come from the North, you know—Philadelphia, where we don't believe in slavery. Or most of us don't."

"Philadelphia?" It seemed she was beginning to relax her guard; her almond eyes widened and she cocked her head inquisitively. "That's where my Daddy lives. He's a free man, now."

"Well, there's a coincidence! You know, I was able to obtain freedom for a slave in Philadelphia once. He's doing quite well, I believe—working in a shop."

Sukey's eyes grew yet wider. She looked about her once more, to reassure herself that no one else was nearby. When she spoke again, it was in a whisper. "I'd give anything, ma'am, to go to Philadelphia, see my Daddy. Be free like him. Could you ... maybe ... *take* me there? Or help me get there, somehow? I've heard there are people who can do that, who"—

"Ah, no—no, I'm afraid I can't do that, it isn't in my power." Her face crumpled like a sheet falling from a clothesline. Poor wretch, I hadn't meant to raise her hopes so high. "But perhaps there is something else I can do for you, to improve your situation."

"Well, I don't know *what*." Her voice was sullen now.

I racked my brain for something to offer her; then, in a flash, I remembered what Thomas had told me, when I met him in the shop. "I could teach you how to read and write."

She gave a sort of snort and put her hands on her hips. "Don't see how that's gonna help me. Besides, it ain't allowed, 'round here, teaching us things like that."

"But no one need know about it. It could be our secret. And reading—why, reading is a wonderful thing to know how to do. Imagine, being able to read signs, and newspapers—even books, after a while. As for writing—well, we could start with your name, but one day, perhaps, you could write an entire letter to your father, in Philadelphia. And if you ever do get your freedom, which I sincerely hope you will, it will be a very handy skill for you, and should help you obtain a decent job—perhaps even in a shop, like that young man I was telling you about."

Sukey stuck out her lower lip, considering. "Anyone finds out, I could be in a heap of trouble."

"No one will find out. I give you my word."

"I get two evenings a week free—plus Sundays, but I'm supposed to be in church then. And the evenings, I generally go across the creek to Hayes, to see my friends. But I reckon I don't have to go *both* evenings."

In short, it was soon arranged that we should meet, behind those very trees, the following evening at seven o'clock. I brought a lantern, and a blanket from the room to sit upon, and some writing paper and a pen and ink. I wrote out the alphabet for her, had her copy it over, then gave her the paper to take with her and memorize. Yesterday evening we met again and, to my amazement, in the space of one week she had learned all twenty-six letters by heart. It is evident that she has a quick wit; and for all her initial reluctance, she seems quite an eager student. Indeed, the delight on her face when I expressed surprise at her accomplishment was exceedingly gratifying to behold. And we have decided, at Sukey's own suggestion, to meet twice a week from now on, so as to speed her progress even further.

I thought it best not to tell Jamie of this little undertaking of mine, for I am not entirely sure he would approve—it being, if Sukey is correct, "not allowed." I had feared that when he saw me leaving the room, at so unusual an hour, so laden with my supplies, he might inquire as to my intentions; but on both occasions he was so immersed in his own affairs—reading over the correspondence and other papers he has collected, jotting down such thoughts as apparently come to him—that he took no notice.

Jamie's health appears to have improved, for which I am grateful, but in other respects he is much the same as before; I still cannot tell when we may be able to quit this place. He has said himself on several occasions that he would like nothing more than to return to the North, and to settle his affairs there in person; but he always adds that there are "circumstances" that render it necessary for him to remain here a while longer. I can only assume that he means the danger of arrest and imprisonment should he return to Philadelphia; but I know better than to pursue that topic with him. I yesterday received a letter from Bird (though I have so far refrained from writing to *him*), setting forth plainly that Mr. Thomas has at last come to agree that Jamie must return to Philadelphia, and convey all his property in trust to his creditors. From the tone of the letter, Bird clearly meant for me to show it to his Papa; and so I shall, though I have no hopes that anything will come of it.

We are still living entirely on credit, for though Mr. Thomas sent a draft for Jamie's salary, there has been some difficulty converting it to cash—I trust Mr. Iredell will assist us in this, when he returns, but unfortunately he is not expected back until the middle of June, Mrs. Iredell says. She has come to call on us two or three times, but it's evident she considers it more of a chore than a pleasure; in any case, she always seems eager to make her escape. And though I feel in great need of friends (I write to Polly, and to the Breck girls, but letters are a poor substitute for conversation), I make no great effort to detain her, for we have so little to say to one another. I certainly cannot describe to her the progress I am making in educating her slave! The only other topic that comes to my mind is news of Mr. Iredell; but if I make only a polite inquiry concerning him, she purses her lips and looks disapproving, and doles out no more than a word or two in reply—as though by merely possessing information about him, I might in some way be stealing him from her. Ah well, no matter: Mr. Iredell is surely a subject best left undiscussed by the two of us.

From James Wilson to Bird Wilson:

Edenton, North Carolina, April 28, 1798

... Mrs. Wilson showed me what you wrote to her on a Subject, concerning which you say Mr. Thomas has altered his opinion. On this Point, I shall give my Sentiments very fully in my next Letter. The Design of this is to acquaint you that I am attentive to ... those Matters, though not yet prepared to write upon them. Mrs. Wilson begs to be remembered to the Family. Remember me likewise ...

Diary of Hannah Iredell

Sukey has been behaving rather strangely of late, and I think I may have discovered the cause. What I first noticed was a general improvement in her Demeanor: her manner more cheerful, her face sometimes lit by a smile, her voice raised in song while she went about her work. To be sure, in many others such Gaiety would be nothing remarkable, but in Sukey it most decidedly is. Nelly has urged me on more than one occasion to sell Sukey, and were it not for my promise to poor Sarah that I would look after the Girl, I would have been sorely tempted to do so. But if she were ever as pleasant as this, I thought, I should find it no sacrifice whatsoever to keep her.

At first I considered only that Sukey had perhaps made her peace with her lot in Life (for she has still not forgiven us for taking her from Hayes, and her Friends), or that she had at last, as I have often urged her, found some solace in Prayer. But last week I happened to meet Elsie, one of the house Negroes at Hayes, who had come across the Creek for some provisions. She asked me if Sukey had been ill, for she hadn't called at Hayes on her free evenings, as has been her custom, for at least two weeks. Why no, I said, Sukey is quite well.

"Well, then," said Elsie with a knowing smile, "she must have found somebody on this side of the Creek to keep company with. Won't poor Marcellus be disappointed! And him thinking they was going to be married someday."

I told Elsie not to let Marcellus give up Hope, for as far as I knew he had no rival. And indeed, I think it is not that at all, for just this morning Sukey asked me—with a sort of studied idleness—whether I had an address for her Father in Philadelphia. I asked why ever she would need one, for Mr. Iredell always brings Peter news of Sukey, when he goes to Philadelphia, and brings her back news of him.

Sukey shrugged and said that she was only curious, that was all, and went about her Business. But what could the wench have been thinking? That she would somehow contrive to run away from here and make her way to Philadelphia? Has she been entertaining some such ridiculous Plan—and is that the cause of her unusually Cheerful mood? Foolish girl, she would almost certainly meet with some terrible Accident if she were to attempt an Escape; and even in the unlikely Event that she reached Philadelphia in one piece, what should await her there? A hard-scrabble existence such as the one poor Peter leads, cutting and carrying wood for Pennies!

Someone has been filling her head with false Hopes, I warrant—some Stranger who cannot comprehend our ways and customs—and I believe I know who that must be. I recall now what Nelly said after that Dinner party before Mr. Iredell left: that Mrs. Wilson kept regarding Sukey with pity, as though her lot were necessarily miserable—when indeed I have treated the Girl with nothing but kindness, and probably more than she deserves. I am nearly certain Sukey has been spending her evenings, not with some dark-skinned Lothario, but with Mrs. Wilson; and that the gleam in her eye is sparked not by thoughts of love, but by tales Mrs. Wilson has spun of a Philadelphia teeming with wealthy and distinguished Negroes! No, it is not enough that she must entice my Husband from me, but she must attempt to steal away my Servant as well.

I am in doubt as to what to do concerning this Situation; for if I were to reveal my suspicions to Sukey, she would certainly deny them. Nor can I level any accusation at Mrs. Wilson without some further proof. But I shall watch and wait; perhaps there will be something, some Evidence, that I can seize upon. I hope to God it will come my way before Sukey is lured into taking some hasty Action that will only bring her misery and grief.

Diary of Hannah Wilson

Saturday, May 12, 1798

I have just had a most unpleasant interview with Mrs. Iredell, and am in such agitation that I scarcely know what to do with myself. In truth, I was not surprised to see her at our door—though she has been a most infrequent visitor of late—for Sukey had warned me that her mistress appeared to have her suspicions.

Alas, poor Sukey—whose skills have already advanced to the point where she can sound out simple words, and even short sentences—had an unfortunate slip a few days ago. Seeing the newspaper lying on a table that she was meant to be dusting, she could not resist bending over it to see if she could make sense of any of its notices. As the advertisements were easier to decipher than the dispatches, she concentrated her efforts on those, and was rewarded with the discovery that a new shipment of flour had arrived at the dock and was selling at Mr. Davis's shop near the harbor for an excellent price. Just then Mrs. Iredell entered the room, and in her excitement Sukey pointed out the advertisement to her mistress, and asked whether she oughtn't to go and buy some straight away. At this Mrs. Iredell drew back and demanded to know how Sukey had managed to understand what was written in the newspaper.

Sukey told me she insisted to Mrs. Iredell that she had only taught herself to read a few words, but that Mrs. Iredell had appeared unconvinced by this; the poor girl was so agitated when we met yesterday evening that she could scarcely attend to her studies. She warned me that this might be our last meeting, for she feared that Mrs. Iredell would soon follow her, to see where she was disappearing to on her free evenings; she had only been prevented from doing so last night by the illness of her elder daughter.

"Mrs. Iredell—she ain't mean, like some mistresses," Sukey said, in what I thought was an exceedingly charitable characterization of one who owned her as though she were no more than a pig or a horse. "But I sure don't think she'd like the idea of this, if she found out."

Indeed, she did not. I don't know if she had somehow pressed Sukey to confess the whole of our endeavor, or if she had only managed to draw her own conclusions, but Mrs. Iredell arrived here shortly after nine o'clock this morning, evidently in high dudgeon, saying it was most urgent that she speak with me immediately. As Jamie was engaged in composing a long letter to Mr. Thomas—and as I thought it best he not be privy to this conversation—we ventured outside and walked briskly and in silence some ways along the waterfront before finding a spot that Mrs. Iredell deemed sufficiently secluded.

"Mrs. Wilson," she said at last with apparent difficulty, as though merely speaking to me required a tremendous effort, "it has come to my notice that you have been interfering in certain domestic matters, matters relating to my family, that are none of your concern."

"Your family?" I thought for a wild moment that she was accusing me of something to do with Mr. Iredell. "To what are you referring, Mrs. Iredell?"

"I believe you know very well, but if I must spell it out for you, I am talking of Sukey."

"And you consider her a member of your family?"

"I do indeed. Your confusion only reveals your limited understanding of our ways, Mrs. Wilson. I consider Sukey to be under my protection—I am responsible for her welfare—and it is my duty to prevent outsiders, strangers, from filling her head with wild notions that can only lead her into making grievous mistakes."

"Wild notions? Why, Mrs. Iredell, I am only teaching her to read and write!"

She turned her head from me for a moment, as though to compose herself, then fixed me once again with her small, anxious brown eyes. "And for what purpose? She has all that she needs, she is well taken care of. What use has she for reading and writing? Learning such things will only give her fanciful hopes for herself, and lead to frustration and disappointment."

"What use? What *use*?" I hardly knew what to say to the woman. "Why, what use have you or I for such things, Mrs. Iredell? Surely you are no stranger to the pleasures of reading. And as for hopes—it seems to me that if anyone is in need of hope, it is one in so hopeless a situation as Sukey. Surely you have noticed a change in her these past few weeks—she is lighter, gayer. Hopeful, if you like. I see no harm in that—indeed, I see a great deal of good."

Mrs. Iredell's thin lips had now nearly disappeared; with her sharp nose and bony face, she resembled nothing so much as a hawk. "Mrs. Wilson, it is evident that we shall never agree on this question, and I therefore see no reason to extend this interview. But I must ask you to terminate this little enterprise of yours. It is for me to decide what is in Sukey's best interests, and what may cause her harm."

"On the contrary," I began, "is it not for *Sukey* to decide"—

"I have forbidden Sukey from continuing to meet with you," she interrupted, "and although I have refrained from meting out any punishment to her at present, I have told her that should she disobey me there will certainly be consequences. If you truly have Sukey's interests at heart, you will do nothing to tempt her to go against my wishes. And now, if you will excuse me ..." She began to turn back towards town, but hesitated. She looked, quite literally, down her beak-like nose at me—for she is quite tall. "If Sukey were to learn to read and write—and I am not at all sure that she should—but *if* she should—it would be for *me* to teach her, Mrs. Wilson, not you."

I stood there shaking with rage, watching her go. Rather than following in her wake, I turned in the opposite direction and walked into the country for nearly a full hour, though the ground was wet and my shoes were soon soaked through; but I was far too distressed to return to that tiny room, and the sound of Jamie's pen scratching away. When at last I did return, sweaty and exhausted, he barely glanced in my direction; he sat there, sharpening his pen with a knife though it was nearly down to the feather, surrounded by balls of crumpled paper.

"Had a nice walk, did you, Nannie?" he said absently before commencing to write again.

"Yes, very nice." What use even to attempt to tell him of what I am suffering: the loss of the one occupation that brought me some satisfaction, some joy—that diverted me from this endless, eternal waiting for a time when I can resume what I used to call my life. And—even worse—the thought of Sukey's being deprived of all hope, all possibility of escape from an existence even drearier than my own; I can imagine, though I probably shall not see, the rapid reversal of the transformation I have witnessed in her, from dull-eyed, resentful drone to curious, quick-witted young woman, who took such joyful pride in her accomplishments.

Even if I had the energy to tell Jamie of all this, he should never have the patience to listen. We are nearly as strangers to one another now, sharing a room and a bed but little else. And yet—there are still times when he emerges from the prison of his poor ravaged mind and calls my name, clasps my hand to his lips, and looks upon me with affection, even love—as though he has forgotten I am here, and then, realizing it, is grateful for my coming all over again.

James Wilson to Joseph Thomas:

Edenton, North Carolina, May 12th, 1798

... I sit down to write to you upon a subject which for some time past has occupied, as it merited, my most serious and deliberate attention. Whether I shall be able to express my sentiments in the manner in which I wish to express them, I cannot say; but the will must be taken for the deed.

You urge me to return ... Many reasons, some respecting my health, concur in forming a strong wish for my return. But against my return at present there are insuperable objections; some respecting Major Butler, others respecting the general conduct of my creditors. If they will agree that, on terms of the best security for them, I shall have it fully in my power to make every personal and intellectual effort for their interest and my own, I will—for I wish to—return whenever the arrangements necessary here shall be made.

... Bird says that contrary to your former opinion, you now think it proper that I should make a conveyance to Trustees in general trust. I confess myself not a little surprised at this change... This measure, as I view it, would effectually preclude me from doing fair and equal justice. It would lay the field open for a system of iniquitous speculation which, I have too much reason to think, has been already contemplated and commenced by some who are, and by some who are not, my creditors, with an avidity cruel, treacherous and insatiable. The consequence would be a loss, heavy and unmerited in some instances; and in others, advantages disproportionate, or totally without just claim. To avoid such consequences, I have submitted and if necessary will submit to every personal indignity and persecution. I have been hunted—I may be hunted—like a wild beast: I have suffered much—I may suffer essentially

in my health and otherwise: But as at present I consider the subject, the last extremity shall never compel my signature to an act which would exclude me from performing the duty, and feeling the pleasure, of doing full and effectual justice to all ...

From many circumstances I think there is reason to believe that the season is approaching when [my] exertions may be crowned with the most abundant success. Perhaps some may suggest that I have not been so active as I might have been about my affairs. My life has not been a life of idleness or indolence. But there are times when nothing, not ruinous, can be done ... . Besides, you know well how many useless and hurtful impediments have been thrown in my way. You can vouch for the many steps I have taken ... This is not the first era of my life in which I have encountered difficulties; and I hope on this, as on a former occasion, I shall be able to surmount those difficulties with safety to all, and advantage to many, who are interested in the situation of my affairs ... .

From James Iredell to Hannah Iredell:

Stateburg, South Carolina, May 19, 1798

... I am detained here by rain today ... . Present my best respects to Mr. and Mrs. Wilson. I am still uneasy about that Writ. You may tell Mrs. Wilson that I have nearly effected my reformation as to swearing and exclaiming, and if I can do it thoroughly shall owe her unspeakable obligations for the friendly frankness with which she corrected those failings.

367

Diary of Hannah Iredell

Tuesday, May 22, 1798

I have decided, despite having scant time to spare, to give Sukey a few lessons in her Letters. Indeed, such Instruction, I have recently discovered, was begun secretly by Mrs. Wilson—my suspicions that the two of them were up to something indeed proved correct. I put a stop to it as soon as I was able to, of course, for who knew what else Mrs. Wilson may have been funneling into Sukey's impressionable young Mind? At first I had no intention of continuing the Lessons myself, but Sukey became so impossible after I forbade her from meeting with Mrs. Wilson—so exceedingly Morose and uncooperative—that I was at a loss as to what to do.

One afternoon—a few days after my rather unpleasant Interview with Mrs. Wilson—when Sukey was supposed to be peeling potatoes in the kitchen, I happened upon her in the Parlor, staring with knitted brow at the pages of a book she had taken down from the shelf; she was so absorbed in her effort that she failed to notice my Presence, and I stood there for a minute or more, watching as a slow tear trickled down her smooth brown cheek. To my surprise, I felt my own eyes begin to water in response; I had not realized the girl was so desperate to read.

When I called her name, she started, and moved quickly to replace the Book on its shelf. The fear I saw in her eyes filled me with Remorse; I remembered my promise to Sarah. And, too, I recalled the way Sappho—Sukey's grandmother—had watched over me with such tenderness: I felt the sturdy warmth of Sappho's arms lifting me when I was a Child, heard the sound of her voice raised in one of her mournful yet comforting Songs. There is indeed something of Sappho about Sukey, something in the shape of her eyes and the tilt of her nose.

"Now, Sukey," I said gently, "if it's so important to you, I can try to teach you to read and write a little. You needn't go running off to Strangers for such things, you know."

Her mouth flew open in a surprised smile, and she clasped her hands to her chest as though at Prayer. "You will, ma'am?" she exclaimed. "Do you really mean it—you will?"

I assured her that I meant it, and told her that we could begin that very Evening, after the chores were done and the Children abed. When I saw what she was capable of doing, I assumed that she and Mrs. Wilson must have been meeting for some two Months, but Sukey assured me it had been no more than three weeks. She is indeed a surprisingly apt Pupil, especially considering her Age—though twenty-three is by no means old for most purposes, for such a task as this it generally puts one at a Disadvantage. But Eagerness and determination of spirit count for at least as much as youthfulness of Mind—one need only contrast Sukey with my Helen to see that. Poor Helen! She finds it difficult to attend for more than two minutes together when I am instructing her—though she can spend hours and hours on her drawings, which are very accomplished for a girl of her age, but also exceedingly strange.

In any event, I had no idea Sukey was capable of such Quickness. And her Attitude and demeanor have improved markedly since I undertook to teach her; she now smiles and sings as she goes about her Work, quite as she did before—and sometimes, when I catch the sound, I am fooled for an absent moment into believing that what I hear is not her Voice at all, but Sappho's. Of course I have instructed Sukey to keep these lessons a Secret, for certainly there are those in these parts who would strongly disapprove.

I have recently received a Letter from Mr. Iredell, crediting Mrs. Wilson with inducing him to desist entirely from his habit of Swearing, and enjoining me to tell her as much. I am in no doubt that Mr. Iredell's reformation is only temporary; nor do I have any intention of adding to that meddlesome Woman's inflated sense of her own Powers by conveying Mr. Iredell's message.

From Pierce Butler to William Slade:

Philadelphia, Pennsylvania, May 24, 1798

... I entirely approve of the steps you have taken with Judge Wilson. He must see, and he ought to feel, how reluctantly I am forced to proceed against him. I have hitherto waited patiently and postponed writing to

you, in daily expectation that his son, or other attorney here, would make me some proposal, but to this hour they have done nothing.

About a fortnight ago, I had a letter from the son, saying that he would in a few days call on me, to make me some Offers. I never heard more from him till the night before last, when he called at near nine O'Clock, but never made me one offer. He confined his visit to reading a Letter from his father to a Mr. Thomas of this place, in which he says, "agreeable to your recommendation and for my health, I am desirous of returning to Philadelphia. But I cannot agree with you in Opinion as to surrendering my Estate into the hands of my Creditors, the malignity of some of whom has Taught me to know that they would tear it to pieces, in order to speculate on my distress."

Here he stopped reading. I repeated to this young man what I had often told him & his father, my wish to avoid proceeding to extremity, and my disposition to contribute to soften his sorrows—I reminded him of my repeated Offers—he made his bow. On parting I told him, I should not wait longer than this day to receive proposals, and If none were made to me, I should write to you to let the Law have its operation. I have not heard from him since. I am therefore In duty to myself and Children ... reluctantly constrained to request that you let the Law have its Operation. His debt to me including the interest due is now $197,000 or more ...

I have again offered his son to extend the time of payment, two & three years, provided they secure it to me. I have no wish to possess his lands, nor the most distant inclination to Speculate on his ruin. I should therefore hope he did not mean to do me the injustice of including or Classing me among his malignant Creditors...

Diary of Hannah Wilson

Tuesday, June 12, 1798

I returned from my walk this morning to hear raised voices coming from the direction of our room—so loud indeed that they were fully audible on the stairs, although I could make out no words. I was greatly alarmed, thinking that some ruffian was engaged in a violent argument with Jamie—though his health has been somewhat better of late, he is still in no condition for excessive excitement—and so I threw open the door without knocking. To my surprise I found that Jamie's presumed assailant was only that lawyer I have seen here before on one or two occasions, Mr. Slade—his face quite red, and his "weapon" merely a paper of some sort that he held rolled up in his hand.

Mr. Slade looked distinctly nonplused to see me, but bowed to me and took his leave. As soon as he had shut the door behind him, Jamie sat down heavily on the wooden desk chair and put his head in his hands. I went to him and began to rub the back of his neck, as he has always liked, and I could feel him begin to relax to my touch. I asked him what Mr. Slade had wanted, and Jamie said it was nothing—but then began to rail on once again about his rapacious creditors wanting to batten on his distress, and how Mr. Greenleaf had turned over his holdings to a trust of his creditors and it had done him no good at all, and so on and on. *Then* he started in on the old refrain about how the time was approaching when all his efforts should at last be crowned with success, et cetera. I couldn't bear to hear it all again, so I interrupted him and told him he must take some rest, that all this excitement was bad for his nerves.

He began to nod, in a sort of tremble, and allowed me to lead him to the bed. I settled him down and kissed his brow, and then, when he seemed to be drifting off to sleep, I crept from the room. I went out again, though it was by now unpleasantly warm, and walked until I found a spot where I might sit unobserved on the bank of the Sound—and there I at last allowed myself to weep, wondering what will become of me, of us.

I see before me nothing but distress and disgrace, poverty and—God forbid it, but I fear it will not be long in coming—impeachment. I shudder to imagine what they are saying of us in Philadelphia now, and what more they will say if Jamie does not attend the Supreme Court in August. Time is running short, and he will not listen to me, or to Bird—or even to Mr. Thomas. But Mr. Iredell is to return from his Circuit within the next few days; the only hope I can cling to is that he will find the words—the magical words, the golden words, the words I cannot discover no matter how I try—to which Jamie will at last hearken.

Diary of Hannah Iredell

Saturday, June 16, 1798

Mr. Iredell arrived home safe at last yesterday, for which I am very grateful, but no sooner had he set foot in the House than he was on his way out again to see the Wilsons. The poor man, fatigued to death from his Journey! And the Children and I, who have waited so long and so patiently to have him again amongst us, scarcely having time to embrace him before he excused himself to go attend to the Affairs of others.

This Morning, yet again, he went off to see Mr. Slade; for apparently Major Butler, though initially approving of the forbearance I had urged, has now lost Patience and again demanded that Mr. Wilson be confined to jail—something to do with an intemperate Letter written by Mr. Wilson, the contents of which I can well imagine after hearing the way he railed at Mr. Slade. I gather it took all Mr. Iredell's considerable powers of Persuasion to preserve Mr. Wilson's relative Liberty; for, in an effort to curry favor with his Client, it seems Mr. Slade has already replied to Major Butler, informing him that the Judge is now imprisoned. Mr. Iredell was obliged to pledge that, should Major Butler discover the Truth, or should Mr. Wilson flee the Town, he himself should take full responsibility for the Decision. It is an exceedingly awkward position for Mr. Iredell to be in, torn in this way between loyalties to Friends; I can see it taking its toll upon him, for he returned from Mr. Slade's looking even wearier than he had the evening before.

I gather that Mrs. Wilson is still uninformed of her Husband's arrest, for Mr. Iredell warned me last night as we were preparing for bed that I was not to mention a Word of all this to her; it seems that Mr. Wilson begged him to keep it secret, just as he did me. I told Mr. Iredell it was unlikely that Mrs. Wilson should discover the Truth from me, as she and I generally had very little to say to one another; and this impulsive remark of mine occasioned an exceedingly distressing exchange between us—though one that I suppose would have occurred eventually in any case.

"I can see that you have taken a dislike to the Lady, my dear," Mr. Iredell said, and he gave a weary sigh. "But I beg you—I appeal to that benevolent and generous Nature with which I know you are blessed—extend a little kindness to her. She finds herself in exceedingly dire circumstances, you know, through no fault of her own—indeed, some might say through an excess of loyalty to her unfortunate Husband. For it was her choice to come here, and few would have condemned her for keeping her distance, at this juncture. And I believe that if you only gave her a chance, you would find her quite charming."

This appeal had an effect on me quite the opposite of what Mr. Iredell intended. "Why the Lady chose to come here is not for me to say," I threw at him in my irritation, "but it is obvious to me that *you* have found her quite charming. That you have been mutually charmed by one another, in fact."

He shook his head and raised his eyes to the ceiling, as though contending with one of poor Helen's unfounded delusions. Then he clasped my hands in his and drew me towards him. "Hannah," he said, meeting my gaze, "I swear to you that I love no Woman but you."

Those words, perhaps, might have been enough for me, once—many years ago, before that Night when I discovered him on the Courthouse Green in the arms of another woman, and after just such protestations. If I looked out our bedroom window now, I could almost see that same Green, through the gathering darkness, and Horniblow's Tavern standing beside it.

Whatever dalliances he may enter into in Charleston, or Savannah, Boston or even Philadelphia while on Circuit I have somehow contrived to put out of my mind; but what I cannot stomach is to see such things here, on display in my own Neighborhood, and not only before myself but also my Friends and relations. The distress, the humiliation, is more than I can bear: when he is here, he must be entirely mine—mine and the Children's. That is all I ask; and even that, it seems, he cannot give me.

Ah, how I wish that the Woman and her poor wretch of a Husband would leave this place, and soon; and yet I know they will not, can not, because of that Writ, and Major Butler. He has condemned us all to live in this Hell with one another, for a few more months at least. And after that, who can tell what is to become of them? God forgive me, but I care not—as long as they remove themselves from here, and return to me the Peace that was mine before they came.

Diary of Hannah Wilson

Thursday, June 21, 1798

Mr. Iredell returned some days ago, but I fear my high hopes for his persuasiveness with Jamie have not been satisfied; foolish of me to expect so much, for he is but a man—an excellent man, indeed, but no magician. I cannot by rights complain of that. But what I can complain of is that we see so little of him, now that he is here. I had hoped we might be invited to another dinner, but as yet we have received no such communication. I suppose, after that incident with poor Sukey, Mrs. Iredell is even less inclined to extend her hospitality to me than she was before; nor, under other circumstances, should I much crave attention from her. It seems to me that we are complete opposites, she and I; and I confess, as well, that when I am in her presence I do feel a little ill at ease, recalling what once passed between Mr. Iredell and myself. But I'm so terribly, so inexpressibly lonely, that I'm sure I should accept any invitation that came my way with alacrity.

What I yearn for is someone to whom I might talk to freely, for there is such feeling dammed up in my heart that I fear it will soon burst. Mrs. Iredell could never be that person, of course; *Mr.* Iredell might, I believe—except that his wife keeps him by her side, when he is here, like a puppy on a short leash. If I cannot have what I truly want, I should at least like a little dinner party to take my mind from my troubles for an hour or two.

My only real diversions are the occasional conversations I have with travelers who stay at this tavern—which is to say, nearly any traveler coming through Edenton who hasn't friends to stay with, for there isn't another public house here even half as decent as this. Sometimes a gentleman comes through from Philadelphia, and I confess I will pump him quite shamelessly for scraps of information, so starved am I for news of home. And last week Jamie's old office boy Hansel was here for two days, on his way from Charleston to Philadelphia; it seems

375

he has done quite well for himself as an agent for various businesses in Philadelphia, and he travels widely. He said he would be at Reading in August, and I asked him to see Charles at his school, if he is still there then. Jamie and Bird have thought it best that Charles not come home just yet, as he is not fully acquainted with the turn our fortunes have taken, though Bird visits him from time to time. It must be hard on the lad to be away from home for so long, and on Polly as well; I do hope those trousers we made for him still fit, and are not entirely in tatters—boys' clothing never seems to last long. In any event, Hansel assured me that if Charles was indeed at Reading, he would make certain that all was well with him. He was very friendly, Hansel was, and tried his best to conceal his dismay at Jamie's appearance, and the conditions of our life here.

I am of a mind to write a letter to Bird, for I do miss him; and I believe enough time has passed that whatever feelings he might once have had for me—feelings so contrary to nature, and distressing to us both—must have cooled. He has been writing to me occasionally, despite my silence, and has said nothing in his letters that sounded amiss. But last week I was greatly disappointed that we received nothing either from him or from Polly—who writes fairly regularly, although of course *her* letters give none of the gossip I should like to find out. I do hope Bird has not given up on me as a correspondent. Perhaps he has become preoccupied with someone else—maybe that young lady we passed in the street, just before I left, the one with the blue eyes (or were they grey?), who greeted him so teasingly. I should be delighted to hear that he has fallen in love; at the same time, of course, I should not like him to forget me entirely.

From Hannah Wilson to Bird Wilson:

Edenton, North Carolina, June 23, 1798

... Your papa and myself were disappointed, my dear Bird, in not receiving any letters by the two last Posts; I expected to have had one from Polly. I know that she is not so averse to writing as you are. I begin to feel quite homesick, but when we shall leave Edenton I do not know. I think if I was once at home, that I should be content never to leave it again.

We are at a very great expense here, and if your papa does not attend the Supreme Court, I feel afraid of the consequence. It was a most unfortunate thing, his leaving Philadelphia; however, Mr. Thomas advised for the best. I dare say something would have been done by this time, but the longer it is put off, the more exasperated the Creditors will be, and the more difficult he will find it to come to any settlement. I am afraid he will not give up his property. He says what advantage has Mr. Greenleaf by doing it—his property sold for one third of the value, and he still in confinement, what reason do the Creditors give for keeping him still confined? I still think it would be but justice for your papa to give up everything, if he cannot settle any other way. I am sure he would feel much happier; but it is a subject that he never wishes to hear mentioned. He says that he knows his own affairs best. Remember my dear Bird, I write in confidence to you.

By accident your papa discovered that his desk was broke open. I was mentioning some quills that he had bought—your papa said that he had some goose quills ... from Hamburg. I told him that I had found three bunches which he did not know he had—he said that he had put them in the desk. He asked me if anyone had got a false key. I told him that it was obliged to be open for some papers that Mr. T. wanted, but that you would take very good care [of] everything—you must put the locks in good order.

I hope to hear by the next letter that you have got a house somewhere or other, and [are] not subject to the ill temper of Mr. Leiper any longer. Your papa has drawn an order on you payable on the fourth July; do not let anything prevent you from paying it, it was money that was paid for our lodgings. I believe it is an ~~order~~ a bill—I do not know whether there is any difference.

Bird, have you seen the lady with the blue or grey eyes since I left home, and have you had the courage to speak to her? I hope she has not proved unkind. Mr. Iredell returned last week. Tell Polly that he desires his best respects to her, and is much obliged to her for the very kind manner in which she mentions him. How are Dr. White's [and] Mr. Breck's ... families? Remember me to them and to Mr. and Mrs. Thomas. I have had but one letter from Boston, but that was a very long one from Mama, she inquired after all the family. You did not mention either Polly or Emily in your last letter, I hope they were not unwell. Tell Polly that she <u>must</u> write, and Emily that it will give me great pleasure to receive a letter <u>from her</u>. Your papa is waiting to hear from you before he writes.

Is Mr. Morris still confined? There is a report here that he has taken to drink, have you heard anything of it? There is a gentleman arrived here from Philadelphia [who says there] is a law lately passed, forbidding all persons to ride on a Sunday, even to Church. I told him that I could not believe it, that I was sure the Clergymen were more liberal. Write me if it is true—Your papa unites with me in love to all of you.

[Has] James got a place yet?

— H. Wilson

Diary of Hannah Iredell

Wednesday, July 4, 1798

We had the Wilsons for tea this afternoon, by way of celebrating the Anniversary of our Nation's independence. We have seen so little of them of late that Mr. Iredell was insistent we invite them; and when I last happened to encounter Mrs. Wilson in the street, a few days ago, the Woman looked so miserable that I was forced to agree it was only the Charitable thing to do. While I cannot imagine that I will ever feel Affection for her, as Mr. Iredell has urged, it is yet impossible for me not to feel some Pity towards her in her present situation.

Today seemed an appropriate Occasion to invite them, as Mr. Wilson was himself a Signer of that Document whose creation we were honoring. And yet, looking at him there—his Clothes nearly in tatters; his manner, when he spoke at all, distracted and disjointed; his eyes displaying a Wild and unsettled aspect, as though at any moment he might explode in a Rage—it was difficult not to discern in his dismaying Decline something symbolic of what has befallen this Country since those heady Days of 1776. Certainly he is a reminder that some of the most honorable Characters of his generation have fallen victim to their own Greed and self-interest—not only Mr. Wilson himself, but also Mr. Morris, the Financier of the Revolution and once a Senator from Pennsylvania, now rotting in a Philadelphia prison and (it is said) pickling himself in the process.

And many who have not had the misfortune, or perhaps the Means, to lose all their Wealth in speculative schemes have exhibited that same destructive self-interest in pursuing Faction and Party. I have read in the Papers of the Government's recent efforts to limit the number of Foreigners admitted to the Country, as they are so likely to foment dangerous criticism of the Government—particularly those shameless Frenchmen. Certainly it seems a proper precautionary Measure; but alas, I fear the worst Vipers are of the domestic variety, nourished by that very

379

Freedom and democracy that they would now attack! Even here in Edenton, one hears the most alarming and disrespectful Comments about President Adams; I am now ashamed to recall that I once laughed—and at a Dinner at the President's House, no less—to hear him described as "His Rotundity."

But I wax political; certainly Mr. Wilson exhibited no inclination to do so this afternoon, as he appeared far more concerned about the state of his Finances than the state of the Nation. It seems he has drawn an order on his Son, payable today, and is quite anxious that it should be honored. I can well understand his Anxiety, considering the Bill that has necessarily been mounting at Horniblow's, and the Wilsons' apparent utter lack of Cash; I'm sure Mr. Iredell has already had a word or two with Mr. Horniblow, pleading for Patience with them. But Mr. Wilson would not let go of the Topic, and began railing about the unreliability of his Son, who he says has been charged with attempting to settle his Affairs in Philadelphia, but who (he maintains) has continually disappointed him, refusing to travel here or even respond to his letters, and now leaving him entirely in the dark as to what efforts are being made in the city on his Behalf. Mrs. Wilson looked distinctly uncomfortable during this Tirade, and attempted to change the Subject several times, but without success.

At length she succeeded in steering the Conversation in the direction of the weather, always—as I remember from my drawing room days in the Capital—a safe topic. Mrs. Wilson complained of the unseasonable Heat, at which I felt compelled to inform her that the Heat was not at all unseasonable, but only what was to be expected in this Climate; and that it would soon grow so much hotter that she would look back upon *this* Weather with regret that it did not last.

"Good heavens, Mrs. Iredell, how do you stand it?" she asked, dabbing at her damp brow with a gray, threadbare handkerchief. "Why, in Boston, they should all wilt within five minutes in this Heat."

"One becomes accustomed to it, I suppose," I replied.

"Or not, as the case may be," interposed Mr. Iredell. "I don't believe I shall *ever* become accustomed to it. The Climate in Philadelphia, though certainly not perfect, is far more agreeable."

"Although not proof against the Yellow Fever," I put in, hoping to forestall yet another Disquisition on how much happier we should all be if only we lived in Philadelphia once again.

"But here, my dear, we're continually subject to the Intermitting Fever," he countered; then turned to the Wilsons to explain, "The season will be upon us soon. I hope, dear Friends, you will take proper precautions against contracting it, for the attacks can be quite serious, even fatal. I would advise you, Mrs. Wilson, to avoid the Morning dew."

She gave Mr. Iredell one of her flirtatious smiles, though it seemed to have lost a little of its old luster. "Oh, I couldn't possibly give up my Morning walks, Mr. Iredell. But I shall be careful, and dry my feet as soon as I return, I promise you."

I did not like the intimate Direction the conversation was now taking, and remarked that Mr. Iredell would be away as usual for the worst of the Sickly season, in order to attend the Supreme Court's August Term. At this, Mrs. Wilson brightened.

"Ah yes, the August Term!" she said. "And if Mr. Wilson's health continues to mend, perhaps we shall be able to accompany you to Philadelphia. Edenton is a lovely place, of course, but for all its charms, I confess I still feel quite homesick."

The rest of us were silent; I dared not glance at Mr. Iredell or Mr. Wilson, but I'm certain we were all painfully conscious that we were in possession of a piece of Intelligence that Mrs. Wilson was not: namely, that Mr. Wilson was obliged to remain in Edenton until Mr. Butler's Suit against him was either settled or decided.

Mr. Wilson's gruff voice broke the silence. "No, we won't be going to Philadelphia—not yet. As I've told Mrs. Wilson before, there are circumstances that make it impossible." Mrs. Wilson's smile suddenly collapsed, and she looked away and put her hand to her temple, as though hiding tears. "But I would ask you, Iredell," Mr. Wilson continued, "when you're there, to perform a favor for me: see that I'm assigned the Southern Circuit in the Fall. As I shall be here anyway, I suppose I might as well take it. And I don't imagine I shall have any serious Rivals for the honor."

We now all looked at Mr. Wilson in surprise—Mrs. Wilson as much as Mr. Iredell or myself, so it seemed evident she had not heard of this Intention before. The thought of Mr. Wilson, in his present sorry Condition, traveling the Circuit and purporting to embody the authority of the Federal government, was one I did not relish—leaving aside questions of how he was to afford the Journey, or whether his Health would hold out, or what might be the outcome of Major Butler's suit against him. It would have been far more sensible in him to request that

Mr. Iredell carry to Philadelphia his resignation from the Court; for it is a certainty that if he does not resign, he will soon be impeached. And what is he intending to do with his Wife? Leave her here alone, for months on end?

"Are you—are you quite sure, Mr. Wilson?" said Mr. Iredell.

"Quite sure, Sir!" said Mr. Wilson with finality, in a barking tone. He now looked distinctly out of sorts, and announced that they must leave. As poor Mrs. Wilson seemed to be having difficulty restraining her Emotions, it seemed in any event the sensible course to take.

As they said their thanks and farewell, I saw Sukey hovering in the front Hall. I had served the tea myself, precisely in order to avoid an encounter between her and Mrs. Wilson. I now held my breath, praying that there would be no unpleasant Scene; for while I have continued Sukey's Lessons, Mrs. Wilson has no way of knowing that. Furthermore, I have allowed Mr. Iredell to believe that educating the girl was my own Idea; he has been quite approving, and it would be awkward for Mrs. Wilson to attempt to claim credit for it. I resolved to scold Sukey for her effrontery as soon as the Wilsons left, for I had given her instructions to remain out of sight.

But there was no Scene, only an exchange of looks: Sukey, holding the door open, first looked directly at Mrs. Wilson and smiled, then cocked her head towards me; Mrs. Wilson, who had returned Sukey's smile, then looked to me with a puzzled expression; I felt my face redden and quickly looked at the Floor—but could not help breaking into a smile of my own. At the sound of Mr. Wilson approaching, saying his last goodbyes to Mr. Iredell, I looked up to see that Mrs. Wilson's puzzlement had only deepened. I suppose she must have imagined I had sold Sukey down the River by now, and could not fathom why the girl was smiling at me!

Diary of Hannah Wilson

Monday, July 16, 1798

Jamie has fallen ill—not in the way he was before, with only weakness and coughing, but with very high fevers, succeeded by chills. I sent for the doctor, but I knew what it must be even before he came, for I have been warned of what they call the intermitting fever. The doctor prescribed Peruvian bark, which tastes quite horrid and has a disturbing effect upon the bowels, but the doctor said there was no other remedy as effective. Indeed, I think Jamie has shown some improvement since he began taking it; but as the effect of it is only temporary, he must take it in every intermission between the paroxysms of fever and ague. I mix it with a little boiled water, which I must retrieve from the kitchen at the back of the tavern.

I sent word to the Iredells of what had befallen Jamie, as I thought Mr. Iredell, at least, would want to know; and was much surprised to find both of them at my door in short order, with a large supply of powdered bark, which they urged me to accept. I was greatly ashamed, but could not say no; for I haven't any idea how I'm to pay the doctor's bill, let alone purchase more bark. Mrs. Iredell said that what they gave me was a particularly effective variety, which had come off a ship that put in here from South America some months ago, and that I must not stint in administering it. I would have suspected that she had accompanied her husband here only to safeguard him from what she undoubtedly believes are my wiles, except that her concern for us appeared quite genuine. She assured me that every member of her family has suffered from the ague and fever repeatedly, and that there is every reason to believe that Jamie will in time make a full recovery. To my surprise, I felt my eyes begin to water, for there was such kindness in her voice; I had not known she was capable of such kindness.

I suppose there is now no hope of either Jamie or myself accompanying Mr. Iredell to Philadelphia, for he must leave at the end of this week. I had nearly determined to return with Mr. Iredell myself, no matter whether Jamie would go or not; I had even gone so far as to broach the subject to Mr. Iredell, who seemed agreeable to the plan, and I wrote in secret to Bird that he might expect me. I hadn't said anything to Jamie, of course, as I knew he should object most violently; but I had resolved to listen to none of his entreaties, for I have felt quite at the end of my patience with the man. And him talking of riding the Southern Circuit this fall—as though he had the money to meet his expenses, as though his children were not awaiting his return to Philadelphia! If his plan is to leave me here (for I couldn't show my face in Charleston or Savannah in the rags that remain to me), I told myself, then why should I not leave *him*, if I have the chance? But this fever has now rendered it unthinkable for me to leave him; when he is so weak and helpless, so entirely dependent on my offices, all vexation seems to drain from me, and in its place floods such tenderness that I can scarcely look at him without weeping.

At least it can be said, with truth, that it is Jamie's health that prevents his attending at court; *that* intelligence, at least, should stave off any demands for his resignation, or (God preserve us from it) his impeachment. But alas—true or not—I'm sure there are not many in Philadelphia who will believe it; I can well imagine the dinners and teas in well-appointed rooms, where voices will lower and interest quicken when the subject of the Wilsons and their misfortunes arises. Those who pretend to confidential knowledge concerning us will quickly command the attention of the rest, no doubt retailing the information that Jamie has taken to drink, and I to depravity, for everyone loves a scandal; and the unvarnished truth is never quite sordid enough. How well I can see and hear it all; for did I not myself, in happier times, batten in the same manner on the distress of the less fortunate?

I can tell that Jamie, too, somewhere in the depths of his distressed mind, has turned his thoughts towards home, for in the delirium brought on by his fever he sometimes mutters about Major Butler and jail, and seems to think he is speaking to Mr. Thomas or Bird. I cannot make much sense of it, but I gather he imagines himself back in Philadelphia. Ah, would that he were, and I with him! It is almost enough to make me wish that this malady had struck me as well, so that I might share in what for me would be a sweet delusion.

But I must leave off now, for Jamie has begun shaking from his chills, and I must cover him with blankets—so odd that he should be chilled, when I am dripping with perspiration, my gown damp and clinging, the air so wet and warm that it is like a silk cloth pressed against my face. The room is invaded by flying things, mosquitoes mostly, but there's no question of shutting the window, which on occasion yields us a barely fluttering breeze. The only time of day the weather is bearable is early in the morning; but I have had to suspend my habit of walking then, for I dare not leave Jamie in his present condition for more than a few minutes. And even if I could, my slippers are nearly worn through now. Ah, but what I would give to be out there, and moving, even in the heat and the dust—just a little free, for just a little while.

From Samuel Johnston to James Iredell:

The Hermitage, Williamston, North Carolina, July 28, 1798

... I feel very much for Judge Wilson. I hear that he has been ill—what on earth will become of him and that unfortunate lady who has attached herself to his fortunes? He discovers no disposition to resign his Office; surely, if his feelings are not rendered altogether callous by his misfortunes, he will not suffer himself to be disgraced by a conviction on an impeachment...

From Hannah Wilson to Bird Wilson:

Edenton, North Carolina, July 28, 1798

I write my dear Bird at your Papa's request; he wishes you to make an apology to Mr. Iredell for his not writing him, but he is too weak to attempt it, though he is much better—he has sat up three hours today. He has had a violent attack ... It will be some days before he recovers his strength, and the weather is very warm. I suppose that Mr. Iredell has told you that it is an intermitting fever which is very common to here. He has not had a return of the fever since Monday. He takes bark constantly; weakness is his chief complaint now. I have kept my health very well. My friends advise me to be very careful as the sickly season is coming on, but I think I shall be proof against it. I am obliged to leave off every minute to wipe the perspiration from my face and hands.

I am very happy to hear there is a prospect of James being placed in a Store...

Mr. Iredell has by this [time] told you what will surprise you, as much as it did me—that your Papa has requested the Southern Circuit. What he means to do with me (as I cannot go with him, as I have no clothes, if it were otherwise convenient) I know not. A single chair & horses will cost three hundred dollars—he certainly never could think of buying a carriage. His clothes are all going to pieces, he has not had anything since he left home, which is fifteen months. It would take 60 dollars at least to furnish him with what would be necessary to go so long a Circuit. Besides the expenses of the journey, your papa has never got a new hat, which was very shabby when you saw it—you may think what 'tis now. He intended to write you fully, and Mr. Iredell, if he had been well enough. He will open his mind to you but not to me, but it is a subject that I have done speaking upon, as we think so differently.

Write me what people say to our not coming home; you need not be afraid of distressing me, as I can hear nothing worse than I expect. Have you much business? Is the matter determined with Leiper? Write me very particularly.

Ask Polly if she will put up your Papa's calico dressing gown, and a pair of slippers that I had made at Bethlehem, and send them to Mr. Iredell, and ask him to put them up with his things that he is going to send by water. They are both in my closet I believe. I want them to walk in the country in, as I mean to walk before breakfast.

My pen is bad, your papa is asleep and I have no one to mend it. I expect a long letter from Polly & Emily by Mr. I.—remember me to him, Mr. & Mrs. Thomas, Dr. White's family, and love to Polly, Emily, & James.

Write me by Mr. I. if you have received this, as I should not like to have it miscarry—your Papa has just waked and desires his love.

H.W.

Diary of Hannah Iredell

Thursday, August 2, 1798

To my surprise, I found Mrs. Wilson at my door this Morning, with what was left of the vial of Bark we had given her, saying that she was returning it with her thanks—Mr. Wilson was now recovered. I explained to her that it was far better that she keep it, for it was likely that she would require it again; she appears not to understand the nature of the Illness, that it is liable to return after seeming to have taken its leave.

She thanked me again and returned the vial to the Pocket that hung from her waist, but seemed reluctant to depart, asking after my Health and that of the Children, and whether I had received any word from Mr. Iredell in Philadelphia. It seemed to me she blushed at the mention of his name, but perhaps it was only the heat, for she immediately added that she only thought he might have conveyed some news of the Wilson Children. I told her that although I was certain Mr. Iredell had written to me, as he is a most faithful Correspondent, I had as yet received nothing.

I couldn't help but notice that the white Navarino bonnet she was wearing was in a shabby state, nearly gray and spotted in several places. Nevertheless, she wore it jauntily, as though to pretend it was new and pristine, which made the Picture all the more pathetic. As she was beginning to say her farewell, something prompted me to remark that I knew of a Method of turning an old bonnet such as hers into what would resemble a brand new Leghorn.

She colored again and fingered the bonnet nervously, as though suddenly aware and ashamed of its Condition. "Really?" she said. "How clever of you. And what is it that needs to be done?"

I began to explain: you simply rip the bonnet to pieces, I told her, wash it with a Sponge and soft water, and then, while it is yet damp, wash it two or three times more with a clean Sponge dipped into a strong Saffron tea, nicely strained. This you repeat until the bonnet is as dark a straw Color as you like, after which you press it on the wrong side with

387

a warm Iron. Mrs. Wilson's expression grew more and more dismayed as I continued, as though I were describing a complicated scientific Experiment instead of a simple exercise in domestic Economy. When I finished, she thanked me and said she might attempt it; but I knew she never would, in her small Tavern room and with her strained resources.

"Mrs. Wilson, I happen to have on hand some Saffron," I called to her as she began to make her way back to Horniblow's. "I could easily make the Bonnet over for you, if you like."

She turned back towards me with an expression of surprised Delight, her small pink mouth formed into an amazed "O." "How very kind of you, Mrs. Iredell! But I couldn't impose"—

"It's no imposition. I wouldn't have made the offer if it were, I assure you."

"Well, then!" She came back to where I was standing in the doorway, smiling and unfastening the ribbon of her Bonnet as she went. "I cannot tell you how grateful I am. It's been ages since I've had anything new."

That much one could see, just by looking at her. Once she'd given me the bonnet, she hurried away quick as she could; unless I'm much mistaken, the poor thing was on the verge of Tears. And all over a silly bonnet! But I've begun the work on it, and employed Helen to assist me (for though the Child won't sit still for her Lessons, she is remarkably good with her hands), and I think it should turn out quite nicely, when it's done.

From James Wilson to Bird Wilson:

Edenton, North Carolina, August 4, 1798

... Yours of the 5ᵗʰ of last Month I received; and, as Mrs. Wilson wrote you, waited to hear from you before I sent another Letter. You "know not what Information I can expect from you." Before the 24ᵗʰ of May last you received a long and, to me, not an unimportant Letter. Mr. Thomas, in a short Letter, acknowledged the Receipt of it; and twice assures me that I shall hear from him fully by the then next Mail. I have never since heard from him—and do you really think that I had no Right to expect any Information from you in Consequence of that Letter? Was it shown to any or to whom of the Creditors? Was any—or what Answer

was given to it—or by whom? Was any Alteration suggested—or by whom? ...

These, and many others, are Articles of Information of some Moment to me. Concerning none of them have I received a single Syllable from you. Some certainly might have been obtained or at least attempted in my Absence as well as in my Presence. Mr. Iredell will return soon after this will reach you. That will be a good opportunity of writing to me fully and particularly upon every Subject. The Time is opening in which, I think, Something very effectual may be done.

I enclose to you a Copy of Major Butler's Letter to his Attorney, dated the very Day on which you wrote to me. You see how he represents Matters concerning your Proposals. I doubt not your Veracity; but hope you will have everything cleared up, as it is now in your Power, about that Business. I am much better, but still weak. Remember Mrs. Wilson and me to all the Family. Show this Letter to Mr. Thomas ...

From James Iredell to Hannah Iredell:

Philadelphia, Pennsylvania, August 6, 1798

... A most astonishing discovery of a private nature was made here on Saturday just after my arrival. Mr. Thomas, Judge Wilson's Attorney ... who had been universally thought a very honest Man (tho' some suspicions, however, have been entertained of him lately) absconded, after having defrauded, among others, some of his most intimate Friends ... The Frauds are supposed to amount to upwards of 60,000 Dollars.

There is not the smallest doubt as to the fact, and the whole city is greatly agitated by it. His poor Wife, who is a very amiable Woman far advanced in her pregnancy, dropped down senseless and remained in that condition for an hour on Officers of Justice coming to search for him...

I am afraid this must unavoidably add to Judge Wilson's distresses, tho' as yet I know ... no particulars ...

From Tom Iredell to James Iredell:

Edenton, North Carolina, August 17, 1798

... I am sorry to say Judge Wilson is by no means well, he takes too little exercise...

Diary of Hannah Wilson

Saturday, August 18, 1798

It is just as Mrs. Iredell warned me, Jamie has had a return of his fever, and it seems worse now—the bark not nearly so efficacious as before; and he sometimes, in his confusion I suppose, flatly refusing to take it. He is sleeping now, though I know not for how long; he sleeps only fitfully and in brief intervals, and when he is awake I scarcely have a moment to myself. I must either be sponging him with cool water, when the fever is upon him, or else piling blankets onto him when he is seized by the chills. And in the brief intervals between these bouts, I must do my best to convince him to take the bark, for it is his only hope of recovery.

I am exceedingly tired—I daresay, more tired than I have ever been in my life before. I have drifted to sleep in every position but recumbent: while sitting in my chair, while kneeling at the bed with my head resting upon its edge, even while standing and leaning against the wall; but always within a few minutes I am startled awake by Jamie's rasping cry of "Nannie, Nannie!" In a way it is better than it was before, when he was stronger; for now I haven't the time or energy to question why I am still here, or think on how I shall ever manage to make my escape.

Mrs. Iredell came to see us this morning, as she had heard of Jamie's relapse, and tried to give me some relief by taking my place for half an hour, so that I might get some fresh air—though it was stifling outside as usual, it was still a blessing to be away from that room. She assured me that all would be well while I was gone, as she was well experienced in tending to victims of this fever; while I'm sure that's true, Jamie was so agitated upon my return—Mrs. Iredell said he had been asking for me the entire time, and despite her assurances seemed convinced that I had abandoned him forever—that I resolved not to leave his side again, if I can help it, till he is recovered. He wants only me, just as my Henry did when he was ill; perhaps Henry, too, believed that if I left him he should never see me again—and then of course, to my

390

everlasting regret, I let them lead me away from him; and my poor babe died without me.

Of course, when Jamie is in the throes of his delirium, he seems often unaware of my presence, or under the impression that I am someone else—I am not always sure who. This morning he looked me square in the face and demanded, "What say you to my proposals, sir?" But when he emerges from his ravings and recognizes me for myself, his joy is so evident that I cannot doubt his affection for me. Indeed, he greets me each time as though I am newly arrived from Philadelphia.

"Nannie, my lass!" he cries, as the shivers begin, and he reaches up, trembling, to caress my face. "Why, here you are."

"Yes, my dear," I reply, blinking back my tears. "I've been right here, all along."

"So good of you, so good," he mutters, marveling; then, with urgent concern, "And you won't leave me, will you, Nannie? You'll stay right here?"

"Of course, my love, right here."

Only then does he allow his head to fall back on the pillow, and his eyes to close. I cannot express the pain it causes me to see him suffer so; it seems that all the misery of the past six months—the agitation of his mind, the fear and uncertainty that have tormented him—has been approaching him like some enormous ball of earth rolling down an incline, gradually increasing in speed and size, until at last it has descended to flatten him entirely.

Now I sometimes see again before me the image that struck such fear into my heart when I was last in Boston, after Dr. Dobel died: Jamie lying cold and lifeless. But when it now comes into my head, what I feel—dare I write the words?—is a great wave of relief washing over me. That he should be at peace at last. And I, though bereft of him and broken-hearted—should I be the worse for it? As for the children—But there he is now, calling for me again.

From Charles Wilson to Bird Wilson:

Reading, Pennsylvania, August 19, 1798

... I seen Hansel this morning, who informed me that Papa was yet very ill, which I was very sorry to hear, and that Mama was very well when he left her. I am hardly fit to be seen, my trousers are so bad, but

I hope I will not be so [for] long. I wish very much to come down to Philadelphia to remain there a week or two with you. I have been very well since you left me. Remember me to all the family. Believe me your affectionate Brother,

C. Wilson

Diary of Hannah Iredell

Monday, August 20, 1798

This morning I reflected that I had not called on the Wilsons yesterday, and they had been in a very bad way when I saw them on Saturday. I was tired and slightly feverish, the Day was unpleasantly warm, Sukey and I had a good deal of washing to do, and two of the Children were ill; but my Conscience pricked at me until at last I told Sukey she must manage without me for a while. I then gathered up some Wild Cherry bark and powdered balm and set out with them to the Tavern.

I had expected to find a Scene of woe and misery, and yet I was still not prepared for what I came upon. Even before I made my way upstairs, Mr. Horniblow shook his head sadly at me.

"Doctor's been and gone already," he said from behind his counter in the tap room. "Quite a row there was, with Judge Wilson raving at the top of his lungs, yelling at the Doctor to leave him be. Seemed to think the Gentleman was trying to poison him."

When Mrs. Wilson answered my knock, I was stunned by the fetid, sickly smell that assaulted my Nostrils—a smell of Vomit and human waste, so thick one could almost see it hanging in the air like a fog. Mr. Wilson appeared to be sleeping on the bed, though his head was tossing to and fro on the pillow, and his lips moving as though he were talking; his Breath came in short wheezes. Mrs. Wilson immediately put a Finger to her lips when she saw me, lest I wake him. She herself was scarcely recognizable: grey circles beneath her reddened eyes, and her hair sadly disheveled.

"Mrs. Wilson," I said, keeping my voice to a whisper in obedience to her Finger, "you must come away, at least for a while—come to my House, take some rest, change your Clothes—we can find someone else to"—

"No!" she whispered back fiercely, then covered her Face with her hands for a moment before looking up. I saw tears brimming at her eyelids. "What I mean to say is … thank you, you're very kind, but I cannot leave him. For if he should wake—*when* he wakes … if he finds I'm not here, he should be … very distressed. He becomes … so afraid. *You* know, you remember."

It seemed a great effort for her to speak, as though she were hoisting up heavy words from some cavern deep within her.

"Yes, but come away only for a little while," I whispered urgently. "If you go on like this much longer, you shall make *Yourself* ill. If he were in his right Senses, he would surely understand."

"Ah yes, but … he isn't in his Senses—I cannot explain to him that I shall return … he cannot understand." Her face became contorted, and her voice choked.

"Nannie, Nannie," came a panicky groan from the Bed. "Are you here?"

"Yes, dear, I'm here, just at the door." She raised her eyebrows at me, as though to say, you see?

"You're not going out!" he cried anxiously.

"No, no, just speaking with Mrs. Iredell, who has kindly come to see us."

He mumbled something and turned on his side, his back to us; it seemed that he was beginning to shiver.

I could see there was no use Arguing further; she is foolish but Stubborn. And indeed, I have been just as Stubborn on occasion, insisting on staying by the sickbed of one of my Children when others begged me to take some rest. Might I not feel the same towards Mr. Iredell, if (God forbid it) he were in such mortal danger? And what if I were successful in convincing her, and Mr. Wilson expired in her absence? Would she not forever hold me responsible, just as Nelly has done?

"As you please, then," I told her, "but send a message if you should change your Mind, or if you need anything. And I have brought you these."

I began to explain to her the method of preparing the Powders, but she looked at them so helplessly—I imagine her exhausted Brain could not comprehend the Instructions—that I desisted and told her I should bring them to Mr. Horniblow's kitchen and have them prepared there. She thanked me again, and then, just as she was about to close the Door, she paused to ask, "Is Mr. Iredell expected home soon?"

I bristled then, as I always do when I hear her speak my Husband's name, but her aspect was so Pitiful that I was able to put suspicion from my mind. "We hope to see him any Day, but I cannot tell for sure. I don't know whether the Court had much business, for we haven't yet had a Letter from Philadelphia. The mails, you know …"

"Yes, yes …of course. But … when he does return, could you ask him to come to us as soon as he is able?"

Again I felt resentment rising, for I did not relish the Idea of our Reunion, after these weeks of anxiety, cut short by a trip to see Mrs. Wilson.

"I don't mean to snatch him from you, of course, but—it's only that Mr. Wilson has been refusing to take the Bark, or any of the other Medicines the Doctor left with us—I daresay he'll even refuse these Remedies you were kind enough to bring. And I thought that … perhaps …" She paused, closed her eyes, and put a hand to her brow before continuing. "Perhaps Mr. Iredell might be able to persuade him, before it's too late, to take something. Mr. Wilson has a very great regard for your Husband, you know."

I suffered an uncomfortable twinge of remorse; the Woman was clearly of no Disposition for flirtation at present. "I'll ask him to come to you directly, I give you my Word."

Mr. Wilson then cried out that he was cold, and she hurriedly excused herself to attend to him. After I had brought the vials of powder to the Kitchen (where there was no need to provide detailed instructions, as Mr. Horniblow's cook knew exactly what to do with them), I returned home and began the tasks that awaited me. But I have not been able to shake my Melancholy—thoughts of the Wilsons hang upon me like the Smell of that room, which still lingers in my Nostrils though I have changed all my clothes.

I cannot puzzle out that Woman. I was certain she had only entered into the Marriage for the material Advantages she fancied it would bring her, for so all her Behavior indicated—including the Intimacy she has been at such pains to establish with my Husband. And yet she came here, and has remained here, when no Advantage is to be gained by it—except perhaps the Sympathy of those who observe her plight. As Mr. Iredell said, surely even the most Skeptical would not have blamed her for staying in Philadelphia, or taking refuge with her Mother, when she has been so ill-used by her Husband. Yet still she clings to him, and nurses him with such selfless Tenderness. Can it be she truly loves the Man?

Diary of Hannah Wilson

Friday, August 24, 1798

It is over now: Jamie gone and at peace, and I still alive, and out of that room at last—here, under the Iredells' roof. Has it truly happened, all of it? It is as though I have waked from some dream—or no, not waked, as I yet have the sense that I am *in* the dream. All seems remote from me: my clothes and hands appear to my eyes as those of someone else, my voice rings strange and distant in my ears. I should be frightened, I suppose, if I were capable of feeling so strong an emotion; but my sentiments, like my senses, are all dulled and deadened—numbed, like a finger pressed too long against a block of ice. But then, I have been sleeping for days now, only leaving my bed long enough to attend the funeral yesterday, and sleep—a deep and dreamless sleep—is all I crave, a sort of death itself.

Can it be but three days that I have been here, three days since I took my final leave of Jamie? It seems a month at least; and yet when I close my eyes all that my mind will conjure is that last evening, as vivid as though it had transpired but a few hours since: I am in our room at Horniblow's, by his bed, pressing a cool cloth to his brow. It has been hours since he has spoken, hours since he has acknowledged my presence. My fatigue is such that I have begun to see things that are not there: Suddenly, for a moment, Jamie's face becomes Henry's, as he looked when he lay sick and dying, and I cry out in joy and horror—joy to see my child once more, and horror to think that he will be taken from me yet again. Then, a moment later, it is Mr. Iredell I see, as he lay before me after his accident at Havre de Grace, shivering and pale.

But now Jamie raises his head from the pillow, a great effort in his weakened state, and all the phantasms are startled away. My mind clears as quickly as a steamy pane of glass wiped clean: this is my husband and no other. Then Jamie says in a voice that is surprisingly clear, "Listen ... very important ..."

I begin to tremble and lean closer, giving him every last ounce of my attention: at last he will tell me … what? I cannot say what I expect, but I have ever felt—despite all the time we have spent in one another's company, despite all that we have been through together—that there is some secret core of him, some inner chamber to which I have always been denied admittance. Is that door now about to open? Will he, with his final breaths (for I know, despite my confusion, that the end is near), reveal to me whatever lies inside?

"Yes, yes, my dearest Jamie, I'm listening." I feel tears descend my cheeks but make no move to wipe them away.

"Sixty-four looms, Mr. Davenport," he says, as calmly and distinctly as though he were conducting a business meeting. "Nine thousand six hundred pieces of duck … eleven dollars and fifty cents a piece."

And then I nod, help him lay his head back on the pillow, allow my muscles and my hopes to fall limp, my tears to spill. It was too much to expect—whatever it was I expected—from someone in his condition. Why should his mind not run back to Wilsonville, and all the plans he once had for the place? He looks at peace now, even with his hair matted and tangled and his face grey and drawn; it seems there is a smile on his lips. I smile too, though the tears still wet my cheeks. For him, it is years ago, and a world of possibility lies at his feet: he is once again a man of vision. Or at least of *visions*, I jest to myself ruefully. But perhaps he will yet open his eyes again, and see me—and know that it is me.

Hours then pass, I know not how many; night falls. I sit there in a daze, watching the rise and fall of his chest, listening to the rasp of his breath, not even lighting a candle; I see all that I need without it. Then I hear voices, footsteps growing closer: Mr. Horniblow's voice, and another's. The doctor? No—a knock, the door creaking open, the glow of a lantern—and there stands Mr. Iredell, home at last: no delusion this time, he is ruddy and warm. Sobs and tears overwhelm me, I fall into his arms. I must look a fright, unmentionable smells cling to my hair and clothes, and yet he holds me close and lets me cry. Mr. Horniblow stands by, holding the lantern, looking at the floor.

"Come, my dear lady, you must come away now," says Mr. Iredell into my ear, in a voice so kind and yet so firm that I want more than anything to obey.

"No, I cannot—if he should wake"— It is Henry, Henry that I think of. If I leave Jamie, as I left him …

"He won't wake, Mrs. Wilson."

I look at Jamie, his breath coming more raggedly and painfully now, and I know that Mr. Iredell is right. Yet I cannot make myself go: I kiss Jamie, on the forehead and the cheeks, for his lips are parched and cracked. I had meant to be there till the end.

"Mrs. Wilson."

Mr. Iredell's hands are on my shoulders, pulling me away.

"Just a minute longer!"

But then suddenly I cannot bear it another minute. I let Mr. Iredell lead me away, and I am glad to be led, glad to be told what I must do.

The rest is already a blur in my mind: a vacant room at the tavern, where I sink onto the bed and fall into a deep sleep; Mr. Iredell coming in when it is light, telling me that the doctor has been there, that Jamie died easy; then that I must come with him, to his house. Oh no, I couldn't, I say, though I haven't any idea where else to go; for I cannot imagine Mrs. Iredell truly wants me there. But Mr. Iredell insists—he says quite pointedly that *both* he and Mrs. Iredell insist. And so I gather up my belongings, there in the room where Jamie is still lying, and follow Mr. Iredell the short distance to his house. Mrs. Iredell at the door, looking anxious—though whether she is anxious on my behalf or because I am there, I cannot tell. Another room, another bed, and Mrs. Iredell brings me a cup of something bitter, that seems to put me in a drowning sort of sleep, and I am grateful for it—for otherwise I am overcome by anxiety and agitation. But Mr. Iredell is somehow always there when I awake, telling me gently that I mustn't worry, that he will see to everything: the arrangements for the funeral, the official notification to the government, the letter to my family in Boston—to Sarah, please, I tell him, not to Mama, as the shock might be too much for her. To your sister, then, he says. He has already taken steps to inform the children—Jamie's children, our children. But, dear to me as they are, are they still *my* children? Where shall I go now: to them? To my mother? What shall I do, what is my place in life? I begin to weep and moan, until someone hands me another cup of something, and a heaviness courses through my veins and brings me more sleep.

Then yesterday there was the funeral, and suddenly I had to rise and face the world; it couldn't wait longer, Mr. Iredell said apologetically, what with the heat—the coffin, in the parlor, was surrounded by saucers full of chloride of lime to purify the air, but even so ... I borrowed a black dress from Mrs. Iredell; she had tried to alter it to suit me, but didn't want to disturb me to take measurements, so the bodice was still too tight, and I kept tripping over the hem. We walked down to the water, the coffin on a cart, and there took canoes across the creek to Mr. Johnston's farm, called Hayes, for he was kind enough to allow us to use the family burial ground—a small green hillock, with a view of the town. There were no more than a dozen of us, I think, including the minister—though in truth, I could not count them, could scarcely take notice of who they were; it took all my effort not to faint in the heat, and with all the thoughts whirling in my head: to lay him here, in this place, for eternity, among these Johnstons and Iredells and Blairs. Imagine the surprise of some future Johnston scion, coming across this interloper of a grave, a hundred years or more from now. What will he know of Jamie? How will James Wilson be remembered—if at all?

To think, if he had died but two years before this, he should have had such a grand funeral in Philadelphia, with a train of friends and dignitaries paying him homage. Now there will be no shrine, no eloquent memorials; all his achievements—and there were, indeed, so many—will count for nothing in the world's tally, when stacked against the few foolish mistakes committed when his great mind, exhausted from a lifetime of exertion, had lost its mooring. Surely, when news of his death reaches the world, there will be little grieving: the government will be rid of a tedious embarrassment; my mother and sisters will tie black bands about their arms but secretly smile in relief; and the creditors, of course, will pounce upon the estate—all his preciously guarded acres—like vultures on a fresh-killed carcass. It is left to me, and to the children, to mourn him as he deserves. For my part, I shall try ever to remember him as I first saw him, that rainy day in Boston: a man of vision and confidence, of learning and wisdom and power—a great man, resplendent in his gilded coach and four—and one entirely in my thrall.

From James Iredell to Sarah Gray:

Edenton, North Carolina, August 25, 1798

... At the desire of your dear and unfortunate Sister, Mrs. Wilson, who is in good health but extreme affliction, I have the pain to acquaint you that Judge Wilson unfortunately died here on the night of the 21st Inst, a few hours after my arrival. Tho' he had been at times in very bad

health, evidently occasioned by distress of mind owing to his pecuniary difficulties, yet the Illness of which he died was of short duration, tho' very sharp, and the greater part of the time he was in a state of delirium during which he would not suffer many things to be done for him which were advised, and might possibly have restored him. Your sister with her usual goodness never quitted him, day or night, until his death was plainly approaching; and then she was parted from him with great difficulty.

It is a mercy for which her friends cannot be too thankful that her health has been so well preserved in such a constant state of anxiety, trouble, and want of rest, as she endured before his death. She was so obliging as to comply with Mrs. Iredell's and my earnest wishes in coming to our house the very next day after this unfortunate event happened; and though for some time her mind was agitated to a most affecting degree, yet I have the satisfaction to assure you that she is now much more composed, and we are at present without any apprehensions about her health. You may be assured of the utmost tenderness and care being shown her by Mrs. I. and myself, who will feel no small satisfaction, though attended by such melancholy circumstances, in enjoying her society as long as it can be afforded to us, looking forward with concern only to the moment of separation, which we shall feel most painfully.

Mrs. W. requested I would write to you and not to her mamma, in order that you may prepare her for the intelligence, to prevent her being too suddenly surprised...

Diary of Hannah Iredell

Sunday, August 26, 1798

She is here, in my own House—a Viper in the nest. God forgive me, for surely she has suffered much and is in need of Succor—and so I have given it to her, though Fanny and my Helen have now fallen ill, and I have yet to entirely recover my own health—and yet I cannot help what I feel. From the moment she appeared at my doorstep—Mr. Iredell having only just returned and then hurried out again to Horniblow's, where he remained the rest of the night (I having kept my word to tell him as soon as he came home that Mrs. Wilson desired him to come to her)—I couldn't bear the sight: his arms about her, cradling her, supporting her.

"How could you have allowed this to happen?" he hissed at me once she had fallen asleep. "Why did you not bring her here before this?"

"I tried," I said, wounded at his tone. "But she would not come—not with me."

"You should have insisted," he said, and then seemed to dismiss me, drawing a chair up to the bed and seating himself just inches from her head, watching for her awakening.

Is it possible that her coming here was all part of some crafty Plan, that she *knew* her Husband would most likely die here, and that she would then throw herself on our Mercy in this way and insinuate herself into the very Bosom of our Family, so that she might sink her Claws into the man on whom we all depend? Certainly that would make sense of her otherwise inexplicable behavior.

But no, but no, I scold myself: did I not see her clinging to her own Husband's side, amidst such filth and squalor, nearly dead herself with exhaustion and Anxiety? Was that all mere show, an elaborate Pantomime concocted in order to delude me? No, I berate myself, as I prepare an infusion of Motherwort or some lettuce water to calm her, or a dram of grated Horseradish root to stimulate her appetite, she is a model of Virtue and you are nothing more than a jealous harridan. And then I enter her room (the room usually shared by Annie and Fanny, who are now crowded in with the younger Girls), and see him there, beside her bed, gazing at her tenderly and speaking to her in low, intimate tones, and all my Suspicions and doubts come rushing back—and I am convinced that *they* are the Truth, just as convinced as I had been moments before that I had done her a grievous Injury by believing them. I can scarcely breathe—the Air seems quite sucked from the room—and it is all I can do to deposit whatever I am carrying without bursting into tears. When I see his head bent so close to hers, I am once again standing on the Green before the Courthouse, staring through the darkness at what I can scarce believe.

Though I know it must have sounded uncharitable, I could not help asking Mr. Iredell how much longer he thought she might remain our guest; for with Mr. Wilson gone, it seems to me there is no impediment to her leaving, once she has regained her strength. To my Dismay he replied that he was at pains to convince her to stay until he returned to Philadelphia in the Winter, so that he might accompany her. Dear Lord, four more months—how shall I bear that Woman's presence in my House for four more Months?

From Charles Wilson to Bird Wilson:

Reading, Pennsylvania, August 29, 1798

... I am very bad off indeed for trousers. These that I have is most off of me. I can get a pair made and it can be charged to Mr. Drake, who told me to tell you that he is very bad off for money and that he would be very glad if you would send him some. The Yellow fever is in town, there is one died here and one or two sick with it. Give my love to all the family and tell Emily that she must write to me...

P.S. Mr. Drake told me to tell you that he would be much obliged to you if you would send him that money and to let him hear from you or he will be very much disappointed.

Diary of Hannah Wilson

Friday, August 31, 1798

I am much stronger now than when I last wrote; although I almost wish I could declare myself an invalid again, and bury myself in sleep. Each day, it seems, has brought some new revelation, some new anxiety. Yesterday it was Mr. Iredell telling me of what he had heard, when he was in Philadelphia, concerning Mr. Thomas—how he had made off with monies belonging to his clients. Though I hadn't liked the man, I never suspected he was capable of such perfidy as this. I now suspect that he counseled Jamie against returning home so that he might steal from him with impunity; and I am certain that he took those papers from Jamie's desk for his own purposes, that day he insisted we break it open—though as whatever he obtained would eventually have gone to the creditors, I suppose it makes little difference. But when Mr. Iredell told me that he had taken as well some two hundred dollars belonging to Bird—money owed him for his work on some of Mr. Thomas's cases—I was moved to angry tears. Bird will somehow have to find a way to make it up, as he is the head of the family now; he will have to exert himself, and apply himself to his law business in earnest.

Bird has been much in my thoughts of late—now that I am able to think. Twice I have tried to write to him, but could not find the words. Does he blame himself, I wonder, for not acceding to his Papa's last wishes (though he could not have known at the time they *would* be his last wishes) and coming to Edenton? To have his father die when there had been such bitterness between them, and with no opportunity for reconciliation! Thank God I need not reproach myself for staying away, or leaving this place (though indeed I have thought of many other things to reproach myself with, lying here in this room). I should like to offer Bird some comfort, to let him know that my presence here was sufficient, and that everything possible was done for his father. And that Jamie is now at peace, his suffering at an end—but to say that without implying any relief on my part that the ordeal is over. When I try to put all this into a letter, my head begins to ache, and the words to swim before my eyes, and I must put down my pen.

It is not only that, however, which has prevented my writing to Bird; it is more that I am in such confusion over what I am to him now, and what my future position will be. Should I sign myself "your Mother"? In truth, I never was his mother—never the mother of any of them, though I tried. But with Bird, of course, it was always more difficult than with the rest of them. And I blame myself for what he felt for me, perhaps still feels—for its having grown from something pure and innocent to something so unnatural that I shudder to think of it; was it not my own vanity and selfishness that prevented me from discouraging it as I should have? Surely I cannot live with him now, under the same roof, as mother and son; and to live with him as anything else is unthinkable. What if he were to propose marriage? Marriage to his own mother! One doesn't find such things even in the pages of the most sensational novels. I cannot begin to imagine the scandal that would ensue—on top of all else that has befallen us. The family would never recover, Bird would never be able to attract any legal business, all would be disgrace and disaster.

I cannot, must not return—though I love them all, and fear for them, and want more than anything to help them. But what help should I be to them, even leaving aside considerations of Bird's intentions towards me? I should only be another mouth to feed, for my skill with a needle is still not such as to earn my keep, and most likely never will be. The best I can do for them, I think, is to keep my distance, and hope they will understand.

If I am no longer a wife, and no longer a mother, I suppose I must again become a daughter, and return home to Boston. I should like to see Mama again, of course—indeed, there have been times, these last few weeks, when I have wanted nothing more—and to see Sarah and poor dear Lucy, and her little daughter. But I shall have to endure those looks, those whispers, the smug smiles of satisfaction that it all ended in disaster, just as they expected—and most likely from the whole town, not just from my family. They will forget in time, though, for some fresher scandal will distract them. And no one will expect me to do needlework, or at least not for money. There will be comfort and security—things I too little valued, before.

But Mr. Iredell says I mustn't think of going anywhere for some time—for he fears that, as it is still the sickly season and my health is not quite entirely restored, I should risk falling ill on the road. He urges that I wait until he himself will be traveling northward, in order to attend the Supreme Court in February, for then he could escort me at least to Philadelphia. It is tempting, indeed, for I don't relish the idea of traveling on my own, or with strangers; and I have such fond memories of our last journey together, when he brought me here.

But when I think back on one part of that journey, of course, I blush; how can I remain for four more months here, in the house of a woman I have wronged? For I see it that way now—I see many things differently now, with a kind of terrible clarity, all my faults and follies. I may have been distraught when we were in Havre de Grace, and not entirely in control of my thoughts or actions; but I cannot take refuge in such excuses: I wronged her nevertheless. And she knows it, or knows something; I can see it in the way her face grows hard whenever Mr. Iredell smiles at me, or even speaks my name.

This morning Mr. Iredell told me something that sent a further shiver of guilt through me: Mrs. Iredell has done me a great favor, and kept it secret all this time. It seems that Jamie had actually been under arrest here, on a writ sworn out by Major Butler and prosecuted by none other than Mr. Slade, and that he had given his word that he should not leave this place before he was due to appear in court, in October. Mr. Iredell said he was sorry that this intelligence had been kept from me, but that Jamie had been most insistent that I know nothing of it, for he feared it would distress me. I was greatly shocked, but more saddened than angered, for it is the last proof of Jamie's concern for me. I quickly saw the events of the past few months in a truer light: Jamie had not been afraid to return to Philadelphia because Major Butler might arrest him there—rather, he had been unable to return because Major Butler had already arrested him *here*. And those things he had said, when the fever was upon him—about jail, and Major Butler—now made more sense to me.

"At least," I said to Mr. Iredell, "Major Butler did not insist on his being put in jail. He could not have borne that, I think."

Mr. Iredell smiled, his eyes narrowing with emotion, and took my hand. "For that, my dear Mrs. Wilson, you have my wife to thank."

"Mrs. Iredell?" Now I was truly shocked.

Mr. Iredell explained that he had been away from home at the time of the arrest, and that Mrs. Iredell had somehow prevailed on Mr. Slade not to carry out Major Butler's directions to have Jamie thrown into prison.

"That was very—very kind of her," I managed to stammer. "I must—I must thank her for that, indeed."

Mr. Iredell nodded. "An excellent idea. She is, in truth, a most generous, kind-hearted creature—she has been most unstinting in the pains she has taken for your health, despite several of the children being ill at present. I fear that, sometimes, her native timidity in the presence of strangers can make her appear distant or … unfriendly. But once one comes to know her, she is really quite"—

"Mr. Iredell." I couldn't listen any more to this pretense; I am done with pretending. "I don't believe it is mere timidity, with me."

He turned from my gaze and reddened slightly. "Still, it could do no harm to thank her."

I promised him I would, and he took his leave; but I cannot imagine how I shall find the strength to seek her out and speak to her, for I can scarcely be in the same room with her without feeling myself begin to tremble. My mind is like a simmering cauldron, bubbles of remorse and self-blame rising to the surface with every second—Henry's dying because I couldn't give him suck; Bird's falling in love with me because I was too selfish to discourage it; Jamie falling into ruin, and then dying, because I could not find a way to make him see the truth of his situation. And when I see Mrs. Iredell, that cauldron of guilt reaches a raging boil, so acutely aware am I of what I have done to her: given her cause for suspicion, of both myself and of her husband, and then subjected her to torments of uncertainty by acting as though there were no basis for it.

I have tried to pray, to seek God's forgiveness; for I know that Bird, if he were here, would assure me that prayer would bring me comfort. But no matter how I try, no matter what effort I put into my prayers, I feel no comfort; indeed, it only makes me feel worse, as I am convinced it is my own fault my prayers leave me uncomforted. Perhaps it is not God's forgiveness I need, but that of Mrs. Iredell; for should not the victim be the one to extend absolution? Now that I know it was her pleading that kept Jamie out of jail, my remorse has grown even sharper, if that were possible; indeed, she has done a great deal for me, certainly more than I deserve. It is too late to undo much of the other damage I have done, but this I might—I need only tell her the entire truth. If I could do that, I think it would ease both our minds; I should cease this constant self-reproach, and begin to feel that there is yet some virtue in me. But how can I, when the only way to prove my virtue is to reveal my very lack of it? How shall I ever find the strength?

From James Iredell to Bird Wilson:

Edenton, North Carolina, September 1, 1798

... I inclose you now a letter from Mrs. Wilson. Her sufferings, tho' uncommonly severe, and accompanied with incessant watching and fatigue and want of rest, have however fortunately not deeply injured her health... She has been so good as to consent to stay at our house, and you may be assured of every possible care and attention being shown her. Her intention is, as soon as she conveniently can, to go to her Mother, but to be first for some little Time in Philadelphia... If she could be satisfied to stay till towards the latter end of December, she would confer a great obligation on Mrs. Iredell and myself, and I could at that time with perfect convenience attend her myself to Philadelphia.

Whenever the time arrives when Mrs. Iredell must part with her she will regret it most painfully. Never was any Lady more respected and esteemed in any place than she has been universally here, nor did any ever experience truer sympathy in misfortune. What she underwent for some days previous to the unfortunate event of anxiety ... and distress, I believe no language could paint. I saw only a small part of it myself, but have received a most affecting account of it from others.

I take the liberty to inform you the amount of the sums due here, so far as I have been able to learn them, and which I believe are all except what is due to the Doctors. Their accounts I will endeavor to obtain and forward next week. Those I know are as follow, viz.

To Mr. John Horniblow (at whose house Mr. and Mrs. Wilson stayed)
£422..7..10 No. Carolina Currency equal to about 845 Dollars
To sundry Persons for Funeral Expenses
£21..2..3—equal to about 42 Dollars 25 Cents

Hannah Wilson to Bird Wilson:

Edenton, North Carolina, September 1, 1798

The shock my dear Bird which you must all have felt by the death of your dear papa affects me sensibly; the separation is a severe trial of my fortitude, but if it was not for you children, I think I should feel resigned to know that his suffering is at an end. But when I think of your situation, it seems too much.

But I hope my dear Bird you will exert yourself; remember you are the only one they have to look up to. And think how much happier your papa is—it would be from a selfish motive if we wished his return. His mind had been in such a state for the last six months, harassed and perplexed, that it was more than he could possibly bear, and brought on a violent nervous fever. I never knew of his arrest till since his death, and now can account for many things he said in his delirium.

I cannot be thankful enough that I did not leave Edenton with Judge Iredell, I never should have forgiven myself if I had left him. When he was sensible he took so much pleasure in seeing me by him, and requested me not to leave him—but that was not five minutes at a time. I had not my clothes off for three days and nights, nor left him till the evening of his death, when I could not bear the scene any longer. I am astonished at myself when I think of what I have gone through. They told me he died easy. I have the satisfaction to know that everything was done that could be, there is a very excellent physician here.

Mr. Iredell did not arrive till the evening of your papa's death, and he was saved the painful intelligence of Mr. Thomas's villainy—but his cruelty to you in taking the two hundred dollars was worse than all the rest, when he knew it was all your support.

Mr. Iredell has been kind beyond everything (his family were all very ill at the time)—he has watched by me night and day. What with the fatigue and anxiety of mind, I was very low when I came here, but I am now much better, and I hope my health will be quite restored. Remember me affectionately to them all; I shall be very anxious to know what you determine upon. I shall return to Boston.

Once more my dear Bird let me entreat you to exert your usual fortitude; this has been a most painful task, but I hope in future I shall write with more composure—but shall always be

Your affectionate mother
H. Wilson

Diary of Hannah Iredell

Monday, September 3, 1798

I saw in a Letter which Mr. Iredell wrote to young Mr. Wilson that he maintained I should be most regretful to part with Mrs. Wilson, when the time comes for her to leave. I suppose it can do no harm to prettify the Picture for a grieving Son, but I warrant that is not Mr. Iredell's only Object, for he seems most determined to foster a Friendship between myself and Mrs. Wilson—telling me that she and I have more in common than I might imagine, and the like. (I bit my tongue and said nothing about what I *feared* we had in common, with regard to himself.)

She sought me out in the Kitchen yesterday afternoon, to thank me for what I had done towards keeping her Husband out of jail, and I have reason to believe it was Mr. Iredell put her up to it—these past few days he has asked me at least three times if Mrs. Wilson had spoken to me, and when he asked the fourth time last Night and at last I told him yes, she had at last, he smiled expectantly, but I said no more to him about it. In fact, Mrs. Wilson and I had a rather longer Interview than we had done in some time, and by the end of it she had played so artfully upon my sympathies that I nearly softened towards her; but by the time of my Conversation with Mr. Iredell I had come to my senses again.

She seemed quite nervous when she began, though perhaps it was only the heat (for the Kitchen, on a September afternoon when the fire has been going, is even hotter than outdoors); she kept tucking at her hair and playing with the collar of her gown (or rather, *my* gown, as I have had to lend her clothes). It meant a great deal to her, she said, my keeping Mr. Wilson out of Jail—and even more to him.

"He had a terrible fear of Jail, you know," she said, "though of course most people do—I mean that he feared it even more than most."

"Yes," I said, poking at a Chicken that was roasting on the fire, "so Mr. Iredell told me."

"He had been in Jail before, you see," she continued, dabbing at the Perspiration on her neck. "Twice, in fact. The first time, in Philadelphia, was very brief, just overnight—I don't believe anyone knew of it, fortunately"—

(Of course people knew of it, even here in Edenton; the poor Woman was deluded—but what purpose would be served by enlightening her?)

"—but it brought him quite low, as he was so proud a Man, you know, and had once ascended to such heights." She swallowed and blinked, and seemed genuinely affected, before composing herself sufficiently to continue. "In any event, I cannot thank you enough—I'm so very ... grateful ..."

She was weeping now, and perspiring heavily as well, but she showed no inclination to leave, nor could I very well dismiss her, considering the state she was in; and as the Heat in the kitchen was doing her no good, I suggested we might retire to the parlor with a cooling drink, as the chicken could look after itself for a while. I suppose I felt rather sorry for her, and uncomfortable at allowing her to think I deserved all the credit for guarding Mr. Wilson's relative freedom. I offered her a tonic of Wild Cherry bark, as it generally has a calming effect, but she made a little face and said that she greatly appreciated my various "Potions," as she called them, but she believed they had done their Work in restoring her health, and might she not have something else instead? Well, I suppose the Wild Cherry, though efficacious, is rather bitter; I gave her some Currant water, and poured some for myself as well.

The Children, who are mostly recovered from their illnesses, were in the Parlor, but I shooed them upstairs and told them they could play at cards there, though it was the Sabbath, and so we had some Peace. There was then a little Silence, while Mrs. Wilson stared into her cup of Currant water, and I thought perhaps I should have stayed with the Chicken; but then she began to speak once more, and a veritable tumble of Words came out: about Mr. Wilson, and how greatly he had suffered; about Mr. Wilson's children, and how each of them was likely to be affected, in different ways, by his loss; how she had resolved to return to her Mother's house, in Boston, as she thought she would only be a burden to the Children if she remained with them.

I nodded and listened, and tried not to think too much on what might be transpiring with the Chicken; for though Mrs. Wilson every now and then made a remark about how she mustn't trespass on my Time, it was obvious that she was loath to end the Conversation.

"I fear my Chin has been wagging shamelessly," she said at length, and bit her lip, "but it's been so long since I've had someone to talk to—another Woman, I mean. It's not the same, talking to a Gentleman, don't you agree?"

She blushed, and I thought of how Mr. Iredell had perhaps heard all this from her before, during his long vigils by her Bed. But I also recollected how I had been so grateful, when I was friendless and alone in Philadelphia, for the company of Mrs. Bond, and her Conversation. It occurred to me that Mrs. Wilson was now in something like the Position I had been in there, removed from all that was Familiar and comforting to her. And I felt the truth of what she said, about talking with a Person of one's own Sex—the little things one needn't explain, the easy intimacy; for that is what I once had not only with Mrs. Bond but with Nelly as well, and what I have missed so sorely, even here in Edenton, these past few years.

Was it possible, I thought with a small internal gasp, that Mr. Iredell was right, that Mrs. Wilson and I might somehow contrive to be friends, despite all that I have suspected of her? Indeed, she has seemed rather different to me these past weeks, after what she has suffered: more serious, less inclined to idle chatter and flirtatious smiles—as though life's buffeting has stripped her of her girlish coquettishness and revealed a Woman underneath. And perhaps that was all it had been, I thought, a mere Veneer. I asked myself, as I have several times before, if I had not misjudged her, confused her in my mind with that Woman of twenty years ago, out on the Courthouse Green; if so, I had done her a grievous Injustice.

I smiled at her and gave her hand a gentle pat. "Yes, I believe I do know what you mean, Mrs. Wilson. But I fear I must now return to my Kitchen and see to Supper. Sukey has gone over to Hayes, as it's her free afternoon."

At the mention of Sukey, I had a sudden impulse to reveal that I had continued the Girl's instruction in her Letters, and that she was making great strides. But the words would not come; and so we rose. As Mrs. Wilson was leaving the room, her elbow somehow managed to knock a China dish onto the floor, where it broke into several Pieces, and she was much alarmed—near Tears, almost. She was quite surprised and relieved when I told her it was no great Matter, that I could easily patch it with a bit of pulverized Lime mixed with the whites of eggs. She then exclaimed at what she called my cleverness, and recalled to me that Bonnet I had fixed up for her so that it looked quite as good as new. Might I be able to do the same, she wondered, with her Slippers, for she was exceedingly fond of them? She then displayed for me a dainty foot sheathed in what had once been, I warrant, the most elegant of footwear—made of pale yellow silk, and embroidered with exquisite tiny flowers, still visible through the accumulated grime. I hadn't seen such delicate work since we were in Bethlehem, years ago—there was that young Lady, that Sister Anna, who had such a way with a needle—but I imagine these Slippers are from some fine shop in Philadelphia, a remnant of more extravagant days. They are now Mud-stained and nearly threadbare (no doubt she foolishly wore them on her walks in the Country), and I doubt I can effect much Improvement in them; but I told her I should see what could be done with a little cold water mixed with Soap, and her eyes quite shone with Gratitude.

But then, at Supper, all this glow of good feeling vanished. For Mrs. Wilson's humor was noticeably lighter than it had been since she arrived here—or indeed, for many weeks before that. At first, believing it was our Conversation that had done it, I was pleased at myself for having brought her some cheer, as well as for having shaken off my uncharitable Suspicions. But as the evening wore on, and some of her old Vivaciousness was on display, I could not ignore the admiring Looks that Mr. Iredell continually cast in her direction, and the smiles and laughter that passed between them. What is she, I demanded of myself—forlorn and friendless Waif, or sly and conniving Vixen? I am quite worn out with trying to settle the Question in my mind.

But it is past thinking about, past pondering. A knot of grief and anger began to form in my Stomach as I watched them, as undeniable as though I had tied it tight with my own two hands.

Diary of Hannah Wilson

Wednesday, September 5, 1798

I've had a letter today from Polly—written three weeks ago, so there was no question of her knowing of her father's death. It seems there has been another outbreak of the yellow fever in the city, this time so serious that Bird and Polly thought it prudent to close up the house and flee to the country. The girls and James have gone to old friends in Germantown, and Bird to relatives in Reading—and while there, I suppose, he will fetch Charles, as I imagine Mr. Drake has lost his patience waiting for the school bills to be paid. I was glad to hear they were all out of harm's way.

But how shall I now leave this place, with the fever raging in Philadelphia? I had resolved to stop there on my way home, to see my old friends the Brecks—and Bird and Polly and the others of course, for I cannot bear the thought that I might never see them again: we must meet and weep and console one another, one last time as a family, before we say our farewells. I cannot imagine that it will be safe to enter the city before late November, so I suppose I must remain here at least till then; and if I am to remain that long, I may as well wait until Mr. Iredell can escort me, as he says he intends to leave in December.

It wouldn't be so bad, I suppose, except that I continue so tormented about Mrs. Iredell. It was easier when I thought her simply a sour old hag, so ill-matched to her charming husband. But the longer I stay here, the more I begin to see her as kind and good-hearted, just as Mr. Iredell says. Certainly I have never seen so patient a mother, tending so carefully to her children's health and education—and not only the education of her own two daughters (the son goes to a school here), but two of her brother's daughters as well. Every morning at the stroke of eight she sets the girls to their various tasks, and these they remain at for two or three hours—the oldest two, Annie and Fanny, reading Mr. Gibbon on the Roman Empire, or Dryden's *Aeneid*, or some such work, and the younger two forming their letters or numbers on slates; and then, in the afternoon, they take turns playing the spinet, while the others paint in watercolors on silk or satin. Such a peaceful, pleasant scene, with Mrs. Iredell offering encouragement and gentle correction!

Yet there is, I think, something seriously amiss with the Iredells' younger daughter, Helen. When she cannot recall a letter or puzzle out a problem, she begins to fuss and whine, until she is soon screaming at full blast. At other times she is quiet as a mouse, yet clearly not attending to the tasks before her, but staring wide-eyed into space; once or twice I have heard her speaking to herself, quite as though she were carrying on a conversation with some invisible being! But I have never seen Mrs. Iredell lose her temper with Helen. When the girl's mind wanders off, she speaks to her quietly but insistently, until she receives some response; and when the child loses her temper, Mrs. Iredell only takes her from the room, so that she won't disturb the others, and rocks her and whispers in her ear until she is calm again. I suppose some would think the girl is being spoiled, and perhaps she is. But there is something so tender in Mrs. Iredell's manner towards her that it brings tears to my eyes, just looking at them.

Then yesterday, when I remarked to Mr. Iredell that I was impressed by his wife's diligence in teaching the girls, he told me a thing I found so remarkable as to be scarcely credible.

"Ah yes," he said with enthusiasm, "Mrs. Iredell is a great believer in the education of girls. And more than that, she has undertaken the education of our Negro serving girl."

"Not … Sukey?"

"Yes, Sukey—Sukey indeed. Mrs. Iredell has been teaching her her letters, and I understand she has proved a remarkably apt pupil. Reading from the Bible already, so Mrs. Iredell tells me." He leaned forward and lowered his voice. "Now there are some in this part of the country, as you may know, who frown on such efforts, so it would be best not to mention it to anyone outside the household. But I'm pleased to say that Mrs. Iredell has more enlightened views."

"Indeed," I managed to say, "that is quite … commendable."

And all this time I'd been feeling sorry for the girl, certain that she'd been punished for our meetings! But now it made sense, all those little smiles and winks Sukey has been giving me, nearly since I arrived in the house: she must have felt constrained from telling me straight out, and this was her attempt to communicate that all was well. Indeed, more than well. At first I was rather vexed, of course, that Mrs. Iredell had apparently portrayed the instruction I had begun—and which she herself had so strenuously opposed—as being entirely her own notion. But on further reflection I considered that the end result was certainly to be approved, so what did it matter how it had been arrived at? I also recalled that Mrs. Iredell had said, in the course of upbraiding me for my efforts, that if anyone were to teach Sukey how to read, it should be herself—and so it has been. And if she has found the time and energy to do it, what with all else that she must do (for she is nearly always in motion, at some task or another), then surely I should put aside my petty irritation and give her my undiluted admiration.

But how can I give her anything, when it seems she is of a mind to receive nothing from me? On Sunday afternoon I managed to find the courage to thank her for what she'd done for Jamie, and for me. It wasn't as difficult as I had anticipated, really, for after I had talked a while of Jamie, and what he had suffered—and rather lost my composure, I fear—I began to see a glow of understanding in her eyes, even of sympathy. And I realized how desperately I craved and yearned not only for her understanding, her forgiveness, but her friendship as well. Is it so impossible a wish? And so I talked, on and on, as though a lock had given way on my heart. And she listened, though I know she had many other things to attend to; she smiled on me and took my hand, and it was as though the sun had broken through a month's worth of clouds—I did not want to part from her. There was a kindness and a benignity to her expression that gave her a kind of beauty, though her face is plain and pock-marked; at that moment, she appeared more beautiful to me than any of the fine ladies of Philadelphia or New York, with their wax and rouge. And when she said she would try to clean my lovely slippers for me, the ones I had made at Bethlehem, I was overcome with gratitude—it was only another household task for her, I suppose, but for me, in the state I was in, it meant all the world.

But then later, after supper, it was suddenly all as it had been before—as though none of it had happened: the ice had returned to her glare, the distance to her manner. Her suspicion was once more trained upon me—on Mr. Iredell and myself—like a musket. It pained me more, now that I knew what it was to have her look upon me kindly. And what must it be for him, to have his wife regard him in that way? It seems I cannot smile at Mr. Iredell, and act towards him in a friendly manner, without triggering her wrath. To win her friendship, must I turn a cold eye on the one person who has unfailingly proved his friendship and his loyalty to me?

And yet who can blame her, when she is right, in part—there *is* of course a secret we are keeping from her, that I am keeping from her (for I know Mr. Iredell should never breathe a word of it, out of consideration for me). I'm sure what she suspects is even more shameful than the truth. And yet, if I told her all, and made a clean breast of it, would she ever again look on me as she did on Sunday afternoon, with sympathy and warmth? Would she ever find it in her heart to consider me her friend? I fear I know the answer.

From Jacob Rush, Chief Judge of Pennsylvania's Third Judicial District, to his brother Benjamin Rush:

Reading, Pennsylvania, September 8, 1798

... The Death of Judge Wilson was to me an unwelcome & unexpected Event—I fear he hastened it by some unjustifiable Means. His Constitution was too good to have sunk in so short a Time under the Weight of mere Intemperance. What a miserable Termination to such distinguished Abilities, and what a dark Cloud overcast the last Days of a Life that had once been marked with uncommon Luster...

From Bishop William White to James Iredell:

Near Philadelphia, Pennsylvania, September 8, 1798

... The melancholy Tidings of which your Letter was intended to give me the first Information had been communicated to me by a Gentleman from the City, on the 5th Inst... . I have written to Polly, to acquaint her with the few Particulars of your Letter which it was material for her to know; & the Letter itself I have enclosed to Mr. Bird Wilson, now at Pottsgrove. It cannot be now unknown to Mrs. Wilson, altho' it must have been so when you wrote, that the Family have shut up the House & are dispersed in Consequence of the prevailing Fever. I sympathize most tenderly with them all on the mournful Occasion, and

shall not be wanting in my Attentions or Services which can tend to alleviate their Sorrows.

My Family desire, with me, to be affectionately remembered to Mrs. Wilson. You do not mention when she intends to return; nor do I know of any Appearances of such a speedy Decline of the Fever, as shall render the City safe to her ...

I doubt not, Sir, it will be a Consolation to the Children that in the Extremity of Mrs. Wilson's Distress, she found a Reception under your hospitable Roof ...

Diary of Hannah Wilson

Thursday, September 20, 1798

I have done it, done what I both yearned to do and dreaded: the secret is out, the sin confessed. But whether my confessor will see fit to pardon me I cannot yet tell; I had hoped to win her trust, but I fear I have only earned her undying enmity.

I don't know that I should have ever found the courage to do it, but for the peculiar events of the last few days. Mrs. Iredell fell quite ill Sunday evening, with fever and chills. I was exceedingly alarmed, especially after having watched Jamie through so similar an illness, and seen the terrible result; but Mrs. Iredell waved away my concern, saying that she had survived many a worse attack—and then she gave me quite a sharp look, as though to discern whether I might not in fact be *hoping* for her demise, which pained me not a little.

The worst of it was that she kept attempting to rise from her bed, though the doctor had left strict instructions that she must have complete rest. Mr. Iredell was nearly at his wit's end, pleading with her to stay in her room and not to concern herself about the children, and the chores—telling her that Sukey was quite capable of managing, and Mrs. Tredwell was coming in as well from time to time to supervise. At last, yesterday morning, after Mrs. Iredell had appeared downstairs several times, pale as death, he asked me if I would do him a great favor, and sit with her to ensure that she abided by the doctor's orders.

"Must it be me?" I asked. "For surely she would prefer someone else."

He explained that there was no one else—that Sukey was needed about the house, that Mrs. Tredwell had her own household to tend to, that Mrs. Johnston was certainly no use—and that he himself had been called away to another town to attend to some urgent business connected with his being executor of an estate, and would to his great regret be gone for several days. I couldn't very well refuse, after having accepted so many favors and kindnesses from the Iredells these past weeks, and yet I was rather alarmed at the thought of remaining by her side for days on end.

"And as for her preferring someone else, my dear Mrs. Wilson," Mr. Iredell continued, "I can only quote you Terence—who, though a writer of comedies, was not without some wisdom—and advise you that from bad beginnings great friendships have often sprung."

I tried to place my faith in the wisdom of Terence; but when I entered Mrs. Iredell's bedroom, I began to feel quite hopeless, for she looked at me once and immediately turned her head to the wall. I sat in the one small chair that was in the room, and asked if there was anything I might bring her—some bark, or perhaps that wild cherry decoction that she puts such faith in? No thank you, she said curtly, and so we sat in awkward silence for some minutes. She then fell asleep, as I could tell from her breathing; fortunately, I had brought a book to occupy my time. When she awoke she was shivering, and I found some blankets in the chest at the foot of the bed and laid them on top of her.

"Perhaps ..." she began, "perhaps I will take some of that wild cherry bark now, if you can bring it to me hot."

I nearly ran from the room, eager to escape—but eager, also, to be of service, to bring her some of what she had so often brought to me. I was fortunate in discovering Sukey in the kitchen, and she knew at once where to find the vial of powdered bark, and how to prepare it. She told me what surprised me, that it was her own grandmother who had instructed Mrs. Iredell in the use of these various herbs and plants. Who would have thought that Mrs. Iredell had acquired all that lore, in which she evidently places a great deal of trust, from one of her family's slaves?

The decoction was still quite hot when I brought it up to her, and it seemed to have a beneficial effect. She thanked me again, and this time there was no curtness to her voice, though neither would one have called it friendly. But after that, she was quite willing to have me do things for her, even without her asking for them. And of course, much of what I did was familiar to me from tending Jamie: a cool damp cloth to her brow when the fever was on her, blankets during the ague, bark in the intervals in between. Several times she said she felt well enough to go downstairs, and see if Sukey knew what to prepare for dinner, or whether the children were doing their lessons; but each time I prevailed on her to let me go instead, and be her eyes and ears.

"You've been most kind," she said when night began to fall, "but now you must go to your bed and take your rest. I won't go wandering tonight, you have my word on it."

But I insisted I would make a pallet on the floor, and sleep on that; for I knew from tending Jamie that the nights were often the worst, and I couldn't think of leaving her alone. And indeed, she suffered quite a bit that night—her brow nearly on fire, her eyes unfocused; she said nothing, but I fear she was in a state of delirium for some minutes. My heart began to beat wildly, as I recalled those days and nights with Jamie, and I was in great anxiety that I might lose her to this malady, as I had him—and never have the chance to speak to her freely, to tell her what she surely deserved to know, what I hoped would ease her heart and mind. I prayed to God to spare her, and vowed that if He did, I should find the strength to unburden myself to her.

I watched all night as she moaned and tossed. Then, shortly before dawn, her fever broke: I could see by the morning light, as she slept peacefully at last, that her color was returning. I felt as though my own fever had broken as well, a fever of anxiety and remorse, and I began to weep.

"Whatever is the matter, Mrs. Wilson?" I heard Mrs. Iredell ask in a weak voice, and I realized I had awakened her.

"Oh nothing, nothing." I hurriedly wiped my cheeks. "Only that you're better, and last night—I was becoming rather anxious."

She gave me an odd sort of smile, quizzical and confused, and a searching look, as though she were trying to see right through my clothes and skin, into my very soul. Then she shook her head slightly, as if to clear it, and closed her eyes, and almost immediately she was back asleep. It was only then I realized how fatigued I was myself, and stretched out on the pallet I had made up on the floor.

Later I was awakened by the sound of her footsteps, and saw her slowly making her way to the door. I convinced her to return to bed, for she was still very weak, and brought her some broth. She thanked me for all my kindness and attention to her, and I told her it was surely no more than she would have done for me, and no more than I owed her; and again she gave me that penetrating look. Tell her, you must tell her, I commanded myself, remembering my vow; but I stood there frozen, unable to speak. Then, to my relief, she asked if I would bring her daughter Helen to her, as she was sure the child had been asking for her—and indeed she had been, most insistently.

The girl was so eager that she barreled up the stairs ahead of me, and before I could enter the room myself she fairly pounced upon poor Mrs. Iredell, who at that moment appeared far too advanced in years to be the mother of such a bouncing, lively child.

"Mama!" Helen cried in a voice far louder than any that had been heard in that room for days. "Come downstairs at once, you've been in bed too long."

She was now pulling on her mother's arm, and I feared she would do her some damage. I would have taken her from the room at once, but Mrs. Iredell shook her head at me as I advanced.

"Come, child," she said to Helen in the gentlest of voices, "come here upon the bed and rest quietly with me."

I saw Helen hesitate, but then she hoisted her skirt up above her knees and with some effort lifted her skinny legs onto the mattress, then snuggled intently against her mother under the quilt like a puppy seeking milk from its dam; and for a moment a wave of grief flooded me, for I suddenly recalled what it was like to have a child's skin against one's own, a small warm body seeking the comfort that only a mother can provide. After a few moments the girl jumped up, but before she skipped away, she tugged at my skirt and said, most solemnly, "Thank you, ma'am, for taking care of my Mama."

"Such an unusual child, your Helen," I said to Mrs. Iredell, when the girl had gone.

"Yes, she has great quantities of energy," she replied, arranging the quilt that the child had kicked off, "and is given to fancies, as you may have noticed. But she has great quantities of affection, as well."

"You're very … understanding with her," I ventured, taking the liberty of sitting on the edge of the mattress. "I'm sure I should never be so good a mother to such a child, myself."

"Ah, but you don't know, do you, until you've had one? Motherhood brings out in us qualities we hadn't known we possessed."

It was true, I thought. "I did have a child once, you know—I don't mean the Wilson children, I mean one of my own."

She nodded, and seemed to know what I was speaking of; I suppose Mr. Iredell had told her. "It's a terrible thing, losing a child," she said, "especially your first. Everyone tries to prepare you for the possibility, but it's no use, you can't help growing attached. I lost my first as well, so I know." I remembered now, what Mr. Iredell had said: how the child—conceived after eleven years of barrenness—had died only a few days after birth. To my surprise, Mrs. Iredell now took my hand and spoke in the same gentle way I'd heard her speak to Helen. "You mustn't blame yourself for it."

I drew back, startled; how had she known? "But it was the milk, you see—if only I'd nursed him from the first, as the doctor advised…"

Mrs. Iredell shook her head. "Every mother finds some reason. I even blamed myself when our Thomas died, though I was so ill during the whole of his brief life that I could scarcely lift my head." She dropped my hand and began to pick at a loose thread on the quilt. "And then there was Mrs. Tredwell's child, Betsey—a lovely child, just a year and a half old. She died under my care, and I felt for a long time that I was to blame for it." She looked up at me again. "But I spent many hours in prayer, and the Lord helped me find a way to forgive myself—to understand that it was His doing, not mine, and that He has His reasons for such things, although they may never be revealed to us." She closed her eyes for a long moment, and I began to think she was returning to sleep; but then, her eyes still closed, she added, "We do all we can, we try our best, and sometimes it's simply not enough. There's no profit in blame; you must try to put it from your mind."

I knew I should never be able to convince myself that the Lord had His reasons for bringing about Henry's death; and yet it was a balm to me, the gentle authority of her words. I wrapped myself in their warmth, as Helen had in her mother's quilt.

"You can never banish the pain of having lost a child, of course," she continued, "but you'll have another one, someday, perhaps many more, and that will be a comfort. You may not want to think of remarriage yet, but you're still quite young, and I'm sure that in time"—

"No, I won't," I said suddenly. "I mean—I don't think I *want* another child. I couldn't bear it again, the possibility of having a creature I loved that way taken from me forever. It was worse …" I hesitated; should I say it? "Worse than losing a husband."

"Yes." I looked at her and saw, not the condemnation I had feared, but that look of understanding in her eyes once more. "But you'll have another one, nonetheless. We all do, eventually."

She reached for my hand, and for a few moments we said nothing. I knew somehow that she was thinking back to her own dead child, as I was to mine—each of us locked into our separate rememberings, and yet connected by them. *Now*, I told myself, tell her now; but again I could not bring the words to my lips.

"Perhaps," she said at last, "you would be so kind as to read to me." She pointed weakly to a book on the table by the bed. "I borrowed this volume from my brother's library and had just begun it before the illness came on me." She paused. "That is, if it's agreeable to you. I fear it has become the subject of some controversy."

I took it from the table and saw the title: *A Vindication of the Rights of Woman*. A peculiar title, and yet familiar; I then remembered hearing it discussed—years ago, a lifetime ago, it seemed—at the very first salon I had attended at Mrs. Bingham's.

"Oh, I should very much like to read this!" I exclaimed, remembering the lively discussion of it that had taken place.

"You've heard of it then?" Mrs. Iredell seemed mildly surprised. "The author, the late Miss Wollstonecraft, appears to have some excellent views on the subject of girls' education, but I understand it has recently been revealed that her private life was quite scandalous."

I told Mrs. Iredell I had no objection on that account, and began to read at the place she had marked. I soon realized to my dismay that the subject was none other than romantic love, and its relationship to marriage: Miss Wollstonecraft seemed to argue that the two could not co-exist for long. A woman who has only been taught "to please," wrote Miss Wollstonecraft, will soon find that her charms no longer have much effect on her husband's heart; when that occurs, such a woman will seek to forget the mortification inflicted on her by her husband's indifference by trying to please other men, and make other conquests.

The words stung, as this was the very conception of me that I feared Mrs. Iredell had so long entertained: that *I* was such a woman, seeking from such men as Mr. Iredell the admiration and flattery that my husband had been too inured, or too distracted, to continue to offer. And was there not some truth to the accusation? I felt a flush rise to my cheeks, and I lowered the book.

"Should I ... should I continue?"

"Please," Mrs. Iredell said mildly; perhaps she was too fatigued to follow closely what I was reading.

I read several more pages that continued on in this vein, with Miss Wollstonecraft roundly criticizing coquettishness and feminine affectation, and arguing that women must put aside pretense, and exercise both their bodies and their minds; for, she wrote, it is only in that way that friendship, rather than indifference, may arise between husband and wife. I was so struck by the force and novelty of these ideas—and the wondering how they might be applicable to my own situation—that I nearly forgot where I was, and to whom I was reading. Then I came to a passage in which Miss Wollstonecraft declared that, after the "fever of love" subsides, "a healthy temperature is thought insipid only by those who have not sufficient intellect to substitute the calm tenderness of friendship, the confidence of respect, instead of blind admiration, and the sensual emotions of fondness."

I put down the book, holding my place with a finger. Surely, I thought, she has shown me some true sympathy during these past few hours, surely she now feels some close connection to me, as I do to her—I had seen it in her eyes, heard it in her voice. If I should ever have the courage to speak, and if she should ever have the forbearance to hear me out, it would be now.

"I believe, Mrs. Iredell," I said, my voice barely more than a whisper, "that you yourself are fortunate in enjoying exactly the situation Miss Wollstonecraft describes."

Mrs. Iredell had closed her eyes while I read, though I could discern that she was not asleep. She now opened them wide and fixed them on me.

"What I mean is," I continued, trembling slightly, "that Mr. Iredell regards you in that way, with"—I glanced back down at the page—" 'the calm tenderness of friendship' and 'the confidence of respect.' "

Her mouth was open slightly and her brow creased; it seemed she did not know whether to take this as compliment or insult. Or perhaps she was merely astonished at my effrontery.

"And how would you know, Mrs. Wilson, how my husband regards me?" she said at last, her voice as low as my own.

"Well, it's evident," I began, "from the way he speaks of you, and looks upon you …"

"I have sometimes thought," she said, turning her face slowly upwards to the ceiling, so that it seemed as though she were speaking more to herself than to me, "that he looks on other women with more admiration, that I"—here she covered her eyes with her hand, and her voice began to break—"that I am not the woman he should have chosen, that he has come to regret"—

"No, no, you mustn't think that!" I swallowed hard, took a breath to fortify myself. "Yes, he likes to flirt from time to time, and flatter other women, if that is what you mean. I've noticed that, of course—but truly, it means nothing. It's only a way to amuse oneself, and pass the time. A parlor game, like cards, that some will like to play at and others won't. And if you grow accustomed to it, well—it can become a habit, difficult to break—like swearing."

I hoped she would understand that these words were true of my own behavior as well. And I thought of Bird, and my efforts to make him play the game; I saw now that it should never suit him, no more than it would suit Mrs. Iredell. One might as well ask a fish to fly.

"You're kind to say such things," she said, her hand still shielding her eyes, "but I have reason to suspect otherwise. Something ... something happened long ago, you see"—

"Mrs. Iredell, there is something you must know," I said quickly. These vague words of reassurance, I could see, would never be enough; I must tell her all, as I had determined to do.

She looked at me then, her eyes watery but hopeful. And so I began to describe what had happened at Havre de Grace—not omitting the part about Mr. Iredell falling through the ice, despite my promise of secrecy, as I thought it necessary in order to explain what occurred later. When I reached the moment of my own shame, I could scarcely continue—it was nearly the most difficult of all the difficult things I have ever done—but I forced myself onward. I had not been in my right mind that day, I told her, not entirely aware of who it was I was pressing my lips against—

"Get out!" she spat at me. I had been so intent on telling my story that I had not realized the effect it was having on her. Her eyes were burning and hard now, her face drawn into such an expression of hatred as I hope never to see again. "Leave my room—leave my house—at once!"

"But you must let me finish!" I dropped to my knees beside her bed; let her despise me, only she must know the full truth. "It was what occurred next—what Mr. Iredell said, and did, that I must tell you."

Her face relaxed slightly, which I took as a sign that I might continue. "He was not unkind to me, yet his voice was quite firm, with not a hint of uncertainty. He told me that he understood my ... distress, but that I must stop." A wave of dizziness came over me, but I knew I must go on, and quickly. "He pushed me from him, and said there was only one woman for him, and that was his wife—that you were his treasure, ever more precious to him as the years passed. That he had once hurt you grievously, when he was young and foolish, and that he had vowed never to do anything of the sort again—and indeed he had not, for he couldn't bear the thought that you might turn from him. He told me of

425

your kindness, your generosity, your cleverness, and your strength—more strength, he said, than you realized you had. He told me that there was a time in Philadelphia, when he was away from home, when you had—with great courage—managed to save the family from a terrible disgrace."

Mrs. Iredell appeared stunned now, transfixed; she said nothing.

"He told me he should never speak to anyone of what had happened between us," I continued. "He was very kind, and assured me that he viewed my behavior as the result of temporary hysteria, brought on by extreme anxiety—which in truth, it was; and that it should be forgotten, and we should remain friends just as before."

Mrs. Iredell closed her eyes and took a deep breath, as though it were a great effort. "Leave me now," she said, her voice almost plaintive. "Please."

She turned her head towards the window, and away from where I stood. I could do nothing but accede to her wishes and take my leave. Certainly she was well enough now—in body at least—to be left alone. As for her mind, I feared I had disturbed it greatly, when I only meant to reassure.

I paused at the door and turned back to her, a thought having suddenly entered my mind. "You have such faith in the Lord, Mrs. Iredell—more faith than I can muster, though I have tried. But I beg you, repose some of that faith, that trust, in your own husband, who I assure you is well deserving of it." I thought of Jamie—of his letters, so curt and business-like, and the way he would retreat into that secret core of himself even when I was by him, and of how I had willed myself to believe that he loved me nonetheless. "We can never entirely satisfy ourselves of what is in the heart of another, not even the one we know better than anyone else. All love, I think, rests on faith." Her head was still turned from me; I could not gauge what effect my words might be having, but I felt there was yet one more thing that had to be said. "And we must have faith in ourselves, that we are worthy of being loved." My voice began to break. "And I assure you, my dear Mrs. Iredell, you are worthy. Worthier than you know."

Her face was still turned from me. I then hurried to my own room, afraid that I should begin to sob, and have remained here this past hour or more, in a state of great agitation. I began to pack my trunk, for I fear Mrs. Iredell may hold to her intention of sending me from the house—though where I shall go, alone and with no money, I cannot say.

At length, I resolved to write down all that had transpired, in hopes that it might calm me, and so I have. But now there comes a knock at the—

Diary of Hannah Iredell

Friday, September 21, 1798

Such a story as I heard from Mrs. Wilson yesterday—I am still feeling the shock of it. I have had an unusually severe attack of the Ague and fever, and in truth I wondered, at first, whether the entire episode had only been a Delusion brought on by the illness. But then I reasoned that it could not be, as my Fever had not returned since the night before; she must have spoken it, every word.

I spent a good deal of time, after she left, trying to fight my way through the tempest of emotions that assaulted me. First I felt such anger as I have never felt before—or not in twenty years, at least: she was a Temptress, a seducer, just as I had suspected all along! And in the previous few hours, I had managed to put aside those suspicions—forever, I thought—for she had been so kind to me in my Illness, so sincerely concerned for me; I had begun to feel true affection for the Woman. Had I discovered the truth earlier, I surely would have been grievously pained; but to hear it at such a juncture, when we stood on the brink of Friendship, felt a sharp betrayal indeed.

But then I recalled what else she had said, which my Brain had nearly been too Exhausted to take in: that Mr. Iredell had declared his faithfulness to me, in a Situation where it seemed I could not doubt his Veracity. I thought over the words Mrs. Wilson had repeated to me—*his* Words: that I was his treasure, that I had only grown more precious to him with the years, that he remembered and appreciated what I had done to settle Mother's debt in Philadelphia—and that he had never, since that terrible Incident twenty years ago, committed an act of Infidelity. The words, turned over and over in my weakened mind, sent a honeyed, golden glow through me, and I began to weep small, quiet tears of relief and Happiness. I went to the glass by the window and examined my gray, tear-stained, ravaged Self: *this* he loves, I told myself, even this he is faithful to. What was it Mrs. Wilson had said, just before she left?

Something about having faith in him, and in myself. I yearned to see him, to throw my arms about him, to beg his forgiveness for tormenting him with my Suspicions all these years—and so I should have, had he not been miles away.

A thought then struck me, and struck from me all my newfound joy: what if she were lying? Perhaps she was only trying to bring some Comfort to a pathetic invalid, plagued by anxiety about her Husband's attachment to her. There had been something about the tale that did not quite convince, if one took a hard look at it—that sounded, for all the world, like a scene from a romantic Novel, or a play. Was it not possible that she viewed the telling of it as one of her Nursing duties, designed to return the patient to robustness?

But no, I told myself, no Woman—no matter how desperate to comfort—would tell a Lie in which she herself appeared to such a Disadvantage. The wonder was that she had told the story at all; and suddenly I realized what a Sacrifice she had made—for it was obvious to me she craved my Friendship and affection, and she must have known that by revealing what she did, she would risk losing those things forever. There was no accounting for it except to say that she had done it for me, and I suppose for Mr. Iredell as well—that she must have known it was the only way I should ever be assured of his Loyalty. True, she had once attempted to seduce my Husband—and despite her protestations of temporary Hysteria, I may never entirely forgive her for that; but if she had not done so—and had not disclosed her own scandalous Behavior—perhaps I should never have known the Truth of what Mr. Iredell feels for me.

I had spent an hour, perhaps, tossed to and fro on the turbulent Sea of my thoughts; but with this realization a calm descended upon me, and I knew I must go to her and say something, though I was not yet sure exactly what—for I had simply sent her away before, too overcome to speak. I found her at the Desk in her room, writing (it seems she keeps a Diary, just as I do, and I can well imagine what she must have been setting down) and with her trunk standing open, halfway packed. She dropped her quill and shut the Diary when I opened the door, and regarded me with great Trepidation—such Power as I seemed to hold over the poor Woman, at that moment! She who has wielded such Power over me these past months, sending an arrow through my heart with every smile she has coaxed from my Husband.

"You must unpack your things, Mrs. Wilson," I said, looking from the trunk to her. "Why, what would Mr. Iredell think, if he returned tomorrow and found you out on the street with your Trunk?"

"Very well, then." She bit her lip, and looked as though she were holding back tears.

"And I"—I hesitated, for there was still some lingering Doubt in my mind; but I could not deny what was in my Heart. "I have no intention of parting with you until it's absolutely necessary."

At this she gave me a brilliant smile, full of surprise and Gratitude, though at the same time, the tears she had been holding back suddenly spilled forward; and I felt the last of my Doubts slip away. I opened my arms to her, and within a moment she was in my Embrace.

From Bird Wilson to James Iredell:

Pottsgrove, Pennsylvania, October 22, 1798

... We are much indebted to you and Mrs. Iredell for the attention that you have paid to Mrs. Wilson, which must have been so grateful and necessary to her in the situation in which she was. Accept, Sir, our thanks for this kindness. Tho' only related to us by marriage, her conduct has so endeared her to us that we cannot help regarding the attention paid to her as a favor conferred on ourselves...

Diary of Hannah Wilson

Sunday, January 6, 1799

To think I have been a guest in this house more than four months now—but in truth, one cannot stay in a house four months and remain a guest. I seem to have become something more akin to a resident aunt or a cousin. I have tried to make myself as useful as possible about the house; Mrs. Iredell has shown me how to remove grease-spots with spirits of turpentine, and how to kill bedbugs with quicksilver and the whites of eggs (though in truth I hope that my future position in life will be such as to render this sort of knowledge unnecessary). And I have undertaken to act as dancing mistress for the children, which has had the result of endearing me to them; indeed Helen Iredell, of whom I have grown rather fond, nearly always cries when I say the lesson is at an end. I wonder if she will cry tomorrow, when we say our farewells.

For I am leaving with Mr. Iredell at last, returning to Philadelphia—and then, after some while, on to Boston. Mr. Iredell would have obliged me by leaving two or three weeks before this, if I had asked him, but it would have been selfish of me to tear him from his family any sooner than was necessary. And, in truth, it wasn't just on his account that I delayed; for I have grown so comfortable here that I was in no great hurry to depart—it was a pleasant, peaceful dream from which I was loath to be awakened. I should never have imagined, before, that I might be happy in a place like Edenton; but I see now that it is a small, neat universe unto itself, more manageable in its way than Philadelphia or New York, almost a large family. It has its little scandals, and triumphs, and tragedies, and one can predict with near confidence who will be at almost any dinner and what will constitute the topics of conversation: the state of Tom Iredell's rheumatism, or Mrs. Johnston's nerves; the unusual severity of the sickly season, and who has been affected by it and to what degree; Mr. Johnston's recent election to the state legislature, and his prospects there. To be sure, the discussion

431

sometimes wanders to the doings on the national stage, and what is transpiring at the seat of government; but it is all at such a remove, any intelligence being at least several weeks old, that it seems something less than real. The miniature events of Edenton—quite invisible to the rest of the world—loom far larger in our minds here.

I believe I understand, now, Mrs. Iredell's reluctance to leave this place—understand it perhaps better than Mr. Iredell does. She need scarcely ever encounter the unexpected, or engage in conversation with a stranger; her life moves as placidly as a canoe skimming across a pond. We have spent many an hour in one another's company, she and I, and she has told me of what she suffered in the Capital—such anguish, such torment at the prospect of calling on Mrs. Jay, or attending a levee at the President's house! At first I could scarcely credit it: why should so clever a woman, one so thoughtful and well-informed, regard such utterly amusing things with terror? Never have I met a person who combined such admirable qualities as Mrs. Iredell with such keen self-doubt. But I have come to realize that it is not for me—or even for Mr. Iredell—to say what should or should not bring her happiness. I cannot help but admire her certitude: it is here her feet are planted, and here she will stay. Some might call it weakness (indeed, I fear that Mrs. Iredell, with her usual penchant for self-denigration, herself regards it so); but I have come to see it more as strength.

And yet—for all I love her and admire her, and believe I understand her—I know that if I myself remained here much longer I should begin to wither and die. A week ago, knowing that the day of my departure was approaching, I was suddenly seized with such yearning for it that I have since then been able to do little else but count the hours and minutes. My heart began to beat faster and my mind to spin: to be in the center of things once more, to share in the gossip and use my wit to parry some pleasantry, to dance till the wee hours at the balls!

I don't believe there's any need to hurry home to Mama, really—a month or two more cannot make a difference to her, and it should mean so much to me. I have arranged to stay with the Brecks in Philadelphia, for they have a large house in town and Spring Hill, their country house, is a lovely place—indeed, it sits adjacent to the Binghams' country place. They know all the best people, and must receive many invitations—I imagine I shall be included as a matter of course, as their guest. And surely dear Lucy will lend me some of her clothes, for we are nearly the same size. She has one gown that I have always coveted, of the palest pink with dark green velvet trim, and cut rather low at the bosom; if she would only allow me to borrow it for a night, or perhaps two! I've had quite enough of wearing black. "Who *is* that lady?" some gentleman will inquire of his companion. "Does she not look familiar?" Ah, the young widow, the companion will explain *sotto voce*—what she has suffered! And so I shall be the object of general fascination.

It seems I am not the only one in this house whose head is filled with dreams of Philadelphia; yesterday morning when Sukey came into my room to fill the basin, she whispered to me quickly that perhaps I should see her there, before long. It seems she has a plan to run away and join her father, come spring; she has written him a letter telling him as much, which Mr. Iredell has promised to deliver for her. I only hope he doesn't become curious about what she has written, and open it himself! So amazed was I by what she told me that I didn't think to warn her that I might no longer be in Philadelphia myself, by springtime. Nor did I tell her what anxiety I felt on her account, thinking of the terrible risks to which she would expose herself. I only wished her Godspeed, for she looked so brimming with hope and expectation that I couldn't bear to discourage her.

I shall truly miss this place, and the friends I have made here: Mrs. Tredwell, and Tom Iredell, the Johnstons, and all the children. And of course Mr. and Mrs. Iredell—dear Mrs. Iredell, whose kindness to me has been more than I deserved, how it pains me to part from her, perhaps forever! But this chapter of my life has come to a close, and a new one must begin—the sooner the better. What I have experienced here—most likely the worst, and perhaps also the best, days of my life—will never leave me, I know; but I must bury it all deep within me, or I shall never be able to go on. Surely, when I imagined my life to be a novel, I never intended it to be a tragedy. This cannot be the end of the tale: no, I only need turn the page, and begin to discover what new adventures await me.

Diary of Hannah Iredell

Monday, January 7, 1799

They left this Morning, Mr. Iredell and Mrs. Wilson, by the stage. It was bitter cold, and I insisted Mrs. Wilson take my heavy Shawl, for the poor Woman has been very ill equipped for Winter. She protested for a while, until I told her it would give her something by which she might remember me, and then she relented—though she regretted she had nothing suitable to give me as a Remembrance of herself.

"No need," I told her, "for there is no possibility of my ever forgetting you."

At this I saw the Tears come to her eyes, and she promised me that nonetheless she should send me some pretty thing from Philadelphia.

"A pretty thing from Philadelphia!" I laughed, though I felt some rising tears myself. "That would indeed remind me of you."

I had feared I would be gripped by my old Jealousies and suspicions, sending the two of them off on the Stage, when I knew what had transpired between them on the Journey southwards. And yet, to my relief, my only fear was for their Safety, and the Hazards of their again crossing the Susquehanna in winter—though I could say nothing of that, when it would only lead to thoughts in the minds of all that had no place there. So I contented myself with a general Injunction to take great care, and guard their health.

It already feels lonely in this House with only the Children and the Negroes for company. Several times today I have thought of something I should like to say to Mrs. Wilson, or thought I heard her step upon the stair, and then realized to my dismay that she was gone. In truth she is a remarkable Lady, with a better heart and Mind than she gives herself credit for.

There was a time I allowed myself to imagine she would choose to stay here—I even fancied she was in love with Tom Iredell, and might become our relation in law as well as in Spirit. But she only laughed when I mentioned it, and asked what had given me such an Idea—for though she liked Mr. Iredell's brother well enough, her flirting with him had been nothing more than idle Amusement, and she trusted he had understood that. I suppose he did, for he never really courted her. But I don't imagine I shall ever fully understand these things, myself.

She would never have remained here, I see that now. This last week, it seemed that she was already gone, in spirit if not in body. I suspect she was imagining herself at some ball in Philadelphia, turning her charm on first one Gentleman and then the next, the eyes of all upon her. She was quite useless the whole week, lost in her Dream—after at last becoming rather handy around the house, under my Tutelage. All she could speak of was some Gown she hoped to borrow from a Friend, which she described to me at greater length than interested me, and what sorts of Invitations she might expect to receive. It seemed that her girlish Veneer had reappeared, again hiding the Woman underneath; or was the girlishness, in fact, far more than a Veneer? Was it perhaps her true Self, or part of it? Was our Friendship no more than a hothouse bloom, that would have quickly withered in the world outside? If we were to meet Years from now, would we find we once again had little to say to one another?

Perhaps; and yet somehow I know the bond between us was real, and all the more precious for its being temporary. It's true what I told her, that I should need no pretty thing by which to remember her, for I am convinced her Sojourn here has left its mark on me. Hardly more than a slip of a Girl, she is, and yet she taught me much—or should I say, rather, we taught one another. She learned from me how to preserve the color in a pocket handkerchief by dipping it in strong salt and water, and how hot coals held close to varnished furniture will take out the spots, and other such useful tricks; and I have learned from her how to love—and how to trust that I am loved.

Epilogue

The stories of the real Iredells and Wilsons—the historical figures whose lives I have imagined with such freedom (may their ghosts forgive me)—did not end at this point, of course. Because some readers may be curious to know what happened next, I will summarize the facts, to the extent that they are known:

James Iredell died only ten months after the end of the story told here, on October 20, 1799. Although the exact nature of his illness is uncertain, he had failed to attend the August sitting of the Supreme Court in 1799, apparently due to exhaustion from the rigors of the preceding spring circuit. Nevertheless, at the request of Justice Bushrod Washington (George Washington's nephew and James Wilson's replacement on the Court), Iredell prepared an extensive summary of a complex and important case over which he had presided; a mistrial had been declared, and Washington was to preside over the retrial. "I certainly should not have made the request …," Washington wrote to Iredell after he had received the summary, "if I could have formed the slightest idea of the labor to which I was about to expose you." The letter was written on the very day that Iredell died. It seems that Iredell's conscientiousness and dedication to his work may have been a contributing factor in his death. Iredell's mother, Margaret McCulloh Iredell, survived her son, but only by a few years; she remained in the care of a country family who lived near Philadelphia until she died in 1802.

Hannah Iredell survived until 1826, dying at the ripe old age (for those days) of 78. She seems to have lived a quiet and generally happy life in Edenton, surrounded by her children and grandchildren, and partially supported by her brother. In 1815 her son James married his cousin Frances Tredwell, one of Nelly's daughters, and the marriage produced eleven children. James was productive in the public as well as the domestic sphere, following his father into the law and ultimately becoming first a governor of North Carolina and then one of its Senators.

It was Hannah's daughters who brought her grief. Annie, by all accounts an intelligent and sweet-tempered young woman who remained close to her mother, never married; plagued by frequent bouts of malaria (the "ague and fever" or "intermittent fever"), she became an invalid and died at the age of thirty. And Hannah's younger daughter, Helen, is said to have "lost her mind" at a young age; a modern diagnosis might be schizophrenia. She would become hysterical, believing herself near death, and apparently suffered from other delusions. Hannah took care of her at home as long as she could, but in 1823 Helen was sent away to live with a Dr. James Chaplin in Cambridgeport, Massachusetts, who specialized in caring for the mentally ill. Two years later, Hannah wrote to her, "Try, I beg of you my beloved child, to get well, that you may return to me." But Helen never recovered, and Hannah never saw her again. Helen lived on through the Civil War, dying in 1869 at the age of seventy-seven.

Hannah Wilson lingered in Philadelphia for some time; in August of 1799, she was still staying with the Brecks at Spring Hill, and writing a chatty letter to James Iredell expressing her disappointment at his not coming to Philadelphia for the August sitting of the Supreme Court ("I do not know what you will say to the length of this letter," she wrote in closing. "It is with writing as with talking: when a woman once begins, she never knows when to leave off.") But at some point she returned to Boston, for it was there, in 1802, that she married for the second time. Her husband was Thomas Bartlett, a retired Boston apothecary and widower who had two daughters and three stepchildren from his first marriage. In September, 1806, Hannah and Thomas had a child of their own, Caroline; but not long after her birth, they sailed for England, leaving the baby with Thomas's parents in Roxbury, Massachusetts. Thomas's two older daughters were sent to boarding school, and a stepdaughter was sent to live with the Wilsons in Philadelphia (an indication that earlier family ties had not been severed). Hannah apparently never saw her daughter again; she died in London in March 1808, when she was only thirty-four.

Bird Wilson did well enough in the practice of law to become a judge: in 1802 he was appointed president of the seventh circuit Pennsylvania court of common pleas. But he was deeply affected, some years later, when called upon to pronounce a sentence of death on a defendant, and in 1817 he resigned from the bench in order to study for the ministry. He left Philadelphia for New York, where he became a professor at, and later dean of, the General Theological Seminary. He died in 1859, at the age of 82.

One might think that nothing more could possibly have happened to James Wilson after his death in 1798. But in 1906, a committee of Philadelphia citizens bent on rehabilitating Wilson's reputation raised the money to have his remains exhumed from the Johnston family burial ground at Hayes and returned to Philadelphia, where they were re-buried at Christ Church. Despite the efforts of the Philadelphia committee, the name of James Wilson is still largely unknown to posterity, his contributions to the United States Constitution and the country's early jurisprudence apparently remaining overshadowed by his later disgrace.

***

I hope that the letters I've included in this novel have helped readers discern which parts of the story are factual and which are fictional. But I wasn't able to include letters and other information that would have illuminated the factual basis for some of the plot details, so I'll try to make up for that now.

Hannah Iredell's painful recollection of James Iredell's infidelity early in their marriage is a mixture of fact and fiction: for a period of about four months in late 1779, James Iredell wrote a series of abject letters to Hannah, begging her forgiveness for an unspecified transgression. From the tone of them, it seems likely that he was guilty of some sort of infidelity—perhaps a flirtation, perhaps a full blown affair. In one of these letters, he proclaimed himself as "deep a Penitent as Man can be," apologized for his "ill behavior," and protested, "You really are in my mind by far the most perfect Woman I know." (The letters are reprinted in volume two of *The Papers of James Iredell*, edited by Don Higginbotham, who comes to a similar conclusion about what must have prompted them.) Hannah also mentions that James Iredell had a speech impediment. This too has a basis in fact, although the exact nature of the impediment has been lost to posterity. The minister who delivered the sermon at Iredell's funeral spoke of Iredell's "natural impediment in his speech, which would have abashed and discouraged weaker minds." (The sermon is quoted in volume one of *The Life and Correspondence of James Iredell*, edited by Griffith McRee, at p. 76.)

The perilous crossing of the frozen Susquehanna River undertaken by James Iredell and Hannah Wilson is based on a similar mishap that actually befell another Supreme Court Justice, Samuel Chase, in February

1800. Chase recounted the experience in a letter to his wife (also named Hannah!) that can be found in volume one of *The Documentary History of the Supreme Court of the United States, 1789-1800*, at page 888.

Both Hannahs did have children who died in infancy. The Iredells' first child, Thomas, was born on October 1, 1784, and died two days later. The details, along with quotations from letters in which Iredell expressed his grief, can be found in *Justice James Iredell*, by Willis P. Whichard. Less is known about the Wilsons' son Henry, but sources indicate that he was born in May 1796 and died while still an infant (see volume three of *The Documentary History of the Supreme Court*, at p. 134, note 4).

Lastly, a word of explanation about the repeated references to "the intermittent fever"—the dread disease endemic to Edenton that ultimately killed James Wilson. These are actually references to what we now call malaria. The "bark," or "Peruvian bark," that Wilson and others took as a remedy was the powdered bark of the cinchona tree, which contains quinine—still in use as a malaria remedy today.

Acknowledgments

This project has been many years in gestation, and a number of people have provided support and encouragement along the way—in some cases, so long ago that they may not even remember doing it. In its very early stages—when the book was little more than an idea—Lea Sloan, Sharon Oard Warner, and Erika Dreifus helped give me the confidence to get started. The members of my two invaluable writing groups—Ellen Bravo, Jenny Brody, Mary Carpenter, Ellen Cassedy, Carolyn Daffron, Anne Glusker, Sally Steenland, and Sara Taber—provided years of astute critiques, perceptive suggestions, and unwavering enthusiasm: without them, this book would certainly never have been written. Nancy Heneson, my most trusted editor (and closest friend), brought her considerable skills to bear on the manuscript; her interest in the unfolding story helped to keep me going. Anne Dubuisson Anderson gave my some excellent ideas for revision. My husband, Jim Feldman, has been the cheering section that every self-doubting writer needs (not to mention the provider of invaluable technical support). And my amazing children, Sophie and Sam, have by their very existence helped me to understand the transformative power of maternal love, an understanding that I certainly drew on in writing the novel.

I have also been gratified and encouraged by the enthusiasm of a number of people who were early readers of the manuscript: Lidya Buzio, Bob Frankel, Maeva Marcus, Jenny Netzer, Dan Pollock, and Anne Whitehouse. I also owe a debt of thanks to Maeva, Bob, Stephen Tull, and all the other members of the staff of the *Documentary History of the Supreme Court of the United States, 1789-1800* who have collected and organized the many documents on which I drew to create the story of *A More Obedient Wife*. And thanks, as well, to the many people I have encountered at dinner parties and other social occasions who expressed interest in reading the novel—this would include the woman at the Segway rental office in Miami Beach several years ago, who practically begged me to finish the book so that she could read it. I hope that it finds its way to at least some of you, and that it does not disappoint.

I owe a debt of a somewhat different kind to Lydia Maria Child, the nineteenth-century author of *The American Frugal Housewife* (1836) and *The Family Nurse* (1837) (she was also the author of the Thanksgiving poem, "Over the River and Through the Woods," and a fervent abolitionist). These books are fascinating compendiums of household hints and home remedies for all sorts of complaints, and—although they were written several decades after the period in which the novel is set—I used their contents freely, particularly in creating the character of Hannah Iredell. In describing dinner at President Washington's house, I borrowed heavily from Senator William Maclay's characteristically acid-tongued account of a similar dinner, which he recorded in his immensely enjoyable diary. And I relied on J. H. Powell's classic, *Bring Out Your Dead*, for details of the 1793 yellow fever epidemic in Philadelphia.

I would also like to thank the various repositories that house the originals of the documents from which I have quoted for granting me permission to publish the excerpts. The repositories are as follows:

The North Carolina Office of Archives and History, Raleigh, North Carolina: Hannah Iredell to James Iredell, May 6, September 15, October 21, and November 11, 1790; James Iredell to Hannah Iredell, May 10, June 18, and September 28, 1790; April 9, September 7, and October 2, 1791; April 8, September 20, October 2, October 13, October 25, and November 1, 1792; April 2, 1793, August 8, 1794, July 2, 1795, March 4, 1796, May 25, 1797, and February 5 and 8, April 5, May 18-19, and August 6, 1798; Nelly Tredwell to Hannah Iredell, June 22, 1790 and July 17, 1791; Hannah Iredell to Nelly Tredwell, February 27 and November 15, 1791, June 18, 1792, and July 22, 1793; Arthur Iredell to James Iredell, July 27 and November 20, 1790; Hannah Iredell to Samuel Tredwell, September 27, 1790; Samuel Johnston to Hannah Iredell, September 27, 1790; John Jay to James Iredell, March 16, 1791; James Iredell to Dr. Tredwell, July 31, 1792; Samuel Johnston to James Iredell, April 10, 1793, February 27, 1796, and July 28, 1798; James Iredell to James Wilson, August 5, 1794 and August 20, 1796; Thomas Iredell to James Iredell, August 17, 1798; James Iredell to Sarah Gray, August 25, 1798; and Bishop William White to James Iredell, September 8, 1798 [all in the Charles E. Johnson Collection]; and [Thomas Blount] to [John Gray Blount], February 16, 1798 and Thomas Blount to [John Gray Blount], February 26, 1798 [both in the John Gray Blount Papers].

The Rare Book, Manuscript, and Special Collections Library of Duke University: James Iredell to Hannah Iredell, May 31, September 5, and November 7, 1790 [James Iredell Sr. and Jr. Papers].

The Library Company of Philadelphia: Jacob Rush to Benjamin Rush, September 8, 1798.

The John Hay Library of Rare Books and Special Collections, Brown University: David Leonard Barnes to Benjamin Bourne, November 8, 1792.

The Historical Society of Pennsylvania: Samuel Wallis to James Wilson, June 14, 1793, James Wilson to Hannah Gray, June 20, 1793, and William Bradford, Jr., to Samuel Bayard, July 16, 1795 [all in the Gratz Collection]; James Wilson to Samuel Wallis, August 7, 1793; Samuel Wallis to James Wilson, November 17, 1793; Henry Hubbell to James Wilson, July 21, 1794; Robert Farmar to James Wilson, July 16, 1795; G.K. Taylor to James Wilson, January 30, 1796; James Wilson to Bird Wilson, June 9 and 27, September 6, and December 17, 1797, and January 17 and 24, 1798; Richard Drake to Bird Wilson, January 13, 1798; Pierce Butler to William Slade, May 24, 1798; Charles Wilson to Bird Wilson, August 19 and 29, 1798; and Hannah Wilson to Bird Wilson, September 1, 1798 [all in the James Wilson Papers]; James Wilson, Manumission of Thomas Pursel, January 12, 1794 [Provincial Delegate Papers]; James Gibson to Pierce Butler, March 22, 1797 [Pierce Butler Papers]; Bird Wilson to James Wilson, June 29, 1797, John Rutledge, Jr., to Edward Rutledge, February 25, 1798, and James Wilson to Bird Wilson, April 28, 1798 [Dreer Collection]; Hannah Wilson to Bird Wilson, November 3, [1797], and June 23, July 28, and September 1, 1798 [James A. Montgomery Collection]; and James Wilson's Proposals for Selling or Mortgaging Some of His Lands, October 4, 1797 [Tench Coxe Papers].

Friends Historical Library, Swarthmore College: James Wilson to Bird Wilson, August 4, 1798, and Bird Wilson to James Iredell, October 22, 1798.

Massachusetts Historical Society: John Quincy Adams to Thomas Boylston Adams, June 23, 1793, and John Adams to Abigail Adams, March 5, 1796 [Adams Family Papers]; and Harrison Gray Otis to Sally Otis, February 18, 1798 [Harrison Gray Otis Papers].